Praise for Jeffe Kennedy
and *Rogue's Pawn*

"A hero with a delicious dangerous streak, a magical world
shimmering with dark beauty...*Rogue's Pawn* is a fun,
fantastical surprise of a book—I loved every minute!"
  —Carolyn Crane, author of The Disillusionists trilogy

"I really cannot say enough about *Rogue's Pawn*.
Jeffe Kennedy has outdone herself in this masterful story of
love, betrayal, power struggles, and magic in a land where
getting what you wish for could be your last mistake."
                                          —*Vampire Romance Books*

"An enthralling, thrilling and seductive ride is the only way
to describe what *Rogue's Pawn* was for me! My first book by
Jeffe Kennedy, and I am 100% trapped within her world."
                                          —*Hardcover Obsession*

"The writing is really good, the characters come through
so vividly, the world vibrates with life and magic, emotion
and action come together beautifully. The end result is a
thoroughly entertaining read, touching and swoon-worthy
as well as active and intriguing, and I for one give it all the
thumbs up I could possibly give it."
                                          —*Butterfly-o-Meter*

"Dazzling writing and crisp, brilliant prose makes
Rogue's Pawn sparkle like the sun on blue water.
Jeffe Kennedy has created a dangerous world full of wit,
charm, and delicious sizzle. I am her captive, and I can't
wait to see what she has up her magical sleeve next!"
  —Darynda Jones, *New York Times* bestselling author of
                                          Third Grave Dead Ahead

"*Rogue's Pawn* delivers a sexy, creepy story in a beautifully
nightmarish world where nothing is what it seems."
  —Marcella Burnard, national bestselling author of
                                          Enemy Within

ROGUE'S PAWN
JEFFE KENNEDY

5485

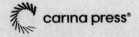
carina press®

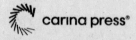

carina press®

ISBN-13: 978-0-373-00383-9

Recycling programs for this product may not exist in your area.

Rogue's Pawn

Copyright © 2012 by Jennifer M. Kennedy

www.CarinaPress.com

Printed in U.S.A.

Dear Reader,

You hold in your hands my first published novel. So much has happened since she left home and ventured into the world, but we never forget any of our children, particularly our firstborns, do we? And now she gets to be in this wonderful box with other amazing books. It's all very exciting and I'm so very pleased and proud.

I often tell people this book came from a dream. When you get to the part about the stolen kiss between tents? That part. I knew from the beginning that I was writing toward that scene. What I didn't anticipate was Rogue walking onstage and taking over both my heroine's life and the entire story. Now I understand that this is exactly what he does—and why I couldn't resist him any better than Gwynn can.

So, welcome to the beginning of this adventure. I hope you enjoy the ride as much as I have.

Best from sunny Santa Fe, New Mexico (yes, even in February!).

Jeffe

To Deedee Boysen, first fan of this story,
whose begging for more chapters kept me going.

ROGUE'S PAWN

Part I

Fundamentals and Context

ONE

In Which I Achieve Escape Velocity

WAGON-WHEEL CHANDELIERS and red velvet. Why on earth every damn hotel in Wyoming seemed compelled to decorate their conference rooms like nineteenth-century saloons escaped me.

But then, everything annoyed me lately.

I shifted, sipping from my glass of Jameson. My feet throbbed from standing around in my heels all evening, and restless irritation crawled across my skin. I'd rather be home, having a quiet evening with my cat, Isabel. I should be in the lab trying to make sense of that last batch of probably worthless data. Being Clive's convenient arm-candy fell pretty low on my list.

And yet, look where I'd ended up. I'd caved to him. Yet again.

The reception was really important to him, and as his fiancée—and here Clive had pulled out the big guns, since he usually only referred to me as his girlfriend—I should be by his side. I always found the energy for *my* job so if I really loved him, I would. On and on and on. Sometimes I think I agreed with him just so I wouldn't have to hear about it anymore.

What the hell was wrong with me these days?

My brain pulsed against my skull. The fragile bones

felt as if they could explode from the sheer pressure of what seethed inside.

I couldn't keep living my life this way.

How did you realize these things? Not in a flash, I thought. Not the epiphany complete with rays of light and singing angels. Instead, it was a slow, creeping restlessness. A depression that sent out fingers of anguished rebellion. You gradually noticed that every morning you dreaded going to your prestigious university research job. Worse, every night you came home to face the guy you thought was The One and you find yourself on the doorstep, hand on the doorknob, and you're suddenly desperate to be *anywhere* but walking into that house.

I suppose I was finally facing the fact that I was miserable. Dreams about a black dog, both compelling and terrifying, had been disrupting my sleep with a message I couldn't interpret.

Or, more precisely, that I didn't want to hear. When I met Clive he'd seemed so different, so mature and, well, like *husband* material. He fit the neat little peghole in the car of my personal Game of Life. Somehow in shining up that image, I'd forgotten that a nice salary and polished shoes didn't make someone a good partner. I'd been just as guilty—letting him see me as the cool, logical scientist. He'd never signed up for a woman with a formless restlessness and these dreams that lately obsessed me.

No, it hadn't been a flash, but standing at that party, it became obvious to me.

I didn't love Clive. Half the time I didn't even like him. Nothing in my life had turned out quite as wonderful as it had seemed when I planned it.

The conversation washed over me. The usual ballyhoo about oil, more drilling, politics, crazy environmentalists. Nothing new. I'd heard the conversation twenty times over and knew better than to argue any of the points. I didn't even think I was listening until I found myself saying, "Oh, Clive, that statistic has been discredited ten times over!"

Clive gaped at me. The other men looked surprised that I spoke.

Try to be softer, my mother said. So far as I could see, soft got you nowhere. Soft got you married to a man who spent his life making up problems to solve and leaving you to sleep alone. Besides, Clive knew I was right. I'd proved him wrong on that point before.

Now we'd have to stay up half the night discussing why I couldn't mind my smart mouth in public and how I didn't have to be always right. He'd explain until I wore down and agreed.

He patted me on the hip—the socially correct version of a pat on the bottom—and said, "It's okay, sweetie, I don't think you really understood the concept of what we were discussing. But love ya, babe!" And with an off-color joke, he guided the group of men away, leaving me standing there.

Maybe I just needed sleep. Probably I shouldn't be drinking whiskey.

With every intention of swapping my empty Jameson glass for some Chardonnay, I headed to the saloon-style bar. Better to have something cool I could sip slowly. Drinking whiskey never contributed to my resolutions to get along with Clive. I appreciated that Clive was a great catch, handsome, successful, charming. Everyone said so. Somehow that just wasn't enough anymore.

Maybe it was me. Perhaps, like my father, nothing could make me happy.

Lately Clive had been saying that logic meant more to me than love. I had to bite my tongue to defy him to prove to me that love existed outside of Hallmark cards and romance novels. Did it register on an oscilloscope or an EEG?

I didn't think so.

I set my highball glass on the bar, nodded to the very cute but very young bartender…and kept walking.

Pulling my coat and purse from the hooks near the reception hall door, I walked out the door. My body carried me away as if it belonged to someone else.

And no one saw me go.

I wasn't thinking about what I was doing until I was driving down the two-lane rural highway, turning up the radio to non-Clive-approved volumes so I could better hear Nickelback assure me that everything would be all right. But just not right now. I sang along, a curious sense of elated freedom lightening my mood. It felt good not to think.

When I did start thinking again, the first thing my brain did was point out that I wasn't on the interstate. Instead it coursed off to my left about half a mile across railroad tracks and prairie, angling away. I hadn't passed any kind of sign in quite a while, but I'd definitely missed the interstate access and was probably going east, not west, in the deepening evening.

Well, shit.

To get on I-90, I'd have to turn around, which I found myself absolutely unable to do. As if I'd gained some kind of escape velocity from the immense gravity well of Clive, from my old life, momentum I couldn't afford to lose. So I just kept driving, feeling the tension bleed away with the rhythm of the highway.

I ended up at Devils Tower.

What can I say? The weathered billboards with the big arrows caught my eye.

They produced a kind of longing in me for something I couldn't quite define. That cold, creeping restlessness in me warmed to the sight of the arrows, like they pointed to the one thing I'd always wanted and never had. I felt compelled to follow them, as I did in those dreams. As if someone was sending messages I couldn't quite hear.

Not logical, but at least it seemed that the plates of my skull might hold together.

Night hung heavy under the trees, a shadowed contrast to the spring sky, which still held a little light. As I wound around the hills, buff-colored sandstone stood out in bright relief to the dark greens of the pines, which in turn made dark silhouettes against the gloaming. Wyoming skies radiate light—one of the best things about the place.

The next bend revealed the tower, starkly outlined against the blue dusk. I might have seen it before, had I been looking in the right place—down instead of up. I'd expected a peak thrusting against the sky, but Devils Tower sits down in a river bottom, carved out of soft sandstone by the Belle Fourche River until only the striated stump of granite remains. As I dropped into its valley, the tower showed black against the darkness, so dark the shadows around it paled to vivid blues.

I found the gates to the park open but unmanned, so I filled out the yellow envelope at the self-pay station with one of those three-inch pencils provided in the bin.

Name, date, car make and year, a ten-dollar bill stuffed
inside. I kept going, excited now, circling the base of
the tower that loomed so immediately above me that I
couldn't see it much anymore.

The road terminated, fittingly, in one final curl—a
circular parking lot at the base of the tower, gleaming in
the growing moonlight. I stood out in the dark, leaning
against the car, as if I was waiting for someone. Like
when you were a teenager and every trip to the mall
held limitless romantic possibilities. I remembered the
champagne giddiness of it all, as if, if you could just
walk around enough, you'd find him. Or he'd find you.

Mule deer wandered nearby, cropping the new green
grass in the center parkway. And that was it. Pretty evening. Peaceful scene. Nothing else happened.

So much for epiphanies.

Oddly disappointed and abruptly exhausted again,
I drove back down the paved road. I didn't know what
I'd been expecting. Something more than deer.

A dirt turnoff to the right was marked by a peeling
sign for Devils Tower Lodge: Friends and Guests Only.
A place to sleep was absolutely what I needed. I turned
in. A sign at a second cattle guard repeated the invitation and warning.

At the end of the road a few buildings clustered beneath the bright light on the pole, the same blue-tinged
spotlight every rural homestead in Wyoming seemed
to have, as if they came free with cattle-guard grates,
woven wire fencing and sheet-metal tool sheds. A new-
looking Jetta was parked in front of the house that didn't
look like a lodge. As I walked up to the door, another
sign said Welcome. Piano music tumbled softly within.

Okay then. I rang the bell.

"Hi there!" said the guy who opened the door, as if I were a neighbor who stopped by frequently.

I hesitated on the doorstep. He wore several beaded chokers around his neck, framed in the open collar of his faded work shirt. A white mustache stood in stark relief to his tanned, wind-roughened face. An ex-hippie.

"I'm Frank," he said, holding out a hand. It seemed he might be about to hug me, but then thought better of it.

"Dr. McGee," I answered automatically.

"You got a first name to go with that title?"

"Oh—sorry. Habit. Obnoxious habit," I amended, embarrassed. "Jennifer."

He shook my hand. "I've always liked Jennifers. Come on in!"

"Is this a lodge? I'm looking for a hotel or something."

"I have four rooms, all empty, you can take your pick. When the rooms are full, you can camp in the yard. Come any time!" He turned and walked back through the mudroom. A shelf ran along the wall with various hiking boots and climbing shoes ranged along it. A scribbled sign said Shoes, with a helpful arrow pointing to the shelf. I slipped off my pumps and set them there with the outdoorsy footwear. Frank waited for me inside the house, by the now-silent piano.

"I'm sorry to come so late, without notice…" I began. Maybe this was a bad idea.

"Hey, I figure everyone who comes to this door is brought by divine inspiration of some kind—Buddha, God, the devil, whatever you believe. It's my job to help you on your way."

Definitely an ex-hippie. But harmless, obviously. I sure wasn't driving any farther tonight if I could help it.

"So, M.D. or vet?"

"Excuse me?"

"Doctor, right?"

"Oh." I waved my hand, regretting my slip. "The PhD kind. I'm a professor at UW." I left out that I studied neurophysiology. Somehow I could never make that come out right. It was like telling people you were actually a rocket scientist. They never looked at you the same again.

Frank nodded to the hallway on my left. "You look tired. Take the Burning Daylight room. It's our honeymoon suite. In the morning you'll see sunrise on Devils Tower." He said it as if there was no greater experience. Maybe to him there wasn't. And I could barely keep my eyes open.

To hell with it.

"Do you need to swipe a credit card?" I reached to open my purse, but Frank just waved a hand at me.

"We can do that in the morning, after pancakes."

I fell asleep to the sound of piano music. Ironic to find myself in the honeymoon suite, when I'd finally walked away from Clive. He was, no doubt, furious over yet another example of my erratic behavior. Illogical and dangerously emotional. Lying in that lodge bed, I really wondered what had possessed me. Maybe I needed to consider seeing a counselor. Out my window, the tower loomed, blacker than the night sky, a silhouette that blocked the stars. An absence of light that somehow still beckoned me.

I dreamed of the Dog, yet again.

The room was warm and steamy, lined with stones.

The floor, ceiling, walls were all formed of rounded cobbles. I stood at the edge of a black pool. At least, it looked opaque in the flickering torchlight. At the shallow edge, near my toes, I could see that the water was transparent. The floor sloped down, the pool growing deeper and darker, until it disappeared into shadow. No end in sight. I must have been planning to bathe, because I was nude.

Then the Dog was there.

The angel hairs on the back of my neck lifted. I spun around. Like a statue of a hound carved out of black glass, the Dog sat on the stone steps that led down from above. Trapped. His amber eyes glinted with relentless hunger, and I wanted to flee but couldn't. His jaws dropped into a canine grin, white fangs echoing sharply pointed ears. I waited for him to attack, knowing I had no other choice.

He cocked his ears and tilted his head, waiting for me to answer a question. I didn't understand what he wanted. I just couldn't quite grasp it.

I AWOKE, DRENCHED in nightmare sweat, to bright light and a sunny Devils Tower. It was always the same dream. Always the edge of disaster. Somehow that made it worse.

After a quick rinse-off in the shower, I dug my contacts out of the water glass I'd soaked them in for the night. I had to put my same panties back on—still slightly damp from the rinsing out the night before. Nothing I could do with my hair and makeup. Not that I'd look a whole lot better even if I had all my stuff. I slipped my necklace and earrings into the pocket of my purse, since the gold was too garish in the morning light. I still looked a little too like a coed doing the walk of shame in last night's cocktail dress and makeup, but there was nothing to be done.

Frank gave me the promised pancakes and said nothing about my appearance, if he even noticed. The windows were filled with Devils Tower—and the spaces between had photos, paintings and etchings of the tower.

"Want me to help you climb it?" Frank asked, pouring strawberry yogurt an inch deep over his pancakes. "I take people up there all the time. I can loan you clothes and shoes."

I mulled that over. "I don't feel a need to climb the tower."

"Afraid of heights?"

"No, I never really have been."

"That's probably why you don't need to climb then. Your fear lies somewhere else."

I shivered and didn't look out the window. Though I knew perfectly well the Dog wasn't there. Then I had to look, just to make sure. Bright sunlight on Devils Tower. Nothing else.

"I'm not sure every fear has to be faced," I told Frank. "Some are just…figments. Bad wiring that got laid down early."

"Or they're not what you think they are," Frank agreed. "I find most things have two faces—like the tower there. Like love and hate. There's a dark and light side. Makes all the difference where you decide to climb."

"Good and evil?" I smiled at him.

"No." Frank cocked his head at me. "Just different aspects of the same thing. It was the Christian settlers who named it Devils Tower, when the natives told them it was the place of dark gods. For the whites, that meant only one guy. Not everybody sees the world that way."

"Who are these dark gods then?"

"Good question." Frank nodded. "Many cultures, of course, have believed in all kinds of supernatural creatures populating the world—both divine and mischievous. Faeries, for example."

"Tinker Bell and her ilk?"

Frank tsked at me. "You come from a Celtic background—you should know better. Our ancestors took messing with the fae very seriously. Of course, once they'd decided to mess with you, there's little recourse."

For no reason, a hot chill washed over me, goose bumps pricking in vestigial response. "I don't believe in any of that."

Frank shrugged. "You don't have to."

I left Frank's, fully intending to get back on the highway, get home and start dealing with my life in a rational way. He hadn't conceded the argument, I realized. Frank had wished me luck in a knowing way, like people do when they think you'll need it.

When I got to the end of his road, I turned left, back to the tower parking lot. I'd come this far, I could at least walk around Devils Tower once. It had nothing to do with facing fear or reconstructing my life, what I did or did not believe in. Or looking for whatever I didn't find last night.

A sprinkling of cars occupied the lot now. Mostly Wyoming plates and a few from nearby South Dakota and Colorado. Locals, more or less, out to see the sights before the serious tourist season began. The immense rock loomed above me.

The blacktop path, bordered by some gray govern-

ment railings, led up into the trees and brush that surged
up against the mountain in a slowly greening tide. If I
could stand for three hours in my heels at one of Clive's
events, I could walk the advertised 1.3 miles around
the tower in them.

I locked my old Honda by pulling out the handle and
flipping the lock, a lazy trick that bypassed the key
and never failed to annoy Clive, who predicted horrific
locked-out-of-my-car predicaments. In deference to the
spring morning chill, I took the fork to the southern side
first, walking as briskly as the slick spots and granite
outcroppings allowed. The sunny face of the mountain
beamed warmth down on me. The air smelled of melting snow over warming pine needles. Swallows swirled
in dizzy patterns overhead, their repetitive chimes ring-
ing against the stark granite. A flicker answered, russet
tail feathers flashing.

Then I rounded the north side to increasing shadows
and snowy patches. Now the tower's dark face brooded
down on me. The calls of birds and rustling of squirrels
gave way to grave quiet. A two-faced mountain, indeed.

A cold breeze sifted through the pines, making the
needles rattle. The small hairs lifted on the back of my
neck. I shivered, fighting the urge to glance over my
shoulder.

The Dog is not behind me. The Dog is not real.

I walked faster. Moldy leaves covered the asphalt
trail, so my footsteps made no sound. Around an outcropping of house-sized boulders, a cluster of aspen
stood in a hollow between the path and the tower. Fe-
tishes and bits of ribbon hung from the limbs. This had
to be where they came, the local tribes, to make their
petitions to the dark gods, whoever they might be.

Fear trilled over me.

Okay, fine, I'd face it then. I stepped off the path. The air thickened as I approached the aspen grove, seeming to promise something. Their luminous trunks gleamed through the damp air, buds thick on their fairy-thin limbs.

Aspens' white bark with jagged scars always looked to me as if lovers had long ago carved their initials into them, careful hearts drawn around, to seal the two together. Silly, romantic and something else I'd never done. The tears that had been rising since I left Frank's pricked at my eyes.

Impatient with myself, I set my purse down on a sharp granite outcropping, pulled off my gloves and dug out a pocket knife. I traced a black pattern that could be my initials, digging in to make them really mine. My blade caught on a stubborn bit, hesitated and bit in.

Bemused by dull pain, I stared at the bright blood welling on my finger where the sharp edge had nicked me. An idea popped into my head, like a bubble bursting.

I swept the fall of my hair around and found a lock from the back of my neck, from the underside, where it wouldn't show, and sawed off a piece about half as big around as my pinky and as long as my forearm. I painted the hair with the blood from my finger.

No, of course I'd never done anything like that before.

Let's not even discuss that the blade wasn't disinfected. Logic and I had parted company when I walked out of Clive's party.

As with that precipitous exit, this felt right. Liberating.

Flipping the knife closed, I tossed it back into my purse, reached up and tied the lock of hair around one fine limb above my initials, so that the ends fluttered free. I stared at it for a moment. Watching its trance-like flutter.

That was the last thing I remembered—the ribbon of bloodstained dirty-blond hair waving from the tree limb, my red Coach purse on the boulder, my leather gloves crumpled next to it, like the discarded skin of a snake.

TWO

In Which I Fall Through the Rabbit Hole

I AWOKE ON soft grass.

This surprised me because I didn't recall falling asleep. As with general anesthesia, when the doctor had you count backward while the fluid flowed into your arm…and then you awoke without ever having been aware of losing consciousness.

I sat up, blinking against the dryness of my contacts, and found myself on a small hill. A glowing green countryside rolled out below, copses of trees scattered about in pleasing clumps. Morning sunlight still shone down on me, but both warmer and softer than the familiar Wyoming variety. Quite a bit warmer. I shrugged out of my heavy red wool coat, leaving my shoulders bare except for the spaghetti straps of the dress. After a moment, I slipped off my heels, too, and dug my toes into the silky grass.

No place I'd been to had this shade of emerald. Or a truly sapphire sky like this. It was as if I'd gone from black and white to Technicolor. Dorothy at the cusp of technology.

In a rush, it came back to me.

Cutting myself—my finger still throbbed, but the slice had scabbed over. And my hair… I reached up and touched the shorn bit at the nape of my neck. Wild, un-reasonable behavior.

And, shit, my purse was nowhere to be seen.

A shudder racked me and a sob welled up. What the hell had happened? This was like some fairy tale, where the hapless heroine wandered into a glen and ended up in a magic land. Maybe my escape velocity had hurled me clear into psychosis, colored heavily by Frank's suggestions of dark faeries.

I instructed myself to get a grip and be logical. What did I know to be true? I listed it in my head.

1. I had no idea where I was.
2. Nothing about myself was changed.
3. I had been unconscious long enough for my finger to scab over.
4. This sure as hell didn't look like Wyoming, much less any place in the world I'd seen. For what that was worth.
5...

I got stuck after that. But at least my heart had calmed.

I hauled myself up and scanned the countryside. Hills, trees, meadows. None of it looked farmed. I turned in a slow circle, ankle-deep in the thick grass. No signs of habitation anywhere. I had hoped to spot some kind of road, to take me to, well, somewhere else. A path, maybe a dirt road of some sort.

I completed my turn—and there it was. Just as I had imagined. The unreality of it slammed through my mind, making the edges of my vision shimmer.

Psychosis—looking more and more likely.

There lay my coat and shoes, just as I'd tossed them,

only now they lay on the verge of a road that had not existed a moment before.

A road that ended—or rather, began—at my bare toes.

This had to be a dream. A new chapter in the old nightmare. Sometimes I'd get so swept up in a dream that I'd think it was real. Until something really illogical happened and I'd think, as I had just now, *Wait! This is a dream, isn't it?* Once I'd caught on to the trick, it was as if I'd solved a puzzle correctly and my subconscious would relent, the dream dissolving away.

No such luck here. The world remained, dazzling, sharp. Improbably vivid, reminding me of the images in mirrors.

Okay then, I had wanted a road and now I'd gotten one. I looped my coat over one arm and picked up my heels in the other hand. While the sun shone warm, I might as well go barefoot—I might be walking for a seriously long time. Hopefully the road wouldn't be too rocky. I found, after a few steps, that the road wasn't rocky at all, but rather a soft dust soothing to my feet.

It felt surprisingly pleasant to simply walk along. Though I grew warm. The coat draped over my arm annoyed me and I shifted it to my other arm. A drink of water would be nice, to offset the dust. That stuff felt good on the feet but not so great on the throat.

As if in answer to my thirst, around the bend a clear brook flowed. It looped out from the trees and back in again, dancing brightly over rounded stones.

I set my shoes down and dropped the coat gratefully, wishing I'd left it back at Devils Tower with the other things. I scooped up some water in my hand, then paused. I sat back on my heels, studying the crystal drops. What about giardia? What about…something worse than that?

The ubiquitous velvety lawn was not Kentucky bluegrass, or any grass I'd ever seen. Botany might not be my forte, but I could recognize most tree species in general—and none of these trees were familiar. The leaves were shaped all wrong, with feathery tips and funny points. And it was quiet. No birds. No insects.

Not real.

Observation Number One still stood: I had no fucking clue where I was.

This might seem to be a fantasy version of Ireland, but it could be Hades' realm, for all I knew. Which would make me Persephone, trapped here forever if I ate or drank anything. Not to be superstitious, but if I admitted that I'd been somehow transported from Devils Tower to Elsewhere—which would be difficult to argue against—then the Underworld could be as possible as anything else. Or Faerie.

I racked my brain for the old tales I'd never paid much attention to. There always seemed to be banquets and falling asleep for hundreds of years.

Regardless, it wasn't wise to drink water I knew nothing about. I went to wipe my hand on my dress but, feeling suddenly paranoid, turned to wipe it on my coat instead.

Which was now gone.

Happily my shoes still lay on the grassy verge, though all alone. As if the coat had never existed.

Or, as if I *had* left it behind with the other things. At last, I had another observation to add to my list.

5. My wishes were coming true.

Deep, cleansing breaths.

I gazed at the water, clearing my mind. *Let the sound of the ripples soothe you. Relax. There must be some explanation for this.*

Then the angel hairs lifted on the back of my neck in familiar dread.

No, it can't be.

The Dog sat on the opposite bank.

A high whine rushed past my ears. My face heated to flashpoint. My stomach dropped in panic and every pore prickled with cold sweat.

He looked unreal, just as in my dreams of the past months, as if carved from volcanic glass. His amber eyes pinned me with fierce intelligence—and satisfaction? Tilting his gleaming head, he seemed to be asking a question. I still didn't know the answer.

"This is a dream," I said out loud. "This is just a new form of the same damn nightmare."

I wasn't naked, though, and not in that bathing chamber. I fervently wished to stay clothed and his jaw parted slightly, revealing a glimpse of white fang, as if he found me amusing.

And there I was, frozen, forever waiting for the attack.

My terror transformed into abrupt rage.

The fury beat against the inside of my forehead. I hated that damn Dog. Stalker Dog. Clearly I had gone over the edge into complete insanity, here in Disney Ireland with Stalker Dog and no birds. And now my wishes were coming true? Fine! Give me some singing birds with my fantasy brook and nightmare Dog!

The Dog's jaw snapped shut, ears lifting. We stared at each other across the bright water, which seemed to laugh with storybook joy, oblivious to the creatures

around it. The stream's chuckles were abruptly drowned
by a crescendo of singing birds. Birds filled the skies
and trees, shrieking song. I clapped my hands over my
ears and ducked my head as robins, cardinals, blue jays,
chickadees, even parrots swooped down, around, darkening the skies.

My stomach sank in horror. I'd done this. Claws
caught my hair. A beak scratched one arm as a mynah
and crow attacked each other.

The Dog still sat on the opposite bank—I saw him in
the breaks of the flights of screaming birds, like a fog
bank shifting and revealing small glimpses. A bubble
seemed to surround him, the birds parting in their wild
passage as water around a boulder.

He stilled and gathered, as if he drew shadows from
the woods behind him. His eyes darkened to a fire-or-
ange—the sparking flames of them bored through the
birds between us. His hackles rose, haunches bunching as his body tensed. The coal-black lips pulled back
again, but in a snarl, teeth somehow sharper-looking
than before.

The attack, at last.

A low growl spiraled from his body, a sub-audible
vibration, a keening wind that at first seemed to be part
of the cacophonic bird calls, then rose to a sharper thunder that shook me. That shook everything.

The birdsong scaled to a single banshee wail, unbearable in intensity. The thunder and keening chorus
became a ululating lamentation that I felt might break
my heart.

Then was gone.

I cautiously opened the eyes I hadn't remembered
closing. Even the brook's babbling had ceased. It, too,
was gone.

The Dog stood an arm's length in front of me. He loomed a good half-a-head above me, where I was still kneeling in the pool of my black skirt. We were the antipode of the virgin and the unicorn. My already straining heart thumped with the tension.

I thought about wishing him gone.

He leaped.

I screamed.

My hands flew up like the frightened birds as his teeth buried in my throat, launching me backward. I braced to die. Being torn apart by a wild animal had always seemed the worst possible death to me. I waited for the tearing pain, wondering how long I'd stay conscious and aware—something I always wondered when I read those horrific news stories—but found myself still pinned under steel jaws while I sobbed.

I fought. Frantic. Shredding myself against him. The Dog pinned me, a relentless strength, a furnace of heat and muscles under glossy fur. Tears ran hot over my cheeks and down my neck.

A panicked shriek bubbled up through the sobs, my chest billowing with it, but the Dog only sank down tighter, stopping my voice, my breath.

A sweet fragment of blue beckoned me, past his great obsidian head. Wishes. I could wish for rescue in this crazy place. I focused on the wish, but the Dog growled softly and closed his jaws slightly more. Stars sparked at the edges of my eyes.

"Please…" I tried to choke out, part sob, part whimper.

Blood-dark gathered at the edges of my vision, seeping in, blurring the circle of blue sky above, then drowning it in blackness.

THREE

In Which I Am Nullified

I AWOKE TO stone walls.

My throat screamed. When I tried to swallow, it seared like the worst strep infection on the face of the earth. Or wherever the hell I was, since I was clearly still Elsewhere. I wasn't dead, at least, unless being dead sucked more than I'd imagined. My contact lenses were glued to my eyeballs, my body was one giant bruise, and the pain in my neck echoed dully through every joint.

Peripheral vision told me I was lying on some sort of bed, on top of a deep blue coverlet. The gray stones of the walls rose to a ceiling high enough to gather shadows. Misty light fell through a window behind my head and I could see a stripe of ashen sky through a window at my feet. The sill looked to be as deep as my forearm and so it cut off most of the view from this angle. There seemed to be no glass in it—nor in the one behind me, judging by the chill breeze coming from that way. It put me in mind of the ruined castles in Scotland. Only somewhat less desolate.

I shifted carefully, to see if moving would make me feel worse. It did. The pain in my throat consumed me. I reached up to touch it, wondering if I would feel a bloody gash, but the drag of chain on my wrist halted the movement. Turned out, both wrists and ankles were chained.

Charming.

I lifted my right hand, rolling my eyes as far as I could to see it better. A silver cuff circled my wrist, attached to what appeared to be several feet of chain running over the edge of the pallet. Attached to the bed or wall somewhere, probably with iron rings cemented into the stones. I kicked up one foot. Same arrangement on my ankle. They probably didn't give me enough slack to sit up, though I wasn't feeling excited about trying that yet. This was fast going from Disney Ireland to Wes Craven's Ireland.

At least I wasn't chained naked to this bed. As it was, I felt acutely aware of the pressure of the cuffs on my skin, the soft slink of the chains as I moved.

With a sigh, I closed my eyes, trying to focus my thoughts. Okay, this could be real or not real. Under "not real" fell all sorts of unpleasant alternatives like concussion, coma, psychosis. I could be locked in my own skull for whatever reason, my neurons struggling to make sense of random signals. Not a pretty prospect. And not one I could control.

The "real" alternative, while spectacularly bizarre, at least left me with some options. If I had moved into some kind of alternate reality or another planet, then most physical laws promised I could go back the other direction. Therefore the most logical thing to do was focus on getting back. Me and Dorothy.

Instead of ruby slippers, it seemed I had wishing as my tool. Time to suspend disbelief and try to master what resources I had.

Concentrating, I wished to be free of the chains. I

pictured myself standing in the aspen grove at Devils
Tower. Or the grassy hillside. I'd take my grassy hill
over this. Or the brook. Not the Dog. *Don't think of the
Dog.* I wished harder.

"It won't work, you know," a bell-like voice said,
tinseled with amusement at my expense.

My eyes flew open and my head snapped around in
shock—or started to, before the waves of agony shot up
through my throat and over my skull. Tears filled my
eyes with blurry heat. A woman towered over me, not
three feet away. Definitely not human. Like a European
model, she stood slim in a way that spoke of a different
bone structure. Curved cheekbones set off rose-petal
lips and gilt almond eyes. Porno-blond hair fringed pix-
ielike around her face. Tinker Bell, right on schedule.

"It won't work," she repeated, "because you have
been nullified. No more romping about the countryside
creating roads, moving perfectly good streams and im-
porting exotic creatures."

I opened my mouth but only a croak leaked through.

She smirked, the expression shattering the loveliness
of her face. "You can't talk either, though that's not the
silver at work. Personally, I think he should have ripped
your throat out like the obscenity you are, instead of just
rendering you unconscious. But my judgments are not
considered." She made that sound like a crime against
the order of the universe.

Nasty Tinker Bell thumped down a tray I hadn't noticed on the ledge of the window, splashing liquid in a
bowl. She yanked the chain attached to my right wrist
and, before I could resist, dragged my hand above my
head, looping the link over a hook. With my arm out of
the way and holding the bowl in one hand, she sat on the

bed, her unbelievably slim hip nudging mine, scooped up some of the liquid and held it to my lips.

Remembering my resolve not to eat or drink in this place, especially now that I was a prisoner, I clamped my lips together. I could at least avoid being drugged. Nasty Tinker Bell's pretty golden eyes sparked. Turning the spoon, she let the liquid dribble over my mouth so that it ran down my cheeks, past my ears and pooled at the back of my neck to join the crusted mess of hair and various dried liquids there.

Careful not to touch the liquid on my lips, I looked directly at her porno prettiness. *Fuck you,* I thought.

I knew Tinker Bell couldn't hear me but I felt better.

"Fine," she snapped, her voice a little bell being rung too hard. Nasty Tinker Bell clearly understood at least the insult in my eyes. She lifted the bowl, with the clear intention of dumping it on my head.

"Enough," a male voice said.

As if I'd ceased to exist, Tinker Bell blinked her eyes and regained her lovely self, face smoothing, shining once again in sunny elegance. Reboot and resume program. She gracefully stood and glided to the tray, set the bowl precisely in the center, lifted the tray and left the room without hesitation.

Booted footsteps crossed the room toward me. Act II, scene ii. Exit Nasty Tinker Bell, Enter God-Only-Knows-What-Now. My face was sticky with whatever the brothy stuff had been, my hair wet and fouled. I stank. I hurt. I was chained to a bed in a place so completely unknown I couldn't begin to understand it. I tried to squeeze my legs closer together, but the chains seemed at the limit of their reach. The energy of my brief triumph evaporated, allowing tears to well up again.

Oh, please, please, please, do not cry. The threatening sting worsened. I closed my eyes and one tear leaked out. He stopped next to me, surveying me.

"You're certainly a mess." His wry voice was rich and smooth.

My eyes snapped open to glare at him through the blur. Fifty different smart remarks flew across my tongue, most along the lines that any failures of appearance on my part could be laid on the doorstep of someone besides myself. But even the buzz of the first word on my vocal chords brought searing agony. Relieved to have a legitimate reason for the tears, I almost welcomed the searing sensation.

"No, don't try to talk—no one needs to hear what you have to say, anyway. Not that we can help it, since you think so loudly. And you have a decision to make. We have a quandary." He began pacing, boots echoing against stone. "No one can heal you while you're bound in silver and we can't release you from the silver until you have yourself under control. Which will take a considerably long time—perhaps years of training—if you're even able to accomplish it at all."

I thought of the birds crashing in increasing cacophony with a small shudder.

"Exactly," he confirmed. "And yes," he said from the window behind my head where he seemed to be gazing out, "I can hear most of your thoughts—another reason to save trying to speak aloud."

My stomach congealed in panic. Had he heard my secret thoughts? *Don't think of them, bury them deep, deep. Think of other things...like what? Think of home, think of Isabel.* Isabel, my cat—Clive hated her. What would happen to her now? How could I not have thought of her until this moment? Abandoned, wondering why I never came home for her... And my mother—she'd be frantic. How long had I been gone? They could be all dead and buried, lost to me forever. The anguish racked me.

"Shh." The man sat on the side of my bed now, heavier than Nasty Tinker Bell. He brushed the hair back from my forehead, then placed his long fingers over my brow and, with his thumbs, rhythmically smoothed along my cheekbones, wiping away the tears that now flowed freely.

I stifled a sob. I had cried more in the past day than I had in years. The sweeping along my cheekbones soothed me, melting warmth through my skull. The rhythm became part of my breathing. Deep breaths. Smooth, easy. The awful tightness in my chest gave a little sigh and released.

"Let's try again, shall we?" The man pulled his hands away. I could hear him brush them against his thighs. Soup, tears and blood. Yuck.

My eyes cleared enough for me to see him. Ebony-blue climbed over half his face. The winding pattern of angular spirals and toothy spikes swirled out of his black hair on the left side of his face, placing sharp fingers along his cheekbone, jaw and brow. For a moment, the tattoo-like pattern dominated everything about him. Ferocious and alien.

Once I adjusted, I could see past the lines. His face echoed Tinker Bell's golden coloring. He could be her fraternal twin, with those same arched cheekbones. But where she was golden dawn, he was darkest night. Mid-

night-blue eyes, that deep blue just before all light was
gone from the sky, when the stars have emerged, but you
could see the black shadows of trees against the night.
He shared Tinker Bell's rose-petal mouth, but with a
curious edge to it. I suppose a man's mouth shouldn't
remind one of a flower, and there was nothing feminine
about this man. Where she wore the pink sugar roses of
debutantes and bridal showers, his lips made me think
of the blooms of late summer, the sharp-ruffled dian-
thus, edges darkening to blood in the heat. His bone
structure was broader than hers but still seemed somehow differently proportioned, his arms hanging a bit
too long from shoulders not quite balanced to his height.
Inky hair pulled back from his face fell in a tail down
his back. One strand had escaped to fall over his shoulder and I could see a blue shimmer in its silk sheen.

He arched his left eyebrow, blueness in the elegant
arch, repeating the deep shades of the fanged lines
around it.

"Shall we?" he repeated.

I stared at him. What was the question?

"Shall we discuss your situation? Attempt to use
some mental discipline and think yes or no, out loud
in your head."

Mental discipline, my ass. *Maybe.*

Then he laughed, an open delighted sound that
brought stars into the midnight of his eyes. "'Maybe'
will work."

I felt momentarily dazzled. Or simply lightheaded
from the throbbing in my neck. Probably serious blood
loss, too.

He stood and resumed pacing, hands folded behind
his back. "I can't hear every thought you've ever had.

Think of it like a lake. The first foot or two is clear. If I row my iittle boat on the lake and look down, I can see fish that come to the surface—especially if they come up for food or even leap out of the water. Deeper than that, I have no idea what fish are in there unless I dive in, which I'm not going to do because who wants to get soaked in someone else's lake water?"

He was lecturing.

"Yes, I often teach," he replied. "There's a good example—your observation that I was falling into a familiar lecture pattern swam up to the surface like a bright goldfish, right up to the bait I dangled in the water—which would be my words to you. The easiest thought to hear is a direct response to your own thoughts, vocalized or not. Especially fully and definitely formed as if you were about to vocalize it. Understand?"

Yes.

"No need to shout." He paused to stand over me again, that eyebrow once again raised in patient disdain. "No need to put any push behind it, just bring the little fishy to the surface for me to see."

Like I was a child.

"You are a child," he snapped—now I could see a flash of Tinker Bell. "Get that through your head right now. You're a toddler with a nuclear warhead, and there are those who will not hesitate to kill you for it. Who even now clamor for your death."

I gaped at him, not that my life being in danger was any surprise, but "nuclear warhead"? Were we in the actual world after all?

"Clear your thoughts, don't panic," he instructed, back in superior teacher mode. "Sort out what you want to ask me from the emotional response—you just about swamped my little rowboat with frantic toothy fish."

Torn between laughing and grinding my teeth, both of which would probably hurt, I pictured a nuclear warhead on my grassy hill and put a question mark next to it. My instructor rolled his eyes, but I caught a glimpse of the stars that brightened the blue of his eyes when he was amused.

"Nice picture, but words, please. We're not babies. Tut, tut—keep the anger out. Emotion only clouds the water."

How did he understand my words anyway—was he speaking English?

"Aha!" He beamed at me, resuming his measured pace around the room. "Now there's our logical girl! No, we do not speak the same language. If you concentrate on only the sound of my voice and not the sense, you'll hear that you don't understand the words I'm saying. But because vocalized words are like ducks on the surface of the lake, you are hearing the sense of my words, not the actual words themselves. You should be able to understand anyone here, except those who are insane or with *very* unclear thoughts. Also, someone who does not mean what they say will confuse you."

Interesting. So maybe he didn't say "nuclear warhead," but something that I translated as my equivalent of whatever that would be here.

"Exactly. Congratulations, we can enter you into kindergarten now."

I started lining up questions to ask, starting with *Where am I and how did I get here?* but he held up one long-fingered hand. Again, out of proportion, fingers just slightly too long for the hand, the whole hand just a little too long for the arm.

"Still your thoughts, let your fish swim deep and listen. Let's return to our original conversation. Answering all of your questions will take many days and we have more pressing concerns to attend to."

He sat on the bed again, frowned at my right hand still chained up to the hook and reached up to release it. He laid my hand down to rest on my stomach, smoothing the small wound on my finger with what I would have called tenderness, if not for the cool remoteness of his face. I could feel anger that wasn't mine, a low tone in the background, along with several other muddier emotions. They were coming from him. He was upset.

"No," he said, hand still over mine. "There's a great deal going on you don't understand, little girl. Can we focus on solving the immediate problem, please? Since it is *your* problem, not anyone else's?"

I tried to be still and thought of a calm lake, no fish.

"That's a start. You're still thinking of *something,* but at least it's something quiet for once." He smirked at me. "Now, it may have escaped your attention, but you were recently savaged by a wild beast. You're injured, you will not eat or drink—yes, I could hear that from downstairs, speaking of shouting—and we cannot use magic to heal you without releasing you from the silver, at which point you would likely destroy us all by accidentally setting off your nuclear warhead."

His words settled into my spinning mind, the implications finally becoming clear. *I can do magic?* I asked the question as quietly and clearly as I could manage.

He regarded me with a mixture of amusement and

sympathy. "Yes. Of course. What did you think you were doing?"

I didn't know. I suppose I'd done my usual thing and had avoided thinking about it directly. Not that I'd had much leisure for contemplation.

"The crux of it is, you are a natural sorceress, but you are not natural to this place. You are like a diseased predator—dangerous and unable to control yourself. That's why you were stopped."

His eyes dark, he leaned forward and gently touched my throat. I gasped and my head spun as the pain reared up. He stood abruptly. Paced across the room, steps a sharp clip. He returned from the far corner with a silver hand mirror.

"Allow me to elucidate." He held up the mirror.

My throat looked like it had been torn out.

FOUR

In Which Quandaries Are Addressed

WHY AREN'T I DEAD?

My instructor sighed.

"At last she comprehends." He started to lower the mirror but I managed to grab it from him, the silver chain chiming softly, and hold it up for myself. "The short answer to that is because you don't want to be. Also I'm reliably informed that it's not quite as bad as it looks. But then, don't you think those Healer types all say that kind of thing?" He sounded irritated but genuinely interested in my opinion.

I tore my eyes away from the reflection, trying to form a clear response from the swirl of my thoughts, but he waved his elegant hand at me.

"Never mind. I digress and you have better things to think about. Go ahead and look your fill."

He resumed his measured pacing, which I'd already come to think of as characteristic, staying quiet while I examined the damage.

It did seem to be somewhat less awful than at first glance. Dried blood—with bright fresh dribbles here and there—formed a contorted mass that obscured most everything else. I reached up with my left hand to gingerly probe the tissue, hissing at the fierce sting. There were definitely deep holes where the teeth had pierced

the skin deep into the underlying muscle. The ridge of
my larynx stood intact but massively bruised. Why it
wasn't crushed or how the Dog missed my carotids on
either side was a miracle. However, unless they communicated telepathically with bacteria here, making
peace treaties with the little beasties, I would be looking at serious infection problems very soon. It seemed
cleaning the damn wound would be a great non-magical
first step and then maybe some old-fashioned stitches.
I laid the mirror facedown on my belly and looked at
the stone ceiling.

Okay, Instructor, what now? I tried to project gently.

"Still too loud," he said from the window. "And call
me Rogue—that's my name." I snorted out a painful
giggle and he paced into my view. "I take it that translated oddly? Show me a picture of what that word means
to you."

I pictured Johnny Depp in *Pirates of the Caribbean,*
scraped and bruised from escapades, a bottle of booze
in one hand and a couple of girls in the other, wicked
mischief on his face.

Rogue laughed, then winked at me. I found myself
staring at his darkly glowing eyes.

"Not far off, really. You do envision detailed pictures—explains a great deal." He sat on the bed again
and smoothly withdrew the mirror from my hands.
"Now to respond to what you were thinking while you
examined your injuries, which I could quite clearly hear
with no effort, since you have an unfortunate tendency
to keep a most audible running commentary in your
head. Yes, you can and likely will get an infection—I
have no idea what the small beasties were that you were
thinking of, though they sound most intriguing. Yes,

we can wash you—believe me we'd love to—and we can stitch you up."

"However—" and now he looked steadily into my eyes, "—it will hurt. Without magic we have no way to deaden the pain."

No anesthetic, of course. Duh.

"Interesting concept, but no, no liquid that can be injected so you don't feel the pain. Normally our healers work with a Familiar that specializes in pain removal—they're quite good. And popular, as I'm sure you can imagine," he added with an impish grin. An image flashed through my mind of a ball with furious endless dancing.

Wait—did I get that image from him?

"Yes, and you could hear more, if only you were quiet long enough to hear something besides your own internal—very loud—babbling."

I pictured Johnny Depp again and smashed the rum bottle over his head, then smiled sweetly at Rogue, though I immediately regretted the searing pull on my neck muscles.

"And *that*, my little chit, is why we don't dare take the silver off of you, and why it will take weeks for you to heal instead of an hour, if you don't die first."

Rogue stood, taking the mirror with him, took a few steps and paused with his back to me, the long tail of his hair caught in a leather tie, then spilling down in a perfect fall of jet. Tension rippled through his shoulders and I cringed. He was genuinely pissed. Maybe not just at me. Being as quiet and still as I could, I reached a finger of myself toward him…and caught an image of me in the aspen grove, tying a lock of my hair to a tree. Triumph. Possessiveness. Followed by…guilt?

What? I thought at him, struggling to sit up, ignoring the searing pain. What happened? Were you there?

Rogue clapped his hands against his skull, dropping the hand mirror, which shattered on the unforgiving stone.

"By Titania, woman!" he roared at me. "Turn the volume *down!*" His eyes blazed blue lightning, the thorns on his cheek accentuating the snarl.

I quailed, my head spinning dizzily. I had failed yet again. At some point, I could quit just reacting and get a grip.

I apologize, I thought in a whisper.

Rogue rubbed his temple and grudgingly nodded. "Better. And no, I won't answer your questions until you demonstrate you can handle the answers. The very fact that you pulled that image out of *my* head—and yes, you yanked it out from a deeper level than you ought to be able to—only further proves what your detractors claim, so you'd better get that control you keep envisioning and never do that kind of thing to anyone else because they will assuredly kill you on the spot." His face was black lines frozen in ice. "Believe me, no one here would mourn your passing."

Guess he wasn't my ally then.

"No," he confirmed. "You are a child in the wilderness. You are without friends." He stalked toward me. "Your only hope lies in getting some level of strength back so you can be trained to be of some use, rather than a threat. Or a liability."

"Now observe." He stepped aside. "Can you see where I dropped the mirror when you so rudely and arrogantly *shrieked* in my head?"

Yes. I shaded the thought with contrition.

"Better, but leave the emotion out." Rogue waved his long-fingered hand at the shards on the floor, then the intact mirror was in his hand, the floor clean as if it never happened. He arched a knife-edged brow at me and set it back on some object across the room.

He clasped his hands behind his back. "That could be you—if only."

If only. If I could keep my thoughts quiet long enough for someone to heal me.

How long? I whispered. How long would I have to keep my head clear?

He watched me gravely. "Five minutes, probably. And don't you dare think that's not a very long time because in this little interview you haven't been able to be quiet for longer than ten to fifteen seconds at a time."

True. I could kid myself I had the mental focus to not think of anything in all that time, but I didn't. I had tried meditating, but I always starting thinking of things to do. Running conversations with people in my head.

"Well, at least you're no fool," Rogue commented, which didn't sound like much of a compliment.

Could I just stay quiet long enough for the magical anesthesiologist to put me out?

Rogue cocked his left eyebrow, the sharp spine above it rising also. "That could work. Though it has to be something you want with all your heart. This would be a deeper unconsciousness than just being knocked out like you were before. We can't afford to have any stray dream-thoughts leak out. If you fight it in any way, you could blast our Healer's Familiar, which I don't think I need to tell you, would not add to your popularity and in fact, would ensure your death sentence."

Yeah, yeah, yeah. Death sentence over my head, I get it already. But I kept the thought deep.

"Close. I almost couldn't hear that."

I was tired. In every way a person could be. Vultures of despair lurked in the corners of my mind, circling. Organize your options, I ordered myself.

1. Endure the pain of cleaning, disinfection and stitches on traumatized deep tissue, then spend weeks convalescing chained to this bed, surrounded by people hoping to kill me.

2. Attempt to control myself long enough to be knocked unconscious, risking the possibility that I could harm someone else and likely be killed.

3. Do nothing and die here of starvation and infection.

Rogue regarded me. "I must say, you do have interesting thoughts when you're not running in circles. So which of your three options will it be?"

I have to try. Will someone be ready to stop me if it looks like I'll lose it and hurt someone?

Rogue nodded. "I'll kill you myself."

FIVE

In Which Surcease Is Offered

So IT CAME to be that I was surrounded by five women, a cat, and Rogue with a silver-bladed knife at my throat. At least none of the women were Nasty Tinker Bell.

"Relax," Rogue murmured in my ear from his position next to my face.

This wasn't easy to do, what with the knife and all. However, I was concentrating on being the most Zen I could be. Which was so not my forte.

They'd pulled the wooden bed out from the wall, and me along with it. As the bed was really just a simple frame with a pallet over it, this made it a good working surface—no headboard or footboard to get in the way. Turned out I was only chained to the bed frame and not to any iron rings in the wall. Why this seemed better, I couldn't say. It just was. Plus, now I had a clear view of the door and everyone who came and went.

If I survived, I should probably start planning some kind of escape. And getting home.

Four of the women came in almost immediately after I agreed to the plan, answering Rogue's verbal call out the door. Maybe not everyone was telepathic. The women were clearly of the same tribe of whatever they were, with long bones and large eyes, though several of them were significantly shorter—perhaps shorter than my own five-four. One of the more petite women had a striking pattern on her face similar to Rogue's but with a different theme, which made me think of moth wings and moonlight.

None of them looked directly at me, as if they were afraid. A short brunette, with a plumper figure and the sensuous mouth of an odalisque, looked with interest at my dress, but she wouldn't meet my eyes. Rogue had directed one to stand at each corner of the bed. He gave each a silver key, then fetched the knife from the table by the far wall, where it had been lying all this time next to the hand mirror. Interview tools.

Rogue knelt down behind my head, knife in his right hand up under my chin, with the blade biased to my left, so he could make a good strong stroke. Then he nodded to the moth-woman and she went to open the door, standing back respectfully for the woman who entered.

I think I would have known her for a healer anywhere. She radiated a sense of restorative serenity that felt like cool water on a hot day, along with the godlike arrogance of a brain surgeon. Draped in layers of green, she glided across the room, earth-brown hair trailing down her back and onto the floor, a train behind her. A tortoiseshell cat trotted by her side. I felt a pang for Isabel but let it sink deep into my Zen-ness.

She sat on the bed next to my hip—I should set out a guest pillow there or something—lifting my hand as she did so, as if checking for my pulse, though her fingers were nowhere near the pulse point, all the while searching my eyes.

"You let it go long," she said to Rogue, with some asperity.

"It couldn't be helped—it was her decision to make."

"Going soft, Lord Rogue?" Then she clicked her tongue and the cat leaped onto her lap, gazing at me with bright inscrutable eyes. "I am Healer and this is Darling."

This literal translation thing was going to be totally unhelpful. Hopefully not all their names would be descriptions of character or professional occupations.

Healer stroked my hand. "Right now you are too injured to understand much."

I caught a definite sense from her that she didn't expect me to be all that bright, even if I wasn't injured. Rogue returned my questioning gaze soberly, just the left side of his mouth cocked up in a twist accentuated by the inky pattern around it.

"Look at me." Healer squeezed my hand to regain my attention. "Rogue, we need her as calm as possible— try to be helpful. Soothe her."

Ha to that. The man had a knife at my throat. I could feel the keen edge of it, just brushing the skin under my ear. Rogue put his cheek down next to mine on the side away from the knife. I didn't want him smelling my disgusting hair and tried to move away, but he put his left hand on my other cheek and held me firm. He lightly rubbed the patterned side of his face against me. Velvet smooth.

The heat of him felt good. With his left hand Rogue stroked my cheekbone. My eyes drifted closed and the hysteria melted away. So tired. I floated.

"Good," Healer murmured. "Now Darling will lie with you. He will only soothe you, just like your own Familiar. Feel that attachment to her and let him settle on you."

The kitty stepped onto my belly, padding delicately

up to sink down on my chest over my heart. His hind
end draped over my stomach. His purr filled my blood
and it felt just like Isabel had crept up to cuddle while
I slept, a warm blanket draped over me.

"Cat's purrs are wonderfully healing. That's why
they survive impact and injury so well. Darling will also
remove your pain and put you to sleep. You'll let him.
Do you trust him? Tell us in your head how you feel."

I trust the kitty. I was relieved to find it was true.

"She's so loud." Healer sounded annoyed.

"You have no idea," Rogue said beside my ear. I
tensed at the irony in his voice. "Shhhh," he said. "Just
relax, no worries." Other words followed, sounds that
had sense in themselves but connected in nonsense like
a lullaby I'd known once but since forgotten. They lulled
me. Darling purred, softly warm on my chest.

"Ladies," said the healer, "insert your keys, but do
not turn them yet." Their cool hands clasped my wrists
and ankles. Metal links softly chimed.

"Now," Healer began. Paused. "Do we know her
name?"

"Gwynn," Rogue murmured beside my head. Something stirred in me to protest that wasn't exactly right,
but he crooned in my ear, "All is well, lovely Gwynn,"
and I sank back down into my half-sleep, yielding to
the exhaustion.

"Yes, so tired, time to sleep, Gwynn," Healer crooned
hypnotically. "Open your eyes, Gwynn, just enough to
see Darling." I struggled to raise my lids to find the cat
had inched up enough that I could look into his eyes.
They were the green of new leaves in spring. *Don't
think.* I tried to let the thoughts spin away.

"Look at Darling. Let him lead you into sleep. Be

without thought. Forget we are here. Quietly and gently, ladies."

The silver fell away and I felt a spark of panic. Rogue tensed, a quiver running through him. Their wariness and fear rose up around me. This had to be how the tiger in the zoo felt, being anesthetized for some surgery or tooth-cleaning. The knife bit into the flesh under my ear.

"Control!" Rogue hissed.

I pressed my cheek into his and dissolved the image of the tiger into tiny bits.

"Look at Darling!" Healer urged. "Follow Darling."

I focused again on the cat's eyes, let go of something tight in myself. I threw it into the green depths, slumberous, beckoning. I could do this little thing. I followed him down and away.

THIS TIME WHEN I woke, at least I knew where I was.

Not in the grander scheme of things, but at least the same stone ceiling greeted me. I appeared to be in the middle of the room still. Amazing what a relief it can be to have the world *not* change while you're unconscious. I stretched and a great rush of well-being filled me. A sense of joy, even. I probably deserved to be happy, since I was still alive and not bleeding out like a kosher lamb. But it was more than that—I felt better than I could ever remember feeling. I touched my throat. Smooth, intact—and encircled by a metal collar.

Nice.

Ready to try the sitting-up thing again, I raised myself on elbows, delighted that my head didn't swim. One happy development—though I once again wore the silver cuffs on my ankles and wrists, they were no

longer attached to chains. Unfortunately, however, my
hair seemed to be still glued to the back of my head in
a disgusting mass. You'd think they could have cleaned
me up a little.

Spotting a mirror on the opposite wall, I hopped off
the bed and padded barefoot over to it. The hand mirror lay on the wooden cabinet. No knife.

I looked like death warmed over.

Maybe death microwaved—because my eyes shone
and my complexion looked fantastic. I could be almost
pretty, if I weren't such a freaking mess. The final tattered remnants of party makeup clung to the corners
of my eyes and ran in smudged dribbles on my cheeks.
The hair and dress were beyond belief. Kind of a Me-
dusa does Ann Taylor look. Not good. The black of the
dress did its best to absorb the bloodstains and various
other fluids I didn't want to contemplate, but it had been
pushed to the limits of the fabric and now looked uncomfortably reminiscent of the battered exoskeleton of
some unfortunate squashed beetle. I wet my fingers and
wiped the cosmetic dregs off as best I could. I tried to
finger-comb my hair, only to fail utterly. The stuff felt
shellacked. How long had I been out?

The door opened and Healer walked in. After un-
locking the door. I was unchained, but not free-range,
apparently.

"You've been out for a full moonrise and moonset,"
she said to me, which explained why the light seemed
much the same. As soon as she left I would look out
the window—said something about me, I guess, that
I'd beelined for the mirror first. "And work on toning
down that volume or Rogue will be in here shortly—
he's not very patient about that sort of thing."

Nor was she, I recalled. *You are without friends.*

"Can you say something?"

"Thank you, Healer," I tried.

"You are most welcome. We can discuss payment later." Approaching me, she held up her hands. "Tilt your head back." Her palms tickled me with little points of heat as she ran them over my throat. She nodded to herself and backed up a step, rubbing her hands briskly, like a surgeon snapping off her latex gloves after an examination.

Payment. What kind of currency could they possibly use—and how would I get some? Escape could solve that problem—get free and ditch the bills in one fell swoop. Not very honorable, but ethics seemed especially gray under the circumstances.

"How can your magic work, if I'm wearing these?" I held up my arms, and the wristbands gleamed dully in the misty light.

Healer smiled serenely, a practiced look that began to grate on me. She had her share of Rogue's and Nasty Tinker Bell's vast superiority. Didn't bode well for me that I was already wearing thin on it.

"There are many things in what you are calling magic, Gwynn. In fact, what you mean right now behind that word doesn't apply at all. It's more like the mind-to-mind talking that you've been doing—"

"Telepathy."

She frowned. "That's almost right. The healing takes magic that can be blocked through certain measures." She gestured to the collar around my throat. "Obviously we couldn't take this precaution before, but around the throat is the second-best possible containment."

I knew right then I never wanted to find out what

they thought the best containment was. Probably something like the man in the iron mask wore. Serious heebie-jeebies on that.

"But in the same way that Lord Rogue and I can still hear your thoughts, I can sense how your body is doing. Which seems to be quite well. I fixed other things while I was at it—you won't need those glass slips in your eyes to assist your vision, though that was a clever idea of yours. And I took out the poisonous mercury in your teeth—was that a punishment for something?"

"What, my fillings?"

"Yes, they packed it into your teeth, which I, naturally, fixed. What a barbaric people you must come from, to punch little holes in your teeth and fill them with poison."

Instead of gritting my teeth, I ran my tongue over them to find they were smooth, without any rough edges. And how had I not noticed my contacts were gone?

"You'll find us much more civilized," she assured me. "Lord Rogue treats his pets very well, in general. Not like some you could be sent to."

She was really too much. Of course, there I was in my little doggie collar, so who was I to argue?

My palms oozed cold sweat and my heart gave a hard thump. Now that I wasn't dying, I had the wit to panic about being trapped. Not caring that Healer watched me, I went to look out the window.

Nothing but fog, deep and impenetrable. Same thing out the other window. The outside wall was the same gray stone as inside, but disappeared into the mist after a few feet. I could possibly crawl out the window, jump onto the lawn and scamper away. Or irretrievably bash my skull on pointed rocks after a forty-story drop. I wondered if they'd heal me again, what the limits of her ability to reconstruct were.

"So, what is this place—where am I?"

"Why, you're in Lord Rogue's castle." She frowned at me, considering, as if she might have missed knitting my brain together.

"I meant in a larger sense—what do you call your... world?"

"Ah." She smiled. "This is the Land of the People."

Of course it was.

I didn't like this. I should be grateful for all Healer had done, but now even my own body wasn't the same. All the information I so desperately needed to make decisions was self-referential. I needed to take some steps to regain control—who am I kidding? *Gain* control—of this situation.

"Well, thanks for everything!" I turned my back to the window and propped my rear against it. I gestured to the dress, my nasty hairdo, trying to look humble. "I know I have no grounds to impose further, but any way I could bathe? Maybe borrow a clean outfit from somebody? Add it to my tab?"

Healer smiled, comfortable now that the pet was wagging her tail. "But of course! You know, we would have bathed you while you were out but we didn't know the customs of your people."

Oh yeah, I could just picture the people I might come from—where blood gook was the new mousse. I made an effort to keep that thought to myself, too, and Healer didn't seem to hear me. Maybe I was getting better at this.

"And, of course, the spell on your dress."

The door opened. Not locked this time—I was keeping track now. Two young men, heads bowed so they could only see the floor, tromped in carrying a brass-looking tub, which they deposited on the floor. They tromped out again as if the room were empty. No lock click behind them.

"That was fast," I remarked.

"Oh yes," Healer agreed. "Rogue's people are very well trained."

"What was that about a spell on my dress?"

"You spelled it so it couldn't be removed. Several people tried. Even Lord Rogue couldn't do it."

What, *Rogue* tried? Asshole.

Healer's eyes flew open in shock. I smiled weakly, imagining the image she'd received from my too-loud thought.

"It would behoove you to learn to think like a lady."

I squashed my response to that one.

"Think back," Healer prompted me. "At some point you wanted to make sure you kept the dress and somehow didn't trust yourself to make certain that would happen…" She was thinking of a silly girl in a torrid embrace being slipped out of her clothes.

As if that kind of thing had ever happened to me, even when I *was* a silly girl.

When could I have done that? Oh yes. The Dog. How could I have forgotten? He'd loomed huge and black on the riverbank and I'd felt a thread of panic. My nightmare in brutal flesh.

"Do *not* think of him here," Healer hissed. The serene lady vanished, Dr. Jekyll abruptly replaced with Ms. Hyde.

"Why not?" I snapped back. "I thought my new jewelry kept me from manifesting my thoughts. Isn't that the whole point of having me shackled like a prisoner?"

Healer's face flushed, pretty lips snarling unpleasantly. "You're an undisciplined peasant wretch! A whore of a magical dilettante. You have no idea what you're dabbling in. And don't think I don't know the filthy source of your power. No decent castle will have you." Her mouth turned down in a final sneer as her eyes swept from my bare feet to my bosom.

The door opened and the plump brunette from the healing session walked in, leading a parade of young girls with buckets. Healer's face fell back into calm serenity as if I'd never seen the woman behind the mask. Just like Nasty Tinker Bell's reboot.

"We'll have your bath ready in a jiffy, Lady Gwynn," the brunette called out, curtseying in my direction.

The activity provided a welcome distraction from my discussion with the Healing Bitch. The girls scurried about, filling the tub, stripping the covers off the bed, which they scooted back against the wall, setting out bottles and towels, building a fire in the stone fireplace at the end of the room. All the while the brunette stood in the middle, reminding me of Mickey Mouse directing his legion of mops.

Darling slipped around the door, which had been left ajar with all the comings and goings. With a pleasant chirrup, he padded up to me and stroked up against my bare legs.

"Hi, Darling." I crouched down to stroke his arched back. It felt blessedly normal to simply pet him, feel his cat vitality. He sniffed at my face. A pink raspy tongue licked my cheek. If I didn't look around, I could be at home.

"Darling, come here to me," Healer said in a tight voice.

As cats will, he simply blinked at her in disinterest, then butted his head against my hand. I obligingly rubbed his ears.

"You *do* understand, don't you," Healer said in her serene voice, but the Nasty Tinker Bell tone threaded underneath, "that he's a Familiar, not a pet? I thought you knew this, since I saw your own Familiar in your head. But it seems I've given you far too much credit." She glanced to see if anyone was listening to us, but the Brunette General was busily herding maids.

I wanted to say, "Well then, you *do* understand that Isabel is just a plain old cat, don't you?" But I kept it very whispery in my head.

Darling purred and rubbed against me again, arching his back in a way that meant he wanted to be held. I gathered my arms around him and stood.

"He doesn't like…!" Healer started and trailed off as Darling's purr filled the room. He rubbed his whiskers on my chin, then tilted his head at Healer, a coy look in his eyes. She stared back, her displeasure obvious under the thin veneer of calm.

Anyone who spent any time with cats should know they love best to be contrary. I had no idea what made a cat a Familiar and not a pet—except Familiars maybe possessed more intelligence, could communicate in some ways. Isabel was certainly a pet.

But then, apparently, so was I.

Darling delicately sniffed the underside of my chin, his cold nose tickling me, then, with a renewed purr, dug his head into my collarbone.

"Lady Gwynn." The brunette appeared at my elbow,

long delicate fingers clasped in front of her generous bosom. "Your bath is ready."

"I shall leave you." Healer tried her serene smile, but it looked gritted out. "See that you eat—I replenished your fluids, but your body needs sustenance after the healing coma."

Healer walked to the door, waited expectantly. I set Darling down on the floor and felt a bit bereft.

"Come along, Darling."

He didn't.

She clucked at him.

He pulled cat attitude and acted as if she were empty air. Instead the freshly made bed became his chief interest. He padded over to it, examined the height and leaped up, landing soft as dandelion down in the center, where he curled up, suddenly exhausted.

By the time I looked at the doorway, Healer had gone.

SIX

In Which I Am Offered Something Even Better than Surcease

"THANK TITANIA THAT one is gone." The brunette sighed, then winked at me. "Now we'll have some peace! Bhrta, Mina, come help Lady Gwynn out of this dress. You'll have to let us, lady. Lord Darling, I'm going to close and lock this door for privacy—do you care to stay or go?"

Darling tucked his head under, stretched, and to all appearances fell into an immediate and deep sleep.

"That answers that. Now release the spell, Lady Gwynn—I'm sure you're perishing to get clean. I know I would be."

"You know, my name isn't Gwynn."

"Lord Rogue says it is, Lady Gwynn. I'm not one to gainsay him."

She stood before me, bright black robin's eyes expectant. The maids, little brown sparrows of girls, waited quietly behind her, eyes cast down, ready to flee. I pulled on the spaghetti straps, but couldn't quite seem to get a grip on them, no more than I could tug on a raised mole. I reached behind me to the zipper. It felt sewn on.

"Lady," Brunette said gently, "release the spell first, then we'll get the zipper for you."

Okay, I'm a dunce.

"I don't know how," I confessed. "Besides, don't these—" I held up my wrists, "—keep me from doing any magic?"

"Undoing is not doing," she assured me gravely. "So my granny always said. Though I've no experience with such things myself. Shall I call Lord Rogue? Surely he'll know."

"No! I mean, I'd rather not involve him in any...well, undressing on my part."

She winked at me again. "No worries, love—I wouldn't let that rascal near my bedchamber either, even were I so lucky as to have him express interest."

The little sparrow girls exchanged a glance, fluttering giggles at each other.

"Let's see." She pursed her lips, clearly marshaling her problem-solving skills. This was a woman— or, whatever, since, though shorter than many, she still sported the odd bone structure they all shared—who knew how to remove obstacles from her path. "The magical types all have different ways of doing what they do. Some use wands, some words, some funny costumes. You just don't know your way yet. Like a youngling first come into power." She raised an eyebrow, waiting politely.

"This is helpful—keep going, please."

"Well, maybe you just need to think about what you did when you cast the spell and work backward. Just as if I spilled soup on the floor—I might think about how I'd get it unspilled, as it were."

"So I kind of need to wipe it up?"

Interesting.

I pictured the Dog standing over me by the brook. Uneasy, I slid my eyes to the group, but no hysterics ensued. They only waited. None of them, thankfully, seemed to hear my thoughts, or at least didn't respond to them.

At a whispered word, Bhrta went to add more hot water to the tub. Thinking about the Dog made my heart clench. Like digging into a wound to find the sliver of glass, I prodded my memory, ignoring the pain. In the fraught swirl of birds and terror and the Dog leaping for my throat, I found an image in my head of wishing the dress to stay on. It glowed there, like a bubble preserved in amber. I could feel the shimmer of—magic?— around it.

I mentally felt around the bubble. It flexed, resilient, part of me and yet not. Experimentally, I popped it. It vanished as if it had never been. I slid one strap of the dress down. Easy peasy. "I think I did it!"

"Of course you did, dear." She bustled behind me to slide the zipper down. "Such a simple thing for a powerful Lady Sorceress as yourself." She slipped the dress down my legs and I stepped out, clad only in the woefully overworn black silk panties. "No wonder Lord Rogue has gone to such lengths. Slip that off, pet, and we'll get you into the tub."

At the brunette's direction, one of the sparrows bundled up the clothes I'd stepped out of and moved to the fireplace. My last anchor to who I had been was about to go up in flames.

"No!" I lunged for them and the little girl quailed, puppy eyes enormous in her panicked face.

"Tsk, Lady Gwynn," Brunette clucked, "no one is taking your things. We'll get them clean. We've a bit of laundry magic, too."

I felt abruptly foolish. Ridiculous. Everything

seemed to be spinning away from me. Had my life seemed lifeless and empty? I no longer recognized that person I'd been. Or who I was now.

The sparrow girl edged away from me and set the bundle by the door. I dropped myself into the hot water, exhaling in relief. This, at least, felt normal. Comforting. Brunette was hustling the girls into warming the towels by the fire, which snapped and crackled in a merry counterpoint to the cool fog out the windows.

"Thank you for your help, Lady…"

"I'm Blackbird, Lady Gwynn. You can leave off the title with me—always seems silly, to keep reminding everyone, don't you think?"

"I wouldn't know, since I've never been nobility of any sort."

"Lord Rogue says you are, dear, so that makes it so. *His* title I am always careful to use—" she winked at me, "—or my granny would tan my behind. Now dunk your head, pet, and give your hair a good soaking, so we can get you clean."

The water muddied immediately with ugly reddish-browns and Blackbird set the sparrow girls to bailing water to dump out the window, while the other brought freshly warmed water from the fireplace. I listened for how far the water fell, but couldn't hear it actually hit the ground. Good thing I hadn't jumped.

"What scents do you prefer, love?" Blackbird settled herself before a tray of bottles.

"Umm, hazelnut?" At least, that was my favorite body butter. Damn, I'd miss that stuff. "Vanilla, cinnamon, mace."

"The dark sweet scents," Blackbird agreed, a wink in her voice. Like an alchemist, she combined drops from various glass bottles. Then scooted a stool behind my head and poured some warm liquid into my hair. She carefully worked her fingers through the snarls, massaging my scalp. It comforted me and I soaked it up. Except I might still be behaving badly.

"Should you be washing my hair? Seems like a noble lady ought to, well, supervise or something."

"Tush." Blackbird poured more liquid into the congealed mass at the nape of my neck. "'Tis a privilege, dear. I volunteered, or was about to when Lord Rogue asked me."

"He asked you to wash my hair?"

She chuckled. "Well, not in so many words, but rather to help you dress for the reception."

"Reception?" I sat up too abruptly, sloshing the water, and she tsked at me.

"Yes, reception and banquet. Your debut. Now close your eyes."

She called Mina over with a bucket and doused my hair, sluicing away the suds. Blackbird poured more goop into my hair and settled in for a second wash. I waited for her to resume our conversation. She changed the subject instead.

"I'm going to add some oil and comb it through to get the tangles out. Then we'll wash once more lightly and we should be done." She handed me a cloth with more of the scented soap in it, so I could scrub myself while she worked. Hopefully it wouldn't be hard on my complexion. Least of my worries, I guessed. My mind was probably grasping at inconsequentials because I couldn't yet grapple with this vastly changed reality. Still, I needed to focus on next steps.

"So when is this reception?"

"Oh, in a little while," Blackbird returned so breezily that I knew she was ducking the subject.

"Will you be there?" I winced as she tugged a wooden comb through the snarls. The comb smelled of sandalwood.

"Only in the background, dear. I'm not so important, thank Titania."

"Is Titania your queen?"

"A ruler?" Blackbird sounded confused as she launched into another shampooing. "No, Titania watches over us. Okay, Bhrta, rinse."

I sat still while the water sluiced over me. "I don't suppose you have some kind of razor?"

"A sharp blade?"

"To shave my legs?" I lifted one leg out of the water and laid it on the rim. The silver ring circling my ankle winked in the light, the same color as the fog. I'd forgotten about it. How quickly one becomes accustomed to shackles.

Rubbing my fingers over the sharp stubble on my leg I could believe it was at least two days' growth. Bhrta and Mina came over, politely curious. Blackbird bent closer, eyes wide.

"Why do you grow hair on your legs?" she asked, completely astonished.

"Not by choice, I assure you. That's why I want to take it off."

She shook her head dubiously. "Maybe better to get Healer to fix that for you."

"Never mind—please tell me I'll have something to wear to this reception? Maybe something long enough that no one will see my legs?"

"Oh yes!" The sparrow girls nodded with her. "Now, stand up and we'll give you a final rinse."

I reluctantly left the warm water and let Mina pour several buckets over me, while Bhrta bailed from the tub. Where was all the water coming from anyway? This was far more than they'd brought in originally and no one had left the room since Blackbird locked it.

Blackbird wrapped me in warm towels—there were advantages to this being-waited-on business—and led me to the fire. The buckets warming there were all full. All except the one Bhrta was still using to empty the tub. The buckets by the fire looked different, some-how. I unfocused my eyes and they almost glowed. That same shimmer as the amber bubble in my mind. This was their "magic." But wasn't magic simply technol-ogy that one didn't fully understand?

"Wrap up your lovely hair in this towel, dear, and we'll get you oiled down."

I bent over and shook my hair out, then wrapped it up tightly. The towels weren't made of the familiar terry but of a silky-feeling fabric. Blackbird bustled back with her tray, slid off the towel I was wrapped in and began rubbing oil into me. Which seemed a bit odd at first, but then no different than a masseuse working on me. She smoothed the oil over my throat particularly, warning me that though it was healed, the skin had been rushed through the process and needed special care. Good to know. The fire warmed my skin, heated the oil so the fragrance of cloves, nuts and cinnamon swam together. Blackbird carefully oiled under the collar and other sil-ver bands as well, then buffed them with a cloth—might as well treat them like jewelry, she observed with char-acteristic cheer.

Then she sat me on a stool, once again draped in a towel, with my back to the fire. She combed my hair, spreading it to the flames, while Bhrta and Mina finished cleaning up the tub. Mina brought over a tray with food of the fruit and cheese variety, maybe some kind of pastry things. I ignored them, though my stomach felt hollow. Not that it would hurt me to burn a little fat.

"Best have something, dear. Lady Healer said you were to eat."

"No, thank you—not at the moment." I tried to think of an excuse. Failed. "Are the water buckets magic?"

"Oh yes—Lord Rogue fixed them up for us, so we wouldn't have to haul water so far. They just stay full all the time, no matter how often we empty them."

"Like the pot of gold that never dwindles."

"I've never heard of such a thing as that, pet. It doesn't sound nearly so useful."

"Tell me more about how magic works. Can you perform magic things or do spells?"

"Me?" She fluttered. "Oh, Titania, no."

"Why not?"

"Lady Gwynn—you should know. Some have the gifts, some do not. It's unkind for someone as powerful as yourself to be so cavalier of your special status."

I turned and caught her hand. "Lady Blackbird— that's the thing. I don't know. I don't know where I am or how I got here."

"Don't you?" Her black eyes glinted, just like her namesake's. "It seems to me you're the person who was there every step of the way."

"I was in my own world and then I was here."

"That's often how it works." She looked sympathetic and tried to pull her hand away.

I sighed at her. "Won't you give me any information?"

"It's really not my place, Lady Gwynn. Lord Rogue would—oh dear."

"What's wrong?"

"Well, I tried to be careful, but I seem to have broken off some of your hair underneath in unsnarling it. I'm so, so sorry for it." Blackbird sounded apprehensive. Of course, with prima donnas of the Nasty Tinker Bell and Lady Healer of Everything Under the Sun ilk running around, I wasn't surprised. I reached back and felt the bristly stub at the right side of my nape.

"Oh, no worries. I did that."

"I see, dear, of course you did. I believe I can braid it in." Blackbird began tugging and weaving, apparently braiding my hair into some kind of up-do. She leaned in close to my ear, whispered, "Did you by chance cut your hair and add blood to it?"

"Yes." My heart thumped, remembering the bizarre impulse—and the vision I'd seen in Rogue's mind about it.

"And were you near a gate?"

"A gate?" I kept my voice and thoughts very quiet.

"A place where, perhaps, in your world odd things occur?"

I nodded.

"That's it then, Lady Gwynn. You spelled yourself here. There's no two ways about it."

"So I could spell myself back?"

"A powerful sorceress such as yourself could do most anything she set her mind to, I would think." A thump sounded behind me and Darling padded over to rub against my legs. I stroked his arched back while he purred.

"He's taken to you, that one," Lady Blackbird chirped out in her normal bright tone, briskly finishing the braids. Confidences were over, I supposed.

Darling left my hand to butt against her legs. "Of course, we are all his servants where ear scratching is involved," she added, leaning over to perform the service. "Now! Let's get you dressed."

With the help of the sparrow twins, Blackbird wrapped me in layers of silk-and linen-ish fabrics, cut into wide strips so they encircled me like a sari or a mummy's wrappings. Strips went between my legs, around my thighs, my belly and waist, secured over my shoulders, then wrapped tightly around my rib cage to bring my breasts together. Good thing they'd offered me the chamber pot behind the screen first, because this underwear was not the do-it-yourself kind.

The chamber pot did the reverse of the water buckets. It magically emptied. Blackbird warned me to be careful not to drop anything in there I liked—several ladies had carelessly lost jewelry that way. When I asked her where the stuff went, couldn't Rogue conjure it back again, she blinked at me and supposed the things went to the same place the water came from.

Silly question.

When they finished, I felt as corseted and stiff as the first Queen Elizabeth looked in her portraits, but I did have impressive cleavage. Now I knew where all the ladies got their figures. And why they'd found my own underwear so titillating. My poor little panties comprised about two percent of the fabric I had on now.

"This isn't for all the time, dear—just formal events, and Lord Rogue wanted you formal tonight."

Blackbird dropped a sheer robe over my head. It draped over me from neck to wrist to toe. She added several more, all light, all in various shades of beige, until I wore seven robes in a straight column of cloth. Mina offered me a pair of ballet-type flats, beige, of course.

I glimpsed myself in the mirror. I looked like a Carmelite Novice. The braided hair was too severe for my face, emphasizing my square jaw. The cinched waist and impressive cleavage were completely obscured. The off-whites did nothing to complement my pale complexion and dishwater hair.

"I am a symphony in neutral," I declared.

"Thank you!" Blackbird beamed.

I tried to think of a way to tell her that wasn't a compliment without hurting her feelings.

"Usually I prefer brighter colors," I tendered.

"Oh no!" Blackbird looked horrified. Turning me away from the mirror, she took my hands. "No colors, no affiliations tonight. You must be neutral, nonthreatening—I thought you knew that. Didn't Lord Rogue explain?"

"When?" I scoffed. I jerked my hands out of hers and paced the room. "After he lambasted me for thinking too loud, but before he held the knife to my throat? I have fifty-three million questions and no answers! I notice he's been markedly absent since I regained my voice, in fact."

"And who would blame me, really?" Rogue drawled from the doorway.

I whirled around to see him lounging against the

doorframe, keen blue gaze sparkling. He was resplendent in black. A velvety outfit that outlined his lean body so that he appeared as sleek as I was puffy. The blade of a knife to my undercooked bratwurst. I contemplated several come-backs, but he waggled a long finger at me.

"Tsk, tsk, temper, darling."

He shrugged away from the doorway as the two tublads reappeared and, heads down, tromped back in, seized the tub and took it away without a word. I was sorry to see it go. Mina and Bhrta hustled after them, padding on silent feet. Darling slipped out, also. Ah, well.

Lady Blackbird swept Rogue a deep curtsey. "Best of the evening to you, sir."

He kissed her hand and she blushed charmingly. "Thank you for your labors, Lady Blackbird. Once again you have exceeded my expectations." He glanced at me. "She could hardly be any less attractive."

"Gosh, thanks."

"Best of luck tonight, Lady Gwynn." She patted my cheek and tucked a wisp of hair behind my ear, whispering, "You'll do just fine, dear—just do whatever Lord Rogue tells you to do."

Oh yeah, great idea. Rogue snorted. I smiled at Blackbird. Then impulsively kissed her on the cheek. "Thank you for your extraordinary kindness to me."

She looked startled, round eyes sharp and bright. "I'll remember this, lady!" She scooted out the door, closing it behind her.

SEVEN

In Which I Make My First Bargain

"I HAD HOPED that your irascible nature was due to the pain and that the healing would have improved your personality," Rogue said as the door shut.

He stood by the fire, arms crossed over his chest. Leather boots came up just over his knees and thick heels for riding added to his height. As if he needed it. He wore the silver knife at his left hip in a sheath glinting with jewels. A black leather belt threaded through the sheath swung low on his narrow hips. I pretended to be only noticing the knife and not the rest. And, oh yes, I was working on keeping my thoughts deep and quiet.

I folded my arms over my own chest—not easy with this many layers. My breasts were beginning to ache with the confinement. The rest of my body pulsed against the tight cloths.

"I'm not going to this party dressed !ike this." I drew my line in the sand. He did the one-eyebrow raise, but didn't move otherwise.

"Stay here then," he returned, "and we'll decide your restitution and future without you."

He didn't move to the door though. Just stood there, acute eyes framed by the thorns on his face and that glass-black hair, watching me.

"Why can't I go but wear something else?"

"Why are you worried about—of all things—what you're wearing? Titania save me from a woman's foolish vanity."

"Look, I don't know much about this world. Where it is, who you are—and I notice no one is eager to answer these questions—but I am not accustomed to being dressed up and trotted about. Contrary to what everyone here seems to think, I am not a pet. I might be a prisoner, but I don't have to be a cheerfully obedient one. Why does it matter what I wear?"

"There are things you don't understand."

"Well, hallelujah, at last we agree on something," I snapped. "Clearly there's some kind of charged sociopolitical thing going on here—do you really think it's a bright idea for me to walk into something like that totally blind?"

"No."

I waited.

The fire crackled.

I returned his stare, refusing to flinch. As far as I was concerned, a monosyllable doesn't count as a valid conversational response so the ball was still in his court.

"We don't have enough time," he finally said.

Ha! Won that round. I pressed my advantage. "How much time do we have? When does this party start?"

"It's not a party. It's a reception and banquet. At which you *will* eat," he added. "And it's starting right now."

I glanced out the windows, where the fog remained the exact same shade of grayness. "How do you know it's time? What time is it, anyway?"

"It's time for the reception to start."

"Okay, now that's just circular reasoning. If I were

inviting you to a party—" he opened his mouth, so I held up a hand, "—a reception and banquet, then. I would say, 'Hey, Rogue, the dinner starts at seven o'clock and it's six fifty-six right now, so we need to be on our way.' Now it's your turn to try it."

He just looked at me.

"Go ahead," I prompted. Never let it be said that I can't be stubborn.

"We don't measure time like that. Things start when they start. Time, however, can be wasted. Just like this. They're waiting. We have to go."

"I want to know at least some basics. We can be five minutes late, or five parsecs or half an inch of melted wax or whatever the hell. I'm calling your bluff—I think you want me there for some reason, so unless you intend to carry me in kicking and screaming, answer a few questions and I'll go."

Rogue started to run one hand through his hair, then apparently remembered it was tied back, so laid his hand against the left side of his face, elbow propped on his fist.

Trust me.

"Why should I? I have no idea what your agenda is. You yourself told me you aren't my friend—right there I'd say that was a fine reason not to."

"Not to what?" He cocked his head to the side as if trying to hear a faint sound.

"Trust you."

"You heard that."

"I'm working at being quieter—you said I'd hear you if I did."

He looked uneasy, glancing away from me for the first time, ostensibly observing the fire. It occurred to me that he hadn't meant me to hear that, which meant what? It was some kind of suggestion, maybe. While he pondered his next move, I lined up my questions, keeping a close eye on him. Rogue really was rather staggeringly gorgeous. His hair was more loosely tied back, caught at the back of his neck in a jeweled band that matched the knife sheath. Something about that lean body made me want to curl up in his arms, let him take care of me…

What had I been thinking about?

I frowned, swirling my thoughts and feelings around, like stirring a pan of milk to bring up the little burned bits. A couple of bits that didn't seem to be mine floated up—I dissolved them as I popped that amber thought bubble. I was kind of getting the knack of this.

Rogue had walked up to me while I was sorting my thoughts and now stood just before me so I had to tilt my head back to look at him.

Too close. If I leaned in a bit, I could lay my body against him. His eyes burned and I felt an answering heat. My nipples peaked against the restraining cloth. A hot shiver ran through me as his gaze dropped to my lips. My heart thumped.

I reveled in that moment, that breathless anticipation where you wondered, hoped, wished, that this beautiful man would lower his head to kiss you.

His breath fluttered against my lips. Cinnamon and sandalwood swirled through my head.

I held my breath, waiting for that first taste of him, waiting for the passion that pressed against the corseting materials to surge over me. I wanted the feel of it.

Wanted him on me and in me. Wanted what he wanted. Wanted him more than anything.

Whoa, since when?

I stepped back quickly. "Are you fucking with my mind?"

Irritation flashed across his face before it fell back into seductive lines.

I found myself shaking my head. "No, no, no—I may be a babe in the woods here, but I know myself at least. And *you* just wasted the five minutes I asked for."

Rogue cursed—I didn't quite catch the meaning, except that it sounded pissed and seemed to have something to do with a cow, which sure as hell had better not be me. Then he started pacing the room, filling the silence with rhythmic boot steps.

Ah, here was the Rogue we knew.

I felt obscurely comforted. My body still seethed and pulsed, but that was all me. As was the bruised disappointment at missing out on the kiss. Probably my only opportunity. I had a habit of blowing the moment. Me and my smart mouth. Still, I felt I'd won a small battle, gained a bit of ground. Go me.

At least I had the sense to know that Rogue didn't really want me. Rogue would probably take what I offered, just as any man would, really, given the opportunity. But what would I be left with once he'd taken it?

It was a mystery to me, what made a man stick around once he'd gotten laid. Maybe the chance to have more at first. Maybe he signed up for the ring and the vows so he could get it regular. *But don't tell me it's love.* Love was just window dressing, to cover up the dirty panes beneath.

At least I was thinking like myself again.

I waited him out while he paced.

"Has anyone ever told you you're irretrievably stubborn, woman?" he finally got out.

"Just about everyone, thanks."

Which was true. It was also true that people called you stubborn when you didn't do what they wanted you to do. I had a pretty good idea that whatever these people wanted me to do wasn't in my best interests.

"You're getting loud with your thoughts again," Rogue said.

"Apologies." Dammit.

"I find myself comforted by the familiarity of it," Rogue answered wryly, in an odd echo of my own thoughts. He walked back up to me. "We're at an impasse, it seems. If I can convince you of the sincerity of my intentions regarding you, will you trust me for the duration of the reception?"

"How will you do that?"

"I'll let you into my thoughts—let you feel my intentions."

"No." I shook my head. "No more mind tricks."

"No mind tricks—you would control this. All you do is look."

"That seems like an invasion of your mental privacy?"

"I'm desperate." His mouth twisted a bit, distorting a black line so it sharpened into a fang.

Desperate could be interesting. I knew he heard my thought from the devastating smile that cracked through the thorns. Now *that* man, with the smile, was the dangerous one. I made certain to keep that observation very much to myself.

"So I look into your head, see that you're on the level,

and then we go to this deal, with me still running blind? I don't think so. I want five questions answered first."

"What's with you and the number five?"

I shrugged. One hand, I don't know.

"No time," Rogue answered, and held up an uncannily long hand when I opened my mouth again. "I feel certain you'd ask hard questions that require long answers. I'll give you three principles—three things you should know to get through the evening."

"Five ground rules."

"I can't think of five."

"You disappoint me."

He flashed me the wicked grin. "I wouldn't have, if you'd let me kiss you."

Ooh, good one. I floundered for a response. Surely I wasn't blushing. Rogue walked away and sat on a chair by the fire, clearly smug with the knowledge he'd beaten me that round. Now he was back to business.

"Four ground rules."

"Why four?"

"Never accept a first offer. Agreed?"

When I nodded, he beckoned me over to stand in front of him. He parted his knees and pulled me between them, hands on my heavily padded waist. "Shhh," he said when I tried to pull back, stroking me into calm, gentling me as he had when I was chained to the bed. "Contact is helpful, even necessary at this point. It's not like I can feel anything through this get-up anyhow."

"And whose fault is that?"

"Ground Rule One," he said, pinning me with his gaze, "you must appear as nonthreatening as possible, like a young girl protected all her life. Virginal, you understand that idea?"

I nodded.

"Be sweet. Be biddable. Be unattractive. Be unsexy. That means they will underestimate you and much rides on that."

"Okay, that helps." I smiled sweetly. "I'll wear the damn outfit."

Didn't want him to forget that was my choice whether to leave the room in it.

"Fingertips on my temples," he instructed.

I laid my hands on his face, my right fingertips over the black swirling lines, the skin equally silken on both sides. His skin seemed unnaturally warm, with a slight buzz to it, as if there were a mild level of static charge. A spark ran through me.

"Look into my eyes."

As if I wasn't already hypnotized by the ardent blue of them. There were gold flecks in his irises, and they were ringed with a thin line of desert black. Rogue drew me in a bit more, fingers flexing on my hips. The fire crackled softly.

Now follow my surface thoughts. Too loud? he asked when I winced.

A bit, I tried quietly.

He chuckled. Yes, ironic. Ha-ha.

This better?

Yes.

Now look around, as if you're looking just under the surface of water.

Like snorkeling. I pictured the Caribbean and felt his interested response.

Then images not my own began to float by—a dark pool in the woods, the water chill, a bright ocean, waves

tumbling, a black-haired, long-legged boy running on
the beach, rocky, uneven.

Now deeper.

I dove down. Private here, quiet. A sense of walking through someone's house at night while they slept.
Scenes flickered, as if in a movie. Me, laughing at him,
my eyes a green flash. My throat torn open, satisfaction shaded with guilt and grief. Me, lying unconscious
on the bed, throat smooth, saved but vulnerable. The
need to protect me shimmered around the image, like
heat waves.

Did I believe it?

I dove deeper.

Something shadowed. A raven's wing swept across
my vision, shrieking whispers. Hot blood in my mouth,
tearing flesh and tears, howls and water. Rogue, drowning in black-and-blue magic, the Dog tearing scarlet
chunks out of his chest until Rogue's howls became
blood themselves.

I wrenched myself away.

Abruptly I was in sunlight.

Or rather, back in the firelit room, chill gray fog out
the windows. Rogue blinked up at me, eyes turbulent.
His fingers dug into my hips, almost all that was holding me upright. It took me a moment to clear the dark
howls from my mind.

"What did you see?"

"You don't know?"

He shook his head. "I kept to my agreement. You
were to look on your own. Hopefully you saw that I
want only to protect you."

"But you said you weren't my friend."

"I'm not."

"Then what are you?"

Rogue stood abruptly, which brought him hard up against me. My hands fell away from his face and I tried to step out of the way, but he held me with one iron arm. Stronger than he looked.

The other hand reached up to toy with the short lock that had escaped from my braids at the nape of my neck. He stared at me fiercely from inches away and my heart pounded. Heat simmered from him and I thrilled to it, despite what I'd seen. Or maybe because of it.

Did the Dog also stalk his dreams?

"Do you trust me now?"

He didn't know all I'd seen in the depth of his heart. Maybe they were things I should not have seen. I wouldn't want anyone to see my nightmares. Especially now that they were real.

"As near to trust as we're going to get right now."

He rewarded me with his brilliant smile. "Excellent!" He released me, then strode over to the table, returning with Blackbird's tray of nibbles. "Have a quick something to eat then and we'll get going."

EIGHT

In Which I Learn to Fence

LIKE A CHILD, I thrust my hands behind my back. My stomach felt wildly hollow all of a sudden, though it hadn't bothered me much before.

"Lovely Gwynn," Rogue said softly, "you need to eat."

His concern washed over me and he raised a finger to my cheek, a feather touch that made me shiver. Now I understood why Persephone broke down and ate the pomegranate seed. She gave in to Hades. Maybe he'd been gorgeous and sexy, too. After all, he was the god of the Underworld, second only to Zeus in power. Kind of the bad boy of the Pantheon. And there I was, wanting to please my diabolical captor, too. But, call me paranoid, it made me deeply suspicious that everyone wanted me to eat from my specially prepared tray.

"My name isn't Gwynn."

"I can be stubborn, too." Rogue waved the tray at me. In case I hadn't noticed it before.

"If you're so worried about time," I countered, "why waste it on me eating? I hear there's a banquet in my future. Or don't you people have food at banquets?"

"Ground Rule Two," he said. "Don't act like you're afraid of being assassinated. You must be nonthreatening enough to be underestimated."

"Not unlike Ground Rule One."

"Lady Gwynn, it's a banquet. You will have to eat. You'll also need your strength." Rogue trailed his finger down my cheekbone again, but I batted it away. Too distracting.

"Stop that. And I'm not a lady and my name isn't Gwynn."

He waved that remark away. "You don't know who you are. Here, eat."

Perversely, I liked the impatient dictatorial Rogue better than the coaxing seductive one. It was true I was going to have to eat at some point. And for all that this magical place wasn't the real world, it also wasn't the Underworld where I could exist only in spirit. Easy not to eat when you didn't have, oh, say, a body to keep alive.

"I'll eat at the banquet—food I see other people eating. Nothing—" I pointed at the tray, "—especially prepared for me."

Rogue glared at me. The tray vanished from his hand.

"Nice parlor trick."

"Meant to demonstrate that food can be altered on its way to your mouth, if a sorcerer desired."

"A sorcerer like you?"

"Any that wished to."

"Nevertheless," I said, "a girl has to have some standards."

"Fine." Rogue strode to the door. "Shall we?"

"I get two more ground rules."

"We'll cover them on the way—it will take a few minutes to walk to the banquet hall."

"Can't you just poof us there?"

Rogue raised that eyebrow at me and held up an arm, every debutante's dream escort.

Sighing, I laid my hand on his forearm. Wiry muscle flexed under the black velvet. We walked out into a short hallway, more gray stones, torches burning merrily in sconces. Then we started down circular stairs. A tower. Of course—where else did you keep prisoners?

"Ground Rule Three. Don't ask questions about magic. Don't act surprised by anything you might see. No one is sure where you come from, what kind of abilities you have. All they know is you are powerful, you lost control and must be taught. Be mysterious."

Mysterious was not my forte, but I could try. Seemed as though keeping my mouth shut as much as possible was a safe bet.

"Understood?"

"Yep, practicing being mysterious and closed-mouthed now."

"Unprecedented."

"Ha-ha."

Rogue grinned down at me and my damn heart lurched. I must be just starved for attention. We emerged from the tower stairs. I hadn't been able to track the number of turns, but it had to be four to five floors' worth, a nice tall tower for prisoner-keeping. A wider gallery opened before us. Arched windows ranged along one side, looking down into an interior courtyard. No fog—wasn't that interesting? It looked to be evening now, with torchlit windows glowing across the way.

"Final ground rule." Rogue paused. I could barely hear the rush of his thoughts as he chose his words. I wasn't going to like this one. "Make the best bargain you can, but watch the wording."

"Meaning?"

"Just that. And remember to keep your thoughts to yourself—half the people here could hear them without trying, and quite a few can hear all they want to with a little effort."

"Ooh, would that be a fifth ground rule?"

"Common sense—I don't have to remind you to keep breathing, do I?"

We turned the corner and huge wooden doors swung open before us. A brightly lit banquet hall lay inside with a fireplace big enough for ten of me to stand in. People dressed to resemble jewels and flowers turned as one to stare at me. I wished I didn't look like an éclair without icing.

Especially when Nasty Tinker Bell swept up, barely draped in strapless gold cloth. It looked as though her pert nipples were all that held up the top. I tried not to look too hard. Could it be Super Glue?

"Welcome to our banquet, Lady Gwynn," Tinker Bell chimed. "We've been so bored, waiting for our guest of honor."

"Lady Gwynn," Rogue said, "may I present Lady Incandescence, whom I believe you've met, but to whom you have not yet been properly introduced." Interesting that Rogue's language seemed to have a more formal cadence.

I took that as my cue to use her correct name.

Damn—I should have gotten coaching on proper greetings. Though it would have been difficult to cover "formally greeting nasty noble folk who've dumped soup on your head."

I gave Nast... Lady Incandescence (say *that* without rolling your eyes) the inclined head nod I used at

my mom's charity balls—tilt head to the right slightly
and dip chin once, agreeable, pleasant. An all-purpose
greeting for non-handshake situations.

Apparently not for this one, however, as she looked
incandescently pissed. Or maybe that was just her usual
face. I was just waiting for that moment when her dress
would eventually lose its purchase.

Nasty Tinker Bell cleared her face with her trademark reboot and, smiling sweetly at me, said, "I hope
everyone votes to kill you in the most painful method
possible." She punctuated the sentence with her bell
of a giggle.

"Well, that's honest, Lady Lightbulb," I answered.
Experiment underway—if I pictured the incandescent
light bulb and used only part of the phrase, would it
translate? The pucker on her charming forehead indicated that it came through slightly wrong, though not
enough to argue with.

Rogue made a choking noise. He could read me well.
But he manfully cleared his throat and said, "Respectfully, Lady Incandescence, recall that Lady Gwynn
does not speak our language, thus hears what you mean,
rather than what you say."

She whitened a bit. Aha! She'd been indulging in
courteous double-talk.

"Rogue, introduce us to your…guest."

A group of three men ringed around behind Tinker
Bell, who seized the opportunity to scuttle away, gold
cloth still miraculously clinging to her nipples. Had to
be magic—wasted too, as no one but me seemed interested in whether it would stick or not. Probably at some
point in the evening, it would come "accidentally" un-
stuck from one or both, to her delighted chagrin. I'd
worked with a gal like that, who managed to lose some

or all of her clothing to some mishap or another, at every social event, including the office Christmas party.

Not everything here was different.

The men were dressed in Rogue's style, in various colored velvets, all snug, all enticing. All were long-limbed, wore daggers and two of them had markings on their faces, though on the right sides. None were as large and complex as Rogue's, and none shared his distinctive coloring. The one with no pattern was ebony dark, the black of his eyes blending into dark holes of pitiless empty space. I shivered, a strange terror crawling up my spine.

Rogue took my left hand and held it forward slightly. "Lady Gwynn, may I present Lords Falcon, Puck and Scourge."

I tried a little curtsey this time, hoping my theater days would see me through, and they bowed solemnly. I tamped down any sarcastic thoughts about the names.

The first who'd spoken stepped forward. Falcon, maybe. Bright yellow eyes stared at me with raptorish intensity above a hooked nose. "Lady Gwynn, do you have a proposal for us?"

"You can't expect her to make terms without hearing our bargaining points first," Rogue said.

Falcon shot him an irritated glance. "Don't assist your pet, Rogue. It makes you look weak. Or is that weakness why you want her?"

"Circumventing etiquette, even with a foreigner, is unworthy of you."

"No point in waiting to break bread if she's going to refuse." The second one, wearing a dizzying ensemble of motley colors, tossed back waves of strawberry hair and grinned at me. This had to be Puck. "What say you, Lady Gwynn? Will you hold out? Yes? No? All of the Above?"

"Lady Gwynn looks forward to dining with us." Rogue looked pointedly at me, replacing my hand on his forearm and covering it with his own.

"Oh, yes." Mindful of Tinker Bell's gaffe, I made an effort to be sincere when I said it. Actually food was sounding better all the time. I was getting a little light-headed.

"Until the meal, then." Falcon made it sound like my funeral. Puck tipped his small, cherry-red top hat, bowed and danced off. The ebony one remained, unmoving.

"Lord Scourge?" Rogue inquired, as if offering him another cup of tea. The fathomless eyes finally lifted from me, flicked to Rogue and then the man smiled, slow and feral, showing glistening pointed black teeth. He ambled off to join Falcon and Puck in a corner, where they talked, glancing in our direction occasionally.

"That guy gives me the serious creeps."

Rogue glanced down at me, seemed about to say something, stopped himself. Fine—I didn't want to talk about him either.

"Who's in charge?" I whispered to Rogue.

"In charge?" He looked as puzzled as Blackbird had, as if the concept didn't quite get through.

"You know, take me to your leader."

"This is my place."

"And who do you answer to—Queen Titania, maybe?"

"Titania?"

I wanted to pull my hair out. Instead I tried for the patient explanation.

"When I thought too loud at you, you said, 'By Titania, woman, keep your voice down.'"

"Volume," he corrected, scanning the room. People watched from various groupings, but no others approached yet.

"Whatever."

"It's an important distinction."

"Okay, okay. But anyway, Blackbird said, 'Thank Titania' about something. To me, Titania is the name of the queen of the fairies and Oberon is the king—from stories. Now I understand these aren't really their names, but if whatever you are saying is translating in my head as the name of the queen, that person must be logically the queen. The leader. The ruler. None of which words you seem to understand."

"Titania isn't a person. She's…" He paused.

"Fictional?"

"No. Never that."

"A goddess?"

"Ah, Lady Healer—your patient is doing admirably," Rogue called out.

"Coward," I muttered under my breath. He patted my hand.

Healer strolled up to us, Darling once more at her side. He blinked at me gravely. She was dolled up, still draped in green but in filmy slices, nothing as revealing as Tinker Bell's seductive outfit. Her tumbled hair wound in complicated twirls and braids with ivy-like leaves intertwined. And she seemed to be wearing cosmetics. Come to think of it, Tinker Bell had been, too—I'd been so busy worrying about her nipples I hadn't registered it at the time. Why hadn't I gotten makeup?

Duh—Rule 1. *How quickly we forget.*

I tried a sweet and biddable smile and a girlish curtsey to Healer's greeting. That went over better.

"You've forsaken Lord Rogue's colors?" She swept
her hand at my outfit.

"I'm sorry?"

"Your black gown. I'm surprised you've refused Lord
Rogue's protection already. Or are you declaring him
unworthy of your loyalty?"

This time, Rogue did not step in, though I could feel
his arm flex. Apparently I was fielding this one alone.

"Lord Rogue has been gracious in his hospitality, but
I thought it best that he not be affected by any penalties
I might face. I represent only myself."

Healer's eyes flicked to Rogue. "So you will not
stand surety for her debts?"

"I am responsible for my own debts, Lady Healer."
After all, I'm a liberated woman, chickie.

"Interesting," she commented, which sounded much
the same as Tinker Bell's "Fine." Masters of the one-
word insult, these gals.

"Well done," Rogue whispered as Healer serenely
glided away, Darling heeling like no cat I'd ever seen.
"Now she has to vote to keep you alive, if she wants
her pound of flesh from you."

"Please tell me that's not a literal translation."

Rogue just looked grim, which was not comforting.

"So, this vote—majority rules?"

He frowned. "What do you mean?"

"Why do I bother asking questions at all?"

"I don't know. You must admit I've tried to dissuade
you."

Another delegation approached us, of three ladies,
all Red Carpet sex goddesses. My inferiority complex

divided and doubled like a zygote. After the ladies, a mixed group stopped to chat. All asked pointed or veiled questions. Rogue remained pretty much silent, only patting my hand occasionally or whispering critiques of my diplomatic skills after they'd moved on.

One woman—and I use the term loosely—floored me by wearing nothing but a pair of enormous butterfly wings. Her nude and hairless body looked girlish, with skin nearly the dusk of an insectile thorax, while the wings soared above her in glimmering monarch oranges. Her hair, a short matching cap, framed large eyes with feathery lashes. I tried to act as though I saw butterfly-women all the time while I ducked her questions about the current war by batting my eyes and saying I left such decisions to the warriors, just being a girl myself. No one seemed to like this answer, but they seemed unsurprised and Rogue approved the maneuver.

"Ostentatious of her," Rogue muttered as she pranced away.

"The wings? Are they real?"

"Did they look like illusion to you?"

"Let me rephrase—are they natural to her? Can she fly with them? If you thought she was being ostentatious, does that mean she doesn't always have them?"

"I thought you were going to stop asking questions."

"I *never* said that," I hissed, but had to desist in the face of another interrogation by a man with Richard Gere silver hair.

A ripple ran through the room. People melted out the doorways, water receding from high tide.

"Banquet time," Rogue said. But we didn't move. We stood in the spot he'd staked out, side by side, my hand still on his arm, as the room emptied.

NINE

In Which I Sell My Soul to the Highest Bidder

APPARENTLY ROGUE WAS going for the late dramatic entrance, because by the time we entered the hall, everyone was seated. Staring at me, of course. I felt like the glazed pig at the banquet. Two empty chairs waited at a raised table.

"Is mine the one with the Sword of Damocles hanging over it?" I whispered as we sedately walked up to the dais.

Rogue didn't deign to answer. Shocking.

The peculiar lads with the bowed heads stood by the heavy wooden chairs. They seemed to be the same ones. Either that or they were part of some servant class that all looked identical. After I sat, my servant guy slid the chair up to the table so that the massive arms sealed to the edge. That, with the low table over my lap, effectively caged me. I might be able to squirm out on my own, but it wouldn't be easy. Coincidence? Oh no, no, no.

I tried to calm myself, to still the feeling that everything had spiraled hopelessly out of control. Here I was, at what appeared to be a faerie banquet out of the old stories. Everything had moved so fast, keeping me off balance. *Concentrate on finding a way out of here.* That was key. Whatever negotiations would occur tonight,

I needed to wrangle a way back to my own world. Regardless of the price.

Rogue ensconced himself at my right, while Lord Puck sat to my left, his back turned while he talked effusively, with much hand-waving, to his companion. Blackbird's voice drifted by and I spotted her next to an archway, directing a stream of servers with bowed heads carrying platters and bowls of food, unified in their sameness. They made my skin crawl and the hair rise on the back of my neck. I slid a glance at Rogue out of the corner of my eye. He was engaged in conversation with a woman on his right I hadn't met, but who seemed to be all shades of pink, from nymphet outfit to eye color. Since he was occupied, I took a good look at the server near me. Healer had referred to them as "Rogue's people." I wondered if he'd created them somehow or manipulated them magically. They seemed…off.

If this were so, he might have manipulated me in the same way, were it not for the silver I wore. I ran my fingertips over the smooth collar, flush with warmth from my skin. Not just restraint but protection. Something to keep in mind. Clearly Rogue was a politician. In my experience, politicians liked people to underestimate them. Or worship them. Flip a coin.

Rogue turned then and looked at me, full blaze-on blue. "You're thinking something, but I didn't quite get it."

I smiled sweetly. Innocently, I hoped. "Following instructions. Being quiet. Waiting to eat my supper like a good girl."

His gaze dropped to my lips, and my breath caught

at the visual caress. Damn, I really hoped I wouldn't regret the not-kissing him when I had a chance.

"No need for regrets, gorgeous Gwynn," Rogue murmured. "You may yet have my lips on you."

Warmth pooled between my legs. Rogue smiled into my eyes again, the blue a hotter shade now and I caught a fleeting edge of his thought. Lips trailing down my throat. And farther. Kissing, hell, this guy could be the best sex I ever had, not that there was a lot of competition there, but still.

Eyes on the prize—don't get distracted by the pretty boy.

"True. Mind your thoughts—you're getting…loud, again."

I wrenched my gaze away as Rogue breathed out a laugh. He set his hand on mine, squeezed lightly and turned back to Pinkie. Platters were set before us, and Rogue waved the lads back, though they dished servings to others. He served himself, then slid the platter to me, so I could choose my own portion. It was so smooth, I could believe this was normal etiquette, but I knew he did it for me.

I gave Rogue a brilliant smile and he winked at me, the left side of his face away from the room. I hadn't noticed before that his marking extended onto his eyelid, with a thorn tipped in amber. I fought the desire to run a fingertip over it.

No silverware of any type. Oh, and no one was eating. All eyes were turned our way, including Puck's avid gaze. He had one brown eye and one of sea-green, a disconcerting imbalance.

"They're waiting for you to eat first," Rogue said *sotto voce.*

"Do I eat with my fingers?" I said through my smile.

"Yes."

I reached for a slice of bread, looked at Puck and pulled off a piece, toasted him with it, and ate. It was really good, honey and sunshine combined. A susurrus ran through the room and everyone began eating and talking. I wolfed the rest of the bread. Puck sighed and tossed a something brightly jeweled at Falcon, who caught it, looking grimly satisfied.

It seemed we ate for hours, course after course of meats in various sauces—which were excellent, fortunately, since I had to lick my fingers clean—fruits, breads, cheeses. No salad course, sadly. I tried a little wine, but it was terribly sweet, like a frothy version of Thunderbird. I needed to keep my wits anyway.

Though I ate ravenously—always from a dish Rogue first served himself—I never felt full. I forgot my circumstances after a bit, heady with the food and merriment. And Rogue's intense regard. *After this we dance all night, I wake up at Devils Tower and a hundred years has gone by.* I should be so lucky.

The room abruptly hushed.

Falcon stood. "I vote for death." And sat again.

Several voices murmured agreement.

And, so much for the merriment.

Wait, I thought to Rogue, *don't I get some discussion first? Bargaining points?*

"Whisper, don't project," he muttered out of the corner of his mouth. "'Spoken' thoughts carry farther."

"That *is* my bargain," Falcon declared, confirming the point.

"Why should I agree to die then?" I asked. *If we're going to deal, let's deal.*

"Why should we agree to let you live?" He looked interested at least.

"Lady Healer still needs to be paid—how can I do that if I'm dead?"

Healer stood from half a dozen places down the table, Darling stretched beside her plate, fishing something off it with a delicate paw. "It's true, I have a debt to reclaim. Her corpse would not be worth as much as she owes."

I would have stood for my answer, but no, I was trapped by the table. A toddler wedged into a highchair amidst the grownups. "I would pay Lady Healer back for her great services to me."

"Services that would have been unnecessary if we'd just let her die and not healed her in the first place." Nasty Tinker Bell popped up like a little gold cork. I thought about throwing a piece of fruit at her, then remembered something.

"But your judgments are not considered," I said, seizing on her remark from before.

"It's true, Lady Incandescence, you know you may not speak." Falcon frowned at her. "Lord Rogue, as host, do you wish to censure her?"

"The lady may leave my table," Rogue answered easily.

Nasty Tinker Bell threw her trademark look my way, with a generous slice for Rogue. Then she poofed, leaving a shower of golden glitter tinkling down on the table. A smattering of polite admiration ruffled through the room, as if that had been a particularly good trick. I raised my eyebrows at Rogue, who returned my gaze with bland indifference.

"Why doesn't she get to vote?" I whispered out of the side of my mouth to Rogue.

Amused interest glittered in his unearthly eyes. "She is in my service—until I release her, she may only do as I say."

Nice system.

The pink gal next to Rogue stood. "Lady Healer, what do you claim as recompense? Lord Rogue has claims of hospitality as well."

"Traditional payment is acceptable—a life in return for her life."

And here I'd been thinking a pot of gold.

"Lord Rogue?"

"Return service is acceptable."

"Lady Gwynn, do you agree to the terms?"

I could see now that Pinkie had rosy wavelike patterns on the right side of her face, reminiscent of the fluted petals of a carnation. I chose my words carefully.

"As you are aware, lady, I am a stranger to your people and naive in the world—I apologize, but I do not understand the specifics of the terms. Can someone elucidate for me?"

Someone in the room laughed and Puck shifted restlessly next to me, but I thought I felt Rogue's approval, though he appeared to be toying with the remains on his plate.

"Enough of this," a voice called out. "She is too powerful. No terms. Death!"

"By dancing!" shouted someone else, which was greeted with general enthusiasm.

"Harnessed to our yoke," Puck said, "she could be a considerable weapon in our glorious battles against the outlander barbarians."

"Harness a lion to your cart, Puck, and see who it scratches!"

This brought on general hilarity, with suggestions shouted out for bedding wildcats, various paraphernalia to be used in the harnessing, and the likely state of Puck's genitalia following certain efforts.

Puck joined in, leering at me. "Perhaps I'll rent her service from Rogue!"

"Can you afford that?" Rogue returned, sweeping a hand at the room, finishing at Healer. "Consider the price of my hospitality."

I was uneasy about what services I might render and suddenly felt much less enthusiastic about the concept of bedding Rogue. The difference between rape and rapture—all in the marketing.

Blackbird approached the table, to my surprise. "Lord Rogue, your guests grow restless. Perhaps those uninvolved in the setting of terms could be excused to begin the dancing? The musicians stand ready."

Rogue gestured with an elegant hand. Noblesse oblige. The room swelled and exhaled, abruptly empty except for about ten people. To my dismay, dark Scourge was one who remained, though he'd yet to say anything.

"Lady Blackbird," Rogue called as she turned away, "please stay."

"Me? I have no voice." She sounded nervous.

"Not that you elect to use. Nevertheless, you were sent to me by your family for a reason, no? Otherwise you'd still be picking apples in your country home while your husband roams the land on foolish quests?"

Blackbird looked sad and lost for a moment. Easy to forget what a jerk Rogue was capable of being at times. She reluctantly took an emptied chair and folded her white hands like birds settling for the night.

"A life for a life, Lady Gwynn," Pinkie took up, as

if there had been no interruption, "is just that. Lady Healer gave you your life back—"

"Plus extended years," Healer inserted, "with removal of existing disease states and poisonous intrusions."

"You always do such excellent work, Lady Healer." Falcon bowed to her, his yellow eyes glittering.

"Including extended years," Pinkie allowed. "But Lady Healer has stated she is willing to accept one life in return. That can be your life, Lady Gwynn, or another's."

"I don't have any lives but my own," I tendered.

"Your children, dear," Blackbird explained gently.

Ah. Firstborn child—right.

"So, since I have no children and probably won't have any, do I give her my life by dying?"

Rogue shifted beside me. I probably should have pretended to know that answer.

"Servitude, Lady Gwynn." Lord Falcon glowered at me. "Don't play dumb. You owe Healer a life of service. You owe Rogue for food, lodging and protection, at such price as he values it. Though we can guess at what he truly wants you for." Darling sidled up the table to me, picking delicately through the dishes and goblets, and trailed under my chin, then sat and looked pointedly at Falcon. "Yes, Lord Darling has a claim of service as well."

I took a deep breath. *There's no place like home, there's no place like home.* Didn't work. Where were the magic slippers when you needed them?

"So, how can I serve more than one person at once?" *And how does one serve a cat?*

"Oh my, what a thought!" Puck laughed with gay abandon.

"I am willing to cede my owed service to Lord Falcon, in payment to him for previous debts, if he finds that acceptable." Healer looked smug.

Though Rogue didn't move, I felt his tension in the back of my mind.

Falcon nodded slowly at her, once, grinned at Rogue, then slid his eyes to me with a rapacious stare that made me shrink away inside the lumpy clothes. Suddenly I was glad for them.

"Puck may see to training her for the war—perhaps she'll be more useful than not," Falcon said, with a dismissive wave of his hand that belied his fixed and predatory gaze.

"I accept." Puck snapped up that ball. "I propose to put Lady Gwynn into immediate training, to quickly bring her into the war effort."

"I would argue," Rogue drawled, trailing a hand down Darling's back, who curved into him, purring, "that Lady Gwynn also owes me a life, beyond hospitality. Without my intervention, she would have died."

"Agreed," Pinkie said.

What? I was stunned.

He raised an impassive ebony eyebrow. He had told me not to mistake him for a friend. "Lady Blackbird was also owed for services, but has been offered a boon, which was accepted."

Jesus, was nothing free around here? Blackbird beamed happily at me. I'd have to find out from her what the boon was.

"Okay." I put up a hand. "Let me get this straight. So far, for Lady Healer's healing, I get to serve in the

military performing magic for Lords Falcon and Puck—
is that right?"

"Is that your proposal?" Lord Falcon pounced, his
face clenched

Okay then. *Be careful of the wording.* Why didn't I
go to law school?

"Let me rephrase. To cancel all liens created by Lady
Healer's service to me, I will attend magical training
under Lord Puck's direction, perform magical military
service for Lord Falcon, and no other services."

"Agreed," Falcon said, while Puck nodded enthu-
siastically.

I didn't look at Rogue, but I could feel his displeasure. Hey, he was the one who wouldn't explain what
I was up against.

"Now, how do we decide how long a lifetime is?"
I asked.

"Until death," Falcon offered.

"But Lady Healer says she extended my life—
shouldn't I only owe until when I would have reasonably died before her intervention? Wasn't my life worth
fewer years then than it is now? And, if I learn magic,
what if I learn to extend my life even more—wouldn't
those years be mine, not owed?"

"Healer," Pinkie asked, "how long would Lady
Gwynn have lived before your work?"

"Seven years," Healer answered. *Seven years?* I must
have looked shocked, because she added, "There were
several conditions progressing that would have led to
her death in that time."

Wow—I guess I really did owe her.

"Lady Gwynn?" Puck prompted me.

"Okay, I propose that the term be seven years." That

didn't sound like so much now, compared to the rest of my life. *And then I go home.* Maybe I'd luck out and time would move differently here.

"Given the brevity of service," Falcon said, "I ask for intensive training."

"Yes." Scourge hissed the word, snake-eyes gleaming. "Marquise and I would be most willing. For the usual side-benefits, naturally."

Without thinking I dug my nails into Rogue's forearm. "What does that mean?"

"Is that necessary?" Rogue demanded.

Falcon smirked. "You'll get yours later. Presumably. I'm within rights, here."

"Agreed," Pinkie ruled. "The stipulation is within the parameters of Lady Gwynn's proposal. Continue, lady. How do you propose to satisfy Lord Rogue?"

About ten smart remarks flew through my mind. I restrained myself. "Maybe I could give him something of value and then I go home?"

"Not acceptable." Rogue pinned me with his stare. "Lady Lillibeth, I put before you that only a firstborn child will satisfy my multiple claims, given that all claimants labored under my aegis."

Falcon sat up straighter, eyes firing.

"It's not ideal," Scourge growled, "but I accept the condition."

"Agreed," said Pinkie.

"Wait a minute!" I would have jumped out of my chair if I could. "*That* is not acceptable."

"Lord Rogue can set his terms," Puck said and they all nodded.

Well, shit.

"I don't have a child and don't plan to." I drew the line at that.

"It will be arranged." Rogue smiled at me and placed his hand over mine, thumb rubbing my palm so that the heat flared in me. I yanked my hand away. Unperturbed, he raised his long fingers up to the nape of my neck, lightly tugging the shorn lock that had escaped Blackbird's braids.

"Oh no," I gasped. I was *not* signing up to be impregnated like some brood cow. Though I didn't like the plummy wine, I grabbed my goblet still sitting mostly full and drank some down.

"You refuse the terms?" Falcon demanded, with an edge of excitement.

"What happens if I do?"

Lady Lillibeth shrugged. "Execution."

Their answer to everything.

Rogue quietly watched me, as if I were deciding which kind of ice cream to buy.

"You said never to accept a first offer," I whispered to him.

His eyes were sober indigo. "Sometimes, one has no other choice. I've done all I could."

He had me neatly trapped. But I would find a loophole. Seven years to do it. If I was a freaking sorceress and would be trained, then I could find a way out of this deal and a way back home.

"Fine." I raised my voice. "To cancel all debts I might owe you, after I finish my service to Lord Puck, in seven years, I will give you my firstborn child, at such time as I may have one." Since I didn't plan to have any kids, that should be easy to deal with.

"*My* child," he stipulated.

I stared at him. Completely aghast. *Oh, I don't think so.* "How exactly would that occur?"

Rogue stroked long fingers down my cheek and over my throat. "Oh, my lovely Gwynn, I would be delighted to demonstrate."

"What if I have someone else's child before then?" I tried to shake off his effect on me.

Something blazed hot in his eyes. "To do so would void the agreement."

"Let me guess—defaulting to death?"

Rogue nodded, lips thinned.

"How do you even know we can interbreed? I don't know if any of you have noticed, but we're not exactly the same species here." I was forgetting to pretend. I put a hand to my temple, my thoughts muzzy.

This observation prompted great hilarity from the group. They laughed, repeating my words to each other. Lady Blackbird went to fetch a pitcher and circled the group, refilling goblets, including mine.

"I may not even be fertile—the women in my family tend not to be."

"Oh, you are now," Healer assured me, smiling sweetly at Rogue. Of course.

"Trust me to handle the rest." Rogue took the goblet from me and set it on the table, keeping hold of my hand. I tried to yank it from him again, but he held it firmly, eyes sparkling dark as star sapphires. He never broke his gaze, even as he kissed the back of my hand. The barely banked heat in me flared.

"You know, I really don't think 'trust' is a good word choice right now."

Rogue looked grim. "Trust in that fact, if not in me," he said, stroking my hand. "Trust that the response of your body will make it pleasurable for you. And that this protects you from far worse things."

"I really do not want to have a baby."

"You don't want to die, either."

"What I want is to go home."

"You can't."

"Can't because it's not physically possible or can't because you won't allow it?"

A shadow crossed his face, darkening the lines even more. What would it be like to see that mask above me in bed? Shadows upon shadows. A shiver ran through me, composed of as much chill as heat. Rogue felt it.

"You are not the only one out of choices, my Lady Gwynn. You have seven years to get used to the idea." He released my hand and seized his own goblet. "The terms are set and agreed upon."

The others were watching us with avid interest, Healer standing behind Falcon, caressing his neck. I just loved being the floor show. A headache throbbed behind my eyes. So much for all that expensive healing.

Darling chirruped and Rogue nodded in my direction. "Lady Lillibeth, we'd best complete the proceedings."

"Only your service to Lord Darling remains, Lady," the pink woman—Lady Lillibeth, apparently—reminded me.

I was exhausted. What else did I have to give? "Okay, what bargain does he offer?"

"Ask him," Rogue said, not looking at me, but rather up to the shadowed depths of the vaulted ceiling.

"What? How?"

Falcon slammed his hand on the table. "Enough with

playing dumb, foreign sorceress. Let's get this done with."

Darling sat on the table in front of me. He blinked at me sweetly, swelling a purr. I saw him in a classroom with me, riding on the back of a horse during battle, then standing at my heel.

"He wants to be my Familiar?"

"Agreed," Lillibeth said.

The cat rubbed his cheek against my chin and padded back down the table. I wanted to ask exactly what I had agreed to, but my thoughts slipped away. Falcon and Healer wandered out of the hall, arm in arm, heads bent together as they laughed merrily over some private joke. Scourge rose to leave.

"Remember what I'm owed, Scourge." Rogue lounged back in his chair, the indolent lord of the feast. "I expect my merchandise returned in appropriate condition."

Scourge stilled. Then gave Rogue a curt nod and left.

"Lord Puck, you will miss the festivities, but you'd best convey your charge to her new home," Lillibeth said breezily.

The bowed-head lads pulled my heavy chair away from the table. Even looking up at them, I couldn't quite get a glimpse of their faces. Was I supposed to stand now? Rogue and Puck pulled me to my feet, so I supposed so. Puck pulled my wrists behind my back, fastening them together by my silver bracelets, then did the same with my feet. I couldn't seem to resist. Why couldn't I think? I teetered there while Rogue steadied me.

"The wine?" I finally got out and Rogue touched my face in that way of his that seemed to be tender.

"Magic can't touch you while you wear silver, but it can touch something you then touch. You could never have protected yourself against it."

"It's better for the journey," Puck added. He clipped a leash to my collar.

For the first time, I really processed that I was going somewhere else, in someone's custody. Damned if I would cry again though, despite the aching emptiness in me that was the loss of everything I'd ever known.

"A moment, please, Lord Puck," Rogue said.

He held me by the shoulders, looking down at me, gaze inscrutable on the placid unmarked right side, intense, almost harsh on the left.

"A deposit on my debt," he said, then pulled me hard against him, one arm sliding around my waist, the other hand cradling my head. His lips touched mine, a soft brush at first. Then moving deeper, parting my mouth with a burning heat, soft and hard at once. Cinnamon, sandalwood and something more. With my hands chained behind my back, inclined against him, nearly off my toes as he held me up by the waist and skull, I had no power to pull back from him.

I couldn't return the kiss. Tried not to.

Tried and failed.

The edges of me blurred and I became the kiss.

I became a goblet held in his arms that he drank from, while the longing in me throbbed, pounding in my breasts and between my legs, melding with the horrible keening loss that also grew.

I knew then, profoundly, that nothing was under my control. Maybe never had been.

Rogue released my lips, eyes fulminous, like the blue flame of a Bunsen burner. He seemed about to say something. Then didn't. Through my haze, I caught roiling regret. He set me down, giving me a little push so that Puck caught me.

Puck tossed me over his shoulder. Upside-down and through the blur of drugged wine, I saw Rogue striding off toward the dancing.

Part II

Higher Education

TEN

In Which I Discover There Is Something Even Worse Than Grad School

I DIDN'T REMEMBER any of the journey. Dimly I recalled arriving at yet another castle, this one silent as stone. Puck carried me down winding stairs and set me with odd gentleness on a hard bench of a bed and clipped my leash to the wall. I blinked at him, bleary, wanting to beg him not to leave me there, though I didn't know what would be inflicted on me.

My blood ran cold with dread.

Puck patted me on the cheek, his green eye slightly luminescent, the brown vanishing in shadow, and whispered in my ear. "'If we shadows have offended, think but this, and all is mended, that you have but slumber'd here, while these visions did appear.'"

I may have dreamed that part, my drugged mind giving him Shakespeare's lines.

They left me alone for the first few days. Completely isolated. I paced my little cell as far as my leash would allow. Though shadowed and windowless, the stones themselves gleamed with an icy gray light, keeping me in an eternal twilight. They'd taken my awful clothes and left me naked, with no blanket to use, but I was neither hot nor cold.

I loathed that cell. I counted the stones that made

the walls and flung the most vile wishes against it that
I could think up. The silver stopped me of course, but
I mentally dismantled that room time and again. Ex-
ploding it away.

And that was just the first few hours.

Those hours strung out into formless time. I had a
bucket of water to drink from and an empty one to void
into. No one brought me food. I slept restlessly, wishing
for darkness, and woke disoriented, craving true light.
Boredom and despair ground into me.

Over and over I replayed the negotiations at the feast,
reviewing the bargain points. They wouldn't just leave
me here. I was to be trained. Rogue wanted me back
intact. They wouldn't let me starve.

Though I knew in my head that this was likely just
the first lesson, as time wore on, the fear that I would
be forgotten wormed into my heart. I'd maybe been
already forgotten back home. A hundred years could
have passed and everyone who knew me was dead. I
could starve and waste away in this little cell and no
one would ever miss me.

I thought about how they were doing it. If you sub-
jected a person to complete darkness, the retinas became so sensitive they could detect a single photon of
light. With the unbroken silence, the featureless stones,
the unvarying light, my senses were becoming more
and more frantic for input. I craved any kind of contact. Anything at all.

By the time the door opened, I keenly felt my own
desperation. Starved in both body and mind, I welcomed the sight of Scourge's cruel ebony face.

"Kneel," he said, in his quiet hiss of a voice. I hesitated and he turned to go, pulling the door behind him.

"Wait!" I cried out. It would do no good to fight this. Clearly no one would rescue me. I knew the terms full well. I would be trained and only then could I return to a semblance of life. I didn't want to die here in this unchanging, claustrophobic room. Scourge watched with cold satisfaction as I knelt.

"You will not stand upright," he explained. "You will not speak. Should either of those things occur again, you will be punished. It will be painful. Understood?"

Taking away my humanity. Check. I nodded, unable to tear my gaze from his matte black eyes.

"Marquise? Come meet your new toy."

With a coo, she came sweeping around him. Marquise was Scourge's alabaster twin. Floor-length white hair blended into the silky sheath she wore around her slender body. "Ooh," she exclaimed, dropping before me in a cloud of mint and fresh air, cupping my cheeks, "she's so cute! You'll be a good widdle girl for Marquise, won't you? Never disappoint me, yes?"

I stared into her exceptionally lovely eyes, layers of white on white, only subtle shadings showing the difference between cornea, pupil and iris, feeling another layer of myself crumble in the face of her attention. The unreality of it all took me just another step farther away. Kneeling there naked, while she petted me, I couldn't quite recall who I was. I only hoped she wouldn't let Scourge hurt me. And that they wouldn't leave me alone again.

"I have something for you." She smiled, white lips curving with joy. She held out a little plate with something resting on it. Something gray and flat. My stomach lurched, desperate for even that unappetizing food. I reached for it.

Scourge's whip cracked on my back. Agony seared through me. I cried out and the whip landed again. I choked back my scream.

"No sounds. No hands," Scourge said, calm and reasonable.

"There, there." Marquise kissed away my tears, her lips cold on my skin. "I'll set it here for you. See?"

She put the plate on the floor and tapped it with an ivory-tipped finger. I stared at it, trying to master the sobs racking me.

"She's not mentally defective, is she?" I heard her ask Scourge with concern.

"I don't think so. She's only a human, of course. Perhaps you should speak more slowly."

"Loook, sweet baby darling," she drew out, "see the yummy food?"

"Eat." Scourge trailed the whip over my tender skin. I obeyed, bending over the plate and lapping up the tasteless patty while Marquise stroked my hair and trilled her delight.

They left me then. Alone with my humiliation and a licked-clean metal plate.

The food was drugged, of course. At least it made the time go faster, the stones around me pulsing in a light fog until I blacked out, waking to a glassy half-existence. By the effects, I thought it must be a hypnotic. Soon I was unable to think at all.

All the better to take suggestion.

Their two next visits went just the same, with me quickly learning what they wanted. Of course, they only wanted easy tricks. Crawl. Sit up. Lie down. Roll over. Just to make me obey. Scourge only struck me with the whip once, when I tried to tuck my hair behind my ear while eating. Otherwise I gratefully gobbled the food they gave me, chagrined to be pleased by Marquise's effusive praise.

On the fourth visit, the door opened when I didn't expect. I'd been pacing at the end of my leash, trying to focus my mind. I dropped to my knees, but not before Scourge saw me.

"You will not stand upright," he said, as if speaking to the mental defective Marquise thought me to be. The whip cracked against my thigh and I clamped my lips on the scream. The whip cracked again. Burying my face in my hands to muffle all my cries, I writhed at his feet while he whipped me, the pain obliterating all else.

It ended when his hard fist wound into my hair and he yanked me to my feet.

"Do you stand?" he asked.

I shook my head frantically, as best I could trying not to reach up to relieve my screaming scalp. I sobbed incoherently. Slowly he lowered me to my knees, still holding me upright by my hair.

"Perhaps you need a reminder. My knife, Marquise."

She glided into view, handing him a golden knife that gleamed sickly in the gray light. She wrapped her arms around Scourge from behind, watching around his shoulder with glowing white eyes that reminded me of Christmas ornaments. A stray thought I couldn't quite grab on to. I tried to remember what a Christmas ornament was and couldn't. I couldn't think of anything as the blade sawed through my hair, roughly ripping it away.

"Kneel straight. Don't move," he said.

I trembled so, I could barely stay still, but I managed as Scourge shaved my head. The blade scraped over my scalp, catching me here and there, but I made sure not to flinch. Tears seeped from under my lashes, but they were like the blood flowing from the wounds on my head—I could not stop either thing. Locks of my hair drifted down, brushing my skin.

Finally, he finished.

"Now, thank me." His eerie flat voice whispered over me. Confused, I sat paralyzed.

"Kiss his feet, darling girl," Marquise said. She lay draped over the bed now, languid and lovely as new-fallen snow. Alien and horrifying in her beauty.

Scourge waited, impassive. Though I'd seen the gleam of pleasure when he whipped me. He liked it when I resisted. They both drank up every moment of my pain and humiliation, bright-eyed and sated with it.

At that moment, I took the last bit of myself and locked it away, down deep where they could never reach it. I turned the key and gave up everything else to being what they wanted.

Otherwise I couldn't survive this.

I bent over and kissed Scourge's boot, pressing my lips to it, numb, blank as a clean slate. Marquise squealed and clapped her hands.

After they left, I ran my hands over my bald head, as if it weren't part of me. When my knees ached from kneeling so long, I crawled over to my bed, which smelled of Marquise.

I slept and the Dog chased me through ragged dreams of shattered delirium. Its eyes were deep sapphire like Rogue's. It seemed both wild and loyal. But I fled, terror driving me into the shadows where Marquise waited for me with her poisonous affection.

Time dragged on, the boundaries of it disappearing

entirely. I waited for my trainers with a kind of eagerness. They had me practice more tricks, Marquise leading me around the little room on a leash while Scourge gave me various commands and I performed like a circus pony. I learned to obey without thought.

I forgot anything but pleasing her and avoiding his whip.

I don't know what made them decide I'd had enough. I had no thoughts at that point. One time—it turned out to be evening—Marquise came to my cell alone and handed me a gray swath of silk and kissed me on the cheek.

"Stand up, sweet baby," she coaxed me.

I started shivering, afraid of the trick.

"Stand up and put this on." She sounded more stern this time, so I found myself obeying. She unclipped my leash from the wall and led me out the door. We walked through a silent corridor, punctuated by a door every so often. We climbed stairs and walked down still hallways. Marquise opened a door to a new chamber.

"Your new room! Isn't it pretty?"

It was. It was grand and large and decorated entirely in shades of gray. My eyes didn't know where to rest. It overwhelmed me and I found myself clinging to Marquise.

"There, there." She held me close, chill fingers brushing over my naked scalp. "Don't be afraid. You're growing up now. Bathe. Eat. Sleep. Tomorrow I'll fetch you for class and you'll be a good pupil, won't you? You'll make me so proud."

She unclipped my leash from the collar and hung it by the door, blew me a kiss and left me in that grand and terrible room.

If she hadn't instructed me to bathe and eat, I likely would have crawled into a corner and stayed there. Instead, I did as she bade me, washing in the warm water left for me, my scalp stinging from the soap and water. A distant part of me observed that not much time must have passed since the shaving.

Time enough.

The food was bland but lacked the tang of the drug. After I ate, I hung up my new dress and slid under the covers, watching the sunset light fade to true night, thinking about nothing at all.

In the morning, I sat nervously on the side of the bed and waited for Marquise, wearing my new dress. She swept in with smiles and a bouquet of flowers for my breakfast table. She watched me eat, praising me all the while, then, when she said it was time to go, attached the leash to my collar and clucked at me to hurry.

She led me to a chamber that looked much like my old cell, except this one gleamed with a metallic sheen. Scourge stood, a black sentinel next to a silver chair positioned in front of a simple table of the same metal. He held the long whip coiled in his dark fist. I couldn't meet his eyes, terrified to be standing up and walking. Marquise went to stand on the other side of the chair.

"Lady Gwynn, welcome." Scourge's gravelly voice rolled across my nerves and I cringed. The silky dress irritated my healing wounds slightly, the whiplashes still raw on my skin. I nodded at him to show my mute obedience and he gave me an approving smile, black teeth gleaming. "We begin with baby steps. We will remove the silver and you will think of nothing. Understood?"

I nodded again.

"Then sit."

They crouched and removed the cuffs from my ankles, then my wrists, the skin blackened and ulcerated
beneath them. Marquise smoothed an affectionate hand
over my bristly scalp and kissed me while she unlocked
the collar. She and he both wore ornate silver jewelry
that stood out against their monochromatic selves.

"Nothing," she reminded me.

I did this easily.

After all, I had no thoughts to think. I sank into the
space I usually occupied, that place without hope or
fear. Simply existing until directed otherwise. It came
naturally to me now.

"I want something from you, Lady Gwynn."
Scourge's voice didn't startle me. I waited for him to
tell me what it was. Anything he wanted. He set a white
crystal on the table in front of me. "I want this to be
black. Make it black for me."

I looked at it without curiosity, uncertain what they
wanted.

"Do you want to please me?" Marquise stroked my
scalp, ivory nails light on the tender skin, and I nodded.
I did. Oh, I wanted to please them both.

"Take that wanting. Visualize the crystal as black.
Connect the two."

I did. And the crystal turned black.

She sighed approval, petting me. He set the whip
aside. I squirmed with joy, then disappointment when
they clicked the silver restraints back on me. But Marquise soothed me. This was enough for today. Back in
my grand chambers, silent servants brought me food
and more flowers, lavish rewards for my small success.

From there the lessons progressed into longer ses-
sions. For days I only turned the crystal from white to

black and back to white. Once, I grew a little bored with
the exercise and turned the crystal pink instead. Before
my horrified eyes even took in what I'd done, Scourge
had bodily lifted me and draped me over his lap while
he took my place in the silver chair.

Blood rushed to my head and an iron hand held me
down. He yanked up my dress and spanked my bare
bottom. I wept helplessly, the pain nothing like the whip
and yet all the worse for being a child's punishment.
And worse because my body roused to the touch, quick-
ening with a rush of shameful desire. When he finally
let me up, I stood before him, hands clasped together,
desperately wishing for a voice to apologize.

Marquise stood beside him, one arm languidly
draped over the back of the chair, her eyes glowing
with arousal.

"Do we even need to discuss your error?" Scourge
asked. I shook my head and he stood. "Then sit."

They kept me there even longer that day, while I
fidgeted on my bruised and throbbing rear end. I didn't
deviate again.

I graduated to changing the crystal into different
shapes. Different materials.

With each triumph, I received more freedoms. I could
wander the castle and even go outside to a walled garden, where I could see the sun and touch living things.
They began to invite me to join them for dinner, where
I sat at the table while they discussed me.

"Her power is not so great as Falcon suggested,"
Scourge commented one evening. They sat facing each
other at the end of a long table while I ate at the other
end, child to their parents. At least I sat in a chair. Al-

ways though, I perched on the edge, ready to slide to my place on the floor.

Marquise surveyed me, her face an exquisite blank. "Well, we haven't really plumbed those depths with her yet."

"Do you think so?"

She shrugged. "For humans, power comes from emotion, particularly sexual. Right now our pet has only wanting to please us."

"That should be power enough." Scourge frowned at me, as if I had failed him. I hunched my shoulder blades. "Besides, she reacted sexually when I spanked her."

"Oh, yes. That was just lovely. We could do more of that. To really evoke her power."

I shuddered inside my skin. I so hoped they wouldn't go there. I turned the thought over, surprised I still hoped for something. That's what those sidelong looks had been about. The "filthy source" of my power was sexual—an answer to so many questions. I tucked the knowledge away. For the day I might be able to be my own person again.

"It's a shame Rogue put such restrictions on this." Scourge looked sour.

"We still get to enjoy her." Marquise pursed her lips and blew me a kiss, then tossed her ivory hair over a slim shoulder. "That's the disadvantage of the intensive method. Falcon knows that. He's a fool, preferring to weaken a tool to gain perfect control."

Rogue's name woke me further. I kept my eyes down, but turned over the new emotion surging into my heart. He knew what they would do to me. He'd kissed me and walked away, sending me to this. Burning hate clawed at my heart.

"Even Rogue cannot control everything. And perhaps he knows something we do not. Sometimes I wonder…"

"What do you wonder, sister-mine?"

Marquise held out a hand to me and obediently I went to kneel at her side, letting her search my eyes and my mind, keeping it carefully clear. Pure gray. "I think sometimes that she's not vanished, but rather sleeping. Hiding."

"Nonsense—our method works perfectly."

"Of course it does, brother. But humans only seem like simple creatures. Their minds are labyrinths of conscious and unconscious thought. They have many places to tuck away bits of themselves in those dense, isolated brains." She held my skull in her hands, pressing thumbs into my cheekbones with agonizing pressure. "What say you, darling? Have you hidden anything from me?"

She rifled through my mind like a sweet breeze, turning over my few, useless thoughts. I closed the door on Rogue and the Dog. They were down below ground, by the bottomless lake. Unreachable to me.

"She is perfect, isn't she?" Scourge studied me with his pitiless gaze and I ducked my head.

"Do you doubt?"

"We haven't really pushed her."

"Oh yes." Marquise flashed me a brilliant and sensual smile. The food roiled in my stomach. "We have a bit of time yet. Let's see where her limits are."

"Time to enjoy the side benefits?" Scourge's voice held a cruel sensuality. I pressed my forehead against Marquise's slim thigh, wishing I could beg them not to. Knowing I was so close to escaping. Just a bit more to endure.

It was the worst part.

They used pain still, yes, but they layered in pleasure now, teaching me to amp up the power.

Scourge would chain me naked to the wall and tease me with the whip while Marquise draped herself over the silver chair, drinking in the sight and holding my dress, sometimes stroking her cheek on it. The stinging whip flicked my nipples, my thighs, and I writhed under the torment. She taunted me softly, offering all I could do to make it stop. The cuffs were iron—I could turn them to water. The whip could be easily vanished. Didn't I want to? It would be easy. Or maybe I didn't want it to stop. Maybe I liked it. Then she'd take it down a dark and foul path of all the things they could do to me and how I couldn't stop them. Or could I?

I knew better. Never did I fall for their tricks.

Only when they gave me a direct order did I obey. When Scourge asked, I immediately gave the whip metal spines that dug into my flesh. I took the glass of water I desperately thirsted for and turned it into a pretty stone at her request. They took great pleasure in teasing me to greater levels of arousal and frustration, seeming to feed off my energy, like sleek and fat lions gorging on a hapless ungulate. They stoked me higher, goading me to perform larger and more complicated magics, delighting in what they could get me to do.

I learned to follow their complex mental instructions as easily as the spoken ones. They let me answer them mentally now, though I was still never allowed to speak.

They pronounced me perfect. I hadn't worn silver in a long time.

My skin felt as if it glowed where the bands had been for the past months. I thought it had been months.

There seemed to be no seasons. Sometimes I thought time didn't pass at all and I would be here forever, in this purgatory. I fought the urge to touch my throat, to keep making sure the collar was really gone.

The end came abruptly, with no forewarning. I sat in my walled garden one evening after another brutal day of school to watch the fading twilight. I held on to that bit of the real world, that the light changed and days really did pass. Garden was a misnomer, though, since only a few scraggly plants grew there. Barely alive. Not unlike myself.

And Darling padded across the stones and leaped onto the bench beside me.

His thoughts poured into my mind, vivacious and brightly colored. His pleasure at seeing me again fell like a balm against my wounded psyche. I petted him and he purred, sitting beside me and agreeing the twilight looked most lovely.

He was the one to tell me that I would be leaving. Heading off to the war with him and the rest of Puck's entourage.

He was bored of being a Familiar for healing, of the leisurely velvet-pillow life. Lady Healer didn't get out of the palace much, it seemed. Darling wanted glory and excitement. He even had a plan for a kind of shiny cat-armor he wanted me to get for him, which apparently would be my job. Darling didn't like talking to many people, so preferred to keep a mouthpiece around.

Bemused, I listened to his tales and speculations. Other thoughts ran through my mind. My own thoughts. Maybe fed by a little trickle of hope.

I would be free.

I would have my revenge.

Part III

Early Experiments

ELEVEN

In Which I Emerge from My Cocoon

THE SUN SHONE brightly on our procession. The sky lay gentle over us, that same rich ultraviolet blue that so struck me the first day I arrived. As a sign of my newly recovered status as an actual person, I rode my own horse—a pretty white mare with a silky stride. No one asked me if I could ride. Just lucky I could. Darling perched behind me on a special pad Lord Puck had arranged for him, eyes slitted in a doze as contented as if he lounged on a window sill.

Marquise and Scourge's castle where I'd stayed these last months seemed so small from the outside, glowing with a sick, greasy light and utterly still. As we rode away, I took a long look at my tower room. Then turned my back on it.

As good as it felt to be released from captivity and my lovingly cruel masters, a spinning sense of panic swirled through me. Agoraphobia, a clinical part of my brain informed me. I seemed to be filling up with thoughts again, an empty well slowly adjusting to a new water table after a long drought. I let the thoughts rise up again behind my tightly controlled wall, presenting my null demeanor to the world. Never would I go back to Marquise and Scourge.

Whatever it took.

I tamped down the anxiety, contenting myself with holding my left wrist in my right hand. It appeared as though I was steadying the hand holding the reins, but it also let me feel my pulse. I was both alive and relatively free. I had things to do.

A battle to win. And not for Falcon.

How easy it had been for Rogue to show me exactly what he wanted me to see. How he'd suckered me in and had me dancing to his tune. He was involved with bringing me to this place. Faerie, I decided to call it, now that I had freedom to think again, to observe and assimilate. Parallel universe, underworld, alternate dimension—the exact definition no longer mattered.

I knew now, better than ever, that power was the only thing that mattered in this world. Magic would give me the power I needed to make sure I never went through anything like that sadistic bootcamp again. Rogue thought to use sex against me, but I wouldn't allow it. Sex was my power to use—I'd learned that much. I'd serve the rest of my sentence and then find my way home. Rogue would never get his baby—I had over six years to make sure of it.

Lord Puck reined up beside me. I cast my eyes down submissively, habitually.

"We'll keep today's ride short, as I imagine you are still…tender."

I said nothing. I didn't have to unless he asked me a direct question. Wisdom lay in saying less.

"We'll stop at Castle Brightness, the ancestral home of Lady Blackbird's family. They're the last decent lodging we'll have for some time. After that it's tents as we travel to the battlefront. You'll see battle within the week, Lady Gwynn, mark my words!" Enthusiasm made him bounce in the saddle.

Darling sent an image of fat mice waddling slowly through golden rooms, accompanied by a lick of pleased anticipation. I sent him back a smile. At least he was excited about our destination. He also wanted a new name but preferred that it emerge in battle. These ideas were accompanied by an image of himself straddling some limp misshapen form, while his own fur dripped blood of the enemy, tail bristling in defiant delight. I didn't point out that his cat body looked more mountain lion-sized in these fantasies.

"You'll understand soon," Lord Puck said, making me start in my skin. "Why Falcon had us do it the way we did. One doesn't cross the Great Lord Falcon, you know."

I slid my eyes carefully up from the brown mane of my horse, to observe his profile through the filmy white scarf covering my head. Lord Puck looked cheerful, as if he might start whistling. Perhaps he was also relieved to have my training done with, and not just because he now could bring a new weapon to the front. To give him a little credit, he'd blanched at my appearance when he came to fetch me. He also stayed far away from Marquise and Scourge, his lighthearted thoughts skittering away from their thin smiles. He didn't know, really, what all had happened inside that castle, had never had a clear idea of what he'd delivered me into.

Unlike Rogue, who'd given me that searing look of regret and warning, then tossed me at Lord Puck and walked off to while away his time dancing while I went through the fires of hell.

Not that I was bitter.

"Lady Gwynn, we ride out in a new day. Your dark time is past. I won't say I'm sorry for my role in it, because it was necessary. However, know this—you may be bound by a debt of service, but you are no slave. Just do your duty by Lord Falcon and take pleasure in your life where you can find it."

I found my voice, so little used lately. "You surprise me, Lord Puck."

"Do I?" A pleased grin flashed across his face. "Good! Living is about surprises. A life without fun isn't worth living. Here." He sidled his horse nearer to mine, fished a little golden bell out of his pocket and affixed it to my horse's bridle. It hung there, jingling with each footstep. "Now you'll arrive with bells on!"

He cocked his head to the side, like a little boy trying to catch my eye. I watched the foolish little bell.

"I'm not sure what to make of this personality change."

"Not a change—just situation-appropriate. We all answer to someone, lady. Inciting merriment among the merry-less is one of my own callings—I take it very seriously."

"Odd that you go to war then."

"Oh no, not at all—it'll be grand fun. You'll see!"

Darling agreed, sending an image of a spiked collar with a brass breastplate for my consideration. Puck launched into a song that seemed to be about apples and pigs, but made no real sense to me.

I let my heart unclench a little.

Castle Brightness did indeed shine brilliantly. Fairy-tale turrets gleamed golden against the emerald hills and verdant apple orchards below. It was the first building I'd approached while conscious in this world. I'd never

even seen Rogue's fortress from the outside, and I'd
been at Marquise and Scourge's for who knows how
long before I saw anything but that tower room.

Taking Puck's advice, I soaked in the view as our
horses stepped lightly on the winding road down the
hill. I still couldn't put my finger on that deeper quality to all the colors. It was like a plasma-screen version
of the world, with just a little more contrast, composed
of cells of light. Rather than reflecting light here, everything seemed to just glow. A kind of otherworld
phosphorescence.

Bright trumpets signaled our arrival, flushing flocks
of blackbirds from the orchards. They swirled, glinting,
a living cloud of mica, then added their fluting calls
to the heralds, as they dove around the fluttering pennants on the towers. Everything seemed suffused with
a dreamlike quality, as if I was still suffering from the
soul-killing timelessness of Marquise and Scourge's
world. As if I'd never fully wakened. I pressed more
firmly on my pulse. It was solid and real, echoing the
soft thuds of my horse's hooves.

A group of people assembled in the wide and gracious courtyard before the castle gates. Darling jumped
down as soon as we reined up, flicking his tail in a casual goodbye, sending me a little reminder image of a
golden floor littered with bloody mice.

And, surprise, there was Lady Blackbird, calling a
hello to Darling and flashing an amused smile when he
ignored her. Then with a delighted greeting she was at
my stirrup, waiting for me to dismount.

Which was, indeed, quite painful.

"The first day riding is always so difficult," she tut-
ted, embracing me.

I tried not to wince when she touched my back. I would be grateful when I finished healing. Puck's people had offered me a healer's services. I had declined.

"I didn't expect you here, Lady Blackbird?"

She folded her hands with a pleased look. "Lord Rogue let me return home, as part of your boon to me." She patted my arm. "Lady Gwynn, may I present to you my daughter, Starling."

"Greetings, Lady Starling." I nodded gravely to the brown-haired woman who stood eagerly at her mother's side, surveying her through the veil. She seemed to be a little older than a teenager, but hard to say what that meant here. If the fairy stories were at all true, these people were immortal, forever youthful. I had yet to see anyone elderly, but there was certainly a maturity difference between Blackbird and Starling.

"Oh not lady, just Starling," she said. "I'm a half-breed, you know."

Interesting. Her limbs did lack that slightly out-of-proportion look. Her cheekbones were more flat, with a scattering of Lucy Liu freckles beneath eyes that matched the snapping dark gloss of her mother's.

"Lady Gwynn," Lord Puck called, "I see the ladies have you in hand. Do what you like this afternoon. We'll see you for the evening meal." He ambled off with a laughing group of men.

With an apology, Blackbird excused herself to see to the feast preparations.

Starling offered to show me to my room. "You'll change out of your traveling clothes and we can have cocktails!" she enthused.

Cocktails—how funny that her word for wine, which I recognized by the sound, translated as "cocktails" in my head. I hadn't had a drink since that sickly plum wine at Rogue's banquet. Talk about enforced rehab.

"I'm afraid I'm a bit of a charity case," I confessed as we walked through the gleaming hallways. "I'm wearing all I have." Though I'd have just loved to ditch the shapeless traveling robe, in my adopted oatmeal color, it was certainly better than what I'd barely been wearing recently.

"Oh, didn't Puck—I mean, Lord Puck—" Starling glanced around to be sure her mother hadn't heard her slip, "—tell you? Since my mother is your seneschal-in-absentia, she took care of assembling your wardrobe." She grabbed my arm excitedly. "All new clothes!"

"Seneschal?" I asked.

Starling did a little dance around me, her filmy gown flaring—she had an enviably slender figure. Of course, I was likely gaunt as a skeleton now.

"Yes! Since you gave her your gratitude, Rogue made her your seneschal. So she'll take care of your business from here until you get your own castle. Or whatever. If I could conjure up anything *I* wanted, I think I'd have a little place by the sea—who wants more fortresses?"

"You have a point there."

"Here we are." Starling opened doors into a sun-filled room all in whites and golds with a row of windows that overlooked the orchards and the green hills beyond. She skipped across the room to an armoire and flung open the doors to a garden of outfits. "See!" She practically squealed. "You can try them all on. See what you like best. I'm very good at helping decide what looks best."

Hesitant, I pulled out something in a pretty jewel-green. It looked reasonable—neither convent nor Frederick's of Hollywood.

"Mother said you prefer brighter colors," Starling said. "I'm calling for cocktails."

I flipped through the gowns, some with divided skirts for riding, all bright jewel tones, all of similar weight. Was it always the same season here? No, couldn't be—not with apples growing outside. Unless those weren't really apples. Ah, well—it was easier to assume normal rules of biology applied. Apple trees were deciduous and required a cold season to fruit. Therefore there must be seasons, right? Though, so far, every day had been the same sunshine, the same clear skies. Bemused, I listened to the roll of my thoughts, more popping up all the time.

"What do I do if there's colder weather?"

Starling returned from the hall, trailed by a young page pushing a sort-of tea cart laden with decanters and a pair of crystal glasses that grabbed the sun and threw shards of light around the room. Starling shooed him out and closed the door, leaning back against it, looking surprised. "I thought you were a sorceress. Can't you just zap yourself warm?" She wiggled her fingers like lightning strikes as an example.

A laugh escaped me, which felt odd. A crack in the granite. "Probably, but wouldn't it be easier just to wear a coat?"

"Unglamorous, if you ask me." She shrugged. "Look in that trunk—I think those are cold-weather supplies. Now do you want honey wine, plum wine or sweet nectar? Or there's this whiskey."

"Whiskey? You have whiskey?"

"Yes, it's common, but Daddy keeps it on the cocktail cart. I don't know why."

"Yes, please, to the whiskey."

She generously filled one crystal goblet and I choked at the sight.

"That much will take all afternoon to drink."

"Good thing we have all afternoon!" Starling poured herself some pink stuff that had to be the nectar and flopped on a white velvet fainting couch. She pointed imperiously at me. "Now start trying on clothes. I've been waiting and waiting to see them. We thought they would never let you out."

Me, too.

"What about the color thing?" I asked, grasping at the memory.

"Color thing?"

"You know, if I wear this color, I'm allied with that person."

"Oh tish tosh." Starling shooed away so much nonsense. "The only ones who believe that are the old-fashioned old-fogies. Wear what you like and screw 'em if they can't take a joke, I say! Only," she added, glancing at the closed door, "don't mention to Mom that I said so. Now get started already!"

The feel of the glass in my hand, the sun streaming in the windows, the taste of whiskey in my mouth—not quite Jameson, but wonderful in its own way—helped settle me back in my skin. Taking my glass with me, I grabbed the green dress and stepped behind the lacquer screen that shielded the chamber pot. Starling didn't need to see the state of my body. I didn't need to answer questions about it.

I nudged the pot aside with my foot, balanced my

glass on a little ledge built into the screen and shrugged out of the oatmeal traveling thing. I tossed the robe over the top of the screen.

"Bravo!" Starling called. "Let's just burn that, shall we?"

"Fine by me, but let's make sure at least one of these fits first."

"Oh they'll fit. Mother never misses."

Fortunately I hadn't been wound into one of those mummy-corsets since that long-ago night of the banquet and only wore what the Elizabethan novels probably meant by *chemise* Just a fine sheer cloth nightgown-style, except the skirt was divided and sewn, so I could ride. I pulled on the green dress, which felt like satiny heaven sliding over me.

Starling gaped at me when I emerged from behind the screen. Her expression made me think I might not be a vision of loveliness.

"Blessed Titania, what happened to your hair?"

I put a hand up to my head. How utterly surreal that I could have forgotten. That I could have pulled off that headscarf with the oatmeal dress and forgotten. I wanted to dash back behind the screen, somehow hide and still pretend that we were having a girlish afternoon trying on clothes.

But I was a deer frozen in the road. Locked in place by Starling's horrified gaze.

She set down her wineglass and edged up to the end of the chaise. She had kicked off her flats and tucked one petite bare foot up under her. Now she folded her hands in her lap, a gesture of her mother's.

"Fix it," she said.

I just stared at her, one hand still on my bristly, scabby scalp.

"Fix it," she insisted. "You're graduated now, right? Free to do whatever magic you want to? And don't tell me it would be easier to wear a wig." She reached back to grab her wineglass. "Now's your opportunity. What kind of hair did you always, always want when you were a little girl? Me? I wanted golden hair. There was this neighbor girl—full breed—like dew-on-the-morning-grass gorgeous, eyes blue as the sky, floating golden hair, delicate pink butterfly wings. Titania, I hated the little bitch."

I laughed, a little. Such a frivolous conversation. Her words eroded my numbness.

Starling leaned forward. "Lady Gwynn—it's hair. Just fix it. Make it what you want."

"I always wanted long black hair."

"Oh, and that would be great with your green eyes, though I imagine you could change those, too, if you wanted to. Do it!"

She was right, I could do this. I was the dog so used to being beaten that I wouldn't leave the yard even though the gate was open. And I needed to practice a great deal, to perfect what I knew and to explore the possibilities. Of course I should do this.

"Is there a mirror?" I asked.

Starling gestured to an alcove. She followed me, avid interest on her face, wineglass in her hand. "Is it okay if I watch? I almost never get to see real magic being performed. Mother doesn't want me getting ideas."

"I don't mind. Just be very quiet and don't distract me."

I focused on my image in the mirror and tried not to

flinch. I looked like Sinead O'Connor after a bad acid trip…and a bar fight.

I should have looked at myself before now. One thing I'd learned—painfully—was that if you were going to muck about with the state of reality via magic, you'd better have a firm grip on what really existed in the first place. There was no room for kidding yourself about what was real. No cutting yourself slack that, oh, you didn't really mean that nasty thought about such and so. Because meaning it, intending it, was what connected the idea to the spark—and it became real like a bomb exploding.

I could be taught.

So first, I had to see my hair as it was now. The old stories had it right, that facing yourself in the mirror as you truly were was the ultimate test of character. Not just to recognize the ugliness, but also the beauty. Everything in its balance. I carefully built the image in my mind of what I wanted and searched my heart for the emotion to make it real. What *I* wanted.

Then I waited.

The magic didn't happen immediately, like in a Las Vegas stage show, with a flash of light and a puff of smoke. No. Real magic flowed on its own timeline.

And there it was. My shaved scalp with its scabs, stubble and awkward bristles was gone as if it had never been. Now shining black hair waved gently around my face, flowing down my back. I'd fixed the bruises on my face while I was at it. I'd fix what I could of the rest later, when I had the leisure to strip.

"Wow," Starling breathed. "That's fascinating. It's not like it happened fast, but it's more that I didn't even notice the change. I *know* in my head that you have different hair now, but a big part of me is convinced you've always been this way. Is that illusion?" She reached out to stroke the silky hair, letting it run through her fingers.

"No. No illusion. This is as real as it gets." I shook my head, letting the new hair settle around me. It was recognizably *my* hair, just a different color and shape, but the same familiar texture. I looked the way I'd always wanted to—the sparkling black accenting a complexion that glowed in snowy smooth contrast. Green eyes blazed at me in the mirror and I recognized the woman who'd had enough and walked out of that cocktail party. And there was the younger woman I'd been, full of ambition and the love of science. For the first time in years, she looked pleased.

Better, she looked powerful.

TWELVE

The Calm Before the Storm

"WHAT WOULDN'T I give to be able to do that?" Starling sighed.

"It's easy to think of sacrifices in theory." My voice sounded a bit too sharp. I took a deep breath. *Let it go.* "In practice you might find yourself... regretting the price you paid."

She nodded gravely. Her gaze rested on my arm, where the tapered sleeve of my gown revealed raised scars the whips had cut into me. I tugged the cuff over the marks and she looked away.

"Where's your whiskey?" she asked in a bright tone, then scooted behind the screen to fetch it. Handing it to me, she clinked her glass against mine. "To the new improved you!"

I joined her in the toast, grateful for the change of subject. I savored the whiskey and studied myself in the mirror to get my new appearance firmly in my head. Wouldn't want to accidentally blur it by thinking of myself in an old way.

"Will it last forever?"

"It should, unless I change it. Things that are close to me, that are constantly in my attention, are much more likely to persist. It's harder to make something I'm not around last in any permanent way. But then, I haven't gotten to experiment with it much."

Rogue could do it—those chamber pots, I suddenly recalled. Maybe he had bespelled those.

"Hmm." Starling sipped at her glass, looking at my hair enviously.

"Why? You want me to change your hair, too?"

"Yes!" She pounced, sloshing her wine. "Can you? Would you? Even if it only lasts until you ride away, it would be worth it."

I loved it—I acquired magical abilities and I was using them for makeovers. Clive would have been disgusted by the girly behavior. My mom would have been the first in line. My heart throbbed, thinking of her now. How long had I been gone? And Isabel, what had become of her? It killed me that she might think I'd abandoned her. A quiet tide of grief surged under the enamel shell of my careful control.

"Can you picture the kind of hair you want—if you don't mind me looking at the image in your head?"

Starling nodded eagerly and folded her hands around her wineglass, closing her eyes as if in prayer. She looked so studious, so serious. We all prayed for our heart's desire. It was a mistake to think that had to be something profound and huge. Very few people really thought of world peace first, in my experience.

I touched my fingertips to her temples as a courtesy, flashed on the night I'd touched Rogue this way and crushed the thought. I dipped lightly into Starling's mind, bright with restless ideas and longings. There on top was the image of the little neighbor girl, long-limbed and ethereal. Attached to it were various sorrows of not belonging, not being good enough. Of failure. I focused on the way the hair looked, like gold embroidery floss, sunlight in spider silk, and carefully stripped away the negative feelings. She didn't need any more of that.

It was easy to find the spark for it—Starling fed me that in spades.

I waited.

"Okay, look and see if it's right."

Starling's eyes popped open. I expected her to whirl around, perhaps squealing, to admire herself in the mirror. Instead she blinked at me, took a breath and cautiously turned, peeking over her shoulder at her reflection. Tears welled up in her dark eyes, threatening to spill over.

"Is it right?" I asked her. "I changed it very slightly, so it wouldn't look like a little girl's hair so much."

Starling nodded. "It's perfect," she whispered.

"Do you want to change your eyes, too? Though I think this combination looks great—my mom always said she thought the brown-eyed blondes had the prettiest coloring."

Starling shook her head. Nodded. Then laughed and gulped down the rest of her wine. The golden hair shimmered softly around her face, brushing her shoulders in a thick paintbrush fringe. Her lightly tanned skin and freckles took on a warmer glow.

"It's perfect," she repeated, not noticing how I flinched at the word. "I'm going to savor every moment of it. It's the first time I've been pleased to look in the mirror. Now, what do I owe you?"

Oh. I hadn't thought of that.

"Can it just be a gift?" I tried.

Starling looked horrified. Not the best option.

"Yes, of course," she said, "but…"

"Never mind," I hastened to reassure her to her obvious relief. She'd been prepared to pay whatever it took when she asked me for the favor, though. And here I didn't know what to ask for. A big part of me still quailed at asking for anything. I thought back to the banquet. "What do you propose?"

"A month of service. After I'm legal."

"That seems like a lot for an overnight hairdo." I wasn't going to ask what "being legal" meant or how long it would take.

She looked again and blew herself a kiss. "I don't care if it's gone in the morning when you ride away. Do you agree?"

"Yes. But I don't think it'll happen like that." I took a moment to survey myself in the green gown. It seemed to fit nicely, though a bit loose over the hips. Rehab and fat camp, all in one brutal engagement. "Of course, I can't see what happens after I've left a place, but I'm pretty sure it'll just gradually revert back to what you're used to. Especially if that's what you're expecting."

"But I can't do magic," Starling replied, eying the green gown. "And I think that one is a definite keeper—great with your eyes."

"Thank you." I set down the whiskey and grabbed a couple more gowns. "You know, where I come from, no one does magic. But I'm surprised how much the rules make sense. I think there's more magic going on than we realize. The world tends to be the way we expect it to be. I think people influence the world around them on a daily basis a lot more than they know."

When had I thought about this? I had no idea. Perhaps part of me had been there all along, hiding and assimilating.

"So, what I'm saying is, if you want to—it wouldn't hurt to try—concentrate on looking like this and see what happens. Maybe if you want it badly enough, the change will persist even after I'm no longer paying attention to it."

When I came out from behind the screen, in a yellow gown, Starling was fiercely staring at herself in the mirror. I hoped she wouldn't break it.

"Easy," I said, handing her a fresh glass of wine. "Just want it with your usual level—believe me, that's plenty. And enjoy it. Let it be welcome in your life." I hesitated. "Be happy when you see it. Don't... When you see your hair, think of yourself and your pleasure in it, never your neighbor. Let that be gone now."

She nodded at me in the mirror, though she didn't look convinced. Then she frowned.

"Problem?"

"Yes."

"What?"

"That color is *really* dreadful on you."

I laughed, forced to agree.

By the time Lady Blackbird joined us, we'd generated two piles, keepers and dreadfuls. The sun was slanting into evening. And we were thoroughly toasted. Not that it took much for me now. The room smelled toasted, too. Tossing the oatmeal dress into the fireplace ended up being quite a bit smokier than we'd planned on. Starling reclined on her chaise, pulling the tips of her hair over her forehead so she dangled them over her eyes. I sat on the floor, going through the trunk of winter things, though I was feeling more sleepy than ambitious at this point.

"Well, look at the two of you, all prettied up!" Black-

bird sang out, as if we were two girls playing dress-up
and changing our hair was an everyday game. She set
down the wooden box she was carrying and cupped her
hands on Starling's cheeks, pursing her lips. "It suits
you, baby bird—you look lovely." And she kissed her
on the nose. "Though I wish you'd forget about that
foolish RosePetal."

"RosePetal?" I snorted and Starling rolled her eyes.

"Lady Gwynn, I have something of yours to return."
Blackbird retrieved her wooden box and set it down next
to me, then poured herself a glass of wine.

I paused in opening the box—hadn't there been only
two glasses on the cart?

Starling saw me looking. "Magic cocktail cart," she
assured me. "Only one like it ever. Daddy got it as a reward. He could pick anything he wanted and the man
picks a cart that never runs out of booze and always has
enough clean glasses for everyone."

Sounded like a man after my own heart. "A reward
for what?"

"The usual heroics." Blackbird waved that away as
unimportant.

"If you're a half-breed, then he's human—like me?"
I looked from mother to daughter, who both nodded solemnly. "How did he get here?"

"There are many of your kind here, Lady Gwynn."

"And, like you, Daddy came from the other world,"
Starling added.

"Where is he? Can I meet him?"

They exchanged exasperated looks. "No," Blackbird
sighed. "Not this time. I'm afraid he's off chasing another rumor on how to get back through the veil. He's

been gone months now. He'll turn up one day and mope around for a while."

"What rumor is he chasing?"

"Nonsense, is what it is." Blackbird sounded gentle but intractable. "Open your box, dear."

I obeyed, my mind chewing on how to meet this man. Then I breathed out a sigh. My Ann Taylor dress. She had promised and I should have never doubted. My silk panties lay neatly folded in there, too. Perched on top, a sedate version of Dorothy's ruby slippers, were my Nine West heels. Already the clothes seemed like an ancestor's relic found in the attic, remnants of another world, another time.

"I've never seen undergarments like that," Starling said. "Mama only let me look at them, not touch."

"So you wouldn't disturb the magic," Blackbird said over her shoulder. "That's why I washed them myself, in rainwater."

"You think my dress is magic because I was wearing it…before?" I still didn't feel comfortable saying "cast a spell"—made me think of the witch in *Snow White* standing on the cliffside, terrifying in purple-black, lightning flashing around her. The idea that something I'd once touched with magic became magic was not something my teachers had discussed—though they had mentioned that magic fixed in objects was something I could explore later. They hadn't mentioned magical cocktail carts, or chamber pots and water pails, for that matter, either.

I never asked questions of them, of course. At last Rogue got what he wanted. Too bad he'd missed it.

"Because you wore it the first time your magic manifested. We always save the garments a child is wearing when their magic first comes alive, refashioning it into charms as the fabric wears over time. It's just tradition—I don't really understand such things."

I was beginning to suspect that any time Blackbird avowed ignorance it was a cover for a deeper insight than she wanted to let on.

"Thank you, Lady Blackbird—it means a great deal to me to have this back, regardless of the purpose. And thank you for all this…" I gestured to the clothes. "I hate to sound ungrateful, or cynical, but I'm wondering about the cost?"

Blackbird chuckled, sipping her wine. "No, you don't owe anything further. You're receiving credit now for your magical services. I just draw from your accounts."

"But I thought that my services were paying off a debt."

"That too."

"So how can I be both paying a debt and earning credit?"

Starling and Blackbird peered quizzically at me with matching bright eyes.

"Never mind," I said, "I'll take your word for it. And the dresses, with grat…appreciation." I was careful not to kiss anyone—though I wasn't sure that was what had done it before.

"We'll leave you then. Come along, Starling, so Lady Gwynn can bathe in peace."

They left the cocktail cart with me, though I protested that I hardly needed to indulge further. I stood at the window, sipping the lovely warm whiskey, watching the shadows lengthen and turn drowsy, while servants—very normal-looking ones—tromped in and out preparing a bath for me. No magic buckets here, no indoor plumbing, no uncanny silence, just heavy manual labor and a significant servant class. Not that I wanted to argue. I was fine with being one of the waited-upon at this point. Much better than my recent status. Amazing how a little—or a lot of—privation can make you happy to be spoiled.

It seemed to be late summer, by the way the apples hung heavy on the trees. But time also passed in a funny way here, and the air always held a bit of cool which the soft sunlight never quite burned away. It seemed Castle Brightness threw off its own radiance, more pronounced now in the gloaming, as the shadows in the trees darkened and the leaves glinted in reflected golden light.

The shadows moved. There, under the edge of the orchard, glass-black separated from the normal shadows.

The Dog. He paced out and sat below my window, amber eyes shining, torches in the night.

I realized I was holding my breath, caught high in my throat, and that I was grasping my neck with one hand, the carotid pulse under my thumb and fingertips tripping a fast and frantic beat. Hatred and terror roared through me. He opened his mouth in a slavering grin. A little whine escaped my lips.

I flung my glass of whiskey at him. My teachers would have punished me greatly for my unreasoned action, but I was free of them and threw it at him with all the childish fear and anger in my heart. The emotion and my desire to hit him with the glass held it to a true course several stories down, but as it sailed, tumbling end over end scattering whiskey in bright drops, the glass slowed. It righted itself in the air and dropped gracefully to land upright before the Dog, as if set there by an invisible hand. The Dog, blazing eyes locked on mine, bent down and delicately licked out the crystal goblet, then licked his chops, savoring every bit.

He grinned at me again and melted back into the shadows. I stared at the empty dark, but didn't see him again.

With a mental shake I took hold of myself. Turning back to the room, I breathed out and dropped my hand from my throat. I clasped my wrist instead, the pulse jumping against my thumb. Then I saw that the cocktail cart had produced a new glass for me, just like the one I'd impulsively thrown.

Almost like. On the thin crystal rim glimmered a drop of bright blood.

THIRTEEN

In Which I Run Off to Join the Circus

"EXPLAIN THE GIFT thing to me," I said to Starling and Blackbird.

We stood in the bright morning light of the castle courtyard, while the glittering birds swirled amidst the pennants above. Starling had just presented me with an elaborately woven headband of gold wire studded with emerald-like stones, to hold my hair back from my face. Her own hair dazzled the eye, a lovely blond that shimmered with platinum glints.

Both women looked at me with consternation.

"Why can you give me a gift and I can't give you one?"

"Lady Sorceress," Blackbird said, "you honor us by accepting what we offer you. You…elevate us." She patted Starling's shoulder. "And no worries, when our daughter reaches her majority, we'll send her to finish her service to you."

"I'm not worried. I look forward to seeing you again, Starling. Thank—I enjoyed our afternoon together. Very much."

"Me too!" Starling enthused, shaking her head so her hair swirled around her shoulders. "I'm concentrating on keeping my hair this way. You'll see. You'll be proud of me."

I didn't quite know what to say. "Starling—you've been a friend to me. When I needed one. There's nothing more important than that."

I mounted my horse—blessedly nearly free of pain, since I'd taken the time to wish everything I could see or feel into faster healing—and added my wish to Starling's.

"For you, my lady sorceress." Blackbird, head bowed, held up something wrapped in a parchment paper cone. I took it and laid it across my lap, while my horse shifted and stamped. I missed being able to loop the reins around the horn, but this was more of an English saddle style. Good thing my riding teacher had made me learn, despite my protests that I'd never use anything but a Western saddle. Blackbird put a hand over the reins, to help steady the mare.

Inside the paper lay a single flower.

Both ostentatious and elegant, the blossom was as big as my head and looked like the Stargazer lilies I'd always loved. Except, instead of a pink throat spreading out to the tips of the ivory petals, this one was blue. Deep indigo ranged through teals to finish in twilight blues, with inky spots scattered throughout. The distinctive Stargazer sweet scent was threaded through with sandalwood. And some other scent, something redolent of mace, that reminded me of the taste of Rogue's mouth. The petals seemed to glow with their own light, almost living flesh.

I knew it wasn't from Blackbird.

From the way she blushed under my gaze, looking carefully down, I knew my stare had grown as hard as my heart felt.

"Lord Rogue sends his regards," Blackbird said.

I seized her by the wrist and leaned down close to her face, the flower heady with scent between us.

"Why does he want a baby with me?" I hissed. The question escaped me unexpectedly, filled with the cold hate that had grown in the recesses of my heart. So many things I could have asked or said—this was what sprang forth.

Blackbird shook her head and tugged a bit. "I can't say, lady." She looked at me then, her bright eyes alien. Her wrist felt spidery under my fingers. I could see Starling over her shoulder, owl-eyed and pale. I loosened my grip so Blackbird could slip her hand out of mine. And I knew by the regret in her face that she meant she was not allowed to say, not that she didn't know.

I nearly threw the blossom to the dirt for my horse to trample, but I hesitated. And she who hesitated was lost. I couldn't destroy that beautiful flower. It had already seduced me with its spiced honey fragrance and outrageous blues.

The lily gave me pleasure, too, as we rode along, Darling behind me on his traveling pad. I already knew it radiated magic, Rogue's magic, as distinct as the flavor of cinnamon, so it was no surprise to find the petals remained dewy fresh, even as the sun climbed overhead.

It occurred to me that having a piece of his magic could turn out useful. At the very least, I could study it.

My hatred for Rogue and what he'd done to me, what he planned to do, sat cold and solid in my gut. If he thought this would soften me, he was sorely mistaken. Perhaps a bit of my feminine heart was charmed by the gift. I liked flowers, particularly this one. I'd known women who took all that a man offered them—dinners and gifts and admiration—then left without a backward glance when they had exhausted him.

I could be that. To punish him.

We rode through more of Disney Ireland. Once we cleared the hill beyond Castle Brightness, I never saw another building. No farms, no towns. Just emerald meadows and chocolate forests. Some of the groves boasted birds. Other sections were conspicuously silent, like the place I'd "landed," and I wondered what it meant. I made a mental note to check those places out sometime.

Puck cheerfully informed me that they marked the frontier. When I responded, "And after the frontier, there be dragons?" he frowned and said, "No, barbarians."

Sometimes we passed a field of flowers that could be on a gardening catalog cover. The blossoms bobbed in exotic beauty, their fragrances tantalizing the air around me.

None, of course, could match my indigo Stargazer. I was sure Rogue would allow nothing less.

Our caravan passed the night in one of the velvety meadows. I perched on a boulder, Stargazer lily draped across my lap, at a bit of a loss, as everyone but me seemed to have a job to do. Even Darling had trotted off somewhere, and a short, stone-faced guy led my mare off as soon as I dismounted, after setting my saddlebags next to me. Puck sent servants to make me a pallet in the grass from a pile of blankets and to give me a platter of these kind of travel biscuits we'd been eating. They tasted of honey and sunshine.

I munched my biscuits and found myself missing Starling's company as the gloaming deepened. I would have liked to stay in that great bed at Castle Brightness, pretend I was a princess and not a prisoner.

But then, I've never been much of a camper.

For lack of anything better to do, I crawled into my blankets. I set the flower next to me, where it would be safe. The others had gathered into various groups, sitting around campfires, singing and dancing in one cluster. Another group laughed so manically my skin crawled. I didn't think I was really invited to join any of them. Not that I wanted to.

No guards seemed to be posted. We were far from any of the groves of silent trees, which gave me some comfort. Would there be anything I could do, should the Dog show up? Probably not. Definitely I shouldn't think about him.

So I lay there and watched the stars brighten.

They spun overhead in stunning glory. As with everything here, the firmament was sharper, more radiant—and they were the same constellations I'd seen all my life. And no Southern Cross, either. This sky shone pure northern hemisphere, Earth perspective. Orion strode boldly high with Sirius trotting at his heels. Leo's question mark exclaimed that this was, indeed, the late summer season. At the sight, my heart first leaped in grateful familiarity. Then the implications hit me. It didn't help that Sirius shone with a green more emerald than any star I'd ever seen. Betelgeuse's usual silver shone almost cobalt.

Was and not was. Neither here nor there, but somewhere else entirely.

I tightened the soft blankets around me and closed my eyes. *Sleep now.*

But I couldn't.

Last night I had slept deep and dreamlessly. Still recovering from all that sleep deprivation. By all rights I should be tired still. I tried to sink down, but my eyes only popped open again. Speared by starlight.

Maybe I slept. It felt as though I hadn't, my dreams filled with hallucinatory night skies. I definitely needed to pee, however. Groggy, I peeled off the blankets and stumbled a few feet away. Some fires were still burning, long-limbed silhouettes gyrating around them.

Where to go in this open meadow?

I trudged off a ways, the lush dew-damp grass brushed my bare feet and pulled at the hem of my white gown. It clung to my calves as I walked, the diaphanous material now sticking to my flesh, now billowing away. My hair hung heavy down my back, a silk cape.

The grass beneath my feet gave way to cool, damp leaf litter when I entered the forest. Trunks of trees stood sentinel around me, starlight sprinkling down though the whispering leaves above. The night glittered with it. My blood sparkled, too.

I lifted the Stargazer lily to my face and breathed in the heavy sweet scent of it. Thick as opium, it made my head swirl. I smiled, my breasts tightening with anticipation.

And there he was.

Black on black, Rogue leaned against a tree. His hair hung loose, like so much satin Spanish moss, blending into the ancient wood behind him. Shadows fingered over him, sliding through the lines on the one side of his face. On the clear side, his dark lips curved into a smile.

"Beautiful Gwynn," he whispered.

The sheer gown shifted over my tight nipples as I walked to him, the blossom clasped in front of me, a bridal bouquet. When I neared, I held it out to him. He wrapped his elegant fingers around my wrist, pulling my hand down to his side, so that I came up against him, stretched against the length of his thighs. I braced myself on his chest, my hand over his heart. I could feel the alien rhythm of it through the black velvet he wore. Almost a waltz beat.

One…two, three.

One…two, three.

He cupped my face with his other hand, holding me as he bent his head. I could see the deep blue of his eyes now. If lava were indigo, it would be like this. Rogue's ebony hair fell around us in a glassy curtain and I swayed at the first touch of his lips. The kiss pulled me under and I drowned eagerly. His lips moved hot and sparking over mine. I fed off of his mouth eagerly, dry dirt soaking up spring rain. Mace filled my head. My bones melted away.

I moaned and he pulled me tight against him.

"My lovely Gwynn," he murmured against my mouth, "I have missed you."

I heard a hissing sound and the gauzy gown I wore fell away, pooling at my feet.

"See?" Rogue said. "Already you are mine."

I looked down and saw the thorns piercing me. Black thorns, glass-sharp, wove into my skin, white in the starlight. My blood trickled from them, dark and glossy.

The flower fell from my hand, tumbling to the ground in slow-motion spirals.

I sat bolt upright, choking on a scream.

Darling blinked at me in disapproval and yawned widely. The sky arched overhead, the stars fading, the horizon brightening with iridescent sunrise. My pulse throbbed through me and I tasted cinnamon in my mouth. I still wore the traveling gown I'd lain down in.

The Stargazer lily rested on top of my bags, luminescent, violently blue in the breaking dawn. A gauntlet thrown down in challenge. The rage rose up through me. A cold and terrible anger. And now he thought to play games with me.

Fine, then. Let's play. Rogue wouldn't know what hit him.

I packed the lily away, not caring how I crushed it into the bottom of my bags.

Even so, I dreamed again the next two nights. Every time I went to him and let him strip me, as helpless as I'd been with my trainers. Every night he showed me that I was already his.

And every morning the lily greeted me, perfect in its sinister beauty.

Though the dreams fell into tatters in the bright light of day, they drained me. As if I had spent every night walking the forest. He thought to take me from one imprisonment to another. Perhaps he, too, thought I had been permanently broken.

He was in for one hell of a surprise.

WHEN WE RODE into Lord Falcon's camp three days after leaving Castle Brightness, the scene hit my bruised senses like a surreal carnival. I had expected something more of a war zone, to which Lord Puck responded that we were well back from the battle lines and so could afford the basic comforts. I didn't know much about war, except for books and movies. This scene was definitely not what I'd pictured.

Tents in an eye-jarring array of colors were jumbled

around a green valley, with a bright brook flowing from
a waterfall down the cliffside beyond. Banners with
fanciful creatures fluttered gaily, music played and a
group of long-limbed figures danced in the meadow. I
half-expected to see unicorns dancing around rainbows.

"See?" Puck said beside me. "Didn't I tell you this
would be grand fun?"

Puck led me to a tent that could have belonged to a
Saudi king. Cream silk swept up and gathered in a rib-
boned knot at the peak. Bright pillows tumbled over the
floor, glowing in the slashes of sunshine falling through
open skylights where the material had been rolled back
above. The only spot not heaped with pillows was one
corner where a girl with dragonfly wings knelt on a
velvety rug by a table with platters of food.

Darling picked his way to a canary-yellow cushion
lying in a sunbeam—bypassing iris-blue and grass-
green ones—and began kneading it. His purr filled the
room. I sent him a picture of a goofy-looking cat drool-
ing like an undignified kitten, but he only agreed happily.

We'd meet for a War Strategy Feast later, Puck promised me, and promptly disappeared, leaving me alone
with the faerie girl.

"Would my lady sorceress like some plum wine or
nectar?" she asked without looking up.

"Is some water a possibility? And don't kneel. You
don't have to kneel."

"I'll fetch some from the stream!" She scampered
up, grabbed a pitcher and slipped out the silk tent flaps,
catching her stiff horizontal wings on both sides. I in-
vestigated the food, finding the same spread of sug-
ared fruits, cheeses and pastries as the snack tray at

chez Rogue. I wished that the food all be nourishing, good for me and not drugged, then plucked out a piece of cheese and surveyed my new home.

Not much to survey.

I tripped on a pillow trying to walk over to the other side of the tent to see if I got a bed. None in sight. Apparently I was intended to loll about like a harem girl draped over pillows.

Dragonfly Girl breezed back in, one silk flap snagged on her right wing. "Shall I pour my lady sorceress some water?" she asked in her tiny voice.

Red-gold curls rumpled around her face, a spring-green pixie outfit barely draped her tiny girlish body. I picked my way across the pillows—this was going to have to change—pulled the silk off her wing so it settled back to flutter in the breeze, then took the cold pitcher from her. Cold enough to be snowmelt. Interesting.

"I need to make sure it's clean first," I told her.

"Oh, it's clean." She nodded earnestly, curls bouncing. "I made sure no dirt went in it."

"A different kind of clean." I really didn't want to try to explain microorganisms and giardia to her, if they even existed here, but better safe than sorry. "A sorceress needs magically clean water."

What a blatant lie, but her eyes grew round and solemn. She nodded gravely. I almost felt bad for misleading her, especially just for my convenience. But not bad enough to explain about germs and disease and why I never wanted another healer near me. Easier to milk the eccentric sorceress gig than reveal my bleeding psyche.

I wished the water pure and poured a glass, studying her over the rim as I sipped. She shifted restlessly, looking uncomfortable. I probably should have let her pour it, so she'd have something to do.

"Are the wings new?"

"Do you like them, Lady Sorceress?"

"Call me Gwynn." As the name left my mouth, I realized what I'd said. Just as well. Let the old me be truly dead. Easier to move on.

"Oh no, Lady Sorceress, I couldn't do that. It would be most improper. Please don't ask that of me." Her gray eyes welled with tears.

That was me, tormenter of little faerie girls.

"All right, no worries. 'Lady Gwynn' is fine." Her tears vanished in a sunrise smile, making me wonder if I'd been had. "And you are?"

"Whatever my lady sorceress wishes to call me."

"If your mother were to walk into this tent right now, what would she call you?"

"But she's not here—she's at home." Dragonfly looked profoundly confused.

I tried another tack. "You've been here in camp for a little while now?"

She nodded.

"Presumably you haven't stayed in this tent the entire time—if you encountered someone you knew on the way to the stream to fetch water, what would they call you?"

"Servant of the Lady Sorceress," she answered.

Oh yes, of course. I could call her whatever I wanted and she would answer, as long as I meant her.

I decided to sit down, not a graceful endeavor on the slick pillows. Dragonfly Girl scurried over, trying to plump up pillows around me. I felt like swatting at her. Especially when one of the iridescent wings nearly poked my eye out.

"Sit," I said, pointing an imperious finger at her, a la Starling. Amazing how quickly the lady-of-the-manor behavior came to you when you were surrounded by the obsequious. She obediently knelt in front of me, then remembered and changed it to a sitting position. Darling drifted over, sniffed at her, then eyed the wing hovering over his head. He batted at it and I tsked at him. Dragonfly looked frightened, though I wasn't sure if it was of me, him or both.

"Darling, leave the girl be," I said to his disdainful look. He settled down into meatloaf position, eyes bright on the wing. I decided to let it go.

"Were you born with the wings?"

"Oh no, Lady Sorceress. Our family magician made them for me so I could be a good servant for you."

"Why do dragonfly wings make you a good servant?"

"Because the Lady Sorceress can't have an ordinary girl!"

"I think I can."

"You don't like me? I've failed already?" Her eyes silvered with tears again. "I haven't even heard your requirements and you're sending me home?"

"Stop with the tears. That's requirement number one."

She sniffled a bit, but dried the tears.

"Can you use the wings—can you fly with them?"

Dragonfly looked astonished, with a nose-wrinkle for my ignorance.

"Never mind. Do you want to keep them? They seem…inconvenient."

"Oh yes, Lady Sorceress. They're way cool."

The faerie version of Valley Girl patter—just what I needed. I blinked against the grittiness of my eyes. If I could just sleep, this would seem less like an acid trip.

If I could sleep without dreaming, I amended to my-self. That meant dealing with that diabolical flower. And maybe an afternoon nap would keep me in slow-wave sleep rather than REM sleep, when dreams oc-curred. My own brain chemistry shouldn't be any different than in the regular world. Hopefully.

And if it had changed, now would be a really good time to find out.

I set Dragonfly to clearing some of the pillows, creat-ing a workspace and finding me something else to sleep on. A futon of sorts. I described the rolled cotton layers of a futon, watching Dragonfly's terror of being unable to please me increase, and realized I could just trans-form some of the pillows into the kind of bed I wanted.

Note to self—magic can be a shortcut. Remember to use it.

On the other hand, sending Dragonfly on a scav-enger hunt for various obscure items for the eccentric foreign sorceress kept her out of my hair. Not unlike sending a bored lab tech off for Erlenmeyer flasks of a certain color in my previous life. Though apparently napping, Darling pictured a few things he'd like to have as well, including a revised version of the spiked collar/breastplate combination. I let him know I'd make that, too. That way I could modify it whenever his whims changed. Which I expected to be often.

Once Dragonfly left, I smoothed some pillows and lay down for a nap in my own sunbeam. I didn't want to tackle the flower while I was muzzy-headed. My trunks had arrived before me, so I packed the lily away in the bottom of one.

Darling curled up next to me in the curve of my body, a habit developed on the road. His purring warmth reminded me of Isabel.

With a last wish that the lily would stay put, I crashed into sleep.

FOURTEEN

Armies and Navies and Dogs, Oh My

"MY LADY SORCERESS?"

I wedged heavy eyelids open to see the tent had cooled and darkened, the bright sunbeams gone. Darling gone. Dragonfly stood over me, her spiky wings a disturbing gray silhouette. I was groggy enough from the hard sleep that I couldn't even feel pleased yet that I hadn't dreamed.

"My lady sorceress?" Dragonfly chirped again, my personal mechanical bird.

"Yes—what?" I sat up and finger-combed my hair.

"Shall I light the candles? It's dark now. And you must go to the evening meal at Lord Falcon's tent."

"Knock yourself out," I said, looking around for my trunks, then it occurred to me to check that my words hadn't translated literally. Fortunately she seemed to have the sense of them. She skipped about lighting little white candles that had been set out in the spaces between cushions. Looked like a fire hazard to me. And there were still too many cushions. I wished one into a philodendron, just to amuse myself. Reveling a little in the freedom. It came out silk, but at least it took up less floor space.

I didn't question how she knew what time the dinner started. For all I knew, she'd been assigned to me pri-

marily as an alarm clock, since I still lacked whatever
plug-in they all had that told them when things started.
They seemed to have a kind of hive mind. Many of
these people, in fact, seemed to have an affinity for insects. But then others tended more toward vertebrates.
Something to ponder.

Nature's call forced me to instead ponder how I
might relieve myself. I found a chamber pot behind a
screen. Instead of looking for Restroom signs in this
place, one apparently looked for a free-standing screen.
I peed, but to my dismay, the pot filled up like any other.
No magical vanishing. No convenient flush. I thought
about wishing it away, but wasn't sure where to send
it. Along the road I'd simply availed myself of the great
outdoors—an option I now missed. This was better than
the bucket in my cell though. Not sure of the protocol,
I left the pot there, covering it with the provided lid. At
least it wouldn't stink.

Finding my trunks tucked against the back wall, I
dug through them for a dress for tonight and immediately put my hand on the lily, wrapped up in a dress that
needed washing. Peeling away the fabric, I watched in
reluctant fascination as the crushed blossom unfurled
its petals, smoothing the creases, returning to its usual
redolence and shimmering with a just-picked glow. And
everyone back home had been excited about how well
Tencel packed.

I longed for a microscope. With even just a dissect-
ing scope I could break petals and watch them reform,
try to pin down the mechanism. Following the rules of
the mundane world, the cellular structures should reca-
pitulate their original formation, in essence regrowing.
But here, would they simply shimmer into place as if

they had always been there, the way it appeared to work
to the naked eye? I should try to make a microscope.
Thanks to Dr. Jenkins I probably understood enough
of the mechanics to do it. He'd believed a microscopist
was only as effective as his or her understanding of the
device. Never truer than now.

For now, I needed to figure out a way to contain
the dangerous blossom. Not that it would go crawling
around the tent in my absence, like some kind of luminous blue spider.

I hoped.

I wished another pillow into a pedestal in the corner.
Maybe the things would come in useful after all—at
least the pillows provided a lot of raw material. I thought
carefully about a bell jar that would fit against a glass
bottom, with a rubberized air seal. Pleased when it came
out just as I wanted, I placed the lily under glass. The
heady sweet scent of it still swirled through the tent,
but ought to diminish over time.

I instructed Dragonfly to leave the overhead flaps
open unless it rained, to ventilate the place. Which
ought to help with keeping candle smoke to a mini-
mum, too.

In any good experiment, you tried to narrow down
the effect of something so you could test one aspect at
a time. This setup should serve to confine the effect of
the lily only to sight. Though the whole magic thing
skewed that—I'd probably have to encase it in silver
to test whether it operated on another plane entirely.

Satisfied for now, and feeling a bit smug about my
solution, I dressed in a ruby-red dress that seemed appropriate for dinner with generals, if not for a strategy

meeting. I mean, did you wear cocktail length or tea length when planning a war?

Things my mom never taught me.

I keenly looked forward to having many questions answered this evening, though likely not that one.

I sat in front of the mirror Dragonfly had obtained, and studied my face while she brushed my hair. The witches in stories always seemed so vain in their obsession with mirrors. Now I understood. In a world where physical manifestations could change in a moment, mirrors were the only objective reality. Sort of objective, anyway.

I'd learned to observe my face as if it were not mine. This became quite simple when you forgot who you were. How it looked when I wasn't doing anything in particular could be informative, kind of like getting a resting pulse. I tried not to notice Dragonfly's left wing brushing dangerously close to a lit candle. The damn things probably had no nerve endings. My face in repose looked sad. Grief with an undercurrent of dread. Shocking.

While Dragonfly affixed Starling's golden headband to my hair, I did my makeup. Through precise and small wishes, I applied the colors, shadows and brighteners I would for any party. I'd tried it first at Castle Brightness with decent results. Clive once told me that he didn't think makeup made me look much different, just "more fuckable." But I felt more confident. Facing Falcon, I needed every boost I could get. I'd undo it again afterward. I wasn't sure why, but it seemed important to retain that ritual of fixing up, then cleansing for bed.

I never could commit to tattooed makeup either.

A horn trumpeted and a stentorian voice announced, "All rejoice at the arrival of Lord Puck!"

I rolled my eyes at myself in the mirror, pleased to see the sparkle of sarcasm wipe away the sorrow. If I had to choose an expression for my face to freeze into, I'd take that one over the mournful-orphan-waiting-to-get-punished look.

With an impressive jingling, Puck pranced into the tent. He wore a bright gold velvet uniform, one that might have been conceived by the costume designer for *The Pirates of Penzance* rather than for any military purpose. Copious medals dangled from bright ribbons, flashing in the candlelight. Puck pirouetted in a distinctly unmilitary way, gave me an elaborate salute, then struck a pose reminiscent of a flamenco dancer. I clapped politely.

"You like it?" he gushed. "Don't I look amazing? I think I shall wear it all the time, now that we've been deployed."

"You are certainly impressive."

"Oh, and you haven't even seen the best part." He untucked a helm from under his arm and plopped it over his bright strawberry curls. The gold of the helm clashed with his hair, but worse was the enormous plume of celadon ostrich-like feathers that now brushed the tent ceiling, though he stood near its peak. Dragonfly squealed with delight.

"I'm speechless," I said with a wide smile. Puck grinned back, with a wink for little Dragonfly.

"You can design your own uniform, too—I've already arranged it." He turned, holding his arm for me, just as Rogue had done. Thankfully I felt no charge when I laid my hand on his forearm as I had with Rogue.

He clearly was the exception to so many things. Puck was looking Dragonfly over.

"Fabulous wings! She'll make an excellent beginning to your entourage." The girl nearly simmered with pleasure. "But you need more pillows in here—better see to that."

"Oh yes, sir, Lord Puck, sir," she breathed.

I didn't bother to protest.

We strolled off through the tents, preceded by Puck's knee-high page, his scrawny body in inverse proportion to his booming voice. The campsite whirled with activity more like a Brazilian street festival than ever. Striped and patterned tents glowed from within. Bewitchingly merry music played. Everywhere people had donned flamboyant costumes that looked vaguely martial. Clearly, understated was not a consideration. Everywhere they danced—whirling, jigging, swinging each other about. Puck grinned in delighted bonhomie at it all.

"Will Lord Rogue be at the dinner?" I tried to sound casual.

"Great Titania, no!" Puck giggled. "Rogue has no use for Falcon's war. Won't come near it. Why Falcon had to go elsewhere for sorcerous aid, you know." He squeezed my arm companionably, then pointed in delight at some gremlin creatures, hands and feet locked to make themselves into a living wheel, rolling by singing a jingling song.

The confines of Lord Falcon's tent were relatively sedate. His dining tent, I should say, as he appeared to have several color-coordinated tents arranged in a little complex at the top of a hill with a magnificent view.

Seemed to me like a magnificent target, too, but what did I know about military strategy?

A long table was elaborately laid with crystal and gold. The people there similarly glittered in wild costumes, giddily telling each other stories of what heroes they would be. In this situation, where people weren't talking directly to me, I could hear the sounds of the language better. If I focused in and dipped lightly over their thoughts, I got the sense of it, but otherwise it was more background music. Puck ditched me immediately after his page announced him—not me—leaving me to fend for myself like a disappointing blind date, while he showed off his truly outstanding uniform.

Only one other female was present that I could see, though it was difficult to tell with the various conversational groups around the mostly empty table and people trickling in still.

I wasn't sure what to do. I squelched the part of me that longed to take refuge in kneeling. I'd break that bit of programming if it killed me. Another part of me—an original part—would rather be back at the tent experimenting with breaking the lily's influence than standing here as just another wallflower at the junior high dance. Clearly this was why I'd spent more of my life in laboratories than at dinner parties.

With one of their hive-mind decisions, the conversational groups dissolved and people sat. I moved toward a chair only to have a fair-haired man in wild purple with legs like stilts seize it, giving me a glass-green stare that made me shrink apologetically. I'd already lost this game of musical chairs. A frisson of dread shook me. Surely they wouldn't try to make me kneel.

"Lady Gwynn, your seat is there," Lord Falcon

growled from the head of the table. I cringed at the censure in his voice. I ducked my head and hesitated in the direction of his sharply pointed finger, toward the lone empty chair near the foot of the long table. "Puck— I thought you were going to train her!"

"Not I, myself, and learn she did," Puck returned happily. "But that doesn't make her any more one of us than any foreign sorceress could ever be."

"We need Rogue for magic, is who we need, not this dubious prize." Falcon frowned at me as I made the long walk down one side of the table.

"You may as well ask Titania herself to kneel at your feet as get that to happen," Puck returned with a jolly laugh.

Trying to hold my head high, proud sorceress not cringing slave, I rounded the foot of the long table and slid into my chair several seats up. The group fell to feasting and toasting as soon as I sat. I sighed to find nectar in my wineglass. The stuff tasted not unlike fermented Hawaiian Punch.

"Lady Gwynn, the fantastic foreign sorceress, are you?" said the man to my left. "I've heard tales of your exploits!"

"As have I," said a gentleman across from me in blush pink with contrasting puce medals. "I heard she defeated an army of barbarians at the Plain of No Trees all by herself."

"With only a bracelet of bells and a feather for tools," said the man on my left, in a more sedate navy color that was, however, meticulously decorated with thousands of little silver sailing ships.

"And turned their ships into swans that then turned and ate them to a man!" This from the blush-and-puce

man's companion, who wore a startling combination of
Christmas red and green.

They rattled on about my supposed exploits while I
nibbled my way through the various portions laid before me. It seemed my PR team, whoever that might
be, had been busy. None of the company seemed to
need any direct information from me to fuel their excitement, so I decided not to contradict their impres-
sions. Couldn't hurt to be thought more than I was.
Also, their words had that curious meaningless quality, like so much white noise. Shallow social talk that
lacked any real thoughts behind it.

"Is it true, Lady Sorceress, that you defeated the
Black Dog?" My companions all stared in delighted
horror at Blush & Puce, who gazed at me with tanta-
lized curiosity, glass in one hand, dripping crimson
tartlet in the other.

"Blessed Titania, man," the gentleman on my right
sputtered. "Watch your mouth!" It almost went by too
fast, but I nearly caught the real name he pronounced.
Shhlynnnsomething.

"Oh, pish tosh! Don't be a superstitious old fart!"
Several others chimed in, squelching the protestor. As
one they turned their bright insectile eyes on me, await-
ing my answer. I carefully licked my fingers clean while
I thought. I tended to agree with the superstitious by
now, and cast a wary eye at the night beyond the open
tent flaps.

"I believe I may have met him. But I think it would
not be accurate to say I defeated him."

"You are not eaten, Lady Gwynn, or don't appear
to be," said Navy Man with a lewd eyebrow waggle.

"Or perhaps he *did* eat you—and thus you seduced him with your sweet flesh." Blush & Puce giggled.

"In that case she would be missing more than a few of her marbles."

"Nonsense," said another voice. "Stories to frighten children with." This was from the woman who sat several places down. The intervening men leaned back so she could bend her imperious gaze on us. Her hair was braided tightly enough that I couldn't make out the color.

"He seemed real enough to me, lady," I said.

"I imagine it would, to someone like yourself."

Someone like myself?

"Lady Strawberry," Falcon said from the head of the table, though he wasn't looking up from his plate, "don't torment the help. My pet foreign sorceress may yet come in handy. In the meanwhile, since you are all bored enough with my feast to dredge up foolish stories to tantalize one another with, let us discuss our war strategy."

Despite Falcon's glowering demeanor, I welcomed this serious attitude. At last we would talk about the actual war and what the hell I was supposed to do. Enough of the frivolity. Falcon might be decked out in what appeared to be a medieval knight's armor of mercury-bright silver—thank goodness for the soft candlelight or we'd have been blinded—but at least he seemed to take his generalship seriously.

"Now," Faicon began, "we shall start off with several land battles—ones with lots of infantry."

"And cavalry," a man close to Falcon urged. He seemed to have a horse's tail, interspersed with glittery strands, coming from his helm. "I'd like the cavalry to come to the rescue at the last moment, at least twice—maybe three times."

Several people agreed to that, generating a small discussion of whose helm decoration would look best streaming through the air as they galloped ferociously at the enemy. Falcon agreed to add in several more cavalry charges at various points in each battle. Lady Strawberry expressed a desire to bring in her stable of monsters to be ridden as well. The table, after much gory storytelling, decided the monsters should be brought into the thickest part of any hand-to-hand ground fight, so as to maximize goring, trampling and the sight of bodies being tossed into the air.

"Lord Falcon," said Navy Man. "You know I've been building my fleet of silver ships—when will we have the naval battles?"

Falcon frowned in thought.

"Now see the great military strategist in action," Navy Man whispered to me.

"To have naval battles," Falcon pronounced, "we will have to move some of the war to the sea."

"Or a large lake would do in a pinch," Navy Man offered helpfully. Falcon nodded gravely.

"So we will have to arrange to be pushed back to the sea—" he held up a hand when Navy Man took a breath, "—or a large lake. Perhaps after the cavalry charge comes in gloriously too late to turn the tide of battle?" This was greeted with great enthusiasm.

"I'm at the Mad Hatter's Tea Party," I muttered to myself.

"We have not forgotten your role, Lady Sorceress," Blush & Puce assured me.

"Lord Puck, of course," Falcon continued, "will be in

charge of all magic." To which Puck nodded enthusias- tically, beaming at me. "All magics will be as spectac- ular as possible and should only occur when the battle is nearly lost. Won't that be glorious? But wait! Lady Gwynn has no uniform at all. Puck! Why isn't she in uniform?"

"We've only arrived today, Lord Falcon," Puck said. "I'll design her and Lord Darling uniforms tomorrow."

I could just see what Puck would come up with for me. No, no, no.

"Actually," I inserted quickly, "in my land, the sor- ceress never wears a uniform, but rather a magic gown." Falcon and Puck frowned uncertainly. "To set her glori- ously apart from the fighters," I added, which smoothed the group's expressions into happy agreement, with sev- eral offering me suggestions for appropriate magical garb.

Then the raucous hilarity fell into abrupt stillness. In one of those uncanny sea changes, the crashing waves of their merriment ceased. They turned their faces all in one direction, apparently staring at the tent wall.

I listened, skimming the thoughts around me for a clue, then heard shouting from outside. Their grave watchfulness ignited into delighted interest. With shouts of merriment, everyone piled out of the tent, knocking over chairs and spilling wineglasses, to see that, just down the hill, one of the enchanting tents was blaz- ing afire.

FIFTEEN

In Which I Discover Some Truths

THE TENT SILK whooshed and billowed with the flames. A number of brightly dressed people gathered around it like college students at a homecoming bonfire, toasting the conflagration with sparkling glasses and shouting advice to one another. With much pointing and excited exclamations, they sent a small servant dashing in through the blazing arch made by the tied-back flaps.

Burning pillows came flying out of the tent, flaming marshmallows flung from the end of a roasting stick. They made bright comets against the night, and the spectators dodged the missiles with whoops and mock-terrified screaming. Once the flaming missiles plopped onto the ground, someone would jump upon it, to the wild encouragement of their fellows, sending sparks flying and puffs of acrid smoke to cloud the night. Falcon's party all galloped down the hill, crying out incoherently.

My heart pounding a greasy sweat out of my pores, I followed more slowly, my soft silken slippers no match for the stones and broken vegetation that poked the soles of my feet. The fire blazed hot on my face as, with a sickening whoosh, a neighboring tent flared with a roman candle of flame. More cries, like the singsong baying of dogs, greeted the spreading fire. I realized then that none of the words made sense to me because there was no meaning behind them. Blazing pillows continued to sail out of the tent, while the game of dodge and stomp intensified. No fire brigade appeared. No one seemed to take any useful action.

My head spun. The surreality of it all hit the back of my brain and rattled around. I wanted to shield my eyes, to crawl under a blanket, to scream out loud.

An especially large pillow rolled out of the first tent.

Oh, gods.

It was the page they'd sent in, burning as brightly and ferociously as the tents and cushions, probably decked in the same billowing silks as the rest. A thin piteous wail came from it, keening with a pain that turned my stomach.

Unable to stand a moment more, through the tears I hadn't known were running down my face, I made a fervent, heartfelt wish.

Abruptly, fire turned to night. Eye-searing light turned to dripping dark. With all light gone from the camp area, stars burst into life above, raining their needles of halogen light upon us. Wet ash and smoke filled the air. Along with the smell of grilled meat. Water dripped like the runoff from gutters after a torrential rainstorm ceases.

Someone seized my arm, the grip a bruising claw.

"What did you do?" he shrieked in my ear. I ripped away, stumbling a few feet. Water soaked through my slippers.

"Well, Lady Sorceress?" Falcon's familiar voice snarled from off to my right. "Your work, I presume?"

Someone tried to light a torch, but it wouldn't take. The starlight showed that the tents that had been merrily burning now sagged with moisture, like dying circus elephants. Charred pillow remains scattered in dissolving pools of charcoal lumps. Moving between tents was a black-on-black sinuous shadow. I caught my breath.

"Lady Gwynn?" Falcon repeated.

I nodded. "I turned the fire into water, to stop the burning."

"Did you have to turn *every* bit of fire in the whole valley to water, you filthy whore?" Lady Strawberry inserted with a bright laugh, a socialite giggling at a party gaffe.

One of the charcoal piles at Falcon's feet choked a cry through watery lumps, pain radiating in an exploding star from its thoughts. I gagged on mucous and tears and horror.

"Help him!" I ordered through my teeth. "Fetch a healer!"

Falcon stared curiously at the dying child. "We have no healer—this is a war zone. It's not the most glorious of deaths, but…"

"Wasn't that just spectacular?" Puck bounced up, nearly stepping on the page. "Did you see what she did? The whole valley, every campfire, torch and candle a puddle of water! Didn't I tell you? I told you, didn't I? This will be amazing!"

"She *still* lacks all control," Falcon snapped. "We're lucky she didn't drown us all."

"You're lucky you didn't fucking burn to death!" I yelled at him. "You're all like children playing a game. In a real war, you have healers to minimize casualties—and you don't send someone into an inferno to rescue pillows!"

They all stared at me in mute astonishment, so I

knelt down in the charred mud next to the page. In the
torchlight I could see blood oozing out of the page's
crackling flesh. I tried to put together a coherent wish
for him, but wasn't sure how to reconstruct his body. I
didn't really know how to do more than wish for healing. And the anger was clouding my thinking. Stupid,
stupid, stupid to let myself get so mad. I shuddered,
thinking that Falcon might try to send me back to that
place. *Think about this dying kid.* If I wished the pain
to stop, would the magic answer by ending his life? It
was funny that way.

Falcon seized my arms and hauled me to my feet. I
choked on my breath, anger transforming to fear.

"Let me help him," I gasped.

He lowered his face close to mine, hawkish nose
sharp against the torchlight, eyes alien black hollows,
the left made sharper by the brown feathery patterns
dancing across the skin, flickering like flapping wings
with the torchlight. I quailed, helpless in his grip.

"Do nothing else," he hissed.

"But…"

"No!" he thundered in my face, as if his mouth might
open into a massive maw that could consume me whole.
His teeth were pointed in a jack-o'-lantern smile. "Why
is she not trained?" He yelled this from inches away,
spittle hitting my face with shrapnel force.

"Scourge and Marquise certified her," Puck said ob-
sequiously, his long fingers tugging at Falcon's sleeve.
I flinched at the sound of their names. "They're most
exacting. Really, she helped not harmed. It was just a
little, well, much, you know?"

"Did your trainers win your obedience, little magi-
cian-slave?" Falcon crooned to me.

"Technically, she's a free…"

"Silence!" Falcon's voice crackled like lightning. Puck subsided. Falcon drew me closer so he spoke against my cheek. As if he might take a bite out of me. "She knows she's all mine for seven years, don't you? Trained to be my pet? That's what I paid for. Answer me, Sorceress. Tell me of your obedience. I know something of what the trainers do. Shall I summon them to come hold your leash and give me a demonstration?"

I shook my head, trembling wildly. He laughed, a cruel sharp cackle.

"Not so full of yourself now, are you?" Falcon pulled back slightly, then gently kissed me on the forehead. "Do as you are told, Sorceress, or I will make good my threat." He stared into my eyes. "Or maybe it's not a threat? Maybe you liked what they did to you? Some do grow addicted, you know, can never know pleasure again without the pain and humiliation. Perhaps I'll show you some of the games I like to play. I don't mind that your magic is sexual." Bending me back, he surveyed my bosom.

He sank his sharp teeth through the ruby velvet into my left breast.

I screamed. But held myself from fighting back. Like one of Pavlov's dogs, I had indeed been carefully conditioned. I might have my thoughts back, but it was as if the circuit in my brain that would allow me to resist had been snapped. *Or rewired,* part of me whispered.

"No magic tricks, lady?" Falcon crooned, watching me closely.

"No," I gasped.

He dropped me in the bloody mud. "Do as you are told. Nothing more. Ever."

Raising his voice, he instructed the others to see that the servants cleaned up the mess, which included carrying off the charred corpse of the page I'd let die instead of finding it in myself to resist Falcon.

I sat in the mud cradling my injured breast, moisture seeping through my dress to settle stickily against my legs. Stars blazed in an icy rainbow above.

"As for you." Falcon nudged me with his toe. "Return to your tent and make yourself useful. Tomorrow, set yourself to creating lights for us that won't burn."

"In different colors!" Puck clapped his hands. "And bright enough so we can still light up the tents from within, like silk lanterns at Festival."

"Yes, most definitely," Falcon agreed. "Off with you, Lady Sorceress. I want nothing more from you tonight."

I strained up, weighed down by my sodden gown, and staggered slowly away, holding my wounded breast tight. It took me a while, wandering through the dark and soggy camp, to find my own tent. Especially since I stayed close to the tent walls, rather than down the open alleyways between. Keeping to the corners and shadows. Gone was the wild party Puck and I had walked through.

I stumbled over a puddle of a campfire and nearly pitched facedown. I stopped and took a moment to breathe. Looking at the stars, I wished the pain in my breast to diminish—I should be able to fix it when I could see it, and until then I didn't want to wish the pain totally away, lest it blunt important information about the state of the wound—then sharpened my night vision.

It was a small defiance, this spell-casting, but I knew I had to continue to go against the programming if I was to have any hope of changing the false wiring

they'd created in me, before my own habits solidified
it forever. Falcon might have scared the living shit out
of me, might have pushed those particular buttons that
short-circuited my free will temporarily, but I would
not allow them to govern my every thought. Not ever
again. I repeated it. My new mantra.

Some things were worse than death. I would take
death over being lost to myself. If Falcon tried to leash
me as he threatened, then they could just try to kill me
and we'd see who won out this time.

Dragonfly met me with squeals and intricate jig-
steps that made her wings and curls bounce fetchingly.
She showed me all her little candles filled with thimbles
of water like it was the best thing ever. I asked Dragonfly if she knew the dead page and she did. She hoped
the war would also bring her such distinction.

I couldn't bear to hear it. I sent her off once she
helped me out of the mess of soaked red velvet. She
could get rid of it, whatever, I didn't care. And go hang
with her servant friends, talk of glory, just leave me
alone with some soap and water for a sponge bath. I'd
see her in the morning. She happily pranced off with
her trophy.

In the cool dark of the tent, still faintly tinged with
the lily's perfume, I wiped myself down of smoke and
mud, reaching under my thin shift, much as a conser-
vative Mormon girl would, obediently dressed even
when bathing. It probably wasn't very effective, but I
couldn't bear to look yet. Bad sign, that.

I remembered a photo that had circulated on the internet, accompanied by a story of how a woman had
gotten a tropical bug bite on her breast that she ban-
daged and ignored. Then she was put off by doctors.

When they finally examined her, finally looked under the bandage, the terrible pain she had been experiencing turned out to be due to the honeycombed parasitic nest her breast had become. The clever picture with it was made by superimposed images, as so many internet urban myths were. This one, however, had managed to choke me with horror before I took refuge in Snopes.com's rational and reassuring breakdown of the hoax.

No one here to tell me it was all urban legend.

Even as my left breast throbbed, I knew most of the pain was fear. I was afraid to look. Afraid to see how deeply those fangs had dug into the tender tissue. Afraid that I might see something horrific as that hollowed-out breast swarming with larvae.

For that reason alone I had to deal. I couldn't risk what my fears might subconsciously create. And I couldn't let a wound go uncleaned. It didn't bear thinking about to see what might grow from the flora of Falcon's nasty maw.

Not giving myself another moment to think about it, I grabbed several of Dragonfly's little votives and dumped the water into a wash basin. I set them on the little vanity table and, slowly and precisely, wished them to light. They flickered into life. The left bosom of the white cloth was soaked in blood, both rusty and bright crimson.

Looking away, I washed my face more thoroughly, then popped the makeup spell. Back to my less-fuckable self, more than a little wan. Though my hair flowed like sparkling black water, just as I first pictured it.

Darling brushed through the tent flaps, just as I had nearly screwed up the courage to yank off the shift. With a stab of guilt I realized I hadn't given him a

thought. Where had he been during the fire? In happy
reply, he sent me pictures of dancing with a group of
people wearing some kind of ribbons. He hadn't seen
the fire but had gotten quite wet. He pictured himself,
soaking and bedraggled, hissing at me.

"Sorry," I said. "If it helps, you're not the only one
pissed and, frankly, your damp fur is the least of my
worries at this point."

Darling leaped up on the vanity, carefully avoiding
the candles, and arched against my belly. Immediately
the throbbing and the fear abated. Forgot how handy
he was that way. I popped the pain-diminishment wish,
too, but left the night vision in place. I scratched Darling's ears and he purred forgiveness, along with a sly
image of him with a horsehair plume like Puck's.

"We'll see." I chuckled, amusement at his foibles
thawing the horror of the night. "Tomorrow we'll see
if I can create light without fire. Then we'll make your
battle armor—whatever you want."

The cat was better than Percocet. Feeling dreamy
and fine, I pulled off the white shift.

Yes, there were the teeth marks, but it wasn't so bad.
They formed an oozing ring around the pink nipple, a
harshly red and inflamed insult to the white globe of my
breast. I washed the wound with the soap and water—
old-fashioned approaches never hurt—and picked out
some white and red fibers clinging here and there. I
wished the wound clean of both fibers and infection, as
I did with water and food. I wished for it to heal quickly.
I hesitated to try to heal it completely myself. I had a
pretty good idea of the glandular tissues involved and
the epidermal layers that covered them, but nothing
precise enough to guarantee a perfect reconstruction.

If I simply healed the skin, I ran the risk of sealing infection inside to fester. It looked better now, anyway.

Darling purred his approval, then sent me an image of myself with enormous breasts. I swatted him.

"No, I like them fine, thank you! And what is a cat doing thinking about human breasts?"

He winked slyly at me, most un-catlike. I really hoped he wouldn't turn out to be some kind of shapeshifter who'd show up in human form someday. Darling perked up and sent me an image of him changing into a handsome man who knelt at my feet with an armload of blossoms.

"So sweet," I said, scratching under his chin. "For your reward, you may share my bed."

In my pre-dinner complacency, I hadn't yet created my futon, and I really didn't want to deal now. Resigned to an aching back in the morning, I grabbed my camp blankets—quilted silk, not army wool—piled together some of the flatter pillows in the corner, and lay down.

I closed my eyes and saw it all play out again, across the screen of my eyelids.

Burning pillows sailing through the night. That little page, hands blistering and cracking as he laid hold of each one, until he, too, was a little stuffed silk luxury ablaze.

I'd better not think about it, as emotional as I was, or I could re-create the whole horrid event.

My gut congealed in an icy fist. Maybe I had unthinkingly created the event in the first place, wondering about the fire hazards of Dragonfly's candles. The magic sometimes worked that way, manifesting general circumstances that you daydreamed about.

It paid to keep your fantasies happy ones.

SIXTEEN

In Which I Return to the Laboratory

THE BELL JAR experiment failed spectacularly. That night I dreamed of Rogue, more vividly than ever.

He sat back on a bed I'd never before seen, massive with wood and velvety materials. Dressed in his customary black, Rogue leaned back against mounded pillows in shades of dark ruby and midnight emerald, his legs crossed at the ankles. His hair fell loose, spilling around his shoulders. His face impassive behind the winding inky lines, he watched me where I stood next to the bed.

In front of me, draped over the velvet coverlet, streamed something in pale lace, nearly white, but blue enough to pick up the navy-dark highlights in all the inky covers of the bed.

Put it on, he told me, though I don't recall hearing his voice.

I slid out of my dress, standing naked in the light of the room before I slipped on the confection of lace. It was the kind of thing that made you feel more nude than simple nakedness. The bodice dropped low over my breasts, hugging the curves so that the lacy swirls just barely covered my nipples. Looking down, I could see them, hard and bright pink, pressing through the fragile strands. The lace fell in streamers down my legs, tantalizing with what it revealed and hid.

Rogue watched me, burning. My skin heated where his gaze traveled and I looked down, vulnerable to the intensity of it. A green silk sash was also draped on the bed. Longing welled up in me, a dark hope that he'd bind my wrists with it. I wanted him to command me to give it to him and then lie on the bed with my wrists crossed over my head while he tied my hands to the headboard. I trembled with the desire, desperate for the command, terrified that he'd taste my desire in my thoughts and do it.

Terrified that he wouldn't do it.

I half-awoke to dreamy sunlight and fierce arousal. Moisture trickled uncomfortably between my thighs. Naked under my blankets, I slid a finger between my legs. It only took a few strokes and I shuddered in the fierce, bright orgasm. The energy of it pulsed through me in long waves, sweet and cleansing. For that drowsy moment, I didn't even mind that it was Rogue's eyes that blazed in my mind, or the scent of sandalwood and lilies that warmed the morning air.

Dragonfly came singing in, breaking the sensual daze.

Fully awake, I now felt the deep bruising in my breast. The surreal horror of the night before. And here I lay, drowning in erotic fantasies about the man who was probably my greatest enemy here.

Well, tossup between him, Falcon, the Dog, the Monochromatic Sadistic Twins. So many nemeses to choose from.

Rogue hadn't stopped playing me. He'd found those dark fantasies hidden in the corners of my heart, the raw wounds still bleeding from my trainers' attentions, and was using it all to try to control me.

Dragonfly brought me a dressing robe I didn't remember ever trying on and I slipped into it. I made myself use the chamber pot, fitting the lid tightly afterward. I thought about taking it somewhere to empty myself but still had no idea where to go. Not exactly a glamorous lifestyle.

I kicked pillows aside as I made my way over to study the Rogue Lily, resplendent inside the glass, dewy fresh and luminous as ever. I sniffed the air, but the scent of lilies and sandalwood had faded. The dusky blue of the flower's throat drew my attention, reminding me of the slow burn in Rogue's eyes watching me in the lace lingerie. Waiting for me to hand him that dammed silk sash.

With a sharp thought fueled by the anger, I shattered the glass.

Dragonfly squealed and I ignored her.

A feeling of power surged through me. Bright and jewel-toned. The daylight side. My own magic. I was no one's pet. No one's sex slave. If I wanted to remain my own person, then I needed to take steps.

Starting with destroying Rogue's "gift."

I understood the gift-thing now. By accepting the lily, I had opened a door between us. By keeping it, I allowed a connection between Rogue and me. One that just happened to be toxic to my well-being. At least Rogue hadn't tried to convince me that it was all about love. There was an honesty in that, I supposed.

This would be my honest answer.

Hopefully Falcon wouldn't be checking up on me too soon. It was possible Dragonfly reported back to

him. I thought I could be convincing, however, that all
my work was research into light-emanating objects.
Lord knew that sort of shell-game worked with grant
agencies.

I set Dragonfly to clearing one end of the tent—
while I grabbed something from the breakfast tray she'd
brought—piling the pillows into neat columns, remov-
ing the broken glass. Some of her fellow worker bees
brought in more tables to be my workbenches. While I
disliked the helplessness of having to ask for everything
I needed, the assistance was definitely a perk.

With the ceiling flaps pinned back, I had good light
to work with. I laid the lily in the bright sunbeam and
studied it. It lay there, sultry and sweet. I twisted my
hair into a knot and studied the treacherous flower. I had
always been most myself when working out a problem.

"My lady sorceress, would you like to bathe and
dress?"

"Later."

"But my lady…"

"Dragonfly," I said, not looking away from the
flower. I tried to think of something better than "go
away."

Failed.

"Go away."

"I don't understand?"

"Go outside of the tent and don't bother me until
I'm done, okay?"

It must have worked because she stopped talking to
me. I examined the lily without touching it. More and
more I thought the wise course would be to incinerate
the thing. My reluctance to do so was probably part of
the magic. But first, there were things I needed to know.

Ironically, the dream had worked me up so much that I had plenty of power to draw from.

I stilled my mind, seeking that quietness that had become my greatest refuge, and dipped into the flower, sinking into the scent, falling through the blues, letting it sweep me up—though I kept my right hand on my left pulse, anchoring to my body, to what was real. Not sure what I was looking for, I drifted through the blossom, feeling the aliveness of it, the magic—oh yes, now that felt like Rogue, the black wings brushing my mind in front of the fire. Not my own light-filled idea-bubbles of magic, this seemed wilder, a beast running beneath the surface.

Sexual, strong, feral and primitive.

Fire with fire, then. I summoned up the arousal he'd cultivated, that desire for him, for the poisonously dark candy he offered. I matched my stride to the beast magic, luring it with my scent, feeling it turn to me as if it was already tuned to me, follow me, follow my lead up into the blaze of light where it suddenly shied. But I had it then, I wrapped it in glass from the bell jar. This one a crystal bubble of magic, unbreakable and pristine. The magic roiled around inside it unhappily, deprived of its quarry.

Bedraggled on my workbench, the lily lay faded and limp, its sweet scent slipping into rot. It was only a flower, long past its bloom, robbed of its sustaining power. I felt as if I'd carelessly plucked it only to let it die out of water. Its beauty gone over to death.

It grieved me to see it dying there and I didn't understand why.

Next to it was a sphere of glass, like a living marble. It was warm to the touch, the smooth surface flawless.

Inside, ebony swirled with midnight highlights, freckles of dusty twilight breaking off only to fall back into the black. Fangs and ravens' wings.

Probably best not to stare into it too long. When I stood, my body creaked in protest and I realized the sun was now past midday. Hours had passed while the lily and I mesmerized one another.

But I felt more myself than I had since I'd come here. All the feelings of desire and anger were gone now. I felt drained, in a good way, as if I'd bled out a poison.

Digging through my trunks, I found the wooden box Blackbird had given me with my dress and shoes. I wrapped the marble in a piece of silk and tucked it into a corner of the box. A little bargaining chip, should Rogue decide he needed that piece of himself back. Careless of him. Tut tut tut.

Dragonfly slid her tousled head through the flaps of the tent entrance. I wouldn't have known it if I hadn't been looking in her direction.

"May I return, my lady sorceress?"

"Sure, come on in."

She held the flap out and turned diagonally to come through without snagging her wings. Hallelujah, she'd been practicing.

"I stood guard the whole time you were spell casting, my lady sorceress. Both Lord Puck and Lord Falcon came to pay a call, but I told them you were deep in work and had forbidden me to allow anyone to disturb you."

"You did? Good initiative—thank you." Okay, I'd been a bitch to her and she hadn't deserved it. "I'm sorry that I was grumpy to you before."

She looked a bit puzzled but pleased.

"So," I asked casually, "did Falcon ask exactly what I was working on?"

"No, my lady sorceress, he seemed satisfied and said he looked forward to having his new non-burning lights this evening. Is that what you're making? How wonderful that will be! No one else has a master as eccentric and powerful as you are. The others were so jealous that I had to sit still outside the tent and not move until you were done." She looked around puzzled. "But where are the lights? Oh! They're invisible until dark? How especially wonderful!"

Okay, we needed to work on communication with the initiative thing. One step at a time.

Right now I needed to eat something. I let Dragonfly brush out my hair while I ate fruit, cheese, nuts and some kind of cold meat from the breakfast tray, not arguing while she fussed that she could have put my hair up for me so that I didn't knot it like that.

"Something out of my face, but not tight," I told her. "I have to finish tweaking the new lights."

She came up with a modified soft ponytail that suited us both, and got me dressed to her satisfaction. Then I sent her off to wash the blankets and clothes, along with chamber-pot emptying, which at least made her happy, even if I still fretted about it. I also suggested that she needed to relax after her guard duty this morning.

I felt good, free, the last dregs of sex and fear clearing from my mind.

But what to do with the dying flower? If I had a book, I'd press it. I decided to dry the flower, hanging it upside down over my workbench with a thread pulled from one of the ubiquitous pillows. I didn't know why I felt the need to preserve it. Something to do with my soft chewy center. After all, it was still a flower from a gorgeous man—and the last gift I could accept from him.

Now to my commissioned project. How to make non-burning lights?

I paced around the tent, ruminating about all the fairy tales I'd read. "Fairy lights" were a common theme, blamed on phosphorescent gases by scientists. Various wizards and so forth had little balls of light they carried on their palms or sent winging around in the air. But that seemed impractical as a long-term solution. It would be better to find some physical object and alter it to emit light.

On my umpteenth circuit around the tent, kicking away yet another pillow that tumbled off a pile and into my path, I considered taking a walk outside. The possibility, however, of running into any number of several someones I didn't want to talk to seemed high. It wasn't that I was hiding out, so much.

What kind of object could I use to make light around the camp?

I didn't want to mess with the existing candles and torches because I already associated them so strongly with fire. And besides, Falcon might believe I'd ducked the assignment, and I couldn't afford that. I needed something innocuous, something readily available. I kicked another pillow aside, which hit one of Dragon-fly's towers so a rainbow of pillows tumbled down in whispers of silk, catching the light.

I laughed.

Glowing pillows. Every tent had too many. The fae loved them. They'd be bright and colorful. You could increase light by adding more, play with the effect by using different colors. Perfect!

But how exactly?

I grabbed a knife from Dragonfly's little buffet table and slit a rectangular lime-green pillow down one seam. There had to be thousands of hand-sewn pillows in this camp alone—who was making them? I pictured a pixie sweatshop, downtrodden gnomes and Dragonfly-girls hunched over pillows, working to earn bizarre body modifications.

The stuffing in the pillow seemed to be some sort of silk floss. Possibly a plant material?

What I wanted was for the pillow fill to glow, like a phosphorescent organism. Ideally it would be light-sensitive in the same way—glow brightening in dusk, perhaps recharging in the light. Except what about when you were ready to go to sleep and you had all the damn pillows radiating away around you?

Though I wasn't exactly sure how phosphorescent organisms emitted light, I remembered a talk at the Neuroscience Convention that discussed how nerve impulses changed the polarity of the membrane around the light-bearing cells. So, I could maybe transform these fibers to do that, so that some kind of action changed their polarity. But then they'd need to be living tissue, which would require nutrition. And excretion.

Feeding and changing the pillows—*I don't think so.*

I needed something like the clapper—clap on, clap off—but how to make something sound-sensitive?

Okay, I was overthinking. *Just experiment with one pillow. Give up trying to control it all and just let the magic find a way.* I thought about what I wanted, the fill to glow as a fiber-optic might, pulling warm light from the sun, lining up to glow when the pillow was clapped, depolarizing to dark with a second clap.

Finally I drew on the sexual charge Rogue had so thoughtfully provided. The little orgasm had barely taken the edge off. How convenient that my poor love life all those years gave me so much practice at sublimating. At least doing magic gave me something productive to do with all that energy. I fed it into the idea I'd constructed. Connected them.

The pillow looked just the same, lime silk sagging around the wound I'd made in it, gray-white silky guts spilling out. I pulled the fabric taut and smacked the pillow. Soft green light shone in the bright sunlight, a purer white from the spilling material.

Eureka!

I strode over to the tent flaps, stepping outside for the first time that day. The camp whirled in the same merry activity, birdsong and music intertwining. I clutched my glowing pillow triumphantly.

"Dragonfly!" I called. "Come see the light I made." *Darling—come see!* I sent him a picture of glowing pillows piled on the floor and heard his lazy response. He sounded unimpressed.

"I'll fetch her, Lady Sorceress." A little guy, one of the hip-high gnomey-looking ones in a ripe blueberry color, sat perched on a tree stump at the corner of my tent.

"Who are you?"

"I'm your page, Lady Sorceress."

"Since when?"

He pulled off his little peaked red cap. That and a red tunic seemed to be all he wore. "Begging your pardon, Lady Sorceress, but I hoped you might take me on. We

all heard how you tried to save poor Loden. I'd like to
return the service as he was my friend, you see."

"I didn't do anything to save him," I said.

"Not every sorcerer is as powerful as Lord Rogue."
Oh. Eep. "Well, I'm sorry for your loss."

The blue guy looked sorrowful. He didn't say anything about glory.

"So do I pay you?" *Do I pay Dragonfly?* I'd forgotten to ask.

"As my lady sorceress wishes."

Puck would know what I should be paying them and
how. Maybe Blackbird as my seneschal should be doing
it. I was acquiring quite the household. I didn't really
need another servant, but I hated to turn him away.

"You're on. Please tell me you have a name already."

"I'm Larch, lady. If it pleases you."

"I'm Gwynn, Larch."

"Yes, Lady Sorceress."

"Have you just been sitting out here all day, waiting
for me to come out?"

"Dragonfly set me to guarding the tent. She told
me to make certain no one interrupted your amazing
magical feats."

His face was completely deadpan, but I was pretty
sure that had been sarcasm under there.

"Look at this, Larch." I smacked the pillow and it
went dark. Then smacked it again and it lit up, though
it was hard to see in the bright sunlight. Larch looked
at me quizzically.

"You try it." I held out the pillow to him. He poked
it with a pudgy finger. "No, no. Smack it. With the flat
of your hand." I demonstrated. He slapped the silk and
the pillow went dark. "See? No more fires in the tents."

He looked at me solemnly, blinking his catlike eyes, the same shade as his skin. Not exactly the enthusiasm I had been looking for.

"Maybe we could name them Loden Pillows?"

He nodded gravely.

"Now, if you would, find Dragonfly and tell her I need needle and thread. I don't suppose you can sew?"

"Yes, all my people can. It's one of our main industries, besides serving nobles such as yourself."

"I'm no noble, Larch. Oh, never mind," I added when a worried look crossed his face. "Is there a name for your people?"

"Oh, yes," he said, proudly. "We are The People."

Of course. Just like everyone. "Say it again, slowly." I concentrated on hearing the sounds, not the sense. "Brooh-nayz?" I tried.

He frowned. Silly me. It wouldn't work for me to ape the sound without the intention behind it and if I put the intention in, he would hear only that and not the sound I made.

Then it hit me— "Wait. Brownies? Are your people Brownies?"

He cocked his head in that appearance of listening for distant music. Then nodded slowly. "That could be right. In another place and time, we've been that. Shall I bring others to sew, Lady Sorceress?"

"Yes—great idea. Tell them to bring pillows from their tents. Lots of pillows."

SEVENTEEN

In Which I Prepare for War

EVENING FOUND MY tent converted to my own third-world sweatshop full of busy Brownies, all in various colors like the pillows. Dragonfly had also fetched several look-alike friends—none with wings, however. Clearly she was a little queen amongst them. Complete with preening.

They all gaily sewed and sang. It could have been a scene from the animated Christmas specials that had populated my childhood. Now I wondered how much of those stories pulled from this world. I asked Larch if any of his people lived in a place that was always ice and snow. He just gave me the standard puzzled look and bent back to his work. At least I had the sense not to ask him about the jolly fat guy in a red outfit.

I'd tweaked the spell a little, so that the stuffing-floss would transfer its properties to like material. Larch assured me it was standard stuffing, made from a shrub that was good for little else. To make a new Loden Pillow, the Brownies took a strand of floss from the mother-pillow—their term, not mine—opened a seam in a daughter-pillow, and tucked the strand deep inside. Once the pillow was resewed, they smacked it hard and said "Loden" three times. The small spark spread from within, replicating outward until the whole pillow glowed. The Dragonfly girlies were allowed to sew seams but not touch the stuffing. Seemed sexist to me, but since the girls didn't protest Larch's arrangement, I stayed out of it.

I hoped the Brownies' belief in the spell might help to sustain the magic in the pillows so it wouldn't wear off when I wasn't around. The philodendron and the pedestal had faded away at some point. Had they become pillows again or just kind of dissolved when I wasn't looking? During my training, whatever I converted or created was usually gone the next day—I never knew exactly what became of it.

Something else to chase down if I was to understand the limits of my own abilities and up my chances of defeating Rogue. And finding a way out of this freakish world. I really needed to start keeping notes.

It seemed to please the Brownies to be making magic. In the stories, their ability to accomplish work like this was magical in and of itself, as I recalled, so in theory they ought to be able to make Loden Pillows forever, without my adding anything more. Then they'd have a business enterprise beside sacrificing pages to fire. I'd also modified the spell so that the light glowed in three levels of brightness—might as well have flexibility in our lighting design.

As the Loden Pillows piled up, Larch called in runners to distribute the light-up cushions back to the camp. Darling, as self-appointed quality tester, pounced repeatedly on the pillows, bouncing them from soft to bright to brightest and off again, which, together with the light flashes from the pillow-creators, created an almost disco effect that oddly complemented the brisk harmonies of the faerie song.

And faerie singing it was. Just as the stories had it.
Luminous, with nearly inaudible harmonies. Birdsong,
the roaring of bears and the insistent buzz of cicadas
wound through in complex counterpoints. It was beautiful, compelling and profoundly disturbing. I found
myself falling into a trancelike state, compulsively repeating the melodies and rhythms in my mind.

Until I came back to myself with an abrupt shake.
Like when you were falling asleep, just sliding into
dream images and your foot went off the step and *boom!*
you startled awake. Common thinking was that it was
probably a kind of brainstem reboot. That your brain
was in danger of shutting down completely, rather than
just into sleep mode.

Interesting that the faerie song had that hypnotic effect on the human brain.

When this happened, revulsion would seize and
sicken me, taking me back to the state of my early training days. Post-traumatic stress, no doubt. Too bad I'd
never learned any clinical psychology. With great effort,
I concentrated on hearing their songs only as uncanny
music. Though, as with Rogue's haunting offers, the potential to slide under its influence continued to nibble
at my less-than-firm state of mind. Really I needed to
get away from it. A problem, since I had nowhere to go.

The revelry outside the tent rose as the sun set,
though the general feel of the camp seemed more sedate than last night. Our runners reported favorable
reactions to the Loden Pillows, with orders placed for
specific colors and shapes. After the first few Brownie-
delivery-boys returned, I spotted Larch and Dragonfly
in deep conference. When I wondered about it, one of

Dragonfly's wingless cohorts chirped that they were
setting up a supply tent.

"What for?" I asked.

"Why, to house all the stuff."

Curious—and seizing the impetus to leave the tent,
I ventured outside for the second time that day. This
time I'd move farther than the grassy space in front.
My breast twinged and I tamped down the fear. *Get a
grip. You are stronger than this.*

Soft evening filled the sky, in dusky hues that reminded me of Rogue's lily. Diabolical lily, I reminded
myself. The air carried a bit of moisture from the waterfall, mixing with the scent of flowers and fruit. No
cooking smells. Where did Dragonfly get her endless
supply of the snack trays that sustained me? Who had
cooked the dinner last night?

It felt good to be out of the crowded tent. I probably
shouldn't be hiding. Yes, I had been working, doing
productive things, but it was also an excuse to brood,
holed up like a frightened cat under the bed. No one
had said I couldn't walk around outside.

I did, however, keep a wary eye out for Falcon as I
circled my tent. The dappled glow of pillow-illumina-
tion colored nearby tents, some flashing rhythmically to
the eerie faerie chants. All we needed was John Travolta
in a white suit to complete the look. Maybe the three-
light level concept wasn't such a great one. Who knew
the Bee Gees' nasal falsetto harmonies were evocative
of faerie song?

Dragonfly and Larch stood in the open area behind
my kaleidoscope tent, supervising the erection of another cream-colored tent. She snapped out orders, a
mini-Napoleon, and he watched gravely as poles were

sunk into the ground. Their apparent minions worked with meek and ferocious speed.

"Be quick there," Dragonfly squealed, rapping one of the knee-high guys with a stick, "or Her Lady Majesty Sorceress will turn you into a toad!"

"Oh?" I said behind her.

Which was a bad idea, since she wheeled around, managing to slap Larch in the face with one wing and nearly overbalancing herself. I stopped her spluttering with a raised hand.

"Be careful what you threaten in my name, Dragonfly." Crystal tears welled up in her eyes, but I drew on the coldness Scourge had instilled in me to steady my resolve. "So, Larch—why do I need a supply tent?"

"Tributes, my lady." He indicated a pile of wooden boxes, cloth, even a basket of fruit. "And we'll need to create more pillows to keep up with demand. Already we've converted nearly a third of the extant pillows in the camp. I've arranged to import silk and stuffing from a nearby tribe."

"Tribe?"

"Of The People."

Interesting that the word translated in my head as *tribe,* not group or town or city. "Okay, so this stuff—" I indicated the pile, "—is in return for our Loden Pillows?"

"Just so."

Right, because otherwise they'd be gifts and would create obligation. I was getting the hang of this.

"I don't suppose anyone sent one of those magic chamber pots?" I asked. To blank response. Ah well, a girl could hope. "Maybe we could just move the pillow-factory into this tent?"

"We should have several tents, my lady sorceress," Dragonfly piped up again. "Lord Falcon has five and you're at least as important as he is, if not more."

"Okay, really, do not repeat that one ever again." I could just imagine Falcon's response to that. I doubt he'd be interested in my excuse that I didn't know how to control Dragonfly's mouth. "But, fine, however many tents you two can arrange is fine—with no threats. If you all could move Santa's workshop into the annex, I can have my own space again?"

My word, their command. Dragonfly and Larch moved the pillow works immediately, returning my tent to blissful emptiness, punctuated by a select few softly glowing pillows in jewel tones of emerald, sapphire and ruby. I could even see the carpet laid over the grass, woven in similar tapestry hues, velvety plush squishing between my toes. Dragonfly was hanging about, a sullen set to her piquant lips. I was about to put her to work on setting me up with a bath of some sort when we heard from Falcon.

Larch escorted the messenger in. The page—not of the Brownie variety, but rather taller and less colorful—bowed deeply. I tried to look regal. However that looked.

"Lord Falcon thanks Lady Sorceress Gwynn for the excellent lights and offers this tribute in return." He held out a small wooden box.

Probably had a viper in it. I took it judiciously, holding it with the very tips of my fingers.

"Further, Lord Falcon, General of the Most High Command, informs Lady Sorceress Gwynn to be ready to ride at first light—" wow, an actual external demarcation of time. For my benefit only? I didn't think so, "—to engage in a most glorious Battle with the Enemy!"

Dragonfly began clapping hands while jumping up and down like a squealing pogo stick. I thanked the messenger and glanced at Larch, who then escorted the page back out, pressing some token into his hand. Finally—someone to handle the tipping. If I hadn't just hired Larch, I'd give him a raise. Though since I had no idea what I was paying him, I might already have done so.

I turned to Dragonfly to ask if a bath could be arranged when Darling sank one claw delicately into my ankle.

"Ouch!" I yelped. "Bad kitty!"

Darling lashed his tail, then firmly sent an image of himself in battle armor.

"Oh, right. I forgot you. Sorry. Bad me." I set down the box from Falcon and picked up Darling, holding him cradled in my arms, nuzzling his belly fur with my nose. He licked my forehead. Then sent me the picture again. "Yes, yes—okay. Dragonfly, can I take a bath somehow?"

"In a tub of water?"

"That's how it's generally done, yes. Unless you can offer me a shower."

"All of the girls have been bathing in the pond, my lady sorceress."

I sighed. "And probably no big, brass tub in the tribute pile, I suppose?"

She shook her head gravely.

"Ah, well, sponge bath it is. Off with you then." At least the magic kept my hair from looking grimy, but my

scalp was starting to itch something fierce. I squelched
the image of lice.

Darling wriggled impatiently in my arms, so I set
him down on my workbench, the drying lily drifting
upside down over his head. I thought he might bat at it
and was ready to stop him, but he only gazed at it. Then
he showed me a picture of Rogue looking disappointed
and sad, gazing out a window at a misty landscape.

"Don't give me that," I answered. "I don't like being
manipulated. I've had my fill of it just lately. Now—
show me exactly what you want. Something practical,
please, that might actually protect you in battle."

He licked the side of one paw, considering. I waited.
The image he gave me finally showed him in a metal
collar with spikes and an attached breastplate. A helmet covered his kitty head, graced with a giant purple
ostrich feather.

"No plume—it'll make you a target. How about
this?"

I imagined the helmet with a short bristle of mottled
brown feathers.

He replaced them with vivid yellow.

"No, yellow is even more visible."

I replaced the yellow with his original purple, in a
zebra pattern. "The broken pattern should help camou-
flage you—harder for the eye to see. At least, I assume
whoever we're fighting has eyes that work like ours."

We agreed on the image—now I just needed some
raw material. My teachers said I ought to be able to conjure things from nothing, but I couldn't get the laws of
thermodynamics out of my head. Conservation of mass.
I just couldn't believe in mass created from nothing.
And unfortunately, this magic business came down to

what I believed was possible. Too bad I'd dispatched Dragonfly. And eliminated all extraneous pillows. I'd have to go to the tribute pile for material myself. Not a big deal. Or it shouldn't be. Still, it was full dark out there and I...dammit, I felt too frightened.

My new life, where I was now really afraid of the dark and what it held.

While I dithered and Darling washed a paw, my eyes fell on the supposed tribute from Falcon. I laid a finger on it but felt nothing unusual. No tingle that living things seem to give off; no feral sexual buzz that marked Rogue's work; no light shock, like from a faulty outlet that I was beginning to associate with other enchanted objects.

"What do you think—is it safe to open?" I asked Darling, who was engaged in full ear-washing now and ignored me. "A lot of help you are. I should call you Unfamiliar."

Without pausing in his washing, he sent me another picture of him in the armor.

"Yes, yes, yes—patience is a virtue, you know."

I turned the little box so it would open away from me and Darling, and not toward anything important. I lifted the hinged lid with the tips of my fingers still, much as I would open a container in the lab that could potentially spew toxic substances.

Nothing came out, so I walked out a few paces and circled to see from a distance what lay inside. My hand had crept up to my throat. I made myself lower it.

In the box, jewels shimmered in the soft pillow light, maybe a topaz-y color. The problem with colored light was you didn't get good color resolution on other objects. The gems seemed inert, so I walked up slowly, watching them with close attention, mental feelers out for anything untoward. It was a necklace of stones. Small, like a choker. No, wait—a collar.

What was *with* these people and their collars?

"Oh, ha-ha," I said, and reached out to snap the lid shut. Darling stopped me with a curious chirrup. "No, we can't use that—it might be a bad idea."

Darling pictured me twirling around, wearing the jeweled collar, fluttering and flirting, petting it with my fingertips.

"Oh yeah—that's me. Like I would ever wear anything from Falcon, much less something that implies I'm his tame pet."

Never again.

"No, I don't want to keep it for myself, but I'm worried there's some kind of trap in it. We should use something else."

Darling patted it with his paw and meowed demandingly.

"You don't get to insist. You're the Unfamiliar and I'm the Ever-So-Powerful Lady Sorceress. Remember who you're talking to."

Darling rumbled a purr and bent down to delicately lick the collar. Then pictured the collar and helmet with shining topazes on them.

"You don't think there could be a hidden trap?"

Darling chirruped, adding more topazes to the image.

"Well, I guess this is your culture and you know it better than I do."

Darling purred agreement.

"Okay, if you're sure. Now this last image—is that your final answer?"

He sent the same picture again, which I took as a yes.

"You don't think the amber of the topazes is a little much with the purple short-plume? No? Fine."

It only took a moment for the breast plate, spiked collar and little helmet to appear, studded with smaller versions of the topaz stones. I'd used the collar as it sat in the wooden box and allowed Darling's armor to manifest in its place, along with a wish for protection and a wash of the cleaning ideas I'd been using on the food and water. It would have been easier to manifest it *on* him, the way he so clearly pictured it, but I wanted to be sure I didn't fuse it to his fur or something else horrible. Fortunately I seemed to be fine with expansion and contraction of mass, conveniently bending that aspect of thermodynamics. And here my advisor had despaired of my tendency to cherry-pick the neurophysiology theories I liked best. Shows him.

"Hold still," I had to remind Darling as I buckled the straps. "Stop preening around. There—got it!"

Immediately Darling dropped from the workbench and trotted across the room to leap onto my vanity. He pranced in delight in front of the mirror, examining himself from all angles, the golden topazes gleaming, the purple ruff spiked with a matching golden zebra mottling. He cocked a gimlet eye at me and sent me a picture of himself ten times taller, grabbing little soldier figures in his sharp teeth and claws, flinging them about like dolls.

I hummed the tune of "Scotland the Brave," and Darling danced in place to the war beat of the song. Snatches of the lyrics ran through my mind, with all the bold hearts, nodding plumes, death and gore.

I shivered at Darling's enthusiasm. Hopefully he understood he was only a small cat in reality. He was truly my only friend here. I reached out to pet him, but he huffed at me and sprang down, heading out to show off his outfit.

"Don't you want me to take it off, so you can sleep?" I called after him.

But he slipped out the tent flaps and I was alone again.

You are without friends. Rogue's voice echoed in my head. So I was.

EIGHTEEN

The Promontory of Magic

WHEN DRAGONFLY WOKE ME an hour before dawn, I stumbled to my clothing trunks and stood there in a bleary haze.

Two things hit me.

I had not dreamed about Rogue. *Oh yeah—go, Powerful Sorceress Gwynn!*

I had completely forgotten to take care of my own "uniform." Not so swift.

I didn't like to contemplate Falcon's reaction if I showed up without one. He'd probably order me squeezed into some *manga* fanatic's idea of a battle-maiden sex-slave.

No, a magic gown I had promised—a magic-seeming gown I would deliver.

Not at my best in the mornings, especially when the supposed dawn looks pretty much the same as night— glowing pillows do not make for perky morning light— I wasted several minutes thinking about how to make one of my gowns look magical and special. Then the obvious solution hit me. I pulled out the box with my Ann Taylor dress and heels. The cold sponge bath left a great deal to be desired, but sliding on the black silk panties instead of the stupid linen long-johns things? Sheer heaven.

Zipping up the dress felt like attaching my own skin again. Another piece of my psyche settled into place. Whether Blackbird was right and the material itself held magic, or the magic was just in the confidence of wearing something I'd picked out on my own and bought with money I knew I'd earned, a sense of right-ness settled over me.

I brushed my hair out and left it loose—seemed more sorceress-y that way—and "did" my makeup as I would for a normal work day. Only I was going to bat-tle, not the university. Oh wait, not that different after all. I chuckled at myself, pleased that my mental tone sounded more firm this morning. Not filled with the uneasy dread of night.

The morning lingered chilly and misty, so I pulled on a cream velvet cloak—and quickly changed it to black. Then to deep red, so I wouldn't look too funereal. Magic was also handy for wardrobe accessorizing.

Larch stood between the blazing torches that still flanked the entrance to my tent, holding the reins of a horse. The same horse I had ridden here, so she must be officially my horse now. She shone creamy white in the flickering light. I sighed to see that now the mare had been decorated with plumes and bells more suited to a parade than a battle.

"What's her name?" I asked Larch.

He shrugged.

I scratched the white forehead under her silky fore-lock and she snuffled sweet hay-breath at me. I tried to dip into her mind for images. A feeling of running and grazing, mixed in a muscular joy. She was pleased to see me again.

"Felicity, then—how's that?"

She arched her neck and did a little prance in place.

"I'll take that as a yes." I mounted, a sense of purpose filling me. I was going to fight a battle. Against whom and why, I had no idea, but still.

Fortunately the skirt was full enough that it only hiked above my knees a bit. Riding in pumps wasn't unlike riding in boots, actually, since the heels sat in the stirrups the same way. Except that my calves would probably chafe. Couldn't be helped. A sorceress had an image to maintain and riding in jeans wasn't it.

Darling leaped up behind me onto his traveling pad, still in full regalia, though it looked as though he might have rolled in some grass while wearing it. I pulled a few of the longer strands off and he let me scratch under the collar. It seemed to fit fine. Larch trotted beside me, leading me to the gathering of the troops.

"You're not wearing my tribute, Lady Gwynn." Falcon glowered. Hawklike shadows haunted his eyes in the gray pre-dawn glow.

I nudged my horse with my knees to change my angle so that Darling was behind me, him and his incriminating topazes out of Falcon's line of sight.

"I cannot express my gratitude for such a tribute," I answered, keeping my words as close to my sincere intentions as I could. Now for the lying: "Surely a priceless necklace like that is not appropriate for me to wear to a battle."

I had to clamp down hard not to add "Like I'd wear your fucking dog-collar, you sadistic bastard" onto the end.

Frankly, I suspected I would never wear anything around my neck again. Just the thought made me twitch, but I kept my hands firmly in my lap, not touching my throat. Or even the pulse at my wrist, though I could have reached my wrist easily, with just a little stretch of my fingers. *Don't give in.*

Falcon's eyes gleamed dull yellow rage. But he grunted and turned away, leaving me to my own devices.

I lingered on the outskirts of the group. A few of my dinner companions, now with full entourages, milled about. They were predictably jolly, busily congratulating one another on the upcoming conflict and their fine uniforms. Their pages' and horses' outfits expanded upon the uniform themes, *ad infinitum*, ad nauseum. You haven't seen fashion risk until you've seen a horse dressed in navy blue with little silver sailing ships.

"We should have dressed you and my horse in basic black," I muttered to Larch.

"It shall be done, my lady."

"I was kidding," I said. "I'm not sure embroidered cotton and spaghetti straps are your thing, anyway. Plus, Ann Taylor would probably find a horse-plume too fussy." Larch gave me his politely confused look. "Besides, wouldn't too much black align me with Lord Rogue?" Shit—careless of me.

"Why would you mind that, lady?" Larch seemed taken aback.

"Um, because I'm not his ally, and consider him a mortal enemy, in fact?"

"You will want to rethink that position, Lady Sorceress," Larch advised, not looking at me. "You are only on loan to Lord Falcon and Lord Puck. You fundamentally belong to Lord Rogue, no matter what color or collar you wear."

I clenched my teeth. "I do not *belong* to Rogue."

"When he claims you six years and some days from now, willing, enthralled, bespelled or enchained, to bear his child, you might find yourself disabused of that notion."

I studied Larch, somewhat startled by his frank response after all the servile posturing. One of these days I'd stop being surprised that everyone seemed to know everything about me. *Never underestimate a hive mind and how information is shared.*

"What if he can't find me?"

"Are we speaking of the same Lord Rogue, my lady?" Larch returned.

Good point.

"What if I refuse? I can fight him. I've learned a great deal."

He looked vaguely shocked but pursed his lips in due consideration. Finally he said, "Surely, my lady sorceress, even in your land there are penalties for those who fail to meet the terms of their bargains."

"Well, not so much," I said, thinking of bankruptcy court.

"A strange land, indeed. Here a debt must be honored. You'll find you have no choice. Learn to wield your abilities—there lies your power. And remember that all must keep their promises to you, as well."

I considered him. Felicity stamped and blew at the bit, anxious to get going, but Larch, a sixteenth of her size, held her easily.

"Whose side are you on?"

"Since I serve both you and Lord Rogue, I need not take sides."

Ha to that.

"You said six years and some days from now—does

that mean you know exactly when my seven years are up?"

Larch nodded, grave as always.

"Is there some way for me to track it?"

"I believe Lord Rogue will inform my lady sorceress of the appropriate day."

I unclenched my teeth. "Before that. So I know how much time I have left?"

To plan accordingly.

An image slid into my mind of six large topazes, four smaller topazes and fifteen small stones, more pale than bronze. I looked in surprise over my shoulder at Darling. "How do you know?"

"He *is* your Familiar, my lady."

Darling blinked fondly at me, again showing me the young man with an armload of roses.

"Unfamiliar, you mean," I said, but I scratched Darling's neck under his collar by way of thanks, obediently moving over a bit when he showed me an itchier spot. "Told you not to sleep in it. You'll be all over itchy by the end of the day."

He swatted my hand, nailing me with a claw and drawing blood.

"Ow! You varmint! See?" I said pointedly to Larch, who looked steadfastly ahead but might have been smirking.

The sun blazed over the horizon, the trumpets blared and the group started to move. Larch slid us into the column of nobles, over a dozen riders back from Falcon's lead group, which suited me just fine. Puck's antifreeze-green plume towered over the rest. We picked up the pace and Larch released the reins, jogging alongside at my stirrup. Other pages did the same.

"Are you coming along?" I asked.

"I am my lady's page, am I not?"

We trotted down the hill and around a bend, into the next valley. I caught my breath at the sight of men marching, four abreast. They wore hard leather and steel. Wild hair streamed, sometimes covered by helmets, sometimes not. Weapons bristled. The scene looked like *Highlander* meets Spartacus.

But what truly caught me, so much so that I could not tear my eyes away, was that these were *men*—humans, to all appearances.

"Where did they come from?" I gasped.

Larch looked up, face a deeper violet from jogging along. "My lady?" he questioned politely, not quite implying that I might have lost my mind.

"Darling, where did these men come from?"

The cat replied with an image of various villages and people working in them and me sitting on the floor with an addled look on my face.

"Why, Virginia," I muttered to myself, "the stork brought them. Now leave mummy alone." Darling added some drool to the addled-me picture, so I reached back and yanked his tail, which made him have to dig in his claws to hang on. The image vanished.

I watched the men, starved for the sight of someone whose limbs looked in the right proportion. I fancied I could smell them, their honest human sweat—no fruits or exotic spices. Just the sight of them soothed my deep loneliness. The men marched along, not looking back at our colorful party as we passed up to the front.

Now I could see other battalions—if that was the word—converging. Some were composed of men. Oth-

ers of various types of fae, some I'd seen already, some
I hadn't.

"Lady Gwynn!" Puck came galloping down the line
to me, towering ostrich feather streaming with drama.
He did look pretty spectacular. "I see you've acquired
a page—most charming." He frowned at Larch. "No
uniforms for your retinue though?"

"At the cleaner's." Apparently the universal sense of
"not accessible to anyone without major difficulties"
came through my wisecrack loud and clear because
Puck looked irritated but resigned. I could see him as
a Wall Street exec, in a celadon Armani suit.

"The Great Lord Falcon will be angry if he sees this."
Puck glanced around, as if expecting Falcon to pounce
on him at any moment.

"Do you all jump to his every whim?"

Puck tilted his head, the plume listing dangerously
to the side. "His punishments can be most...unpleas-
ant. I don't care to repeat them. I'm surprised you do."

I looked away, swallowing back my gorge at the
thought of Falcon sinking his teeth into my vulnerable
breast. Maybe I was lucky he hadn't torn a chunk off
and eaten it in front of me.

"We're moving out to the Promontory of Magic,"
Puck declared, forever resilient and careful to pro-
nounce the capitals. "Follow me!" He angled off to the
left, toward a rise of hills, virulent plume waving.

I kicked my horse into a canter—such a relief, as
cantering was infinitely more comfortable than endless
trotting—and looked to see how Larch kept up. He ran
alongside easily, though his blue sheen had deepened
to a decided deep purple.

Darling clung like a cocklebur to the saddle behind

me, beneath the fluttering canopy of my cloak, and I
leaned lower over Felicity's neck, her white mane lash-
ing my face and flying past to mingle with my dark
hair. The sun spilled over the horizon, blazing unnatural gold.

My heart pounded with exhilaration at the ride, the
morning, the warming damp air, the smooth cadence
of hooves on grass. Perhaps I picked up on the battle
ambience, because I felt fierce and excited. Maybe this
would be a *Lord of the Rings*/Narnia-type war, full of
heroics and flags—we certainly had the costumes for
it—rather than a muddy, grueling Private Ryan/Platoon
kind of thing. I'd definitely take glorious over gritty. I
laughed at myself. Laughed at the wind in my hair and
the blood pumping hot in me.

The conversation with Larch had Rogue circling my
thoughts again. Fortunately I didn't have the dream-
dregs to contend with, too.

*...when he drags you off enthralled, bespelled or
enchained...*

I fought down the uneasy arousal that image stirred
in me. But I could feel my body's interest, my awakened tissues vibrating with the ride, rubbing deliciously
against the hard press of the saddle. Some part of me
craved it, even as I knew in my head that I had been
in chains and it was no sex party. Had Marquise and
Scourge programmed this response, or had I always
carried it, deep inside, far from the light of day and
equal rights?

I thought back to that sense that Rogue felt responsible for my being here. His determination to possess
me. Had he somehow known this about me, even from
the other side of the veil? Had he somehow sniffed out

that in this land I could be a sorceress, that I had this dark sexual thing inside?

Not pleasant to contemplate, but that might contain the key to getting myself home.

Felicity slowed as we closed on Puck, now picking his way up a rocky trail on a wooded hillside that seemed made of some kind of chalk or white sedimentary stone. My cloak settled back into a deep red drape that I adjusted to spill over one side of the horse at Darling's indignant squawk. I let Felicity find her own way through the white stones, Larch falling behind to trail her. Ferns covered the shaded ground under thick trees reminiscent of an Alaskan forest landscape. I thought I could smell the hot prick of needle litter, but that was likely my imagination constructing something of home.

We emerged from the tunnel of shade, white stones and green ferns, up over a last lip of rock, into a vast dome of startling blue. Puck sat his horse, grinning at me, sweeping his arms out as if he'd created the spot just for me.

"The Promontory of Magic!" he declared.

No trees stood on the windswept top, as big around as a basketball court, the white rock showing through in many places, with the mossy grass only clinging to dips and hollows. The deep-green fringe of the forest canopy stopped short of the plateau, making for a spectacular 360-degree view. In a Victorian novel, the cast of characters would have taken carriages up here to have a picnic.

Darling leaped down to explore, armor clinking. Larch followed, picking his way across like a mountain goat.

On the plain below, I could see our army. Armies.

Rivers of people from several directions, all heading around the bend of the ridge line. The next watershed over was filled with another army, an angry, seething sea.

"The enemy," Puck pointed out to me.

"Who are they?" I asked, studying the shifting mass. From this distance I could make out little detail.

"Barbarians," Puck intoned.

"Aren't they always?" I returned, but Puck only nodded agreement.

"Isn't this perfect? Lord Falcon agreed to have the first battle here, so we could use this spot as the Promontory of Magic. We plan to have the first clash of infantry in that charming meadow there." Puck pointed to a spot roughly between the leading edges of the two armies.

"And so I shall leave you." Puck wheeled his horse around back toward the path. With great bounds, Darling ran after him and leaped up onto the back of Puck's saddle.

"Wait!"

He stopped, looking impatient. "What, Lady Gwynn? I must away—the battle commences!"

"You're leaving me here alone? What do I do?"

Puck sighed. "We've been over this. What you're told, remember?"

I blew out an exasperated breath. "Yes, yes, yes, I know—" *yada yada yada*, "—but how do I know what that is? Remember that I don't just know along with you!"

"We'll send messages," Puck said, speaking clearly so the dummy could understand. "Victory to you!" he called over his shoulder.

Darling didn't even say goodbye.

"And also with you," I grumbled. I looked around. "I thought there'd be more flags."

Under that acid blue sky I amused only myself.

NINETEEN

In Which I Am Covered in Glory and Other Obnoxious Fluids

PAGES WERE HANDY creatures to have around, especially because they were the ones who remembered to bring refreshments to war.

Larch had stowed a picnic worthy of a Victorian novel in Felicity's saddlebags, unbeknownst to me. My new lifestyle as a pampered lady. I'd have giddily ridden up here and spent the day with nothing to eat and nothing to do except chase my horse to keep her from taking off to be with the other horses in the valley below.

Instead, Larch had efficiently hobbled her and set her to grazing so I could wander around the promontory, trying to look officially occupied. I picked out an observation spot where I could watch the slow progress of the two forces as they wound their way to the charming meadow.

I was a character in *The Thin Red Line* after all, bored and running a dull internal monologue. I'd had to watch the damn movie three times, Clive liked it so much. He thought it a great movie because it showed how monotonous much of war was. Anyone who could make Christian Slater boring had certainly accomplished something, but I was thinking it wasn't a great thing.

To occupy myself with something besides mentally reviewing every war movie I'd ever seen, and the fewer war books I'd read—most of which were sword and sorcery and not nonfiction, anyway—I mulled over what magics I'd perform, given the leeway. If I wasn't to do anything until the battle was nearly lost, this was going to be a long day. How long did battles take anyway? Long, grueling hours, by all accounts.

Left to me, I'd rather have tried to divert the enemy forces before they reached the charming meadow and prevent the battle altogether.

But Falcon and the others seemed to be scripting their war for last-minute, tide-turning action. They wanted spectacular, so I should do something fireworks-y, something loud and colorful. Except I wasn't excited about killing anyone. Yes, yes—I knew it was freaking war, but I was a girly-girl. There was a reason I left the room during the brutal stuff.

Good thing I had lots of time to think about this. But then, there was restfulness—and an absolution of guilt, maybe—in simply doing what one was told. I could just follow instructions for once and not have to think up my own strategy. That would be playing it safe. The cowed and obedient part of me loved this idea.

That alone was reason not to do it.

I'd also learned better. Most of the fae did not seem possessed of noble intentions. Playful at best, cruel at worst—they operated on a totally different ethical system. What they could take by hook or crook, they would. If you believed their lies, too bad for you.

Simply doing as I was told could make me an accomplice—or the instigator—of something I would never support. And it wouldn't help me heal.

When Larch called me to eat an early lunch, I sat gratefully on the little circle of mossy grass he'd picked out. The armies should close on each other within the hour, though they seemed to have slowed to nearly a standstill. I slipped off my shoes and laid them to the side, resting my arches. We made odd picnicking partners, while a war assembled below us.

"Tell me something, Larch." I laid cheese on apple slices—at least that was how they tasted. "What is the goal of this war?"

"To defeat the barbarians of course."

"To accomplish what? Gain land? Property? Prove a religious point?"

Larch looked up at the sky. "You're asking me for a real reason?"

"Yes."

His blueberry eyes met mine. "They grow bored from time to time, Lady Gwynn. This is the latest diversion."

"And our enemy—the barbarians?"

Larch handed me a basket of rolls. "The same."

"So, there's no real purpose to this war?"

"I wouldn't say that. For immortal folk, jockeying for power is everything. Falcon is making a bold move with this war. Many are waiting to see how he succeeds."

I set the rolls down, too queasy to eat. "But people will die down there—yours and mine, both."

"Yes. But they won't. That's all that matters to them."

Groping for words, I studied the black embroidery of my dress. I'd dressed up for this, made plans. "Why do you all go along with it?" I finally asked.

"Why, my lady?" Larch sounded suddenly angry.

He scrambled up on stocky legs. "You, puppet of the nobles, ask me that?"

I stared at him, steeling myself not to flinch at displeasing him.

"The power is all theirs, Lady Gwynn," he said more gently. "Best to learn it now."

He began packing up our lunch, so I slipped my shoes back on, brushed off my dress and made myself scarce. I'd long since ditched the cloak in deference to the hot sunshine. Larch must have efficiently packed it. At least now I could be confident that I hadn't inadvertently zapped it away somewhere.

Okay, I knew what I needed to do.

I changed a loose rock at my observation point into a barstool. It manifested fused to the rock below, in all its chalky magnificence. Careless imagining on my part. Though fine for stability, it looked like something out of Monty Python. I decided to leave it as it was, sat on the stool—after I modified the top to make it into a cushion—and hooked my heels over the rungs. Larch declined my offer of another stool and squatted down next to me.

I'd thought maybe a live war would make more sense than the movie ones, where I could never seem to keep track of the action. But I quickly lost track of who was who—complicated by the fact that the Enemy Men seemed to be very much the same as our own Men. Were the same, from what Larch had said.

"So, the humans here—they're like me?"

Larch snorted. "Humans rarely can do magic. Something about you folks from the other side makes you special."

"What is it?"

"You're asking me? It's your world."

The leading edges of leather and metal flung them-selves against each other, boiled up, then smoothed once more into a flowing sea of movement. Two rivers meet-ing. If I watched the current closely, I could make out the line where the two joined, more defined in some places than others. But that line broke apart, splintered and swirled as some groups pushed forward and oth-ers back.

I kept good thoughts for all involved, in case that helped, focusing on them being strong and courageous, being careful not to exceed my instructions. I felt like the ten-year-old cheerleader in sagging socks again, peering past the coaches, trying to figure out enough of what was going on in the game to know which cheer to use.

Blood didn't spurt up into the air or anything, but bodies dropped, disappearing beneath the melee, an ominous vanishing. The cavalry charged in from the side—plumes nodding indeed—and I picked out Puck's celadon outfit easily. I couldn't see whether Darling was with him and when I tried to query the cat, I got noth-ing back—whether due to distance, his preoccupation or worse, I didn't know.

After a bit, I was able to identify the knot of nobles, mostly by tracking the paths of the bright uniforms run-ning back and forth from it. Figures seemed to forage out briefly and, after having grabbed a taste of battle for themselves, scurry back to their fortified hill, sur-rounded by a bastion of colorful pages.

There was a similar grouping at the end of the other valley. I toyed with sending a little spell their way, but no—*do what you're told.* This time I deliberately stroked my throat. Remember. Work within parameters. I could do this. My rebellions needed to be carefully chosen. And hidden.

Then they brought out Lady Strawberry's beasts, and monstrous they were.

Now the blood did fly as four great rhinoceros-sized creatures waded through the infantry. I watched in congealing horror, glad I hadn't eaten any more than I had. A page-jockey perched on the neck of each one. Massive horns gored and tossed. Maybe it was my own confusion, but the monsters looked to be rampaging equally through both armies. The line between them grew more diffused, blurring as soldiers ran in all directions from the beasts.

Preoccupied with the nightmare of it all, I didn't see the dragons until they flew right overhead.

They thundered in from behind me and dropped into the belly of the valley below. The wake turbulence of their great passage nearly threw me from the stool and, as I clutched the sides of my seat, I saw Larch's blueberry face raised in shock and terror. Glinting in the afternoon light, the two dragons swooped like raptors falling onto their prey. They seized the rhino-creatures, two each, carrying them into the sky, pages tumbling as they fell from their mounts.

The dragons spiraled up, the pumping of their wings flattening both armies for a moment as the men crouched under the blast of hot wind. Then the dragons wheeled and roared directly over our plateau again. I crouched at the base of the stool, clutching Larch, as the bloody dripping carcasses of the rhinos dangling from the enormous dragon claws barely cleared us. Red and yellow mucousy gore rained down on us, along with a

clump of flesh that hit my bare shoulder and slid greas-
ily off.

As quickly as the dragons arrived, they were gone
again. Lady Strawberry's monsters had been removed
from the playing field like illegal chess pieces. The
armies seemed at a loss for a moment, perhaps as
stunned as I.

They stood from their crouches.

Regarded one another.

Then fell to fighting again, prodded by who knows
what. What could be worse for them than facing this?

Larch offered me a cleaning cloth from his never-
ending supply of noble-tending materials. I tried to wipe
myself clean while Larch did the same.

The fluids were oddly sticky. I felt as if I was trying
to remove maple syrup with tissue—fibers of the gray
cleaning cloths sticking to the smearing stains. I wiped
harder with no better success. The stuff stank, too, like
pond water and xylene mixed. What if it was toxic?

Having had enough, I wished us both clean, which
helped considerably, though not completely. I frowned
at the yellow streaks still sprinkling down the skirt of
my dress.

"Dragon blood, Lady Sorceress," Larch offered.
"One of Lady Strawberry's monsters must have gored
one. Or perhaps an arrow. Magic doesn't work on dragons," he added as I continued to stare at him.

"Why ever not?" I asked, to which he only shrugged
in that fatalistic way. "That makes no sense. Aren't
they subject to the same physical laws as everything
else here?"

"Why can some perform magic and others not?"
Larch countered.

"Excellent question—why is that?"

"Surely it's not so different in your land. Some have power. Some don't. Why is that?" Larch snapped back, which made me realize he'd dropped all obsequious servant attitude. Apparently he also caught himself, because he lowered his head and began muttering that he might be able to concoct a cleaning solution from some of the mosses in the area, combined with some water, liberally sprinkling the explanation with *myla-dysorceresses.*

"Cut the crap, Larch." We were both on edge, watching the horrors below. "You know I don't care whether you 'my lady' me—what do you know of magic and where I'm from? If you know the answers to my questions, I sure as hell want to hear them. I've had it up to here with circuitous answers."

"Then why did you walk away from the one person who could answer them?" His bright eyes pierced me.

"Who—Rogue?" Suddenly suspicious, I grabbed his little arm. "You work for Rogue, don't you?"

"I thought I worked for you, my lady sorceress." His tone was deferential but he wrenched his arm from my grasp and stalked away.

I studied Larch as he yanked various supplies from his packs.

"He abandoned me. To torture, I might add. And being drugged and packed off over someone's shoulder hardly counts as walking away."

Larch snorted. The interruption gave me a chance to steady my voice, which had started to get wobbly. *Don't you dare cry.*

"He knew what would be done to me and consigned me to the worst of hells." He kissed me and deserted me. I sounded pitiful, even to myself. Time to focus on someone else's problems. Just as well, since Larch apparently had no come-back to that.

The battlefield appeared to be in utter chaos, with the two sides virtually indistinguishable except for the two gaily bannered camps at each far end of the valleys. The cavalry charged in, gloriously, only to charge back out. The purpose of the battle remained unclear to me, whether we meant to advance down the valley or prevent them from doing so. More and more I dreaded what Falcon's instructions would be. How could I possibly perform a magic that wouldn't make me into a mass murderer?

When Larch silently handed me a damp cloth, I took it without a word and began wiping my arm and shoulder. It wasn't perfect, but his concoction removed most of the yellow stuff and all of the smell. He promised to refine the formula at day's end so that my dress could be cleaned. I wrapped the damp cloth around the sticky section of my hair and held it there, nodding absently to his remarks, as if completely absorbed in the battle instead of nursing my wounded soul.

Larch stood when a raptor winged in our direction, silhouetted against the lengthening light. A hawk or falcon by the size, I thought. The bird swooped in and settled on Larch's upraised arm, black eyes fixed on me with dark intelligence and a wickedly curved beak. More of a hawk, but colored a more vivid russet than any species I knew. The hawk and Larch bent their heads to each other, almost an affectionate curve.

"Spectacular explosions, blindness, bodies flying through the air," Larch described slowly. "Something that looks like spirals?"

The hawk peeped softly in agreement.

"That's it?" I asked. "Let me see." I tried looking in Larch's thoughts and hit a big wall.

"I don't think so, my lady," Larch said softly.

"Great. I love having my fate resting on not getting clear instructions."

"Lord Falcon can't kill you or permanently disfigure you without disrupting Lord Rogue's claim. My lady's fate does not ride on this."

"Believe me, there's worse things than that," I returned, fingering my neck. "Can I try directly with the hawk?"

The great bird mantled a bit, but seemed more amenable than Larch, who looked decidedly grumpy. "My lady's arms would be scored by the talons."

"You hold him. I'll come to you."

I knelt down, coincidentally bringing myself to head height with Larch. From this perspective, I could see that his face, his head loomed out of proportion with the rest of his body. Uneasy, I looked away, focusing on the hawk instead. I dipped into its mind, and instantly dropped into spiraling vertigo, hot flight, tearing blood. Gasping, I yanked myself back out.

Larch watched me with a sardonic look that reminded me of Rogue. But all he said was, "Raptors can be difficult to talk to."

I stood, as much to remove myself from the view of Larch's odd proportions as to regain some dignity.

"Okay—let's do this empirically. What is the unmistakable essence of my instructions?"

Larch blinked his catlike eyes at me solemnly. "Little in life is unmistakable, Lady Sorceress."

"You're beginning to sound like Yoda."

"My lady?"

"Yeah, yeah, always in motion is the future, I get it. What do you *think* I am required to do?"

Larch frowned at the hawk. I reached for Darling while I waited. Maybe I could get him just to ask Puck directly. No answer still. And no way to leave a voice mail, either.

"Big, bright explosions spiraling in the sky that blind the enemy," Larch finally said.

"What about the side effects of blinding our guys? Or us, up here on the hill for that matter?"

Larch squinted before conceding that wasn't specified. I found myself picking at the dried dragon goo in my hair. "Does it specify permanent blindness? Or that the blinding must be a direct result of the sky explosions?"

When Larch allowed that neither of these things were specified, I had my plan.

I slipped off my shoes and clambered up to stand on the stool, which was nice and stable. Maybe I had known what I was doing after all when I fused it to the bedrock. The hawk showed no inclination to leave, so it and Larch watched me from below. I needed something more showy, like a wand or a few shouted words, but oh well.

I pictured Fourth of July fireworks, a whole half-hour show's worth—granted not all of those would spiral, but I did make sure to include those ones that swirl down in fuzzy worms and then break into starbursts. I set that going and was startled by the burst of music that accompanied it. Apparently my mental movie of fireworks shows carried the typical soundtrack of patriotic songs. Done deal now. *Talk about not being able to run away from yourself.*

While the disembodied voice belted out his thanks to be an American and how at least he knew he was free, the fireworks exploded with gratifying brightness—though it would have been better with full dark. The battle had ground mostly to a halt below, with men either cowering down or staring in wonder and fear, or both. Only a few stolidly still hacked at one another. I implemented Phase II, converting sparks from an expanding starburst into myriad tiny fruit flies, implanted with a desire for salt instead of sugar.

With each explosion, another swarm of dark flies descended on the men, going for any exposed skin, attracted by the sweat on their faces and around the eyes vulnerable from the openings in their helmets. I made sure clouds of the irritating insects headed toward both cadres of colorful nobles, too.

Oops, my bad. Just a happy coincidence that those little flies didn't like to ascend to heights like ours.

The fireworks continued through their set, unfortunately to the same loop of country song—the only thing worse than manifesting a bad song was that you didn't know it well enough to at least play it all the way through. Earworm syndrome.

"The Star-Spangled Banner" had to have been played, too—why wasn't *that* booming through the valley? At least I knew all the words to that. I toyed with disconnecting the soundtrack from the spell but thought I might disrupt the whole thing.

Men scattered, pulling off their helmets and wiping their eyes. The cavalry horses were crying out, rear-ing and bucking—that was definitely an unintended consequence.

Apologies, horses. Both armies began to withdraw, trumpets sounding orderly calls to retreat that only highlighted the great disorder. I laughed to see the nobles hightailing it away from the battlefield, surprised to hear Larch chortling along with me.

Both armies seemed to be closing up shop for the night, so I let the fireworks end when their half-hour cycle was up. I'd made the fruit flies all male, so they wouldn't breed, and made them old enough that they should die off in the next few hours. Pleased with myself, I let Larch help me down from the stool and slipped my heels back on.

"What now?" I asked. "Do we send a message back? Wait for Puck to come fetch us?"

Larch opened his mouth to reply, but he clamped his mouth shut, gaze locked past me in frozen alarm. The hawk mantled and I wheeled around to see the Black Dog, like a piece of night forest with white-bladed teeth, charging at full speed toward us.

TWENTY

In Which We Celebrate the First Pyrrhic Victory

No!

The scream welled up in my throat, though it had no time to make it past my lips.

No! It wasn't an accident this time. It was a job. I was made to do it. Not like the birds, not like the birds!

I glimpsed what I thought was Larch moving to throw himself in front of me, but all I saw were the slavering jaws coming for me, for my blood. The mirrored glass coat of the Dog reflected night against the crepuscular shadows.

I saw my death in it.

I braced myself, mind racing for some image, some spell to stop it, but before I formed something cohesive from the shrieking birds of my thoughts, even as the Dog leaped for me, a thudding pain dropped me to the ground.

Remnants of the fireworks sprang around the dark edges of my vision, bright pinpoints sparkling against blood red. I heard Larch screaming in thin wails, as Loden had. I couldn't see through my eyelids. Sounds were muffled, distant.

Of their own accord it seemed, my eyelids fluttered open to show me the unnatural ultramarine of the sky, wheeling with streaks of bright sunset.

My stomach quailed and a headache throbbed between my eyes, piercing deeper with each of Larch's cries. And someone else's screams, too. At first I thought the hoarse shouts of battle still echoed in my head, those few that drifted up to us on the warm air currents. When I realized these were just beyond me, very immediate, their loudness penetrating the veil of my confusion, it galvanized me.

Like a cat out of bath water, I sprang up and landed curled in a crouch before I finished the thought that I should move.

It took a moment to make sense of what I saw. My visual cortex struggled to right the images, to make sense of the flailing limbs. Instead of seeing Larch convulse as the Black Dog gutted him, I saw men on the ground, Larch pinning one with a spearlike thing through the neck. The Black Dog tore the throat out of another man as I watched, the blood arcing in a violet stream against the graying sage of the mosses and white rocks. I heard the skirl of the hawk, circling above.

The Dog stood on the chest of the man he'd just killed, and I caught my breath remembering the great weight of him. That vicious dark muzzle lowered and he sniffed the man's congealing face.

My stomach wrenched. Fear flowed through me, my blood turned to mercury, thin and hot. I tucked my feet up, ready to stand, to run, to do something. One shoe was gone. Magic—I needed a spell against the Dog.

Even as I thought it, the Dog raised his head, a hound scenting prey, and looked over his glossy shoulder.

At me.

Blood dripping from his muzzle, the Dog's lambent amber eyes glared at me. Daring me. He licked his glossy muzzle and delicately stepped off the corpse, padding toward me like a panther.

"No magic, Lady Gwynn, please," Larch whispered, still clutching the spear that impaled the other body. As the Dog stalked toward me, I glimpsed another bloodied corpse just beyond the others. "Trust me. No magic."

"He'll kill me," I said.

"No. He's protecting you."

I strangled a sob as the Dog stopped in front of me. I could smell blood and meat on his hot breath as he panted gently. My breast throbbed, each healing tooth mark a pinpoint resounding with my adrenaline-fueled heartbeat. The prey in me wanted to run, to break cover, to heart-poundingly try for some safety even while I knew I couldn't escape him.

"He attacked me once before."

"To save you from yourself."

Oh.

The Black Dog's jaws fell wider into a canine laugh. He took one more step forward and I moaned, deep in my throat, lunch acrid in my stomach. He cocked his head, touched his muzzle to my temple in a soft warm whuffing. I patted his head, feeling awkward. He licked my wrist, rubbing his head against my hand. Back to friendly Lab mode. Then he vaulted over my head and trotted into the deepening forest.

We watched him go in silence.

"Who is he?"

Larch glanced at me sideways. "Guardian. Passer of boundaries. Gatekeeper, guide and reaper."

"Reaper?" I strangled on the word. "I'm not dead." *Am I?*

"There are many ways and worlds to cross."

"Why is he protecting me?"

Larch grinned at me, unexpected and somewhat eerie on his stolid blue face. "I suspect that's a question more than one person would like the answer to. Shall we return to camp, my lady sorceress?"

I nodded, blowing my breath out in one long exhale.

Riding back down the hill, navy-dark Larch following as my horse picked her way along the shadowed descent, I fingered the tender bump under my hair, where one man had struck me. They'd crept up from behind to attack. Drag me off or murder me—it mattered little which. And the Dog had likely saved my life. Again. Though the first occasion seemed considerably muddier.

"Who were those men on the hill?" I asked Larch.

"Barbarians," he confirmed.

"Sent to kill me?"

"Or capture. We were careless."

Okay then.

We caught up with the long train of men marching back to some camp along the river. They strung along the road, looking fierce and exhausted. A mutter ran through them as we came alongside, passing rapidly, my horse's fresh canter far exceeding their battle-weary tread. Some looked askance, others openly stared.

I wanted to say hello, ask questions. This was clearly not the time. So I just rode alongside, soaking up the comfort of being near my own kind.

A chant sprang up from a few throats, guttural rhythm to their heavy steps. Others joined in, the song spreading up and down the column, seeping like water through the tired faces. The words made no sense— instead I received a barrage of ideas, flashes of battle scenes, the dragons, the monsters, the fireworks from below, the blinding flies. Me, a small figure in black high up on the hill, midnight hair flying.

I tried to close off the input and concentrated on the sound instead.

Ahm prohd... Tbhee... Mehrkan
Ahtleest... Ahnoh... Ahmfree

It was the soundtrack.

They couldn't have understood the meaning behind the words, but they'd heard the awful loop enough times that the sounds had sunk in. They went on, male voices rising and falling in the cadence of the nonsense words. If only I had thought ahead, I could have given them something better. "Scotland the Brave," with bold hearts and nodding plumes.

By the time we reached camp, full night had descended and the tents were brilliantly lit with the disco patterns of the glowing pillows. Larch's contingent of non-page workers and Dragonfly's idle maids had clearly been busy. Not a corner of the camp wasn't glowing. Already music was playing, different tunes from various tent groupings, reminding me of the fraternity stereo wars in college, with each house blasting a different song from speakers propped in the windows.

"Lady Sorceress!" A brownish page I didn't recognize bowed in front of me.

"Yes?"

"Brilliantly fought battle, Lady Sorceress."

"Thank you." I said it drily, but he seemed not to notice. I nudged my horse onward.

"Lady Sorceress!"

I sighed. "How can I help you?"

"I am sent to ask for Lord Darling's services in the dancing tonight."

"I haven't seen Lord Darling, yet—did you look at the tent?"

"I believe he has returned from glorious battle. Just as your victorious self has done."

Victorious? I hadn't thought yet about whether we'd won.

"As Lord Darling's liege, you must give your permission for him to provide services to the camp," Larch told me.

"Oh, well, Darling is his own cat. Whatever services he wishes to provide are fine by me. Will he be helping to treat the wounded?"

"No, Lady Sorceress." The page twitched from foot to foot with overweening impatience. "The *dancing*."

Of course.

"Fine. Whatever. Permission granted. Knock yourselves out."

The page dashed off happily and we resumed our trek to the tent.

Dragonfly greeted me with the delirious news that a large brass bathtub had appeared in the tribute tent, to her great amazement. I sent a silent thank you to the magic that seemed to ensure that the things I wanted managed to find their way to me, even without my direct intervention.

I was just about to strip down and sink into the enticingly steamy water of the bath Dragonfly had prepared, when a commotion out front caught my attention. I heard Larch informing someone that the lady sorceress was engaged in private study and could not be interrupted. He was still on guard duty apparently—did the guy never sleep? Actually maybe he didn't need to. What did I know of Brownie physiology?

I pushed through the silken flaps to find Larch holding the brown page by the scruff of the neck so his toes dangled above the ground—quite the feat since they matched in height. The brown page, though, didn't struggle, simply dangled like a recalcitrant kitten caught in its mother's teeth. He saw me and moaned.

"If it please you, Lady Sorceress…"

"What? I said Darling could go play with you."

"Yes, and many thanks, Great and Powerful Lady Sorceress."

"But?"

"But, if it please you, Lady Sorceress…" Larch gave him a shake, making his eyes goggle a bit.

"Larch, set the poor thing down so he can give me his message and let me get back to my arcane magical studies." I cocked an eyebrow at Larch, who simply sighed and set the brown guy down.

"Many thanks, many, many thanks, Gracious and Great…"

"You're welcome. Message please?"

"Lord Darling, he—well, he's dead, Lady Sorceress. Magically choked to death."

Part IV
Hypothesis Testing

TWENTY-ONE

In Which We Pick Up Where We Left Off

THE NECKLACE FROM FALCON.

Even as I ran barefooted through the camp, dodging dancers and merrymakers who juggled flashing pillows, I knew what had happened. I should never have used it. It had been a trap, with the trigger somehow pulled on Darling.

I had been tragically negligent.

The brown page halted our mad dash, pointing the way to a knot of nobles and pages—some still spattered with dried blood and gore. At Larch's booming proclamation that I had arrived, they opened up, forming an aisle for me. In the center of the group, Darling lay stretched out on a high table, on top of a glowing dark blue pillow, silent musicians standing around him in a doleful huddle. A page was diligently festooning Darling's body with ivory flowers. He still wore his armor, an unnaturally stiff structure standing out around his lax furry limbs.

I pushed the page aside and swept the flowers off, running my hands over Darling, ignoring the indignant cries around me. He was still warm, but oh so limp. I felt for the femoral pulse in his leg, difficult to find in cats anyway, impossible with my own heart thundering in my ears and my hands shaking. I turned him over so

I could lay my ear against his little chest, his limbs still
so pliant. Maybe I could hear something. Maybe I only
wanted to too badly. Around me discussions flared over
Darling's death, his brave deeds on the battlefield, what
sort of funeral would be most glorious.

Snarling at them all, I gathered Darling up in my
arms. "Clear the way, Larch."

They all stared at me, shocked, but also delighted
with the unexpected turn of events.

"Make way for the Great and Powerful Lady Sorceress carrying the burden of her dead Familiar!" Larch
thundered.

I clenched my teeth on a sob and plowed through
the titillated sea. Falcon waited for me at the end of the
aisle. He still wore his blinding armor, flame-gold now
in the reflected light of the torches borne by the pages
who flanked him.

"Lord Darling is dead, Lady Gwynn. Won't you let
him rest in peace?"

"Murderer," I whispered. As if this said anything
pertinent.

"Oh no, lady. It was not I who placed the collar
around his neck. So pretty, such lovely stones." He
brushed his finger over one and raised the eyebrow on
the patterned side of his face, his blazing eye the same
color as the jewels.

I hugged Darling to my breast, feeling where Falcon's
teeth had sunk in, pinned beneath his sharp gaze. Anger
and despair, two sides of the same coin, burned through
the mental and emotional barriers instilled in me.

*Marquise may have been right to question the tight-
ness of my bonds.*

"So sorry you took out the wrong target, but I have things to do." I slipped around Falcon and he let me.

"Don't fret, lady," he called after me. "I can have the stones reset into a necklace for you. You won't be without it long."

I buried my face in Darling's fur, blindly following Larch. Noticing his fur was wet, I realized I was crying. Crying silently and effortlessly, like I had when my old cat had died of cancer. All that winter afternoon and into the night I'd held her, thinking each ratcheting breath would be the last. Waiting for her to slip away. Until she began convulsing, crying in pain, and I called the emergency vet in the middle of the night, going to that cold sterile room to buy that final shot for her. I hadn't been sure which of us was being put out of her misery.

There was no one for me to call now.

When I reached the tent, Larch held the flap open for me, while Dragonfly anxiously bounced up, a solicitous pillow in each hand. My bath still stood, waiting for me. Cold.

"Night off, Dragonfly," I said.

I strode past her to my workbench, tenderly laying Darling on the surface. I ran my hands through his fur. Think. *Think.* Something rustled, distracting me.

"Everybody out," I ordered. "I swear, if anyone disturbs me, I'll strike them dead where they stand."

"Good threat," said a silky voice behind me, "but can you back it up?"

I spun around, my body coiling.

"Rogue."

He sprawled across the pillows in the otherwise empty tent. Languid, even indolent, he poured like ink over the gaily covered cushions, blue-black against their soft glow.

"I like your pillows. Cute idea." He smacked one, making it glow brighter. "Aren't you going to strike me dead? I'm agog to see your technique."

"I don't have time for you and your games," I snapped. "Go torment someone else."

I turned my back on him and ran my hands over Darling again, feeling his muscle tone, feeling for life. Cooler than he had been, but still limp. No rigor mortis. How long did that take in a cat? I laid my ear on his chest again. Maybe I could hear for a heartbeat better without the armor. I reached for the buckles.

"I wouldn't do that," Rogue breathed in my ear.

Proud of myself for not startling, I refused to look at him, knowing his face was right over my shoulder. The scent of cinnamon and sandalwood teased along my cheek.

"Why not?"

"His life is linked to it now. Without it, he'll die in truth."

A dry sob suddenly escaped me. I clamped down, digging my fingers into Darling's fur.

"He's not dead then?"

"Death wears many faces."

I spun around to face him. Then stepped back, he loomed so closely over me. "Can you heal him?"

"What are you willing to give me?"

Nothing without a price. I stared at him, the green ribbon from my dreams flashing through my mind. From the sapphire flare in Rogue's eyes, I knew he caught it.

Rogue cocked his head at me in acknowledgement, the long tail of his inky hair sliding over one shoulder.

"No." But it came out a whisper.

"Then what?"

"This isn't some kind of game of sex and power! We can flirt all you want after you deal with Darling."

"I accept your bargain."

Damn, damn and damn.

"And, lovely Gwynn—" Rogue trailed an elegant finger down my cheek, "—everything is a game of sex and power."

I tried to compose myself. It didn't pay to lose my temper. I slowly and pointedly removed his finger.

"I believe we just agreed to after we deal with Darling?" I was pleased with my arch tone. "Wouldn't want to violate the bargain, would you?"

Rogue sighed elaborately. "Falcon gave you a preset trap. As soon as you invoke magic, it...grabs you. Not death, but not life either."

"Some kind of stasis."

He nodded thoughtfully.

"But Darling wasn't with the wounded, what magic would he have invoked?"

"I thought you gave permission for him to facilitate the dancing?"

"What does dancing have to do with it?"

Rogue rolled his eyes dramatically and reached up to flick a long finger against the drying lily over the bench. We both watched it spin, its dusky indigos undiminished, a sweet crumbling scent wafting out with its movement. I tore my gaze away from it to find Rogue eyeing me, eyes glinting darkly.

"Despite your innovative little tricks, there is much you don't understand."

"No argument there."

"Lord Darling's gift is to offer freedom from pain, you do remember that?"

"Yes." I was being patient.

"How do you imagine anyone can dance all night long without a little assistance that way?"

"Oh." I glanced at Darling. "I hadn't thought."

"You never do."

"Ha-ha."

He was watching the lily again, its inverted dance dying out. He looked almost sorrowful. I felt the urge to apologize but clamped down on it ruthlessly.

"Why are you here, Rogue? How do you know what's been going on—the necklace from Falcon and me saying Darling could help with the dancing?" I asked it softly. *How could you let them do all that to me?* I tucked that last question away where he couldn't hear it.

Not something I wanted to hear the answer to.

"I pay attention to my investments."

"Thanks for that illuminating response."

He grinned at me, a bright flash of teeth twisting the sharp lines around his mouth. "Maybe I've missed you, Lovely Gwynn." He stepped toward me, reaching to tuck a strand of hair behind my ear. "The black is ravishing, but you didn't have to do it for me."

"I didn't. And we're not flirting—we haven't dealt with Darling."

"He's not going anywhere. And you failed to define 'deal'—he's been dealt with."

I looked at the cat's body on the table, inert, lifeless. Tears pricked my eyes and I stuffed them back. "But now what? What was Falcon's plan if it had been me? Why not just kill me?"

"Falcon doesn't forget what I am owed, even if you do."

My eyes flew to Rogue's—which were too damn close. I walked away, pacing. He leaned against the workbench, booted ankles crossed, an amused look on his face.

"That's a little under six and a half years away."

"Ah, my lady has been counting the days."

I glared at him. "So I know how much time I have to figure a way out of it."

He was at my side in a movement so fast I didn't see it. I must have thrown up a hand to ward him off, because he seized my wrist and pulled the hand up over my head, while his other arm crushed me against his chest. Had I thought Falcon's gaze was sharp? Rogue's predatory eyes bored into me, midnight space, the sable lines stark against his skin.

"Don't even imagine the possibility," he whispered.

"Let me go."

"That's the point—my answer is no."

"I won't be your brood mare."

"No, you'll be infinitely more than that."

He almost crooned the words. I closed my eyes against his proximity and I felt his lips, blazing hot against my cheek. I tried to yank my hand away but failed to move it even slightly. My whole body arched against him, thrumming with tension. Emotion rocked through me. The rollercoaster of the day had left me unbalanced. More so than usual, anyway. Rogue's lips trailed to my throat, the light brushing singing through my nerves, burning through me. But I managed to hold myself still, as if uninterested.

I felt Rogue raise his head and I opened my eyes to find his, dark Pacific blue, nearly black and swimming deep. The three-three beat of his heart pounded in counterpoint to mine.

"You promised to flirt, Gwynn. This feels like resistance."

"Doesn't it bother you that I hate you with all my heart?"

"But I know you don't."

I had no response to that. Except to open that little door between us and let him feel the hot rush of it.

Rogue closed his eyes, as if savoring a fine wine. "The strength of your passion is enough for me. It's connection enough for what I need from you. And—" he opened his eyes again, spearing me with their blue blaze, "—you are now failing the terms of our bargain. Which means you will owe me a forfeit. Are you prepared for that?"

"Oh no—we didn't define the terms of the bargain. You failed to define flirting. And," I repeated myself in measured tones, "we haven't dealt with Darling yet."

"Observe, darling Gwynn."

His eyes darkened and I felt something gather in the air around us, like an electrical storm of the navy-black energy I'd pulled from the lily. I could taste Rogue's magic in the air. I craned my neck to see Darling. With a subaudible chime, the topazes poofed into amber smoke, the armor following suit. Darling sat up, shook himself and meowed at Rogue.

"No—the lovely Lady Gwynn has paid for it. Now leave us so I can collect."

Darling sent me a salacious image, but it felt tired. He sauntered out of the tent, all dignity, his tail drooping slightly.

"Perhaps I should—"

"Pay attention to your bargain with me? Yes. Anything else to deal with—regarding Darling, of course?"

I tried to think of something, shifted a bit to see if Rogue would release his grip, but it was like being held by granite. Really warm, satin granite.

Giddy relief that Darling was okay surged through me. My blood heated at the press of Rogue's lithe muscled body. This was not good at all. "I could think better if you'd let me go."

"No. Darling questions now or we…move on."

Okay then. I tried to divorce my mind. Focus on what I needed to know.

"Why didn't Darling know the stones were enchanted? He talked me into using them."

"If Darling were perspicacious enough to avoid such traps, he wouldn't be a cat now."

"You mean he's not really a cat—he's a man? Or a faerie, I mean?"

"Both. Anything else?"

"Why wasn't the spell in the necklace nullified when I transformed it into armor?"

"Because you're an amateur. You didn't properly stabilize the spell so it would stay itself."

"Oh." How interesting. "Like your chamber pots. How do you do that?"

Rogue's eyes gleamed with an acquisitive light. "I could teach you—for a price."

"Sorry, I'm clearly already in debt up to my eyeballs."

Rogue nipped my ear lobe lightly. "You're stalling. Do we have anything else to 'deal' with, in your estimation?"

"Define flirting."

"It was your own offer—you define it."

I frowned at him. "I can't think in this position."

"That would be your problem."

"Acting like you're interested in someone...romantically."

"I can accept that." Rogue trailed his lips along my cheek. "I look forward to your interest in me."

"How could you do it?" I whispered. "Send me to that...place."

"That is not a question about Darling."

I caught his gaze. "Nevertheless, I need to know."

"I told you. Not everything is within my power, lovely Gwynn. I knew you would survive it. And that you would come out stronger. I did what I could to make the terms bearable."

"You made sure they couldn't actually use me—sexually."

"Yes." He nearly growled the word. "That is only for me. I long for you. Let me have you."

His eyes burned with an intensity I couldn't face. I looked away and wiggled the fingers of my right hand. "My hand is falling asleep."

"Pity. I'll have to rub it for you." He slid his body sinuously along mine in demonstration. My nipples chafed and peaked. Rogue's eyes roved down to where the straight neckline of my dress threatened to drag too low. He tightened the arm around my waist, lifting me up a bit, which only pulled the dress lower. He bent, placing a trailing kiss along my bosom. I dragged in a breath, trying to still my response.

"This isn't flirting," I gasped out.

"What do you call it?" he asked lazily, as a lock of his hair fell across my breast, stark against the white curve.

I held back a whimper as his tongue dipped below the fabric dangerously close to a nipple. Longing surged through me.

"I don't agree to this. I agreed to flirting, nothing more."

Rogue chuckled and raised his head. With a heated stare at my breasts pushing above the top of my dress, he placed a last kiss just over my heart.

And set me on my feet. He watched me with close interest while I pulled the fabric back into place. He cocked his head when I set to massaging the feeling back into my hand.

"Shall I help?"

"No thanks. No more touching."

"Flirting means no touching to you?"

"Correct."

"I want touching. To me, flirting involves some touching. It's not acting as if you're interested otherwise."

"That would be your problem," I quipped back, all sweetness.

"Okay, we can void the agreement and I'll proceed as I wish—you don't seem to be very good at fighting me off."

Humiliating but true. Though I didn't think he'd rape me, I could tell by the need already throbbing through me that I wouldn't resist him forever if he made a concerted effort. I hated him—why wasn't that helping?

Instead I felt alive and alert. Stimulated. And by more than just the foreplay. I enjoyed the banter. *He's not your friend,* I reminded myself.

"Limited touching. No lips, no…body parts."

His lips quirked at my unwillingness to name the parts.

"*Some* body parts, surely—hands?"

"One hand only," I allowed grudgingly. "Outside the clothes."

"And any publicly exposed skin," he qualified.

I didn't like it, but I thought it might be the best deal I'd get.

"Agreed."

TWENTY-TWO

In Which I Fulfill One Bargain

WE STOOD THERE, glowing pillows scattered at our feet. Rogue quirked a gloss-black eyebrow at me. "Well?"

"Well what?"

"Aren't you going to flirt with me now?"

"I really hate to tell you this, Rogue, but you're barking up the wrong skirt here—I'm a lab rat from way back. I've dated exactly three men in my life and have absolutely *no* idea how to flirt."

He sighed expressively, then held out his elegant hands in a palms-up gesture. "What shall we do? You promised flirting." His eyes fell on the full bathtub. "You could take your bath and I'll watch."

"I don't think so."

"It would be a flirtatious thing to do…"

"It would be exhibitionism on my part and voyeurism on yours. Besides which, I am not stupid enough to add to the skin that's already publicly exposed."

"But your feet are dirty."

He was right. Dust and mud mixed with unmentionable fluids caked my toes and spattered up my legs from my run through the camp. Ick.

While Rogue watched with great interest I walked over and stepped into the tub, holding my skirt up out of the water and shivering at the tepid temperature.

Bunching the fabric carefully between my legs, I sat on the uncomfortable narrow rim and began scrubbing.

Rogue piled up a few pillows, smacking them to his desired brightness and arranged himself as if for viewing a show. He peeled off his leather boots and, reaching back, he pulled the tie off his tail of hair, releasing it to spill around him. He looked like a raven Viking, all masculine cheekbones and streaming hair, his bare feet as long and elegant as his hands.

"Tug the skirt up higher," he suggested, "and blow me a kiss."

"No."

"It would be a mild flirtation and you've yet to do anything that qualifies as vaguely flirtatious."

I tugged my skirt up a grudging inch and pursed my lips at him.

His eyes flared. "Is the water warm enough for you? I could heat it up."

"So can I," I retorted and wished it a little warmer. "Rogue, we need to talk."

"No, no, no." He waggled a long finger at me. "That's anti-flirtation. 'We need to talk' is the death of romance. I don't think you're taking this bargain seriously. I'm close to crying foul."

A smile curved his lips, but his eyes were deadly intent. I tried to think up something flirtatious.

"Surely a big, strong, handsome man like you wouldn't take advantage of little ol' me," I fluttered with a peachy accent.

"Amazing. You really are bad at this."

I stood, clutching the fabric balled in my lap. "Look, Rogue…"

As I moved to step out of the tub, he was there in a

flash, holding my hand to help me balance. One hand only, I noticed.

"Oh, believe me, I am looking," he assured me. "You are lovelier than ever, saucy Gwynn." He let go of my hand to run his fingers over my hair. "Come, sit with me. I'll teach you how to flirt, as I've taught you so much else."

"Barely an ounce of what I need to know," I grumbled, but allowed him to help lower me to some pillows when he gave me a significant look. I stretched out on my side, propped up on one elbow.

He stood over me. "Observe." He swept his hands in a grand flourish and presented me with a flower. Another Stargazer lily—if anything, larger, sweeter and more intensely blue in the throat than the first had been. "Now, when a gentleman gives a lady a gift, to evince interest in him, she might trail it along her cheek to show him how lovely it feels against her skin, to give him ideas of how he might touch her."

He sank down onto the pillows, not close enough to touch, eyes intent on me, glowing bluer than the blossom. There was no harm in playing this game, theoretically. Unable to tear my eyes from his, I inhaled the fragrance, then brushed the velvet petals along my cheek. The light flared in his eyes and, emboldened, I trailed the flower down my throat to brush with exquisite delicacy over the upper curves of my breasts.

"Very well done." His voice sounded a bit hoarse.

"This seems more like seduction to me." My voice had a whiskey quality, too.

"Oh yes," he murmured, easing himself to lie down to face me, mirroring my pose, but still not too close. "Flirtation is seduction with clothes on, sex without sex, back and forth. You are ravishingly seductive, Lady Gwynn."

"You just want me for my eggs," I teased.

"I plan to enjoy much more than that on my way to them."

"Why me?" I asked softly. Just as I'd asked the Black Dog.

"Never question a man's desires, Gwynn. Especially when he's flirting with you." He slipped the lily out of my hand and laid it between us, then lifted my fingers in his, rubbing his thumb over them lightly. "I should never have agreed to no lips."

"It's not your fault," I offered generously. "You were outwitted."

"Is that what happened?" He stared at me, burning blue. Then laid my hand back on the flower and leaned over to trace my cheek. Then down my throat, following the path of the lily. I held my breath as he stroked over the upper curves of my bosom. "Much can be done with one hand, Gwynn." His sensitive fingertips trailed over the cotton of my dress, circling my breast. A breath shuddered out of me and I closed my eyes. "Watch, Gwynn," he whispered, "see how you want me, too."

His fingers, pale against my dress, gracefully swirled over my breast. Ever smaller circles, until they brushed over the painfully hard point of my nipple. I nearly convulsed in response, a sharp cry escaping my lips. I started to pull back, but his fingers closed on my nipple through the fabric.

"Resisting, Gwynn? Will you deny me what you granted?"

"Oh, please…" I whimpered, but held myself still.

"What do you plead for?" he asked, massaging the nipple with his clever fingertips.

My head spun thick and sweet. My elbow seemed to collapse and I laid my head down. I couldn't form a response. I did want him. To my great peril.

Rogue released my nipple to resume his circling, moving to include the other breast now offered up as I lay back. I gazed blurrily at the night sky through the open flaps above, until his face moved over mine. Propped on his elbow still, he watched me, seeming to drink me in. Jet-black hair, glinting navy and rose from the pillows, fell around his face, shadowing it. A few long locks fell across the hand lying by my side. I surreptitiously wound them around my fingers, clutching at the silk of them. It reminded me not to reach up and wrap my arms around him.

I was pushing my breast into his hand now, fighting the overwhelming urge to spread my legs just a little. It had to be hardwired into women's brains—enough arousal and we wanted to open right up. *Nothing like making it easy for them.*

"I'm not having sex with you," I gritted out.

"Did I ask?" He sounded amused. He also never stopped teasing my breast. "Though if you wish to cry off the bargain, I'd be happy to oblige you."

I was going to explode, but I didn't think I could actually climax this way. Only endless buildup. My vision reddened and I clutched at the pillows beneath me. I should have taken my chances with fighting him off. Allowing this was unbearable.

"I can't take any more."

"Oh, I think you can. We've only just started, lovely

Gwynn." He breathed along my cheek, not quite touching his lips to me. "Do you wish to cry off?"

I moaned in despair.

"Is that a yes?" Rogue watched me, the lines of his face seeming to oscillate in the light. Maybe that was my own frantic pulse, pounding through the fragile vessels of my retinas.

"No," I gasped, then whimpered when he increased the pressure on one breast, the pleasure keen as pain. I realized it was my left breast, Falcon's bite marks throbbing anew under the stimulus, the pain flaring up. "You're hurting me, Rogue."

He frowned but lightened his touch. "Why? That shouldn't hurt."

I tried to sit up, but he held me still, searching my eyes. I looked away uncomfortably.

"Tell me Gwynn. Now."

I felt a nudging against my thoughts, so I gave him the image of Falcon bending over me, his razor teeth sinking into me. Vastly easier than describing it.

"He took a taste of you?" Rogue's voice was eerily calm, devoid of emotion. He ran his hand lightly over my breast. "Let me see."

I sat up, clasping the fabric to my chest. "Absolutely not."

"Think of me as a healer—I need to see if it's okay." Something glinted in his eyes, however. Anything I uncovered would fall under the "exposed areas portion" of our agreement. I didn't want to find out how I'd respond to him touching my bare flesh, if the fabric-muffled version had been so intense.

"No, it's healing fine. I can tell that much."

He studied me for a moment, then sighed, resigned.

That was too easy. He looked too relaxed, too at ease. He radiated satisfaction, not the frustration of a man denied. It appeared Falcon's trick had at least gotten me out of this snare, but Rogue had something else up his sleeve.

"It's late and you need to sleep. We can continue tomorrow." He gathered his hair into the tail again. "Take your bath and get your dress washed—the dragon blood is a little much."

I watched him, trying to crank my thinking back into gear. "Tomorrow? What's tomorrow?"

"Why, my lovely Gwynn—more flirting!" Rogue gave me a wicked smile and lightly tugged on my hair where it spilled over one shoulder.

"Wait…" Geez, I seriously needed to clear my head. Rogue looked suspiciously alert and unaffected by our little tryst. "More flirting? I didn't agree to more than tonight."

"In point of fact—" Rogue stood and held up a professorial finger, "—you did not place a time limit on the bargain. You said, and I quote, 'we can flirt all you want after you deal with Darling.' It's still after."

I stared at him, trying to assemble a coherent argument. I could not go through this all day, every day. I knew myself. I'd cave eventually. An image of myself begging him to take me, promising all sorts of things, asking for that green silk binding, crossed my mind. Like a dose of cold water, it hit me. Here I was, hurtling toward another slavery.

"But," he allowed in a generous tone of voice, "I'm willing to settle for the standard night and a day. At sunset tomorrow you may return to denying and sniping at me with the bargain fulfilled."

I pulled my knees up to my chest under the skirt, wrapping my arms around them. He looked entirely too pleased with himself.

"I might have a battle tomorrow."

"No." Rogue shook his head, pulling his boots on. "Falcon and I will be meeting. He can pursue his war later."

"Don't forget your flower." I nodded at the lily still lying next to me, beguiling me with its scent.

A slight frown creased Rogue's brow. "It is a gift for you—I'm hopeful you won't destroy this one so willfully."

"I've learned to be wary of gifts. And this is no magic chamber pot. Is this one also a spying device?"

"If you're with me, lovely Gwynn, why would I need to spy on you?"

"I'll be with you?"

"After tomorrow," he said, with great confidence, even smugness. "Falcon will have no choice but to cede possession to me early, after this stunt."

"The stasis spell in the necklace?"

"Oh yes, that, too. But he broke the rules by damaging you, foolish Gwynn." He smiled at me fondly. "Also he failed to safeguard you during battle today. You were nearly killed, so I'm entitled to safeguard my investment." His smile faded.

"What if I don't wish to cede possession of myself to you?" I asked in a steady voice, trying to keep the pissed-off out of it. He hadn't called me on not-flirting, yet. In fact, he seemed like the cat that ate the canary.

Rogue dropped down beside me, running his hand over my hair and down my bosom to toy with the nipple on my uninjured breast. I made myself hold still for it.

"Seductive Gwynn, you can't fight your nature. After a day of my...attentions, by tomorrow night you'll be begging me to take you." His eyelids lowered in intent pleasure as he massaged my breast and I leaned into his hand. "Once we have bedded one another, you will know what we can have. You will never want to leave me."

I believed it, too. He filled my head like the lily, sweet and bewitching. Bewitching indeed. An image of that dream bedchamber crossed my mind, the green sash lying on the bed.

"I won't lose myself to you," I whispered.

"What's to lose? This isn't much of a life. I'll keep you safe, lovely Gwynn," he promised. "Not even the passage of time will touch you."

I shuddered, and it wasn't sexual this time. The prospect of timeless imprisonment congealed in my belly with a chill. Despair filled me. A gilded cage was still a cage. No matter how appealing my jailer might be. A captive breeding program for exotic human sorceresses. Was that why he wanted the baby I would possibly have?

He was right that I would cave. The physical longing to have him inside me, possessing and filling me, washed over the caution. I needed something else to keep him from that moment when I would collapse and let him in.

Then I caught an idea, glimpsed a path through.

"There's just one thing." I opened my eyes and smiled dreamily at him. The cat with cream on his lips indeed. "I think you were right the first time. Our bargain did not have a time limitation. It would be unfair of me to require you to end it after only a night and a day. We should stick to our original agreement."

Rogue stilled. Then anger began to filter through his eyes, amber sparking in the lapis.

I smiled sweetly and pressed my breast more firmly into his hand. "Outside the clothes, one hand, no body parts…forever. You might be able to make me go with you, but, crafty Rogue, however do you plan to impregnate me?"

I watched, fascinated, as the eyes iced over, cold fury creeping through them.

"You will cry off eventually," he said, his tone steel. "You are a sexual creature—you cannot resist the demands of your body for long."

I shook my head at him, kept shaking it, slow and measured. "I am also a creature of the mind and will, Rogue. If not before, then the training I went through saw to that. If it means my freedom from sexual slavery and my maybe-child from some unknown, possibly horrific, fate? That gives me plenty of incentive to resist."

I hoped.

But he must have read the truth of it in my eyes, because he stood again, gazing down at me with aristocratic disdain.

"I saved your life," he got out. "You owe me."

"Oh yes, you certainly did." I smiled, careful to look flirtatious. "But how is it my fault that you agreed to a bargain that supersedes the previous one?" That was a gambit—I wasn't sure which took precedence, chronological order or immediacy. But it seemed he wasn't going to argue that point.

"Don't set yourself up to battle me, Gwynn. You can't win."

"I'll settle for not losing, frankly."

"You'll stay here, surrounded by enemies, out of childish fear of the pleasure I can give you?"

"The pleasure you offer comes with a hell of a lot of strings, Rogue. Chains even. I haven't heard you deny it yet."

He drew himself together, holding still, but his fingers flexed rhythmically at his sides. I admired the long lines of him. At least I didn't have to fake the interest.

"You won't be able to resist me for long."

"I guess we'll find out, won't we?"

"If you don't get yourself killed. Or worse." He gestured to my breast.

"I can take care of myself."

"Oh, yes," he sneered, "you've been doing a fabulous job of that so far. You can't even protect your own Familiar."

I felt myself blanch. "That was a low blow, Rogue." An accurate one. "But cloistering me in your fortress like some kind of Rapunzel fuck-toy is not what I consider a fantastic solution."

Rogue folded his arms while color suffused his skin, angry blood filling in around the black lines. "You have a filthy mouth."

"I told you from the beginning that I'm no lady. You were just in denial."

"I know who you are, Gwynn."

"Then why do you get my name wrong?"

He raised the eyebrow on the clear side of his face, but otherwise did not move. He appeared to be restraining himself from throttling me.

"I know who you are, far better than you know who I am," he murmured. "Be careful not to underestimate me, Gwynhwyvar."

I stood, bringing the gorgeous lily with me. I tucked it into the fold of his arms, then let my hand, one hand only, trail down his leanly muscled arm, dropping to his hip. Found the hard upthrust line of him under the velvet with my fingertips and rubbed lightly. Not so impassive after all. His eyes flared.

I raised my eyebrows at him. "Likewise. Pleasant dreams, lover."

And he disappeared. Right out from under my hand.

"Poof!" I said to the thin air. "Figured you could do that."

I stared at the spot where he'd been, telling myself I'd done the right thing. That I wasn't even the tiniest bit disappointed.

TWENTY-THREE

Détente and Circumstances

I AWOKE ALONE the next morning, having slept myself out. Last night's threats to the "staff" to leave me undisturbed clearly had been effective. The morning had advanced along, bright sun shining in my open skylights. My body felt sluggish, blood pooled in all the wrong places.

Darling hadn't returned, and both lilies had poofed along with Rogue last night. I wanted to take a bath, but I was too nervous that Rogue might reappear. I tried to distract myself with plans for wishing up something decent to get drunk on—whiskey, Chardonnay, *something*.

Shockingly enough, trying to remember the chemical structure of alcohol didn't do much for distraction from emotional turmoil.

As it was, I had lain in the dark while my mind raced. When I finally slept, it was one of those sleeps where you kept thinking you were still awake. Except that I was running around saving kittens from dragons, plucking them out of goo and trying to clear the stuff from their pink noses while they cried piteously.

No need to psychoanalyze that one.

Rogue hadn't shown up yet to renew his assaults. Surprising, given the lateness of the morning. I'd even worn something to sleep in, which normally annoyed the hell out of me, just in case he did show. Couldn't afford to have accessible skin around him. Though with the stakes this high, perhaps I could resist.

God, I hoped I could resist. I really did not want to find out what would become of me—and my maybe-baby—if I didn't.

Hauling myself up, I stopped on the way to my clothing trunks to examine myself in the mirror. Dark circles shadowed under my eyes. I looked exhausted, the white cotton nightgown barely whiter than my pale skin. And I felt depressed. I had come far too close to getting Darling killed. White was the color of mourning in the Orient. I should start wearing white all the time. Better than black, that was for sure. Rogue needed no advantages.

"Regrets?" I asked myself.

"No," I answered myself. "The price is too high and you know it."

We both nodded, knowing it to be true.

I brushed out my hair. Wished some shine into it and added a bit of makeup. Time-tested female armor for bolstering oneself for a tough day ahead.

Then, casting a look around the tent once more for unexpected visitors—maybe I could make some kind of Rogue-keep-out spell? Now there was an idea—I unbuttoned the neckline of my nightgown and let it fall to my waist, so I could check on Falcon's bite mark in the bright light of day. Rogue's apparent concern—feigned or not—over the matter had me worried.

I felt like the breast-exam woman, standing in front of the mirror, hands on hips, studying the relative shape and size of my two breasts. Red dimples circled the aureole on the left side, but they didn't look inflamed. The left breast looked as round and smooth as the other—no sign of necrosis, no red streaking of blood poisoning. The freshly brushed black strands of my hair streamed down, curving slightly, dark contrast to my white skin and icing-pink nipples. I could be the witch queen from any number of tales. The thought heartened me considerably. Better the villainess than the victim any day. *Don't try to stick me in a glass coffin!*

"No wonder Falcon wanted a taste."

I squealed in a most unpowerful, very damsel-in-distress kind of way. I even clamped my arms over my breasts to hide my charms like any silly movie maiden.

"God*dammit*, Rogue! You can't just appear in my private tent any damn time you please."

He grinned easily at me, butt propped against the workbench, in his customary relaxed pose. "But, I *can,* ravishing Gwynn—see?" He gestured to himself and the tent.

"We'll see about that," I muttered.

I turned my back to him and, careful to face away from the mirror, slid my arms back into the nightgown's sleeves and buttoned it up to the high neckline, silently thanking Starling and Blackbird for the modest sleepwear. Then I pulled a deep green velvety robe from the trunk and added it for good measure, though the late morning was a bit warm for it. Why Rogue hadn't taken immediate advantage of my nudity, I didn't know, but I wasn't taking further chances.

"I see you're back to your usual fine fettle this morning."

Rogue shrugged, all nonchalance, but something dark shadowed beneath it. "I brought you a present."

"Is it a hollow wooden horse?"

"I don't believe you requested one of those." With a

flourish, he gestured to an enameled chamber pot sitting on my workbench.

I must confess I squealed a little. Maybe skipped a bit over to the bench and ran my hands over the rather gorgeous pot, shining brass and gold, with blue lilies all over. Of course. I lifted the lid and peered inside. It gleamed empty brass. I wanted to poke my finger in, find out if the metal felt the same from the inside.

"I wouldn't do that. And don't drop anything you like in it."

"So I've been warned." I contemplated Rogue, who looked decidedly irritated under the glib facade. The black lines on the sinister side of his face seemed darker this morning, and perhaps sharper. "And what's the price tag on this?"

"It's a gift, Gwynn, since you don't like my flowers."

"I don't like the strings on your flowers," I specified. Then added, to be perfectly clear: "Or on any gifts. Where are the strings on this?"

He sighed, brows forking down. I got the distinct impression that had he been a man of my world, he would have said "yada yada yada." Instead, he said, "Titania give me patience."

"The price?" I persisted.

"Not everything has a price, Gwynn."

"You know, my experiences thus far in your world indicate otherwise."

"Then give me something in return."

"Aha. This is the part I was concerned about."

"Alas."

Too bad I hadn't rummaged through the tribute tent yet. I glanced around, looking for something I could give him, something of equivalent value. He watched me in amusement, a lock of shining hair falling over his shoulder. Blue glinted in the black with the morning light.

"A kiss?" he suggested.

Here we go. "Not a good idea—and a deal-breaker, recall?"

"A one-time exemption, no hands, lips only." His eyes darkened and he tucked his hands ostentatiously behind his back. "Come give me a kiss, Gwynn."

I studied him uncertainly. "Our agreement stands? This momentary exemption in no way alters any other standing bargains?"

"Agreed."

"And in return for this one kiss, lips only, no hands, this one time, I get to keep this magical chamber pot, which will be wholly mine and not connected to you in any way."

"Agreed. Come give me a kiss, Gwynn."

"I can't help but think this has to be a bad idea."

Rogue simply regarded me steadily. His lips, the sweet Val Kilmer curve of them, drew my eye. It didn't help that I wanted to kiss him. And the irony didn't escape me that I had turned out to be the sort of woman seduced not by flowers but by convenient hygiene—along with an opportunity to study how he did the spell stabilization. But kisses—weren't they magically potent? I flipped through stories in my head. Sleeping Beauty's kiss, Snow White's kiss. Judas's kiss. Awakenings, pledges, betrayals.

"One kiss, as a thank-you. It means nothing else?"

"It might mean little to you, Gwynn," he replied softly, not moving.

"What might it mean to you?" I jumped on the point.

But he only smiled, a slow curve of those enticing lips. "You have your parameters, Gwynn. A kiss, another gift of similar value. Or," he added with a raised eyebrow, "you can owe me."

"I don't see how one lousy kiss has much value anyway," I muttered.

"There you are then. Something you can easily part with. And it would go a long ways toward being flirtatious. Come give me a kiss, Gwynn."

Even with his hands behind his back, Rogue looked dangerous. Tempting dark candy. Unable to shake the feeling this was a bad idea, but unable to intellectually pin it down to anything, I finally put my hesitation to fear of my own weaknesses. I stepped up to Rogue, who watched me gravely. His long legs crossed at the ankle made it difficult for me to get close enough—would I have to straddle him? No way.

I stepped in from the side, to reach him from that angle, but with a flash of his predatory grin, Rogue drew up his legs and opened them wide, so that I had no choice but to move between them. As I inched up enough to get close enough to kiss, I realized that, even with him partially sitting on the bench, I couldn't match his height without leaning on him.

"You'll have to lean forward," I said, "for me to reach you with lips only."

He obligingly angled toward me, his tail of hair sliding back over his shoulder as he moved. I felt awkward, with my hands fluttering in the air, no place to ground, so I finally folded them behind my back, too, and raised on my toes to place my lips on his.

Seductive and sweet, the soft steely heat of him moved through me. Sandalwood and Stargazers swirled in my head, and I kissed him longer than I'd meant to, angling my head to savor him better. He responded with a deep hum and opened to me, drinking me in, as he had before. During our other kiss, when my hands had also been behind my back, but chained there.

The memory brought up the flooding arousal and despair of that moment.

I broke away, stepping back with an abruptness that elicited a soft snarl from him, black lines spiking around his eye with a certain savagery.

"Let me have you, Gwynn," he demanded.

I took another step back.

"No." I tensed to run, because he seemed as if he might launch himself at me, but then he coiled the tension into himself.

"Don't you have servants? The little faerie with the ridiculous wings?" Rogue was suddenly the insouciant courtier. "Refreshments would be appreciated."

I struggled to catch up. "Um, what would you like?"

"Just some wine. Some food."

Trying to move sedately, I walked over to unlayer the tent flaps and poke my head out. Larch stood sentry and Dragonfly crouched morosely at his feet.

"My lady sorceress!" She sprang up, knocking Larch in the side of the head with one stiff wing. He rolled his eyes in disgust. "How may I serve you?"

"Could we get a refreshment tray, wine, fruit, stuff like that?"

"Immediately, lady." Dragonfly pranced off happily.

"Larch, your...liege is inside—you want to come in, get instructions maybe?"

He cocked his head, looked up at me from the corner of his eye. "I serve you, my lady." Then returned his gaze to scanning the rows of tents.

Yeah, right. But I let him be.

"Okay, breakfast, brunch, whatever, is on its way," I said as I came back in, to find Rogue pacing. A sign we were back to business then. "So where do you and I stand now? I'm losing track." The kiss still hovered in the air, a tangible cord between us. I almost felt I could close my eyes and track the ripple of it.

"Falcon and I have arrived at an understanding."

"Which is?"

"Boring. Politics are so dreary, don't you think?" As he paced, he kicked a few pillows out of the way, which flickered into light as they flew.

"I think they get more interesting when your life and freedom hang on the decisions," I said in a dry tone.

"Which you wouldn't have to worry about if you'd just quit being stubborn and let me take care of you."

"Oh yeah! And the price for *that* would be, what? Only the loss of everything I am? And everything my maybe-baby might be? Slavery in exchange for sex and security. I don't think so."

"Apparently your training did not make you any more biddable."

"What?" Cold betrayal bottomed out my stomach. Some part of me had held out hope, apparently, that he hadn't really known what they would do. "That's what you wanted? This is truly what you want from me?"

"Given up on flirting with me, have you?"

I gritted my teeth, not only because he was right. "This situation is untenable."

He closed the distance between us, close enough that I had to tilt my head back to look into his face.

"Yes. Yes it is, obstinate Gwynn," he whispered, frustration contorting his face. "And you have brought us to it as surely as I have."

"Then you admit…"

"Enough." He held one finger to my lips, lightly pressing them. I squelched the impulse to kiss it. Which only roiled me up further. How could I want so much and feel so repelled at the same time?

Dragonfly came capering in and I took the opportunity to walk away, supposedly to supervise her activities. For her part, Dragonfly made no effort to pretend she wasn't enthralled by Rogue.

"Esteemed Lord Rogue," she breathed, "you honor us with your presence."

Rogue cocked an eyebrow at me, as if to point out the difference in our behaviors. Then turned his back to me to survey the blonde fairy. "Wine, lovely little girl," he told her.

She poured some and walked on dancing feet to him, curls bouncing, head cocked coyly. She presented him the goblet from a deep curtsey, head bowed. When he took it from her, she shivered. I grabbed an apple-like fruit and bit in, trying not to roll my eyes.

Dragonfly remained folded at Rogue's feet, a tumble of gilded pink against the stark black lines of him.

"Is there anything else I can do for you, esteemed lord? Anything at all?" she breathed, looking up at him, her mouth conveniently close to his groin.

Rogue glanced at me, direct blue smolder. *Ah. A new game commences.* Oh no, I wouldn't bite on this one.

"Hey, *mi casa es su casa,* apparently. If you want to molest the help, who am I to naysay you?"

Rogue thoughtfully fingered the midnight velvet at

his waist while he sipped his wine, as if contemplating opening what passed for his fly. Dragonfly trembled in anticipation, visibly heating under his intense regard.

"I do find myself in need of relief. Something you are unwilling to give me," he murmured.

"I thought that was Nasty Tinker Bell's job," I shot back.

He looked momentarily puzzled, then laughed. "No, Lady Incandescence serves me in other ways, nothing so pleasurable for her."

"Are you so sure it would be?"

His face sharpened, gaze pinning me. "You have no idea what I'm offering you."

"I do," Dragonfly chimed in and he caressed her curls.

"Well, then," I said in a bright voice, "I'll just leave you two alone then, shall I?"

"You don't want to watch?" Rogue sipped from his wine, watching me over the rim, even as Dragonfly reached up with her delicate fingers to undo the fabric covering that hard ridge I'd touched last night.

"Golly, gee whiz, what a neat idea, but no—I'll pass." I turned around and looked for some shoes. I was tempted to call Dragonfly to find them, but that would be petty.

"You do realize, darling Gwynn, that if you continue your games, I can always go elsewhere. Where will you go?"

"There are other men." I scrambled around in my wardrobe. *God, not the heels right now.*

"If you conceive by another man—and you would, given what Healer has done for you—you would be in violation of our agreement."

"So noted." I found my shoes, laid them out with one hand and stepped into them, still holding my apple in the other, juices running down my arm. Then I paused. "No, wait. This is *my* tent. You two can go elsewhere."

"I am…otherwise occupied at the moment."

His voice was a taunt to make me look, but I refused to turn around. I bit again into the fruit, crunching loudly so I couldn't hear any potential…noises. The image in my head was vivid enough. Dark blood suffusing his face with pleasure, the tension riding his body. And I had to admit, if only to myself, that I burned with curiosity—and not a little prurience—to see what his organ looked like. I'd only ever seen circumcised men in the flesh and I doubted that the covenant of Abraham had made it here. For all I knew, Rogue had a forked penis, being the snake he was. I was pissed enough to deliberately leak the thought.

Rogue chuckled, then groaned in pleasure, leaking back an image to me of Dragonfly's adorable upturned face. Unable to stand it, I stormed out of the tent, nearly bowling Larch over. For once, I was glad of the training—the torments they dreamed up if I allowed anything magical to manifest to defend myself. I could feel that cool barrier even now, between the anger—*not* hurt—and the manifestation.

I would control myself.

No matter how much I wanted to be not just the witch-queen but also the black and purple dragon on the cliff, calling lightning strikes down.

TWENTY-FOUR

In Which I'm Shown a Thing or Two

I STRODE FAST, strong, out of that dammed camp, ignoring the startled and titillated looks thrown my way. I headed toward the waterfall I'd seen when we rode in, toward green, which had always been my refuge. Not like me—the former me—not to wander out to see the natural.

Of course, I wasn't that person anymore, was I? In some ways I still crouched in my little cell. Not really free at all. Trapped by my own fears.

Larch trotted at my heels and I wheeled around and hissed at him to go away. He watched me impassively.

"Go take your master a hanky or something!"

"It's not safe for my lady to be alone out of camp."

"Don't worry—i'm thinking lightning strikes at anything that moves at the moment, including annoying little Brownies."

Larch considered me for a moment. "I'm surprised you let him manipulate you like this."

I huffed, at a loss. Hurled the apple at nothing in particular, then turned and continued walking. Larch followed. I was tempted to give him a little shock, just to jolt him out of his confidence, but I didn't want to risk really hurting him. Maybe I'd practice on Dragonfly.

Larch had a point though. Rogue was deliberately

pushing my buttons, which I saw coming a mile off and still walked right into.

And I couldn't escape the parallel, that here I was, storming off to take a walk around rocks and trees, all because I couldn't face some guy again. Though the deadly dark image of Rogue leaning against my bench, dangerous velvet framed by jewel-tone pillows and hot morning light while that pink-and-gold faerie…tended to him was wildly removed from Clive spouting convenient statistics to his cronies.

Finding a secluded spot under a tree, with a lovely view of the falls, I plopped myself down, wiping the sticky juice off my hand on the lush grass.

"Please go away," I begged Larch. He looked dubious. "If Rogue leaves and I'm still here later, you can sign me up for karate lessons or whatever, okay? For now, give me a knife or something."

"Do you even know how to use one?"

"What's to know? You stick the sharp pointy part into people you don't like, right?"

"Getting it into the proper position takes a bit more trouble than that." But I could tell he was amused.

"Look, I've used thousands of scalpels and I've cut up more chickens and veggies than that. Give me a knife and if someone gets close enough to me to hurt me, that'll be close enough to slice them up."

He didn't look happy but bowed gravely and handed me a gray-handled knife on open palms, like a ceremonial offering. I set it on the grass beside me and watched absently as he headed back the way we came. Wedging my back against the tree, I drew up my knees and hugged them, then laid a cheek on my knee, watching the bright splash of water.

I tried some calming breaths, but my heart still roiled.

I was losing track of my role in this game and needed to keep my eye on the prize. Get out of my bargain with Rogue—and Falcon, if possible—and get myself back home. Getting myself home would solve all of these problems. *Focus.*

In some ways, it would be so easy, so gratifying to just give in. Just eat the pomegranate seed— *aren't you hungry? So juicy and sweet...* Hades was both Persephone's captor and her husband, enemy and lover together. Perhaps the Greeks understood that message—two faces of the same coin. And then I would be as lost as Persephone, facing the winter of her heart.

"You missed the show."

I sighed and didn't look up. "Speak of the devil."

"Sulking?"

"Thinking."

"Well, get up—I want to show you one more thing."

I turned my head and squinted up at Rogue, the high sun outlining him in cerulean. He held one long-fingered hand down to me, to help me up. The way he was silhouetted, I couldn't tell if he was still hard or not, if it had been a trick or real. I hadn't been sitting there all that long. But then, how long did it take? Not long, in my experience.

I decided it didn't matter and I needed to keep compliant with our bargain. I gave him my hand and let him haul me to my feet. His fingers caressed the sensitive skin under my wrist. I clamped down on my shivering response. At least I was wearing more than I had been last night, even if they were technically nightclothes.

"Now what?" I asked. "What's your new battle strategy?" That would decide mine. For the moment. Then I'd develop a long-term plan. "I should warn you that last trick didn't advance your cause."

"That all depends on what my cause is, doesn't it?"

"You know, you could just explain…"

"Spread your legs."

I gaped at him. Closed my mouth. Pursed my lips.

"No," I said slowly. "I don't think so."

Irritation crossed his face, maybe had never left it since he appeared in my tent this morning.

"One hand, over the clothes, you allow it or the bargain is moot. Don't make me warn you again, Gwynn. The consequences for oath-breakers are not ones you should take lightly. Even I cannot protect you from that." Rogue leaned in, crowding me against the tree without touching me, beyond the rhythmic stroking fingers on my wrist. His touch on my skin sent whispers of longing into me. Intensifying as he caressed my palm. Then he interlaced his fingers with mine.

"Gwynn," he whispered, "let me touch you. You have before. Flirt with me, keep to your bargain."

Nervous, I tried to look for witnesses, but I couldn't see around Rogue's tall figure. He had his hair pulled back, cheekbones stark under the gold skin and snaking black pattern. Tears pricked the backs of my eyes. Of course, I could just give in now. Go with him and have a bed and tender kisses in privacy to soften the edges.

No. That was pet-Gwynn talking. Give in. Just do what they want. So much easier to be numb and lap up the crumbs of pleasure any of them cared to toss me. *They have all the power,* Larch's words echoed in my head.

Oh no, they did not. Not while I had breath left in my body.

I nodded and triumph lit his eyes. *Sure, Rogue—underestimate me again. Please.*

Rogue lifted my hand—for a moment I thought he'd kiss it, but he restrained himself—then raised it above my head and gently guided my fingers around the tree branch over my head.

"You might want to hold on with both hands." He set his own right hand next to mine on the branch, fingers so long they wrapped nearly all the way around while mine made it barely halfway—and I had fingers long enough to easily reach an octave stretch on the piano. "Spread your legs," he reminded me, voice husky, eyes midnight dark.

I decided to go ahead and hold on to the limb with both hands. And inched my feet apart.

A sudden smile flashed across his face. He stroked my cheek with one long finger. "Wider, Gwynn."

I looked away. He traced down my jaw, fingers and thumb bracketing my throat, where I was sure he could feel my pulse pounding. Oddly, it soothed me to feel his touch there, not unlike my own habit of feeling for the absence of the silver collar.

"Open for me just a little more, precious Gwynhwyvar," he crooned. "White shadow, white ghost, pale shade of things to come." The bark was gritty and real under my hands, but otherwise I hung suspended in his voice, caught in the blaze of his eyes.

I spread my legs for him.

His croon dropped into a wordless hum, hand dropping down over the green velvet, lingering briefly over the rise of my breasts, then smoothing over the curve of my waist and hip. I nearly lost my nerve and had to fight not to close my legs. So vulnerable, standing open like that. *You can take this. You've withstood far worse.*

As his hand traced down the outside of my thigh, and then inevitably back up the tender inner thigh, I dropped my eyes, thoroughly unable to bear the intensity of it. Rogue leaned in, so I could feel his hot breath on my cheek. Cinnamon and mace.

"If you can't take any more, just give me the word," he whispered. "At any time, just tell me that you'll give yourself to me. That's all it takes."

Like hell, I thought. I opened my mouth to tell Rogue that he could go straight there…and lost all my breath in a convulsive rush when he slipped his hand up.

He cupped my mound firmly, pressing the soft cloth against me. My head fell back and I shuddered, staring at my white fingers digging into the bark, trying to slow my heart and regain my breath. I knew he was watching me and I wished fervently for a way to hide. I turned my face into the folds of the full sleeve of the robe, where it gathered around my shoulder, my forearms rising like pale flower stems, a fragile tether to the branch above.

"I can still see you." The low hum of his voice filled me. "You cannot hide your ardor from me, passionate Gwynn."

I hung there, suspended between the branch and his hand, refusing to look. Concentrating everything on keeping still, not squirming, not writhing. I focused on keeping my breath deep and even, no moaning allowed. All I had to do was not move. Deep, even breaths. *Think of something else.*

Rogue's crooning to me became a low song that seemed to penetrate my blood. Another variation on the faerie singing. I tried to block it out the way I had before, but it seemed to seep through my pores, a distant thunder resonating in my bones. And, for some reason, it didn't bother me in the same way. Instead it felt…alluring. The heat in my groin grew, and Rogue's hand—long fingers cupping me, penetrating hot, nearly bearing my weight—became the center of the vibration, streaking into the swollen tissues like heat lightning. My whole body clenched and my shocked gaze flew up to find his only a breath away. His eyes were molten blue, chromium on boil.

I nearly convulsed again as the hot oscillation filled me. I tried to be still, to absorb it, bleed the building tension away.

Breathe it out.

But then another rill of sensation would rock me. Building in unbearable pressure. Climbing so that I was going to orgasm, right here, back against a tree, the bright light of day burning on my face while he watched.

"Please…" I gasped.

"You know how to stop it." His voice resonant, lips seductive. "Give in to me, my Gwynn. Come with me and leave this horrible place." His words hummed in my blood, hypnotic. So help me, I wanted to say yes.

I longed to fasten myself to his lips, throw myself around him and give in, open, yield. Giving way would be easier.

So much easier.

Another wrenching wave of pleasure racked me, bringing a keening cry. Rogue was driving me up, beyond where I could deny my own release. His long fingers burned into me as if delving into my deepest parts, wrenching the climax from me, dragging it into the bright light of day for him to devour. His face, so close to mine, shone with avid hunger, the obsidian pattern pulsing.

The lines gathered, filling my vision, as darkness rushed in from the edges of my retinas. Black filled with pounding red, spiked with bright stars of wildly flashing neurons.

Everything in me engorged with blood, filled to bursting.

I screamed when the blood dam broke.

Screamed out to the sky all my frustration and exaltation and rage.

I rode Rogue's hand like a plunging horse, careening through the pulsing waves of his magic. The words were on my lips, ready to tumble out.

Yes, I wanted to scream. Yes, take me, do whatever you wish with me.

It terrified me. *Never again!*

So I seized the emotion. Seized it, tore down the cool barrier and threw that impulse, that final surge of yielding so profound that the self was immolated, into the vast sky.

And it roared back down on us, a lightning bolt sundering the tree.

TWENTY-FIVE

In Which I Learn a Thing or Two

AT LEAST, SO I was told.

The thing about being hit by lightning—even one's own—was that the enormous electrical surge scrambled the nervous system. Senses, thinking processes, organs—everything connected to that nervous system—got hard-booted in the most wrenching way possible. So all you really got of the experience was how you felt afterward.

If you survived.

Rogue regained consciousness first—which only confirmed my suspicions that he had nerves made of steel, or at least some sort of aluminum alloy. Immortality was an enviable thing.

I awoke to find him crouched over me on all fours, holding my hand wrapped in his so that our wrists spiraled around each other, just over my heart. His face loomed over mine as he breathed into my face. For a confused moment, I thought the Black Dog had me pinned, but my blurred vision resolved and Rogue's gorgeous face appeared.

My heart thundering in a beat too rapid to feel possible, I gasped for breath. Every rib protested the movement. This had to be how a hummingbird felt, just before its heart exploded from stress.

Rogue squeezed my hand hard, drawing me back from the precipice.

Oh yeah, don't imagine your own heart exploding, dammit. I calmed myself, shrugging the well of nothing around me. His hair was singed and still vaguely smoking. He blew steady breath between my lips—even now only touching me with one hand and no lips, I noticed with wry humor. His breath streamed into me like mountain run-off. Like the oxygen-saturated chunks of glacier dropping into the ocean in Alaska, effervescent as Alka-Seltzer, releasing primordial air back into the world, fresh, clean, powerful and ancient.

I drank it in and my heart slowed. My ribs moved. My lungs drew air.

At last Rogue sat back, drawing me to a sitting position as he did so. Then he released me, drew up his knees and, echoing my earlier position, wrapped his long arms around them, steadily studying me.

I didn't know what to say.

Apparently he didn't either.

I watched Rogue, waiting for an acid comment, but he only gazed back, weary and faded.

I felt curiously depleted, so I tried standing and, though my legs were shaky, managed to get to my feet and turn to look at the tree. Rogue had either dragged me or we'd been thrown about fifteen feet away. The tree was neatly cleaved in half, limbs draped over the ground as though a drunken debutante passed out in her own voluminous skirts.

I turned back to Rogue, who still sat, eyes unfocused. He seemed to be concentrating on something. Holding something tightly inside. It made me uneasy. I looked at the tree again.

"In the stories," I said, "of places like this—there are dryads, spirits who live in the trees."

He nodded.

"Was there one here?"

He shrugged.

I began to wonder if he'd lost his voice. It occurred to me to ask if he was okay, but that seemed foolish, because what could I do? And I thought about asking if the cat got his tongue, but I wasn't feeling flip enough. Maybe his nerves were less steely than I thought.

At a loss, I paced over to the tree, across the carpet of shredded leaves. The soft toe of my shoe clunked against something and I looked down to see one end of the gray-handled knife poking out, still lying where I left it. But when I picked it up, I saw that the blade had warped, the sharp edge running in rivulets like tears. Not a promising sign. I tossed it away again. I'd get Larch another.

A deep hole split the middle of the tree and I tried to peer in. Sharp splinters arrayed the edges, but deep shadows pooled inside. I thought I could make out something pale.

I stretched an arm down and hissed as a splinter dug into my triceps. Standing on tiptoes, I tried again but couldn't reach. I looked around for Rogue, who still sat, facing mostly away, as if in a trance.

"Rogue!"

He didn't move. I walked over to him, laid a hand on his shoulder. He seemed to warm a bit to my touch and slowly tilted his head to look up at me.

"Lord Rogue," I said gently, "would you help me?"

I held my hand down to him, acutely aware of the role reversal. He raised one eyebrow, an arc of wry comment in the fanged lines around it, and stood in one uncoiling movement. I snatched my hand back and tucked it behind my back, like a child startled by the sudden springing of a jack-in-the-box.

His full lips curled at one corner, but the smile lacked his usual insouciant curve. He slipped past me and strode to the tree, reached in with one long arm and withdrew a pale, fleshy mass that just overflowed the one hand he held it in. Rogue turned back to me and, for a moment, I thought he might toss it to me and I panicked a bit in my heart.

"Now what, my powerful lady sorceress?" he asked.

The silky disdain gave me pause, but I eased up to him to peer at what he held. Up close I couldn't make any more sense of it than I had from ten feet away. It was flesh-like, a healthy-seeming pink color. But featureless, kind of ovoid.

"I'm out of my depth here."

"Oh," he drawled, "do you really think so?"

I sighed. "I apologize for the lightning. I won't even mention that you drove me to it. So to speak," I had to add.

He tilted his head to the side like a raptor changing sight lines to get better depth perception.

"I may have erred," he said softly, "in not killing you after the bird incident."

"You mean, not letting me die," I corrected.

Rogue didn't comment—he simply held out the object to me, clearly intending me to take it. Well, yes, I'd asked him to get it. So I took it with the ginger care I would an infant, wrapping it in the tattered remains of my robe and gown. A little bigger than a football, it seemed to be living flesh but undifferentiated.

"This...is the dryad?"

"What remains."

"Does she—it—live?"

"If the tree lives, she lives. And the reverse. Heal the tree, you heal her."

I turned to face the tree, holding my bundle of grief against my bosom. "I can do that."

"Can you?"

I glanced at Rogue, who'd folded his arms. His face was remote, still.

"Yes, I can fix a tree—especially when it's just putting it back together."

He waved a gracious hand at the tree, inviting me to proceed. I focused my thoughts, imagined the xylem and phloem running with sap, the tree whole and mighty as it had been, connected it to my desire to see it right again, and...nothing.

No spark. Nada.

I pretended to be still working at it, unwilling to see the smug vindication on Rogue's face. I tried to look as though I was concentrating, while I madly scrambled within myself for some hint of the well of magic that had coursed through me ever since I first woke up on that grassy hill. Maybe even, as Larch had suggested, before that.

Rogue, shockingly enough, was not fooled by my dissembling. He reached over and tipped up my chin with one elegant finger and shook his head at me. Then he slipped the fleshy bundle from my arms and returned her to the tree, settling her deep inside again. He turned back to me and suddenly the tree behind him was whole and full again.

Rogue swooped a shredded leaf from the ground and presented it to me with a bow.

Then turned and walked away.

Part V
Preliminary Conclusions

TWENTY-SIX

The Blood of the Dragon

I SANK TO the ground and sat there for a long time, holding that leaf.

Twirling it in my fingers, watching the uneven spin of it, the singed and torn bits fluttering as it spun. Utterly depleted, I stayed long enough for the afternoon to give way to the long shadows of twilight. The forked shadows reminded me of the black patterns on Rogue's face.

Apparently I had won. At least for the moment, Rogue was leaving me alone. No more teasing. No more seduction. No more trying to move up the timetable for my impregnation.

And here I sat in my nightgown and dressing robe, hollowed out and empty, bereft of even the magic that was the first gift I received here. Funny that I hadn't thought of it as a gift before. So cliché of me, not to appreciate it until it was gone.

I steeled myself against the staining of regret. This was what I'd wanted. By the time Rogue thought to try again, I'd be long gone. I didn't need magic to get home. I hadn't been a sorceress when I came here, so it followed I didn't need to be one to get back. If I was well and truly fried, then perhaps I could persuade Falcon that I no longer held any use for him.

I walked back to my tent. After all, where else did I have to go? Not to mention promises to keep. Plans to make.

Our camp spread out before me in the valley in all its colorful eccentricity. The usual music and tumbling glittered here and there. Falcon's mini-village sat on a hill across the way, silks fluttering gaily in the slight breeze.

My tent was dark and empty. Neither Larch nor Dragonfly was in evidence and all the pillows were out. Still no sign of Darling. I sent an inquiring thought at him and got sulky cat grumpiness back. I slapped a few pillows into life and desperately wished the tub would just be full of hot water, though if the magic was gone… but there, suddenly the tub was full of steaming water.

"Thank you, magic," I whispered in the quiet of the tent, as another wave of exhaustion washed over me. It began to make sense to me. When I was full of sexual energy, I had plenty for magic. But fully releasing it, as Rogue had driven me to do, pushing me so high, so far, and then the way I'd emptied myself, both in orgasm and with the lighting… No wonder I'd had nothing left.

I scavenged the remains of the brunch tray Dragonfly had brought for Rogue, and guzzled from the pitcher of water. The decanter of too-sweet wine I took into the tub with me.

In the morning, I had a slight headache from too much wine but awoke with that peaceful feeling of sound rest and well-being. The way you felt waking up after a terrible fight with your boyfriend the night before, when at first you felt good and peaceful and you wondered why that was so surprising and then you remembered how awful you felt when you went to sleep and it all came flooding back, but somehow muted, less immediate and ferocious than it was before you slept.

Darling, curled up next to me, stretched and purred. I dug my fingers through his plush fur. He sent me contented thoughts.

"I'm sorry you got hurt," I whispered.

He licked my hand with a raspy tongue and sent an image of a disemboweled Falcon.

"Not a bad idea, if we can pull it off."

Feeling better, I found some clothes for the day and stripped off the tattered nightgown, dumping it on the pile of tattered robe I'd left the night before. I pulled on the new dress quickly, though Rogue likely would not put in another appearance—not this morning, nor any other, if I read him right. I brushed out my hair and tried some tentative deliberate magic to do my makeup— which worked just fine.

"Today is the first day of the rest of your very strange and twisted life," I told my reflection, attempting the jaunty tone I imagined people who practiced affirmations used. Darling, engaged in an intensive washing, snorted at me mentally.

I opened all the tent flaps, dumped out the dried remains of the food tray and neatly stacked the pillows into the corners. I even made my bed. My black dress still lay on the workbench where I'd left it after the molestation session with Rogue. The dragon blood gleamed an uncomfortable yellow. I needed to find a way to get that out. Either that or burn the dress, which I just couldn't face doing.

No Larch out front still. After wishing the water away to the foot of the dryad's tree, I dragged the brass tub out the back of the tent to dry in the sunshine. A little UV disinfection never hurt anything. Darling hopped up on the rim, balanced a moment on tiptoes, then plopped inside. Clearly he was much more cat than man. He flicked a tail tip at me in disdain.

And, since I was out there already, and determined not to spend any more days hiding in my tent, I marched myself over to the pillow factory.

There was Larch, his buddies and the girls, busily working and chirping away. Ants to my grasshopper. They all glanced up, surprise on their pixie or gnarled faces alike.

I didn't see Dragonfly.

"My lady." Larch bowed to me. "We thought you had left."

"Off with Rogue, you thought?" I asked archly.

He bowed again.

"No." I took a breath to say something more. Blew it out again.

"I'd like to see the tribute tent, Larch, and—seeing as how Rogue is gone and I'm still here—I'm keeping my word. You want to set me up for self-defense lessons for this afternoon?"

I wouldn't let myself think about how much *those* lessons would probably suck. Instead of gritty Hilary Swank, I'd be girly Sarah Jessica Parker—okay, size 8 to her size 2—facing an impossibly long and steely fae version of Clint Eastwood. But Rogue's accusation had hit home. I was not doing a good job of taking care of myself. Or the people dependent on me. That, at least, I could control. An idea hit me.

"I'd like to learn from other people like me—are some nearby?"

"Yes, my lady. I know of an excellent human fighting teacher."

Excellent—two birds with one stone.

"Where is Dragonfly?"

"We thought she'd gone with you, my lady."

Oh, I knew who she'd gone with all right.

"Well, may he have joy of her," I muttered. "And that reminds me—I kind of melted your knife. Maybe there's one in the tribute tent you could have to replace it?"

"Yes, my lady sorceress."

Gotta love a place where you could admit you melted a knife and no one blinked.

I followed Larch to another tent, this one with the sides all securely tied down. A couple of gnomey guys bobbed and bowed at me, nimble fingers undoing the knots on the tent flaps. They helpfully slapped some pillows into life, setting them in strategic spots so the dim interior was illuminated. Darling slunk through and immediately disappeared down a narrow aisle.

"Wow," I breathed. "All this from less than a week?"

The place was crammed full, items stacked in uncanny towers that defied gravity. Immediately by the door something that looked very like a Persian Empire hookah worked in brass and burgundy velvet teetered atop a pile of fabrics interspersed with carved wooden pieces and a bit of yellow poking out that I would have identified as a rubber ducky, if that weren't so completely out of context. And that was just the near tower.

I edged farther into the tent, careful not to upset any stacks. What appeared to be a copper fire pit lurked in the corner filled with jeweled pear-shaped objects.

"This is all in exchange for pillows?"

"Well, and tribute, of course, to curry favor with you."

That sounded promising. Surely I could use that somehow.

"Was my lady sorceress looking for anything in particular?"

"I need a basin. Can we empty the jeweled pears of that copper fire pit thing? And I need a blank book, if there is one."

"A book?"

"You know, pages inside a binder, something I can write notes on."

Larch cocked his head at me.

"Never mind. Maybe I can make one."

I dumped the hookah on the ground, ignoring Larch's wince, and tossed some fabric bundles onto a statue of a unicorn. I grabbed the carved wooden box now on top and the—yes, it really was a yellow rubber ducky—fell, bouncing off my foot. Darling shot out of the shadows and pounced on it, batting it across the ground.

"I'm not even going to contemplate that one," I muttered to myself.

Larch retrieved the duck, earning a displeased look from Darling, and reverently added it to the pile of jeweled pears he was making, by way of emptying the copper fire pit. I opened the box. Nothing inside.

"Any reason I can't monkey with this?" I asked him. Larch frowned up at me. "Empty wooden box?" I demonstrated, shaking it upside down.

"Well, does it look valuable to you?" He pointed in disdain.

"No, but neither does the rubber ducky, other than as evidence that I'm experiencing a psychotic break rather than an honest-to-goodness trip to fairyland." I paused under his solemn gaze. "Which, when I say it out loud like that, just makes me realize there's no point in worrying which one it is. This box will work then."

I needed ink, too. Or something to put ink in. I examined a cloisonné bowl that I might be able to fill with water that could be magicked into ink.

"How about something like a quill?" I caught Larch's bewildered look. "Something to dip in ink to make pretty designs with?" Larch looked dubious, but handed me a handful of paintbrushes he dug out from behind a pile of furry things.

Darling swatted the yellow rubber ducky out of the bowl and batted it soccer-ball style to my feet. Obligingly, I added it to my pile of things. Yep—looked, felt and even smelled like a regular rubber duck. Maybe Darling had a point. If the ducky had traveled from my world to this, it might contain a clue toward reversing the path.

By the time Larch and some of his fellows carried in the copper fire pit, I had started my notes, the rubber ducky sitting on the workbench next to me, Darling curled up sound asleep with one paw on it.

I'd managed to change the box into a blank book and filled my bowl with water turned to ink. The book still looked largely like a box, as I'd kept the wooden sides intact all around. It gave it a satisfying grimoire look. I even contrived to create the pages with a thick parchmenty feel. It wasn't the graph-paper-filled lab book my high school chemistry teacher taught me to use, and which I'd used for lab notes until I switched to a computer, but I found I liked the feel of the vast blankness of the page.

The first page I titled Dr. Jennifer McGee's Big Book of Fairyland. It made me smile to see it.

Knowledge is power. And this would be my first step. Perhaps through the process of cataloguing all my observations, I could begin to make sense of this world. And find a way out of it.

A little judicious wishing got the tip of the brush hardened sufficiently for reasonably neat printing, though the bristles didn't hold ink as well as I'd like. I labeled several pages with headers such as Rules of Magic, Rules of Bargaining, Faerie Species Identified, The Black Dog, Flora and Fauna, Objects with Magical Properties, etc. I left generous pages between headers, expecting to fill them all eventually. I devoted an entire section to Rogue, though I was perversely tempted to make him a sub header under Flora and Fauna. If I could have ensured he'd see it, I would have done it, too, if only to take his ego down a notch.

No dwelling on Rogue.

I flipped to Rules of Magic, made a subsection for Sex & Magic, and began writing out what had happened at the dryad's tree. Larch and the guys brought in the copper fire pit, plopping it where the bathtub had stood.

"Right here, please." I gestured to a spot I'd cleared next to the bench. Larch gave a sigh of the long-suffering and they heaved it over to my chosen location.

"Thank you, boys," I said with an effort at charm. The other Brownies blushed and smiled, but Larch frowned at me suspiciously.

"What task are you engaged in, my lady?" he asked.

"Oh, this and that, puttering about." I flipped to the title page, reflexively keeping my ruminations private.

His eyes fell on the book.

"What is this?" He peered at it, then touched the page gently with a stubby fingertip. He reminded me of Isabel poking at her cat food with a testing paw, as if dubious that it wouldn't bite back.

"I'm making notes—organizing my thoughts."

He looked puzzled.

"You know, writing things down?"

He shook his head, as if shooing away gnats. "I've never heard of such a thing, my lady."

"Books? Writing?"

Larch continued to shake his head. He looked suspicious, even superstitious. "No, Lady Gwynn, this is a powerful magic beyond my ken."

Interesting.

"And so it is," I agreed. "Please make sure that no one disturbs my…grimoire," I said with great satisfaction. "Am I signed up for self-defense?"

"Arranged. I shall escort you."

"Never mind." I waved my hand. "Fetch me when the time comes."

I thoughtfully chewed the end of my paintbrush. No written language. This world seemed suddenly more empty without the prospect of books. At least I could be uninhibited in what I wrote, now that I knew no one but me would ever read it.

I flipped to the back page of the book and labeled the top To Do List.

1.

And stared at it for a while.

When overwhelmed, just make a list, my mother always said. If you have to, start with the things you already accomplished and cross them out.

1. *Figure out a way to keep Rogue from impregnating me.*
2. *Get dragon blood out of dress (find use for dragon blood?)*
3. *Find out about humans in this world*
4. *Study the tie between sex & magic*
5. *Deal with Falcon*
6. *Get home—Rubber Ducky? Black Dog?*

It would be ironic if, like the shoes on my feet, the creature that had dogged me along would turn out to be my way home. Crosser of boundaries. The Black Dog was the only being, besides me, I'd seen in both worlds. I really wondered who the rubber duck tribute came from.

Several of the girls brought me lunch, along with a couple of buckets of waterfall water. I put down my pen and set to filling the copper basin of the gleaming fire pit with water.

Time to get after my list.

I retrieved the Ann Taylor dress, which smelled of some kind of musty sweet patchouli. Setting the dress into the water to soak, I sat cross-legged on the floor and munched on cheese and chicken-type things. I had thought about lighting a fire under the basin. In Mary Stewart's books, Merlin said that creating flame was the first of his gifts to come and the last to go. As much as I had admired Merlin and wanted to be like him, I hadn't even tried the creating-flame trick. Not even during sadism boot camp—though that was because my trainers had never asked that particular thing of me.

As I still felt uneasy about fire in the tents, I promised myself I'd try some fire-starting later. Hell, if I

could pull lightning—though I still wasn't exactly sure
how I'd done it—I could certainly create a little flame.

But for now I concentrated on the water gradually
warming up, while I poked at the dress occasionally
with my finger, to sink the puffy parts under the water.
When the water was hot, but not boiling, I added a bit
of swirling, while I focused on the dragon blood leaving
the dress and entering the water. Which didn't work—I
could actually feel the null resistance of it. The classic
immovable object.

So instead I thought about the dress pulling away,
leaving the blood behind, and, yes, that sang right. The
dress spun around the basin, black embroidery catching the light here and there. My own little washing ma-
chine, if I cared to do it this way. Which I didn't. This
was more about organic chemistry than housekeeping,
though I'd always been struck by the similarities.

I finally lifted the dress out manually. It would have
been neat to raise it magically, but I wanted to be sure
not to mess this up. I did wish a hook into the tent post
next to the basin and hung the dripping dress on it, so
that the liquid fell back into the basin. Then I carefully
poured fresh water over the dress, rinsing it clean.

Three rinses in distilled water to clean glassware for
sterilization, three steps for magic in the stories—coincidence? I didn't think so.

I wrung the dress out one last time and took it out
back, draping it over the bathtub to dry in the sun.
Concentrating on the basin of water again, I warmed
it up enough to simmer gently but not boil. Who knew
at what temperature dragon blood denatured? I'd need
better equipment than this to find out. Better to treat
this like a wine sauce—just enough heat to reduce, not

enough to evaporate the best parts of the alcohol. Eesh, what if there were valuable volatiles I'd be losing to the air, or worse, nasty toxins swirling about to poison us all? Couldn't have that.

I grabbed my ink bowl and dumped out the fluid. I could always make more. On a scrap piece of paper, I sketched my orgo lab distillation apparatus as best I remembered it, keeping it very simple. Fewer things to screw up. Focusing carefully on the design, I transformed the erstwhile ink bottle into a glass funnel that fitted to the top of the basin, complete with cooling chamber and output hose to another bottle.

Resisting a mad scientist cackle, I set the distillation into motion.

TWENTY-SEVEN

The Sun, the Moon and a Man

BY THE TIME Larch came to fetch me for my self-defense lesson, I'd eaten and made several useful entries in my grimoire. I was really beginning to long for some kind of database capability so I could more easily revisit and cross-reference, but alas for that.

The camp seemed bright with activity, a bit more purposeful than usual. Excited dancing about accompanied Larch's broadcast of my name, with various greetings thrown my way and, in one case, manic juggling of what looked to be at least nine flashing pillows. Darling trotted along with us, tail held high and proud. He regally acknowledged the shouts of good wishes. No one seemed all that surprised to find him alive again.

Of course, likely all sorts of conflated tales of the miracle circulated.

We walked for a ways, around Falcon's grassy hill, down across the stream, and then over a ridge on the far side. I drew in a surprised breath at the vista below— a whole other camp lay before me. A camp of people like me. I wanted to wander the tent alleys below, saying "Hi! Human are you? Me too!"

Larch had started down the hill and looked back at me with a politely servile but still pointed, waiting expression. Eager to see more, I trotted after him, soaking in the familiarity of sights and sounds. To my disappointment, Larch led me around the outskirts of the camp. I found, though, that I could easily pick up the human thoughts, like the scent of cooking on the breeze.

I could smell the battle from a few days ago, the sweat and blood in their memories. The grinding pain of the gravely wounded, the triumph and resolution of the more successful. More than anything though, the air eddied with resigned boredom—the scent of active men waiting. In places the mental babble became a thick soup and I understood why Rogue had been so annoyed with my loud thoughts that first day.

Besides being an intolerant megalomaniac, anyway.

At the end of a long row of tents lay an area pounded into the soil, the grass trampled flat and worn thin in places. Racks of weapons stood to one side, canvas draping shrugged along the ground ready to be pulled over them in case of rain. A tall man with bronze curls and a weathered face waited there, looking in our direction, then squinted at the position of the sun.

"I thought we agreed on three hours past midday, Larch!" he called out as we approached.

Larch titled his head to the side and shrugged. I caught the man's irritation layering over a desire to kick the Brownie. Oh yes, it felt good to be around my own kind.

"I understand time," I said. "From now on you and I can agree on a meeting and I can make sure to get here at the right time."

He measured me up and down, his expression carefully polite and formal, but I caught the warm buzz of masculine appreciation. Darling pranced over to circle him.

"Can you now, Lady Sorceress? Not many of our kind end up working the magic with the fae folk."

"None," Larch said.

"Call me Gwynn." Funny how I didn't even hesitate over the name anymore. Maybe it helped keep the scientist and the sorceress separate in my mind. "I appreciate you agreeing to teach me something about keeping my head attached."

"Officer Liam." He bowed to me. "I don't know anything about magic, but I can show you a thing or two to keep you on your feet long enough to shoot off some fireworks." He grinned at me.

I blushed at the thought that passed through his mind and wondered if I should warn him that I could quite clearly get what he was thinking he'd like to do to me. The sensual electricity fed into me though, refilling that well. More study on the connection between sex and magic would be a good thing, so I said nothing. Besides, I had questions for Officer Liam.

"Larch." I turned to him. "Thank you for bringing me." I tried to think of a polite way to get him to leave. "Larch, don't you have somewhere to be?"

He frowned at me.

I glanced at Liam. "I'm going to be here, what, an hour?"

Liam squinted at the sun again. "Aye, an hour. Get here an hour earlier tomorrow and we can make it about two. You look pretty soft, in a most attractive way—but I doubt you can take much more than that, to begin with. But we'll whip you into shape." That sunny grin again.

Be still, my heart.

"The Lady Sorceress…" Larch began, his voice

sinking into the stentorian tones that cleaved through crowds."

"Larch, it's fine. Go do something and come back… later."

Larch bowed, nearly breaking in half with it, then stalked off.

"He's not going far," I speculated.

"They never do, Lady Sorceress," Liam agreed. Darling wound between his feet and he looked bemused. "You brought your kitty with you?"

I opened my mouth, paused, shrugged. "What can I say? He follows me everywhere."

Darling flashed me an irritated swat and I crouched down to scratch his ears. "Who's a good puddy tat— hmm? Who's my precious kitty?"

He narrowed his eyes, puffed up his tail and stalked away, picturing me running myself through with my own sword. Not unlikely.

"Let's pick you out a weapon."

I followed him over to the weapons rack. "Have you been in the military all your life? Were you born here?"

Liam paused and glanced at me over his shoulder. "The village I was born in lies about twenty days' ride to the north, and I became a soldier as a young man, yes. Why do you ask?"

"I come from—farther away. I don't know much about the people here."

He shrugged, turning back to survey the weapons. "There's not much to know. We're people like any other, I suppose."

"Not like mine."

Liam smiled at me. "I'd love to hear all about your

people, but this isn't teaching you to keep your head attached."

He pulled out a pair of glittering metal wheels as big as—no, including the spikes, bigger than—my head. I stepped back. He held them up thoughtfully, measuring against me with one eye squinched, and nodded in satisfaction. He set those down and grabbed a staff longer than my arm.

"Why not just a simple little knife?" I squeaked.

"Simple question, easy answer." He pulled out a wooden practice dagger and handed it to me. "Okay, stick me with it. Anywhere that looks like a good spot."

I took a step forward, careful not to step on my skirt, and sliced at his throat. Before I got the knife there, his hand was clamped on my wrist, stopping me cold, which was no surprise. "Now look down, Lady Gwynn."

I looked to see that he had another wooden dagger pressed just below my sternum, poised to strike upward.

"See?" he said. "You have to get too close to a man to do any damage. Most everyone is going to have a longer reach than you do—any man would have you stalemated at best and gutted at worst before you got your blade near him. You want something that gives you an advantage." He tapped the wrist he held meaningfully.

"I could learn to throw it."

"Yes, but then you've thrown away your weapon."

"Oh."

"Keep that practice dagger, though. Knives can be good for desperation maneuvers—when you're already in close and got nothing left. We'll teach you a few. Keep one under your skirt." Liam's tone was all respect but, oh, the ideas in his head. I screened them out so I could concentrate.

"Now these beauties…" He seized the metal disks. "These make it real damn hard for even a much larger man to get near you."

I took the wheels by the leather-wrapped handles, taken aback by their dense weight that pulled on my shoulder sockets. The polished metal shone blindingly. A sharpened crescent inside protected the back of my hand, while the outer curve of the disk sported blades radiating outward at regular intervals. Liam showed me how every surface was sharp—no matter how I poked or sliced, these would keep an attacker far away, and could I cast spells while I was moving? I should work on that, he told me sternly.

I tried an initial swipe with the disk. And immediately caught it in my clothes, slicing a big rip in my skirt and just missing my own thigh. Liam, who had jumped back, stepped nimbly in and removed the weapons from my hands.

"That, Lady Sorceress, is why we start you out with a stick. We'll work with the sun-and-moon wheels down the road."

Liam taught me how to swing the short staff in simple figure-eight patterns that created a shield across the front of my body. He showed me how to place my feet for the best strength and balance. And laughed when I managed to clonk myself in the head with the stick.

Liam looked bemused. "It's probably a good thing you can do magic—you're not much of a fighter."

"I've always been a klutz," I muttered. "And this is my first time."

"Your people don't learn to fight?"

"Some do. Most don't."

"You mean, all of the men, but just some of the

women?" He nodded to himself. "I've heard of villages like that."

"No, some of our men don't either. Are there women soldiers? I haven't seen any." I cast my mind over the camp, but it felt solidly male.

Liam studied me. "No, our women stay home to defend the villages, since all the men must go to war."

"Why do you do it? Fight in these fae wars? There's no purpose to them except to entertain the nobles."

A look of infinite sorrow crossed his face, like cloud swooping over the sun. "Your people must indeed be far away, for you to ask a question like that."

"Yes." I almost said more, thought better of it. "So, why?"

"Surely you understand that they have all the advantages over us—physical strength, magic, numbers." He ticked the points off on his calloused fingers. "Besides, we have many vows constraining us."

"What's the deal with oath-keeping anyway? What happens to someone who breaks a bargain?"

"I hope you never find out, Lady Sorceress." A horrific image dashed across his thoughts, but he suppressed it. Not so I couldn't see, but because he couldn't bear it. "Now let's focus on what's at hand. Try the figure-eight again."

"I'll probably just klonk myself."

"Aren't you glad that wasn't a sharp-edged blade then?" He grinned, back to his sunny self. "Run it again."

Larch found me tired, sweaty and bruised in several places by the time he returned. The stick was lighter than the sun-and-moon wheels, but not by much, and my shoulder cried with relief when I set it down. Liam slid my wheels into a leather carrier and handed them to me, along with my stick.

"I thought I'd just leave them here? Rather than dragging everything back and forth?"

"No, Lady Gwynn." Liam winked at me. "Keep your weapons with you. Get used to having them around, at your fingertips like your magic wand. Beside your bed, under your pillow."

I didn't tell him I didn't have a magic wand. Though it would be cool.

He turned back to straightening the weapons rack after telling me to meet the next day, if there wasn't a battle. I felt his eyes, and thoughts, on me as I walked away. His desire fed and filled me.

Uneasily, I wondered what I was becoming.

TWENTY-EIGHT

In Which I Receive an Unexpected Guest

LARCH AND I walked in companionable silence back to the tent. I felt pleasantly tired out. Maybe some healthy exercise was what I really needed. Wash that man out of my hair and all that. Nothing like being around a healthy, red-blooded human man to make a girl feel better in her skin. And to fill up her well of magic.

"I shall return later, to escort you to dinner, my lady sorceress," Larch told me on parting.

"What? What dinner?"

"With General Falcon. He requests your presence at dinner."

Great, another mad war tea party.

"Okay," I sighed. "I'll get ready."

I dragged the tub back into the tent, happily filling it with steaming water with a thought. At least the magic had come back. Who I would be here without it didn't bear considering.

Pulling off the dress, I examined the now raggedly torn and dirty hem. I'd stepped on it more than once.

Cocktail length for war then.

Grimacing at my rapidly stiffening muscles, I climbed into the tub, sighing as the heat penetrated the soreness. I let my head rest against the high back of the tub.

"We're living in a *tent?*"

I started out of my skin, water sloshing onto the floor. "Jesus, Starling! What the hell are you doing here?"

Starling twirled in place, skirts spinning out, blond locks shining. "I've arrived!"

"So I see."

"They diverted me here just as soon as we heard, and here I am! No, no, don't get out of the tub. Gracious, where are your servants? The page out front told me to come in, but not that you'd been abandoned without serving girls. Are you being punished?" Starling's hands flew to her mouth in dismay. "You didn't accidentally turn them into butterflies or something, did you?"

"What? No! There was Dragonfly, but she's gone and I'm fine without servants. Now what are you doing?"

Starling had carelessly tossed her cape onto my workbench, tapped the rubber ducky on the head with a cooed "How cute!" and swooped down behind me.

"Washing your hair for you. And super-neat pillows! Now dunk to wet your hair."

"I'm still soaking."

"No, you're not. Your page said you have dinner with the general. You have to get ready."

Resigned, I dunked. Starling immediately started in on my hair with Blackbird's nutty shampoos. The scent made me smile, remembering that day she'd washed my hair in my tower room at Rogue's. "Who diverted you from where, once you heard what?"

"Lord Rogue. He'd already sent for me to meet you at his castle, to help you settle in, when he sent word that you were staying here and needed me."

"So you were on your way to Castle Mistiness to

meet me? I thought you had to reach your majority before you could…come serve me."

"Dispensation," she sang out. "Oh, and you didn't notice!" Starling pranced into view, tossing her hair like a young starlet.

I wiped the soap out of my eyes. "I did so notice. Blond and beautiful."

"I know!" She nearly squealed it. "It's *so* sticking. Your advice was perfect."

"Well, it's only been, what, a week now?" So much had happened. I dunked again, rinsing my hair, and climbed out. Starling met me with a drying cloth and started to rub me down. "Starling, you don't need to do this."

She stopped. Stared with glistening dark eyes. "You won't let me serve you?"

This again.

"No. I mean, yes. Stay. Love having you here." I wrapped myself in the cloth and sat at the vanity, taking up my comb.

She sagged in exaggerated relief. "Oh good. We'll have the best time."

"You talked to Rogue then?" I tried to sound casual as I combed out the tangles in my hair. Starling slipped the comb from my fingers and took over the task. I sat back and enjoyed the sensation. There was something wonderful about being tended to.

"Mmm," Starling hummed a noncommittal answer, her thoughts very blank.

"What does that mean?"

"My lady sorceress," Larch intoned from the doorway, "Lord Falcon awaits you."

"I'm hurrying."

Starling selected a gown for me—a lovely gold one with a soft Marilyn Monroe bodice. Even though I protested that it was too much, she insisted that I needed to look my best and just to put it on already.

"Why are all your dresses in the trunk still?" Starling complained. "Why haven't your servant girls gotten you a wardrobe and hung these up?"

"I can just wish the wrinkles out—don't fret."

A quick look in the mirror showed that the gently gathered bodice flattered me. I wished it to the right length along with a bit of wrinkle-removal. But now the black pumps were just too low-heeled for the dress. I looked clunky, dammit. And the outfit needed jewelry. Mine had been in the purse I left behind at Devils Tower. Left behind with the other relics of who I used to be.

I had too many weird feelings about jewelry now, to think about wishing up any, but with a judicious thought, I grew my heels, picturing the sleek, stiletto look I wanted. Maybe I didn't have gazelle-like legs, but I could hold my head up high.

"You shortened your dress? It's really not appropriate for a lady…"

"Starling—I am just so not a lady, you can't even imagine."

"Yes, but the others…"

"Call me eccentric, whatever, I don't care. Tell them it's not proper in my land for dresses to be long."

"Like your sorceress's robes." Starling was peering at my now-dry dress that I'd tossed on the workbench. "What did you do to it? And what *is* that stuff?"

I peered with her at the dragon blood distillate. The liquid was clear, with a silver sheen that reminded me

of mercury. I took a moment to disconnect my distillate flask and seal over the top with a wish—better than
any stopper, that. I set the flask on my workbench, carefully back in a corner where it couldn't be knocked off.

"Dragon's blood. Or a refined version of it. Kind of
cool, huh?"

Starling looked at me dubiously.

"I'll ask Larch to get the guys to drag the dragon
blood equipment outside." We probably didn't need it
in the tent overnight. I'd clean up the bowls, etc., tomorrow morning.

"I can do that."

"Aren't you coming to dinner?"

"Oh, no, Lady Sorceress. That is not my place. I
wouldn't be welcome. Besides, there's lots to do here."
She wrinkled up her nose.

"Gwynn."

"I beg your pardon?"

"You call me Gwynn or I won't let you stay."

Starling opened her mouth to protest but I jumped in.

"I mean it. I can only take so much in one day. Don't
you do it to me, too."

"Yes… Gwynn. I'll see that this is all picked up."

"Thanks, Starling—but don't let anyone touch the
vial or the residue in the basin. I need to make sure
they're not poisonous or anything."

Maybe I needed a workshop tent of my own, too,
if I planned on messing with anything else that would
prove an unpleasant sleeping companion. And Starling
would probably be living here, too, now.

I sighed for my short-lived privacy.

"My lady sorceress," Larch said, yet again.

"What? Will he expire from hunger?"

"Lord Falcon…"

"Okay, okay. I'm ready."

But I paused at the doorway, while Larch huffed with impatience.

"Starling?"

She smiled questioningly at me.

"I'm really glad you're here." I waved a hand loftily at Larch. "Proceed, James," I declared with a posh accent, and grinned when Starling rolled her eyes behind his back.

TWENTY-NINE

My Dinner with Falcon

THE SHORT TREK across camp was becoming familiar. Homelike, in an odd way. It felt good, too, to walk on seriously high heels again. A certain confidence came from that, from the gliding hip-swaying steps those heels required. I was glad now, that Starling got me to dress up. Armor came in many forms.

I had a pretty good idea how I wanted to play this meeting. And, no, it did not involve agreeing to him having all the power.

A group of giggling pages of indeterminate sex danced around me for a moment singing an ethereally high-pitched song, presented me with a flower and scampered off. In the varied light of the moon, campfires and flickering pillows, it reminded me of a rose. Smelled like a rose, too. I spun it in my fingertips as I followed Larch's proclamations of my progress, and felt nothing more than flower in it. Green plant energy.

Sometimes a flower was just a flower, I supposed.

"Lady Gwynn." Falcon swept a bow to me when I entered his tent.

"Falcon." I nodded at him.

He raised an eyebrow on the clear side of his face. "Are you my superior, then, to neglect my title?"

"I'm not all that interested in titles," I answered with

a careless air, tossing my rose down onto the small square dinner table. Intimate and set for two, with the place settings on two adjoining sides, rather than across from each other. "Is this a date?"

"You refused Rogue's offer. I assumed you had come to certain…decisions." Falcon wore buff leather tonight, which clung to the long sinewy lines of him, the color one eerie shade lighter than his eyes.

"Did you now?" I flicked a glance at Larch, who stared steadily out the tent flaps, undoubtedly watching for marauding barbarians. Then I slid out the chair at my chosen place-setting and sat, crossing my legs, gathering my thoughts.

Falcon sat in the other chair, brushing my foot as he slid past. He filled my crystal goblet from a carafe, then filled his own. He held his goblet up, the faceted lines of it reflecting bloodred in the candlelight. "To us."

"Happy days," I answered with my grandmother's traditional toast, lifting my own sanguine goblet and clinking it lightly to his. I waited for him to sip first before I tasted mine, and grimaced at it. Even sweeter than the white stuff. It didn't seem possible. And I'd thought the Manischewitz wine at my college roommate's Passover dinner was bad.

I leaned back in my chair, bringing my wineglass with me, and toyed with the rose lying by my plate, admiring its creamy warmth against the dark red cloth of Falcon's table. I thought back to my first dinner here and the bargains I'd made that night.

"So, do you have a proposal for me?"

"You already belong to me. I'm willing to take you in, now that Rogue has discarded you."

"Take me in?" I raised my eyebrows. Falcon leaned

in, running his fingers down the inside of my wrist, his fingers long like Rogue's but the nails a hard and pointed aged-ivory. The wine in my glass shivered with my trepidation.

"I don't mind the filthy source of your power." Falcon chuckled. "We can play games, you and I, that will keep you fully charged for battle. I know how to keep a woman like you on edge without draining the magic away."

"I don't believe my agreement with Rogue is void at this point," I said with care. I sipped from my glass so I could slip out of Falcon's touch. "What about his baby?"

Falcon waved a negligent hand. "You can pleasure me, pet, without danger of impregnation. And if Rogue survives until then, he can still claim you at the appointed time. As if that will save him."

"Save him?"

"You were wise to refuse him." Falcon laid his hand on my knee, inching the hem of my dress up a bit higher. "Even now the Black Dog escapes his control. The odds are against him surviving until your contract is up with me. You'll be far better off as my pet than his."

I studied the flaring triumph in Falcon's yellow eyes. "You know, where I come from, sometimes people try to make pets of the wrong animals. They bring home a bobcat kitten or a part-wolf pup. At first everything is fine. Then they grow up and things change. One day, without warning, their cute little tamed pet is a vicious, savage beast."

I held his eyes a moment, then shrugged and lifted my wine again and sat back, uncrossing my legs and recrossing them the other direction, again shaking off that clawed touch.

"Sadly, it often takes a serious injury or even death to open their eyes to the fact that Mittens the kitten is a wild and dangerous beast, with all the deadly power a true predator possesses."

"Do you have a point, Lady Gwynn?" Falcon asked. I was pleased to see him drain his wine and refill the glass from the carafe.

"I thought you might enjoy debating the difference between a pet and a wild animal that is caged——" I touched my fingertips to my throat, "——and what happens when it is no longer restrained."

Falcon seized my wrist, yanking me so the wine in my glass sloshed over the faceted rim, spilling down my arm in bloody rivulets. His pointed nails, nearly talons, dug in, drawing my own dark blood to the surface to join the mix. "Have a care, pet. Restraint can be immediately arranged."

"I'm sick of your threats, Falcon," I whispered, a sweet smile curving my lips. "I've endured more pain than this—thanks for that, by the way—and dealt with department chairs more malicious than you. With more power."

I hurled a brief and pointed desire his way, connecting it to all that dull rage I'd accumulated over the years, from every totalitarian senior professor, every smug condescension from Clive, each of Falcon's maneuvers to cow me. With a shriek, Falcon yanked his hand away as if burned, clutching his hand to his chest.

Burned he was. The hand that had touched me sizzled charcoal, visibly smoking. The smell of cooked flesh filled the air.

It turned my stomach. Too much like that poor dead page—should have thought of that. But I clamped down on my own horror. Sometimes power lay in seeming not to care. No weeping during major magical power struggles.

I sat back in my chair, poured myself some wine. At least the cough-syrupy scent of it was thick enough to screen the smell of burning fae.

Falcon was shrieking for his servants. His pages bustled around him, slathering his arm with something, then wrapping it in silk. I stood, idly wandering the tent while they worked, keeping one ear on Falcon's thoughts. Startled birds wheeling through the sky.

One strawberry-smoothie-pink fellow trotted up to me and offered a cloth and bowl of water to clean my arm. I thanked him but declined. The wound helped focus my thoughts. I raised my arm, watching the dark crimson drops well up and ooze down my arm in slow spirals. The wine might have been going to my head, but the sound of Falcon's whimpers, my strength in the face of his crushed swagger, gave me a dizzying sense of power.

I strolled over to watch the first-aid efforts, enjoying Falcon's cringe as I stood over him.

"You know, they always say that wild animals are more afraid of you than you are of them. And that may be true. But when people get attacked? That's because the animal decides it has no choice but to fight. When destruction seems imminent from every direction, there is no disadvantage to giving every drop of life to the hope of survival, or at least mutual destruction."

"I told Puck, that idiot, that you weren't trained," Falcon hissed, kicking one of the pages away.

"Not mindless, anyway."

"I can still summon Marquise and Scourge to re-collar you. In slavery to silver you'll find yourself less cocky, human monster."

I put down my wineglass. "Try it. Just know this— I'll fight. With everything I have. To the death, rather than go back to that. Which means I'll take as much as I can with me—and you're first in line, Birdboy."

"You would be an oathbreaker!"

I looked around the lavish tent in mock surprise. "You know, I keep hearing about the dire consequences of breaking bargains, but I'm not seeing it."

"You are a fool," Falcon hissed.

"It seems to me," I continued, "that you and I need to come to some agreements. To set the flavor of our future working relationship. I'll serve out my time with you, but I decide what magic I do and how. You tell me what you want accomplished and I'll decide how to do it. And this—" I gestured to the table. "No more of this. I'm no one's pet. Not Rogue's. Not yours."

"Agreed, Lady Gwynn." Falcon began unwinding the silk from his arm. The silk slipped apart, sliding easily, no blood or gore caking it together. "Do your magic as you see fit—I'm not interested to interfere."

A buff golden color showed through the folds of the silk bandage, banded with browns and blacks, a hint of cream. Falcon stood, shaking the last of the wrapping away, flaring the wing his arm had become, feathers snapping to with a whoosh like a parachute grabbing wind. The candles on the table flickered and went out in the sudden draft.

My wounded arm suddenly throbbed in sympathy.

Falcon's eyes had lost their pupils, gone to the clear cadmium yellow of the raptor. "As long as battle goes my way. Consider me duly cautious of awaking the beast within you."

His face lengthened, sharpened beaklike, his voice growing oddly strident.

"But, Lady Gwynn, exercise caution yourself." His clothing morphed into feathers. "See that you keep your word in the next battle, or you will have failed to serve me. Then you will see what it means to break your oath to the fae."

With a clap of air rushing into a vacuum, he collapsed into a small falcon shape, then disappeared.

THIRTY

In Which a Goddess Puts In an Unpleasant Appearance

THE NEXT DAY, Starling started organizing me.

She made it easy for me, I must confess. Her mother's daughter, Starling brought a polished level of organization to the carnival atmosphere of the war camp. At least, to our little corner of it. She marshaled the Brownie forces to set her up a tent next to mine, seeming to know without me telling her how much I valued my privacy. She set up a little area for Darling, too, with a place for him to keep the souvenirs he picked up around camp.

And I found myself following Starling's schedule without her telling me.

She even arranged for regular meals, with actual nourishing food rather than the endless supply of pastries and fruit Dragonfly had provided. Pillow-making was proceeding apace. Everybody seemed cheerfully occupied.

Even those of us sublimating our emotions into work. I should have been pleased with my little victory over Falcon, but his closing warning had left me uneasy. I'd been very careful to follow the letter of my agreements with Rogue, but admittedly not much more than that. However, he was not my friend or my lover, but my enemy. How that all fell into my personal code of ethics, I wasn't at all sure.

Then Starling had to bring up Dragonfly.

"It's a good thing you dismissed her," Starling said.

She had acquired a standing wardrobe for me and was hanging up dresses the Brownies had laundered. I hated to bother them about it, but Starling had just shaken her head at me. "You have to give them work to do or they wither away." The images in her head showed me she meant that literally.

"I didn't, actually," I replied from my workbench. "She took off with Rogue."

"With Lord Rogue?"

"At least, so I believe."

"She did not!"

"The circumstantial evidence is pretty compelling."

"Tell me."

"There's nothing to tell." I tried to concentrate on the spell I was working up for the upcoming battle. I didn't want to be winging it this time. Dancing along the line Falcon drew would make it interesting.

"Then it won't take long." Starling plopped her butt down next to my grimoire, like a kid waiting for a fairytale story.

"Why is it that you're all 'whatever my lady wants' until you're bugging me about something?"

Starling grinned happily at me and wiggled her rear farther back. "Mother told me my primary responsibility is taking care of you, whatever that takes. What happened?"

My gut clenched, thinking about it. I rubbed my hands over my face and into my hair, massaging my scalp. "No, we are not having this conversation."

"Gwynn." Starling reached out and lightly touched my wrist, a glancing touch and retreat. "Trust me. Maybe I can help you."

It was on the tip of my tongue to tell her I didn't need help. The incident still burned bitterly in my heart. I found myself picking at it in my mind, replaying the images and waiting for them to hurt less. Remembering how I'd come for him like that. Wondering exactly what had happened. Why he left.

Was it the lightning?

And why the hell did I even care?

"Rogue was here…" Starling prompted.

"And he was mad at me."

Starling nodded, biting her lip with one pearly eye-tooth.

"Because I wouldn't…we had this deal where…" I stood up, started pacing. "Look, it's a long freaking story, Starling. Suffice to say that I chose not to put out and give in to whatever the hell his diabolical plan is, and Dragonfly stepped up to the plate, as it were."

Starling held up a pale hand, as if to halt my tirade, though I'd already finished.

"You're saying Dragonfly had intercourse with Lord Rogue?"

"I don't know. I left the tent."

"So you didn't see."

"Not exactly, but he made it clear what direction things were going. She was kneeling down, you know. All eager to…"

"Oh."

"Exactly."

"And then what?"

I sighed, rolling my shoulders. "Umm. I left, he came

after me a while later, we talked about some stuff out by the oak tree. He left for good, and when I got back to the tent, Dragonfly was a gone Johnson."

"I'm sorry." Starling said it quietly, her chocolate-brown eyes grave.

"No. Not at all. I refused his attentions so he was free to go elsewhere. That's how it works."

"No, I'm sorry to tell you this, but… I think Titania took her."

"Titania? As in a real person, or are you saying something like 'she returned to the arms of the Lord'?"

Starling cocked her head at me. I could almost see her thoughts swirling around her head. "Dragonfly agreed to serve you. You must have said it was okay for her to make that offer to Rogue?"

Yeah, I guess I had. Starling read it in my face.

"But you didn't really mean it—and it's not your fault, really, because how could you? You were feeling all hurt and stuff…"

"I wasn't…"

"But that's what happens with true love. There are misunderstandings, and lovers fight. So you were feeling all hurt and you said it was okay, but it wasn't, so Dragonfly—who was stupid, by the way, she should have known better—broke her agreement to you and now, well, Titania's got her."

I stared at Starling, flabbergasted. It took me a moment to get my breath back. "Okay. One, I am not in love with Rogue. You have no idea the kinds of things he's done—and tried to do—to me. Two, he certainly does not love me, and I'd be a fool to set myself up for that. And three, what the hell does that mean, 'Titania's got her'? The image I'm getting in my head is like some kind of…what my people think of as damnation."

Starling fiddled with the folds of her dress. "The consequences for oath-breaking can be dire."

I dropped my face into my hands, digging my fingers across my scalp. "Fabulous."

"Good morning, beautiful damsels!" Puck popped his tousled strawberry head through the tent flaps. "Anyone not decent—I hope?"

"You might have checked *before* you looked," I answered drily.

"No fun in that, is there!"

Starling had already slipped off the table, and Puck gallantly bowed over her hand, kissing it with an elaborate flourish.

"Lady Starling of Castle Brightness, you grow more ravishing with every sunrise, surpassing even the glow of your ancestral home."

I managed not to roll my eyes as Starling giggled at him.

"And Most Powerful Lady Sorceress!" Puck left Starling to sweep me a bow. "You grow more…absolutely terrifying. What have you done to your hair, dear lady?"

"Puck—do you have a reason to be here, besides being the fashion police?"

"Indeed. I am here to inform the Mighty Sorceress Gwynn, and her lovely attendant—" he winked at Starling, "—of impending battle tomorrow. There will be cavalry! Gore! Glory for all!" Puck performed an intricate box step, ending with a flourish. "Be ready at first light."

He popped out again, as quickly as he'd appeared,

leaving Starling and I staring at each other in be-
musement.

Starling opened her mouth and I stepped in before
she could say anything.

"No, let's not discuss this any more right now. Just
get it out of your head that this is some kind of love
story here." I found my voice unaccountably choked up.

Starling took a step toward me, her brow furrowed.
"But I know Lord Rogue saved you after the Battle of
the Birds. He performed great magics to save your life
and, in return, you pledged him your eternal love. Everyone knows the story."

I threw my hands up in the air. "Incredible how you
people believe your own press! You need to grow up,
Starling. There is no such thing as true love. It's a fantasy. And what is going on between Rogue and me is
all about power."

"Well, I'm sure he's not easy to love, but…"

"I. Do. Not. Love. Rogue." I said it slowly and with
as much intent as I could muster behind it so she could
understand.

Starling blinked at me, worry clouding her eyes. "But
you're here for him. That's why you brought yourself
over from your world. You dreamed of him, loved him
even then, and sacrificed everything to come here and
be with him. To answer him in his time of need."

"What need? His need to impregnate a human
woman and make the baby into some kind of change-
ling? Starling, that is just not something a person signs
up for."

"But your magic! That's why you're so powerful, because of the intimate connection with him!"

I sighed. "Look around you, Starling. Do you see

him? No, you don't. Because I refused him and ran him
off. I won. Do you see? It doesn't matter what stories
everyone is telling. *This* is the reality. My being here
is an accident and I'm going back home. I didn't come
here to save anybody, least of all Rogue. It was just stupid happenstance. There are people I left behind who
love me and need me."

From his favorite violet pillow, Darling sent a question about Isabel.

"Yes, you would have liked her. Though she's all cat
with nothing…extra about her." I picked up my hair-
brush, working out the snarls I'd put in. I would get
back to them. If they weren't all dead. To Isabel and my
mother. If I could face down Rogue and Falcon, then I
could break up with Clive in person. Maybe I'd apply for
jobs at another university, move up. Back in the world
I belonged to, where things made sense. My heart felt
satisfyingly hard again. Impervious. "And I'll tell you
what—if this Titania took Dragonfly and is punishing
her because that silly little faerie let me down somehow,
then I'd like her to come here and explain."

A frisson ran over the room. If a wave of energy that
felt like blistering drought could be called that. The
cheerfully noisy camp fell silent.

Starling's face whitened. "What have you done,
Gwynn?"

I hadn't meant to make the wish. I'd gotten caught up
in thinking in my old ways. It wasn't even really a clear
wish, but I could feel it manifest. As if something had
been waiting for the opportunity to pounce. Be careful
what you wish for, all right.

We pushed out of the tent and into the deathly silent

camp. Not a fae, pixie, page or Brownie was in sight. Only Titania riding up the velvety green hill to see me.

She rode a white horse with a cotton-candy-pink mane and tail. Titania herself—she could be no other— was naked, her voluptuous body featureless as a Barbie doll's. Long silver hair flowed over the horse and trailed on the ground behind.

Her pale eyes fixed on me.

Parching heat flowed out of her, prickling my skin. I wished a protective wall between her and us, just in case. She smiled at me, sweet, charming, and canceled it. She tore the magic out of me, making me gasp out loud.

All around me, the thoughts had stilled. Like the endless buzz of cicadas ceasing before a storm, the eerie silence filled me with dread.

"Lady Sorceress." Titania's voice filled my mind, a symphony of bass chords and high flutes. Her pretty lips never lost their smile. "You asked for an explanation."

Well, holy shit. I grasped for words that flew away. I reached for the silence Marquise and Scourge had taught me. Nothing. Everything in me wanted to scream and run away.

She put long fingers to her lips, as if to stifle a giggle. They had several extra joints, a spider's hand.

"I'm missing my maidservant, Dragonfly."

"She broke her oath to you. That makes her mine."

"It was a mistake."

The heat roared up. I tried not to flinch. Behind me, Starling whimpered. Darling pressed against my ankle, but not a whisper of thought came from him.

"I do not make mistakes, Sorceress. Oaths and oath-breakers are mine. Isn't that so, Lord Darling? How do you enjoy your new body?"

Darling pressed against me, shivering.

"I meant that it was my mistake." *Your highness.* How does one address a deity?

The heat dropped a little. My face felt burnt.

"You make many mistakes, Sorceress."

"Yes."

"I've been watching you. I suspect you'll be mine as well."

"I've obeyed my agreements."

That yellow gaze burned through the dark shadows in my mind.

"Barely." Her doubt hummed through me. "Dancing the edge. Foolish human girl. Rogue is a fool, to rest so much on one so…unreliable."

"I never asked to be here."

"Didn't you?" She spun her segmented fingers in the air and Dragonfly appeared on the horse in front of her. The girl stared at me in mute terror. "This game will be over too easily, Sorceress, if you lose so soon. So, here's a caution for you."

The spidery hand closed on one of Dragonfly's silly wings. With a sickening crunch, Titania pulled it off, dripping goo trailing. She tossed it at my feet while Dragonfly screamed piteously. The second wing followed.

"A memento for you. To remember me by." Titania stopped smiling. "Or do you require further explanations?"

I shook my head, too horrified to answer. Dragonfly sagged in Titania's lap, held up by one spidery arm while Titania licked her fingers clean of the yellow ooze.

"I'll see you soon, Sorceress."

And she was gone.

THIRTY-ONE

In Which I Fight a Couple of Battles of My Own

STARLING AWAKENED ME in the pre-dawn darkness for the battle, ready with my black dress and heels, along with some kind of eggs for us to eat. The heels were still in stiletto mode, but they matched my mood so I left them that way. We perched on the pillows, cross-legged, eating in silence.

"Starling—I'm sorry about yesterday."

"Don't discuss *her*."

After Titania vanished, the camp had immediately returned to its usual level of hilarity. Starling nattered on about nothing. Even Darling refused to discuss what had happened, distracting me by attacking the yellow rubber ducky instead. I didn't blame them, really, but I found their denial disconcerting.

"No, I know you won't talk about that. I meant, mostly, about Rogue and what I said. I'm sorry if I was abrupt with you."

Starling shook her head at me, her hair pink in the pillow light. "Gwynn, this isn't about me. It's you I'm worried about. Especially now."

"Well then," I answered brightly, standing up, "we have no problems because I am perfectly fine." I would be fine, too. I was sorry for them, living under an onus like Titania's, but this was not my world. More than ever, I wanted out of this insane place.

Larch met me with Felicity outside the tent and she snorted at me in greeting. I stroked her silky white mane, pleased to see her, too. Darling was already waiting on the traveling pad.

"No armor this time?"

He flicked his tail at me and looked away.

Starling handed me my stick and dagger to strap to the saddle. Liam didn't trust me not to slice myself open with the sun-and-moon wheels yet, so those were staying behind.

"I'll see you at the victory feast tonight," she said.

"There's already a victory feast planned? What if we lose?"

Starling and Larch laughed. Silly me.

"General Falcon wants the camp moved to the front and then everyone will celebrate the advance tonight," Larch put in. "They're setting up special tents for everyone. We're to be there in armor, with evidence of glorious battle upon us."

Charming.

"You guys have to move all this stuff in one day?" Now I kind of felt bad that I'd created and accumulated so much stuff. "I could poof some of it."

"It'll be fine, Lady Sorceress," Starling said.

"Be careful with the dragon's blood—both the vial and that residue. I'm still not sure if it's toxic or what."

"Don't worry."

"Maybe I should put my grimoire in my saddlebags?"

"Lady Sorceress Gwynn, we'll handle it." Now Starling sounded more like her usual brisk self. "This is our job—now go do yours."

"Um—about those wings."

Larch looked grim. "We've stored them. Best that you keep them. Just in case."

Boy howdy.

We rode out and I craned back for a last look, feeling oddly nostalgic to leave my brief home. If I'd known, I would have walked out to visit the dryad at the oak tree last night. Not that she would care. Still, I'd kept the leaf Rogue had handed me. Pressed it between the pages of the grimoire.

Silly, I know.

I maintained my cool shell, but under it, all these conflicting emotions roiled.

Titania's words haunted me. What had Rogue risked with me? And why the hell would I spend a moment feeling, what? Was this guilt? It certainly wasn't love, no matter what the Starlings of the world thought. He'd tried to make me a pawn in his games. It would be a terrible thing, if his own bargains were with Titania. But if he failed, that was on him.

What really ate at me was, would trying to get home be breaking my oath to Rogue? Probably. But Titania's power would be limited to this world. So if I wanted to get home, I'd have to make sure I transitioned really damn quick, so I wouldn't be an oathbreaker in this world long enough for her to get me.

And do her version of plucking my wings out.

Logically, I owed Rogue less than nothing. It seemed more and more clear he'd dragged me into Faerie to suit his own purposes. Or the Black Dog had, clearly at his direction.

This game will be over too easily, if you lose so soon.

She expected me to break my bargain with Rogue.

Eventually. No wonder he'd been so eager to get going on delivering that impregnation. *Guess what, boys and girls? I'm not playing your games.*

When we converged with the human soldiers, I looked for Liam as a distraction from my dark thoughts. I'd thought I could pick out his bronze curls in the rising light, but so many of them were wearing their helms. The air around the men buzzed with excitement for the coming battle. Cheers rose up when the men spotted me. It felt wrong to be kind of thrilled by it, especially given everything that had happened. They saw me as some kind of romantic heroine, which was a lot better than my recent roles. Hell, I should play that up. Enjoy the sorceress gig for the moment.

"Lady Sorceress!"

"Officer Liam!" I trotted Felicity over to where Liam led his unit. He was some sort of sergeant or lieutenant, then, because he marched just outside the ranks of men. I didn't really understand the military hierarchy—here or back home.

"You have your dagger and your stick then, lady?" Liam eyed the weapons tied to my saddle with approval. "Though you'd be smarter to have the dagger in your hand as you ride. It would take you far too long to get at it there."

"Yes, sir." I grinned.

"Be careful today, Lady Gwynn." Liam eyed the men, verifying their disciplined march. "I'm told we're to have an easy victory, but don't get lulled into a false sense of security. Always be on the lookout."

"I will."

"If you get tired of fae wine, send your man to us. We'll set you up with a real drink."

"Now there's an offer to warm a girl's heart," I told him. "Are we talking whiskey, here?"

"You mean there's another real drink besides that?"

I laughed. "No, surely there's not. You be careful today, too."

"I don't have to be careful—why's that?"

I opened my mouth, my confusion cut off by the roar of the men.

"We're strong! We're vigilant! All fall before us!"

Liam winked at me. "Now be off with you, Most Valiant and Powerful Lady Sorceress, lest you insult my men again."

"We're strong! We're vigilant! All fall before us!" They boomed again. A kind of good luck charm against the coming conflict.

I kind of wanted to salute the men, then realized it probably made no sense here. Oh, well. So I waved and trotted off as if I knew where I was going. Behind me, the bastardized "Proud to Be an American" chant welled up. Whee—my theme song. That was where I belonged—with humans.

We rode for a couple of hours this time, so the sun was well into mid-sky before Puck fetched me to ride up with the pack of nobles, all in their circus armor. No Promontory of Magic for me this time.

"Lady Gwynn." Falcon greeted me with a somber nod. He appeared no different for having turned into a bird lately. I wanted to ask how long he'd stayed that way, and if he'd meant to shape-shift or if it was an involuntary response to the injury I'd caused. From the hints he'd dropped about Rogue, my current hypothesis was that the change to this magical animal form was subconsciously triggered.

"Good morning, General Falcon."

"I trust you're planning to abide by instructions today?"

Ulp. Oh yes, indeed.

"To the best of my ability, General."

He gave me a narrow look, so I knew my uncertainty had leaked through my careful wording.

"Very well, then." Falcon turned his horse and the nobles parted, all watching me with great interest. I moved Felicity up next to Falcon at his pointed glance. Our group sat on the edge of a bluff. Golden fields spread out below, bordered by scrubby brush here and there. In the distance glimmered the sea, dazzling aquamarine.

The enemy streamed into the plain below, obediently lining up for the coming conflict. I didn't see our men, but thought they must be coming around from the side somewhere.

"Push them to the sea, Lady Gwynn."

I glanced obliquely at Falcon. His craggy profile pointed to the distant water.

"Push them?"

"To the sea."

And he turned his horse to rejoin the rest of the nobles, a spectator's distance back, leaving me at the edge of the bluff. Even Larch stood back with them. Apparently I didn't need much protecting at the moment.

So much for all those spells I'd planned for blinding, frightening or otherwise quelling the enemy.

I studied the army filling the plain.

How to move them? Preferably without bringing on the dragons.

"Lady Sorceress Gwynn! I shall never get my naval battle at this rate—could you hurry it up?"

"She's baffled. We should bring in my monsters. That will move this army."

"Perhaps we should break out lunch? Have our picnic now while we wait?"

Ah, my fan club's voices behind me.

"Lady Gwynn." There was Falcon's malicious drawl. "Are you reneging on our agreement?"

Shit, shit, shit.

This was like the bad dream, where you were taking an exam and hadn't gone to class for the entire semester. Felicity stamped restlessly, huffing into her bit. Darling sent me a picture of me as a blank-eyed idiot.

"Lady Gwynn?"

"Just working out some of the subtleties of the spell—it requires concentration."

"All hold silent while the Powerful Sorceress Gwynn works her magic!" Larch's surprising baritone rang out.

They all subsided. Even Felicity. *Thank you, Larch.*

If only I could make the opposing army want to go so easily.

Okay, *think.* Push, Falcon had said, but pulling could work, too. What could pull them to the sea?

Darling pictured a mermaid. Never mind that he thought about chomping into her fishy tail.

Sirens. The irresistible lure. Of course they had mermaids here. They had everything else from every story I'd ever read. I rubbed Darling's ears and he purred. But were they in *this* ocean? Darling mentally shrugged and washed a paw, wondering if they tasted more like fish or girl.

I glanced behind me. The fae all held statue-still and

silent. As if made of wax, just a plume rippling in the breeze here and there.

"Umm, Larch? Could you come hold Felicity?"

Larch scampered alertly up, taking the horse by the bridle. I dismounted, slightly wobbly on the stilettos. I made a show of stretching and turned my back on the nobles.

"In the ocean there," I muttered under my breath, "are there mermaids, sirens—that kind of thing?"

"If my lady wishes it to be so, I'm sure there shall be."

I wanted to snap back that I could hardly create a whole race of creatures. Besides, Larch had a point. Just trust in it.

I wished for mermaids. I pictured them on diamond-white sand, their jeweled tails in the surf, waves tangling their long locks as they sang. Sing for the men, I thought. Sing your songs for the soldiers. No fighting today. Bring them to the sea. When the first man reaches the shore, stop. Let them wander the beach, but take none of them with you.

I threaded it through with my own longing. Caribbean blue days and tropical nights. The whimsical beat of steel drums. Sunshine flooding my skin. The sexual heat of magic flowed through me, into the spell.

It called to me. Sweet with simple pleasure.

The enemy army reversed its flow, streaming away again, like a river running to the delta. The men followed the siren call. All the men—ours, too.

I followed behind them, drunk on the song.

We all followed.

THIRTY-TWO

In Which I Quench My Thirst

FORTUNATELY MY SPELL worked exactly right.

As soon as the first soldier set foot on the diamond-white sand, the song stopped. At least, it seemed clear that was what happened, because it had to have been one of theirs who got there first.

At any rate, our army fetched up midstride when the song ceased. The sun declined in a grand blaze of peach and red wine over the water. And serendipity had us at the site of the new camp. Fortunately, none of the camp-setting-up folks were sucked in by the siren song. I'd kind of forgotten they would also have been in range.

As it turned out, it was as if I'd planned the whole thing.

At Falcon's table, they toasted me, the guest of honor. And I was pleased enough with myself to enjoy the moment. So nice to have something go right for a change, I didn't even care that the only point of pushing the enemy to the ocean was to get to play with boats. Even the nonsensical conversation didn't bother me as much. Victory was indeed sweet.

So was the damn wine. Way too sweet. I wanted whiskey in the worst way. I didn't want to send Larch for it either. I wanted to get it myself. Be around the humans. Say hi to my handsome Officer Liam.

For research purposes, of course.

Starling, who sat far down the table, stood when I did. I waved that she could stay where she was. She looked lovely in a dawn-pink dress, her glossy hair warm gold in the combined pillow and torchlight. I didn't really want to mention where I was going, since she'd undoubtedly disapprove, given her fantasy about me and Rogue.

Besides, she looked like she was having fun and I could use a little walk by myself. Fortunately, Darling had taken off in search of a mermaid who might give him a nibble. I told him that they were probably all off swimming, but he seemed undeterred. He deserved his own version of celebrating. Not unlike my idea.

The camp rang out with more hilarity than usual. Pathways between the tents were lined with glowing pillows, some pulsing with the music. There had to be thousands of the things now. How they'd been set to auto-pulse, I had no idea.

A cluster of Dragonfly girls scurried past, naked and giggling hysterically. Recognizing a familiar tune from the next tent, I hummed along.

The human side of camp wasn't hard to find, now that I knew what to look for. I moved through the buffer of night separating the two, a brief respite of quiet starsong. Which was interrupted by the rough songs of humans and the squeals of camp followers. No blinking pillows here. I slipped around the edges, making for the bright torches of what I hoped was the main party area.

A number of younger soldiers manned the tent, no doubt set on sober keg duty for some infraction. But they looked cheerful enough, pouring ale into the tin cups, mugs and drinking horns of the men who came through.

I stepped into the light of the tent. The roar of male laughter abruptly died and they all snapped to attention, party forgotten.

"Lady Sorceress!" One saluted me as the others followed suit. "How may we serve you? Are you lost—"

His question ended on a choke as his companion sharply elbowed him, muttering, "She's a bloody sorceress, numbskull—she can't get lost!"

I smiled easily, charmingly I hoped, and held out the crystal glass I'd brought from Falcon's table. "They're serving that awful sweet wine in our tent. Officer Liam promised me whiskey if I stopped by. Is he around?"

Silence.

My stomach sank. I hadn't thought.

"Oh no—he wasn't injured today, was he? I'd heard we had no fighting at all."

They gaped at me, clearly at a total loss, sliding looks at each other.

"Snap to, boys!" a deep voice behind me rang out, while the boys did indeed snap to even sharper attention, if it were possible. "The Lady Sorceress has asked a simple question—what is the delay?"

"Officer Liam, yes, sir!"

"Is there a reason we can't give the Lady Sorceress what she's looking for?" Liam gave me a warm grin of welcome.

The soldier who knew I couldn't get lost—if only that were true—stepped forward, bowed and reverently eased the goblet from my hand. I tried to catch his eye, but he flushed and ducked away.

"Thank you, Officer Liam." I smiled up at his car-amel-brown eyes.

"Lady Sorceress." He bowed deeply. "We are be-holden to you for a peaceful maneuver today."

The young soldier handed me the glass again with a whispered, "My lady sorceress." I thanked him, then frowned at the lightness of the glass before I thought to school my face. Officer Liam peered at the bare half-inch of whiskey in the bottom.

"Would you prefer more than that, Lady Sorceress?"

Despite his look of grave inquiry, I could swear he suppressed a grin. For a moment I wasn't the Sorceress, victor of the Battle of the Birds, not to mention the Plain of No Trees, sworn to love Rogue eternally. Instead I was the college girl I'd once been, standing over a keg with a cute guy. Oh yes, I wanted him to get me more.

"Yes, please—it *is* a bit of a walk over here."

The boys scrambled to retrieve the tankard, mutter-ing frantic apologies, while I watched with great dig-nity—coed pretending to be sorceress. They filled the glass nearly to the brim this time—an amount I doubted even I could drink. But it should last me a while, any-way.

I sipped. Then sipped again, closing my eyes as the smooth warmth fell through to my stomach and spread with lovely fingers into my bloodstream. The ebb of it dissolved away the edges of my horror over Titania and the residual bitter taste of Rogue. The sensual buzz of the magic today rode through my blood with it.

I opened my eyes to see the men all watching me, smoky lust drifting across the floor.

I was in control again. Better. I nodded at them with noble serenity and they settled back into their roles.

"It's lovely, gentle soldiers. I thank you, and I'll take my leave of you."

They bowed deeply, yet again, clearly waiting for my departure so they could attend to the growing queue of jubilant men wanting their share. I stepped back out of the ring of light.

"Lady Sorceress." Liam followed me. "May I escort you back to the nobles' feast tent?"

"It's not necessary, officer. I can find my way."

He offered his right arm. "I hear our sorceress has the eyes of a cat, but allow a humble warrior the satisfaction of knowing you safely seated with nary a drop of whiskey spilled." His tone was all humility, but I felt the thread of laughter through it. "Besides, General Falcon would have my hide if I did not assist you."

With a bit of a thrill, I slipped my left arm through his. He felt warm and muscled, totally unlike Rogue's wiry steel. I couldn't help remembering how his body brushed mine in weapons practice. I took another sip of whiskey, raised my glass to the carnival lights of the fae side of camp. "Let us proceed."

We picked our way across the hummocky ground and I found myself clinging to him as my heels sank into the damp earth while I balanced the precious whiskey. I could hear him wondering why I didn't have an escort. Or why I hadn't sent Larch to fetch for me.

"I like doing for myself. And I had a powerful thirst."

He glanced down, a cautious smile playing on his lips. "I should mind my thoughts around you."

"Apologies." Since we seemed on even ground for a moment, I took another sip of whiskey. "I don't try to pick up thoughts, but sometimes they waft by, like the smell of dinner cooking."

He nodded thoughtfully and we continued quietly for a bit longer. I didn't mention I'd picked up much more salacious stuff from him than that.

"Was that terribly out of line," I wondered out loud, "for me to come to the soldiers' tent?"

Now his laugh boomed out, generous and vital. "I think my men may never recover from the shock, Lady Sorceress. They've only seen barmaids tipple whiskey—and I wager none drank so deeply, with such a look…" He trailed off, remembering himself.

"What look?" I nudged the arm he escorted me by, my fingers tapping his ridged forearm. "What look—you've come this far." In the dark between the human and the fae camps, a strange intimacy settled.

This felt simple and easy. Familiar, even. No games. Or, only the usual kind.

"Like a woman looks when a man touches her," he admitted softly, a bit rough.

He stared resolutely forward into the night when I glanced up at him, looking down only when I stopped walking. "I've offended you—forgive my impertinence, Lady Sorceress—drunk on siren song and a beautiful woman on my arm…" He shook his head. "I've lost my head."

Warmth coiled in my stomach as I watched his mouth in the reflected light of the torches on one side and pillows on the other. I wanted just a taste of him. I had made no vows to Rogue that I wouldn't kiss anyone else, just that I wouldn't bear anyone else's child first.

One kiss broke no promises.

This was for me and no one else. I needed something for me.

I slipped my arm from Liam's and he moved as if

to step back, but I reached up to touch him, my fingertips white against his sun-bronzed cheekbone. He hesitated a moment, then bent his head so I could touch
my lips to his.

Ah, the breath of a man on my tongue, that first
touch of flesh I'd never before felt. His taste, a wisp of
smoke, tang of musk, filled me. Making me nostalgic
for a simple man.

The magic surged up, wanting a place to go.

I tore myself away. "It's my turn to ask forgiveness.
I'm not sure why I—"

Liam slipped his hand behind my neck, his fierce
kiss stopping my words. He kissed me hard, thoroughly.
I clutched at his arm with one hand, the other still bal-
ancing the whiskey. His lips were hard and soft, a day's
growth of beard sharpening the edges, a rough delight.
He drew away, eyes gleaming darkly.

"I know I made the invitation," I whispered, "but I
have to go back to the feast. I'm expected."

He nodded, understanding duty. His warrior's fingers
brushed the nape of my neck as he slid his hand away,
and I released his powerful arm. We stood a moment.

Then he held his arm out as before—"Lady Sorceress?"—and I draped my fingers across his forearm
again and we walked in stately formality toward Falcon's tent cluster.

Kissing Liam had been lovely. Unthreatening. Should
Rogue return, I could cope with him better if I had
taken the edge off. As many teenagers could attest,
there was plenty to do without actual intercourse. And
I could investigate—under more controlled circumstances—the effect of orgasm on magic.

It was on my list, after all.

I glanced up at Liam and he met my look. Then stopped. We were just outside Falcon's tent. Dappled pillow light glinted off Liam's bright curls.

"If I could find a place tonight," he whispered, "someplace completely discreet, where no one would ever, ever know, would you…?"

"Yes." I answered without hesitation, without thought. And the grin I'd felt in him before flashed across his face like the sunshine he was born of.

"Just like that," he whispered in wonder.

"But, it can only be tonight and there will be rules. I can't…" *go all the way.* Okay, that would sound really dorky.

"A good warrior always knows his limitations. I will send someone to your tent later, to guide you."

With a wry look he handed me into the torchlight, where Falcon hailed me.

"Ah, Lady Gwynn, we were about to send out a search party, but I see our noble Officer Liam has rescued you already."

Everyone laughed uproariously. A fine joke at the human's expense.

"Thank you, officer." I inclined my head at Liam as he bowed.

"My pleasure, Lady Sorceress," he murmured correctly.

"Well served, officer. Now off with you—I'm sure you have your men to attend to."

Falcon waved him away, just as I'd waved Starling to stay where she was. Liam disappeared back into the darkness, while I settled onto my seat to nurse my whiskey through the remainder of the feast, careful not to look directly into Starling's inquiring gaze.

THIRTY-THREE

In Which I Am Taken by Surprise

"OH, FOR HEAVENS' SAKE, Starling, I just went to get some whiskey."

"You should have taken me with you." Starling walked with stiff stubbornness beside me, ostensibly to show me the new tent location.

"What, you're my babysitter now?"

Starling stopped. Her face crumpled. Was it me, or did her hair look less blond suddenly?

"Hey—" I reached out to touch her arm. "I'm sorry. I just…" I rubbed my face with my hands. "I don't know what's wrong with me."

Starling wiped away a tear. "You're just under a lot of pressure." She placed her hand over mine. "I understand. I really do."

I let it go, even as I was tempted to confide in her. As we continued our walk, Starling fell silent and I indulged in the sweet sizzle of anticipation of seeing Liam later. Or tried. Now that the moment had passed, I felt a bit less enthused. Hopefully this wasn't a bad idea. And me, for the one-night stand?

Not really in character for me.

Of course, none of this was, anymore. I had been reborn into a new world. I could be whoever the hell I wanted to be. One orgasm with a man—a human man—

and I'd have another data point on the sex-and-magic thing.

I ignored the sneaky voice whispering that I wasn't being exactly rational. Who could blame me? I deserved a little fun, didn't I?

Still, when it came time to sneak out like some guilty teenager, my stomach clenched. The camp was as silent as it ever became, which wasn't much. Starling, though, had long since gone to bed and I'd dismissed Larch's guys. Good thing I'd already established a rep for being temperamental and sending servants packing, willy-nilly.

I kept the Ann Taylor sorceress dress on, so I could pretend to be working still, if anyone checked on me. And fiddled at my workbench for the same reason. My grimoire had been set in a place of honor, writing tools next to it. The vial of dragon's blood stood off to the side, where it couldn't be carelessly bumped.

I didn't feel like messing with either one.

On a sudden thought, I jumped up and rummaged through my trunk. My heart fluttered in a bit of panic, until my fingers closed over the wooden box. I yanked it out and unwrapped the glass globe from its cocoon of silk.

Undisturbed by the move, the crystal swirled with living night, glinting feral blue. I could feel the silk sweep of Rogue's obsidian hair, almost scent him through the glass.

Shaking off the sense that I was somehow being unfaithful to Rogue, I nevertheless tucked the marble into the pocket of my skirt, even as I turned at the slight noise behind me.

A kind of creature I hadn't seen before stood inside my tent flaps.

He was a shriveled, sooty skeleton. Like a doll made of pipe cleaners that had been set on fire and quickly doused. My skin crawled at the sight.

The creature beckoned me with a silent gesture. I stopped and pulled on my cloak, wishing it to black for discretion. I kept the heels high, though my feet ached from being in them all day. This was, after all, a date. I looked in the mirror and tried to drum up my earlier excitement, but the woman in it stared back at me with dark green sobriety.

The glass marble in my pocket felt obscurely comforting. Odd since Rogue would likely not wish to bolster me on this particular project. I turned back and grabbed my dagger, putting it in my cloak pocket for good measure.

I followed the thing through the shadowed back pathways of camp. We avoided the parties that still continued. The shrieking, dancing and merrymaking faded to the edges.

Beyond the twin circles of light from both camps, a shrouded figure stood next to a dark horse. Liam tipped back his hood, his curls silver in the starlight. He held out a hand to me and I took it, the size of it startling me. Had I expected long, slim fingers?

Get a goddamn grip.

He drew me toward him and I hesitated, glancing to see where the stick creature went.

I might also have checked for amber eyes watching from the shadows.

"I hope you don't mind the golem, Lady Sorceress," Liam said softly. Of course his sharp warrior's eyes would notice me checking for attack. "I borrowed it from a friend. Some people don't like it, but with you being a sorceress and all…"

"It's fine. Totally fine."

"Let's go then." Liam stopped. Turned back and touched my cheek with reverence. "This night—it means everything to me, Lady Sorceress," he whispered with rough passion.

"Jennifer," I said.

"Lady?"

"The other name—that's what the fae call me."

"Of course, Jynnfahr. Thank you for that privilege."

I restrained myself from rolling my eyes when he turned his back to climb on the horse and managed a smile for him when he held down a hand for me to mount behind him. I settled in, wrapping my arms around him for stability. Fortunate that he hadn't wanted me in front of him. That might have led to groping and, well, I just wasn't quite in the mood, yet. Never mind that the image of Dragonfly wilting on the front of Titania's horse still haunted me.

This is a mistake.

This is important research and don't you dare chicken out now.

"Second thoughts?" Liam asked softly.

I turned my cheek into his woolish cloak. It smelled of leather and man, sweat and horse. Not unpleasant. Liam's horse had a smooth gait and the night flew past.

"No." I barely whispered it.

"Lady—I mean, Jen?"

"No." I said it louder. "Just anxious to get there."

Liam chuckled. A satisfied, masculine sound.

I could hear the waves crashing on the shore by the

time we pulled up at a dark cottage. Liam held out an arm for me to steady myself as I dismounted. He swung down and brought the reins around to tie off the horse on a stunted tree in front. My hand slid into my cloak pocket, fingers wrapping around the now-familiar dagger handle. Just as Liam had taught me.

Nothing like making yourself vulnerable to the guy who taught you everything you know about hand-to-hand. I'd better be ready with some spells.

"Isn't the enemy camp nearby?" I asked Liam.

He turned to me. "You don't trust me? Why are you here if you don't trust me?"

I didn't know what to say.

"We rode out at a diagonal—the enemy camp is on the other side of the strand." Liam's face was stone. "And I think I should take you back now."

"No!" I grabbed a handful of his cloak. "I'm just… nervous. You know. It's been a long day."

Liam softened, tipped the hood of my cloak back and cupped my face with his hands. Two hands at a time, I thought—cheating.

No, this was good. No bargains here. No deceit. Oh, except maybe on my part. *Not enough to break an oath, that's what matters.*

I held still as Liam lowered his bronze head. Then, better, slid my hands into his parted cloak and set them on his waist. He grunted in satisfaction and kissed me.

A soft brush of his lips, followed by deeper kisses, urging me to my earlier heat. He'd shaved smooth now and smelled of what I would have called bay rum in my old world. I opened my mouth to him, and he kissed me deeply.

I tried to give over to it. Waited for the swimming spin of desire.

Not quite there.

"Let's go inside. I'll build you a fire and we can do this properly."

I realized then I was shivering slightly.

Liam untied his weapons from the horse and urged me inside, one hand at the small of my back. He knelt at the hearth of a stone fireplace that seemed large for the tiny cottage. Wrapped in my cloak still, I watched Liam work at lighting the fire on the cold hearth. Clearly no one had been here for some time. Another chill ran through me.

Liam cursed softly as the tiny flame he nursed went out yet again.

With a heartfelt wish, I lit the fire. Not difficult at all.

Liam started back in astonishment, then looked over his shoulder at me. "That's the second time I forgot the company I'm keeping."

"Liam—about those rules. You should know—"

He rose and walked up to me. Calloused fingers touched my cheek. "Whatever part you wish to give." He ran his fingers over my hair, the way he might gentle a horse. "Shiny as a raven's wing," he whispered. "Trust me, Lady Sorceress."

I nodded, unable to speak. His fingers tightened in my hair and his lips dove to claim mine. I tried to relax into it.

"Would my Lady Sorceress remove her cloak?" He raised his head, watching my face intently.

I unfastened the cloak and let it drop to the floor. His eyes darkened and he ran his hands down my bare arms.

"I hoped you'd be wearing this dress still, which

clings to you like night itself." He bent to rain kisses on my shoulders, then my throat when my head dropped back. His arms slid behind my back to support me and I gave myself up to them.

"A lot of poetic words for a soldier," I remarked, losing the words in a gasp as his mouth brushed the upper curves of my breasts. I tried not to think of Rogue holding me like this. Of the profound thrill of his lips on my skin.

Stay in the moment.

"All warriors are poets, don't you think?" He raised his head, caramel eyes serious. "We deal death—what is more profound than that? And this. This a warrior also knows—the other side of death's coin." He dropped his eyes to my bosom. Holding me arched back in his muscled left arm, he raised his right hand to lightly trace the curves, then looked into my eyes with a wicked gleam. "This is what I wanted to do in the feast tent, when I saw your nipples peaked for me."

He slid one finger between my breasts and pulled the dress down abruptly so my breasts sprang free. I gasped and his grip tightened on me. He licked lavish strokes around my nipples, on the so-sensitive undersides of my breasts, then returned to the nipples to lip at them. I fell back in his arms, concentrating on enjoying this. I strangled a startled cry when he nipped one nipple, then drew it into his mouth hard and fast.

"You can call out," he muttered. "There's no one near enough to hear."

I must have tensed at that because he looked at me, then set me on my feet. I struggled to pull my head together, strangely embarrassed to stand in front of him with my breasts bare, shining wet from his attentions.

"You still look for ambush here?" he asked, face grave.

I closed my eyes, then gave in and folded my hands over my bosom, hiding myself from his too-intent stare. He waited.

"Yes," I finally said. "I'm not what you call a trusting soul." Scarred, broken and bleeding was what I was. Funny how Rogue seemed to understand that about me, alternately bullying and coaxing me, not letting me think too much.

All mind-reading, most likely.

And why the hell was I thinking about goddamned Rogue?

Liam ran his hand down my hair, until the ends filtered through his fingertips.

"I want this." I made my tone firm. *Convincing yourself?* whispered the sneaky voice. "Tonight I don't want to be a sorceress. I just want to feel like an ordinary woman again."

"I haven't much experience in the ways of sorcery." He brushed his fingers over my hands, then slowly guided them down to my sides. "But I know something about pleasuring women. Let me pleasure you, Lady Sorceress." He knelt down so his head was level with my bosom and dipped his head to lay a kiss on each trembling pink nipple, like a hummingbird tasting flowers.

"Call me Jennifer."

"Lady Jyn." His voice slid around the kisses. "Let me undress you."

I turned and held up my hair, explaining how to draw down the foreign zipper. His nibbling kisses slid down my spine as the black dress fell away from me. Liam

turned me and gave me his hand to step out of the pool
of my dress. Still kneeling, his head came to my chin,
even in my heels. As he swept my nearly naked body
then met my eyes with that wicked smile, the surge of
desire from him hit me like a drug. I soaked it in, shaking off the uncomfortable memory of Marquise watching me with avid Christmas-ornament eyes.

"Will you leave the shoes on for me, for now? I've
never seen anything like them, but they seem made
for a naked woman, for sex." His hands tugged in my
hair, pulling my head back while he feasted on my rib
cage, on my belly.

"Where I come from," I told him, "some people call
them come-fuck-me shoes."

"I like that," he growled. "I like your foreign garments and all of your invitations, Lady Sorceress." Then
he released my hair, slid my panties down to my ankles
and dug his fingers into my ass, holding my groin to
be consumed next.

Funny, his hunger for me had become more interesting than what I felt. When he nuzzled my thighs apart,
I let him, distantly observing that the stroking of his
tongue, while pleasant, didn't hold a candle to the rush
of feeling him want me. With Rogue, my own desire
had risen up to match his. I began to wonder if this experiment would fail. I put a hand on Liam's head, ready
to disappoint him.

With a crack of ebony, the room broke in two.

Liam dropped me and I fell in a disgraceful heap,
askew on my heels, tangled in my panties.

Rogue stood over us, a slash of cobalt black, a silver
sword blazing in the now-billowing firelight.

THIRTY-FOUR

On the Beach

WITH A SEASONED warrior's reflexes, Liam ducked the lethal swing of Rogue's sword.

And with shocking alacrity, he grabbed his own sword and shot out the door.

"Hello, Gwynn," Rogue said with ice-blue calm. "You're looking...lovely tonight." The black lines crawled over the left side of his face like vipers.

I wrenched out of the one heel still clinging to my toes, scrabbled my feet under me and crouched, shielding myself from his deadly glare.

"Don't fret, you'll have time to dress yourself while I dispatch that impertinent human. Then you and I have things to discuss." He paused, dark thoughts swirling that I couldn't quite catch. Was he...hurt? Surely not. "We need to talk."

Rogue turned and strode out the door before I could gasp out another word.

Liam. Oh, no.

"Rogue! Don't you dare hurt him!" I yelled out, yanking up my panties. Where they should have stayed, dammit, if I had any sense. I pulled on my dress and flung myself out the cottage door, trying to get the zipper at least partway up and scanning the night for the sounds of conflict.

All I could hear was surf.

Clouds scudded across the sky, dashing themselves against the moon and fleeing again.

I ran for the beach, the snaky grasses grabbing at my toes, slicing at my ankles. The soil turned to sand under my tender soles and I burst like a wild thing onto the clear shore. The moonlight reflected cool blue on the fine sand.

Rogue and Liam fought, silhouetted against the phosphorescent surf.

Liam surged in close, his shorter, stockier frame wedging up underneath Rogue's sword arm, grappling with him in a maneuver even I could see was desperate. As I struggled through the sinking sand toward them, Rogue yanked Liam's head back by his hair. Liam thrashed, but Rogue held him with ease. He took a step back and stretched Liam out, holding him with unnatural strength while he brought his sword around, and laid the tip against Liam's chest.

I remembered who had all the power.

"No!" I screamed.

The crashing surf swallowed the sound.

But Rogue looked up at me. His eyes captured the moonlight and shone with an impossible cobalt reflection. He cast Liam aside, a rag doll on the sand.

He strode toward me, an avenging demon, the wind whipping his long black hair, those eyes shining as bright as the sword he carried.

I lost all breath.

He seized me by the throat with his left hand, firm but not hurting me. Even now, one hand only.

"Why?" he thundered in my face. His skin gleamed glacier-cold in the moonlight. The black pattern of his face looked larger, more complex. As if it were visibly growing. "All the time I watched you, waited for you. How is it that you don't feel what is between us? You drive me to despair, Gwynn. How could you deny me the least crumb and offer that dreg of a human everything?"

Not even a squeak escaped my throat. I had no ability to answer.

Oh, but I did.

So I showed him. My terror and desire. The rage I felt at his betrayal. How I was still spiraling down the rabbit hole he'd shoved me into. The sickening fear of what he might do to a child I bore. What Titania might do. I threw all my thoughts and emotions at Rogue, fierce and as loud as I could make it.

He threw back his head and howled to the sky. Despair, yes. It raked cold claws through my heart.

Spikes of ebony lines crawled up his chest, over his neck and spread across his face like a virus.

His hand clenched convulsively on my throat and I scrabbled at it, suddenly desperate for air. Through the crack of the surf, another wet splitting noise filled my ears. The sound of bones snapping, the sickening snap of flesh rending.

Rogue's howl of pain sharpened into true anguish, physical and emotional. I felt it more keenly than if it happened to me.

His hand released and I fell to the chill sand, staring up in utter horror as Rogue's body bent back into a crescent, splitting open in a spray of midnight blood.

Glossy black, the blood fountained impossibly up, arcing to fall on the sand. Rogue's body collapsed back, shredded and empty, more blood than any body could

hold, creating a grotesque rainbow, gathering, coalesc-
ing into a shape.

Until, shining in the moonlight, the Dog crouched
with me on the sand, the shattered remnants of Rogue
and the silver sword between us. My heart shattered,
too.

Amber eyes shone.

He cocked his head at me, that square head massive
in the moonlight. He stood, stretching, languid as a cat,
and paced to me. The smell of bloody flesh caught his
attention, and he paused to sniff at the fleshy bits that
had been Rogue.

"Goddammit, no!"

The snarl burst out of me and I found myself launching at the Dog. In fury, I slammed into it. Rage at myself for not seeing the truth. At Rogue for not telling
me. We rolled on the sand, snarling and grappling. Its
growls mixed with the surf. I shrieked and pounded its
hot sleek hide.

A wild thing.

Cold saltwater hit me, swamped my lungs. The Dog
was abruptly gone and I struggled to hold on to the
sand. Singing filled my ears, far off in the distance.
The waves tugged at my dress, begging me to come
out to sea. The old passions of infinite souls poured
through me. So easy to go, to fall under and away. Suc-
cumb to the cold waters of the despair that had dragged
Rogue under.

All my fault.

The sharp grains of sand bit under my nails as I
crawled out of the water.

A chill breeze hit me. Thunder rumbled in the dis-

tance. The clouds dashing around the sky gathered together, competing to hide the moon.

Dark streaks of blood marred my arms and breasts
where the Dog's fangs had snagged me. The fragile spaghetti straps of my dress had snapped. Too much strain.
I tugged at the soaked bodice, managing to wrestle it
back in place somewhat. The salt stung in my wounds.

I crawled up the sand, sodden hair in snarled threads
around my face. I found Rogue's body. Impossibly rent.
A small keening noise escaped me. And I'd thought
he was indestructible. Had counted on it, somewhere
deep inside. But I'd turned out to be his weakness. I
wondered why he hadn't carried out his threat to kill
me. The Dog crouched over him. Guardian. Crosser
of boundaries. Would he escort Rogue's spirit to yet
another realm? Or was Rogue in there, somewhere,
trapped by his own subconscious?

The wind tugged at my wet dress, slapping the
soaked tendrils of my hair against my stinging skin.
This world was just as real as the one I'd left. More
real, in many ways. Just as Rogue connected with me
more vividly, more viscerally than any man I'd known.
Surely that meant something.

It couldn't be too late.

I stared down the Dog. Oh no. I had no intention of
losing now.

Or, maybe losing was what it took to win.

THIRTY-FIVE

In Which I Find a Way to Surrender

"LADY SORCERESS—DON'T MOVE."

I sagged at the sound of Liam's voice behind me. A miracle that he wasn't dead already, but he would get himself killed for sure now.

The Dog turned, growled, eyes bleeding into red. He bared his teeth, flashing in the night.

"Liam," I said in an even voice. "You need to back away. Go back to your horse and ride to camp."

"I cannot leave you. I'll protect you with my life. That creature, you don't know—"

"Yes, I do."

The Black Dog blinked, one slow, satisfied gesture of agreement.

I stood, keeping an eye on the Dog. Liam laid a warm hand on my bare arm. The Dog's hackles shot up, and the low growl grew into an openmouthed roar. I shook Liam off. Stepped back and laid a hand on the Dog's glossy head.

The Dog's hackles lowered and he rubbed his head against my hand with a soft whimper.

"Go, Liam." I thought it at him, too. Fairly loud.

Liam was covered in sand, bleeding from nicks in a few places. He stared at me, astonished. Horrified, even.

"What are you?" he breathed.

I didn't bother to point out that I was the same woman he'd put his mouth on. It wouldn't change what he now saw. I wasn't really human anymore. Time to face what Rogue had known. I stroked the Dog.

"Just go."

Liam backed away. I watched his careful retreat up the sand until his dark shape disappeared into the shrouding shadows of the grass-covered dunes. I listened to the frantic whirl of his thoughts as he found the horse and rode away.

I could see myself there, soaked, the dress barely hanging off my breasts, my hair in ropes, spattered with seawater and Rogue's black blood, my face wild with tears, the massive Dog beside me, my eyes glowing with unnatural light. I couldn't go back to being what I'd been, mild-mannered professor, frozen in my own life. The changes I'd gone through were too deep, too wrenching. You can't go home again, they say. Now I knew what they meant. More. I knew I didn't want to.

It couldn't be too late.

I knelt beside the Dog. He tilted his head at me, eyes shadowed. Clouds were gathering around the moon, deepening the night.

"Rogue?" I whispered it, reaching for any sense of him inside.

The Dog's tongue lolled out, pleased as any puppy. I let my hand slide around to his thick chest, feeling the strong heart beating beneath.

The Dog's thoughts flowed formless, like Felicity's or the hawk's. They swirled with fierce motion. The surf, the smell of blood and me. The race of aggression and the hunger for the shreds of flesh beside us.

Veils between worlds shredding, flying into tattered remnants. I dug deeper, the Dog still under my hand.

Raven's wings swept across my vision, shrieking whispers. Hot blood in my mouth, tearing flesh and tears, howls and water. Rogue, drowning in black and blue magic, the Dog tearing scarlet chunks out of his chest until Rogue's howls became blood themselves. I wrenched myself away.

I had seen this before, in Rogue's mind. Before the fireplace. But I couldn't find Rogue himself.

Thunder rumbled again. The moon shot through the tumbling clouds, now lighting them, then succumbing to their dark whirl. Legs of lighting walked across the ocean's horizon.

Falcon's transformation hadn't been like this. It seemed gentle in comparison. I felt a sickening fear that Rogue had somehow irrevocably lost himself.

The fear that had ridden him. The hope that had surrounded the idea of me. The despair that finally dragged him under.

This was the center of why I was here. The Dog had brought me, chasing me through nightmares until I ran to Devils Tower, helping me to cross that boundary. But it was Rogue's need that drove it. Watching me. Waiting for me.

Somehow I hadn't seen that he was at the center of it. I had made the blood sacrifice to reach him, understanding on a subconscious level what my conscious mind had never grasped. He was the one I'd been looking for all this time. Not a happy, easy love. But one who recognized me for who I was.

I pulled the glass marble out of my pocket.

Had I forgotten it was there? Perhaps. And yet, part

of me held on to it, had reached for it as I left the tent and brought it out now. The same part of me that had driven the knife into my finger half a year ago. The part of me who belonged here. With him.

I focused on the sphere, dipping into it, allowing the macabre dance inside to entrance me. It was inimitably Rogue in a way the Dog was not. Sharp, sensuous, deadly seductive. Obsidian through sapphire.

I rolled the marble in the cooling blood of Rogue's remains, then wrapped my left hand around the sword lying on the sand, just like Liam had shown me not to do. My blood welled up, hot against my chilled skin. I held the crystal in my hand, letting our spirits mingle.

I sank into memory. Of how I felt when Rogue held me. *I know who you are,* he'd told me, but I hadn't believed. The touch of his skin, the sardonic twist of his eyebrow. The scent of mace and Stargazers. The lily I'd destroyed in order to tear myself away from this connection. My stubbornness and fear.

Instead I let the lust boil up. The sex and magic filled me.

I gave it all up and let myself drift.

I stood at the edge of the pool. Naked, my hair flowing down my back and sliding over my shoulders in a silky caress. I knew it was black now. Even in my dreams. Shining like the inky water before me. The arches of my feet were warmed and stretched by the curve of the worn stones, just at the edge of the water, not quite touching.

The angel hairs on the back of my neck lifted, so I knew the Dog had arrived. That he sat behind me on the stairs, as if carved from obsidian, but alive with hunger.

There he sat. Glossy, shimmering night against the

paler shadows. Flash of white fang, glistening with saliva. He shimmered. Shifted.

And Rogue uncoiled. Long hair streaming like ink spilled on leather. Cloak swirling around him.

He descended the steps with that uncanny elegance, stalking on long legs, effulgent eyes so intense that the sapphire was lost in ebony. As he paced toward me, he held something in his hand. The green silk cord. Longing in his beautiful face.

I quailed but held the marble in the palm of my hand. An offering.

Rogue stopped in front of me, sleek as a cobra, the pattern on his face once again still and cool. He slid the bloody sphere from my unresisting fingers. The eyebrow on the clear side of his face arched, Rogue held the glass sphere up to the misty light, turning it to see the bruised swirling within.

His eyes glittered like mica as they ran over my face. His elegant fingers folded around it. When he opened his hand again, it was gone.

Then he held his other hand up to me, the green silk cord trailing across it. A challenge. A question.

My breath caught and a tremor ran through me. I couldn't bear it.

"Do I have to?" I whispered. I searched his eyes. Regret and triumph chased each other through their depths. He trailed a long finger down my cheek and I shuddered.

"Beautiful Gwynhwyvar. You are both the omen and the fulfillment of it. You have seen how fighting this will only shatter us. Please. I need you."

Rogue sank to one knee, his cloak settling in a sensuous swirl. He held up the silken cord like an engagement ring.

"Gwynn, I cannot survive without you. Will you accept my bonds?"

My heart thundered, my brain swimming in heated blood, my breasts tight and sex throbbing. I couldn't think. But I didn't need to. I'd already made the choice.

It mattered that it was my choice.

I held out my wrists.

Without rising, Rogue knotted the green silk. First around one wrist, then the other. I trembled to feel it tighten around my skin. The sensation arrowed through me in helpless arousal. The ends dangled down, a twisted bridal bouquet.

My breath escalated. Excitement spiraling out of control.

Thrilled to the core, I let it go.

Weaving the dangling cords between his fingers, Rogue drew me down to bend over him. He offered his mouth to me and I kissed him, starving, insatiable. I dropped into his hot, sweet lips, my wrists tethered to his hands.

I sank to my knees, reveling in the heat of him against my naked skin, my nipples unbearably teased by the velvet he wore. I let him plunder my mouth.

When he raised his head, brilliant eyes fired, I tilted my head back, exposing my throat to his teeth in surrender.

With a growl, he slid his lips along my throat. I moaned, my thighs slick with moisture. He trailed nipping kisses down my neck and I sparked to his touch.

When he sank his teeth into the junction between my neck and shoulder, I convulsed. Rogue released my wrists, pulled me tight against him with one arm, slid his elegant fingers between my thighs into my swollen sex.

I convulsed again, screaming, and his mouth closed over mine.

My climax poured into him and he drank me in. Inhaled me, and poured it back.

This was right. This was how it should go.

Drowning in the volcanic tide, I was filled with Rogue. My heart swelled, pounding through me, burning through the sky in supernova.

On a crescendo of longing, I wished for him to live.

And collapsed into darkness.

THIRTY-SIX

In Which It Rains

I AWOKE IN Rogue's arms.

Dawn was breaking in a gray light. A misting rain fell over us, where we lay on the sand, wrapped in his cloak.

Rogue gazed at me, eyes quiet. The black pattern spiked over the left side of his face in more branches, more complex swirls, a thicket of blackthorn twining around his exotic indigo eye. But it seemed docile again, still and quiet. No longer feral. I trailed my fingers over it and felt only his skin.

Then I raised my hand to see no cord bound my wrist.

He raised an eyebrow at me, waiting for me to ask the question. Unaccountably, I blushed. Did he remember it all?

"What now?" I asked, instead.

"Whatever you wish for, beautiful Gwynn."

"I've learned to be careful of that."

"And in this case?"

"I think I don't know what to wish for."

"Wish for simple things. That's best."

Rogue shrugged and sat up. I shivered, bereft of his cloak and warm presence. The sodden dress still barely clung to me. He uncoiled to his feet and held a long hand down to me, just as he had under the dryad's tree. I slid my hand into his, trying not to think of how those elegant fingers had driven into me. Then and in the dream last night.

Tried not to think about how much I wanted all of him inside me.

"Dreams are just a different reality, lovely Gwynn. You should understand that by now."

"But our bargain…"

"Valid still." His lips twisted. "You are still safe from having my child. For the moment. Or until you change your mind."

I wrapped my clammy arms around myself.

"Allow me." With a flourish, Rogue produced a dark cloak out of thin air and wrapped it around my shoulders. The cords on it were knotted green silk.

I studied the shockingly gorgeous planes of his face, the dianthus-edge of his lips. The inky lines on the patterned side of his face seemed as if they could run in the rain.

"Why?" I finally asked him.

He sighed. Taking my hand, he drew me beside him. We walked along the sand, the soft rain falling, the surf quiet. The beach curved around the grassy bluff, disappearing in the mist. I felt curiously at peace, despite it all. As if we might head back to a cozy home soon and settle in with a glass of wine before the fire.

"You gave me the gift of your trust last night."

"Did I?"

Rogue glanced at me and wrapped his fingers around my wrist. I shuddered and he smiled.

"So I'm putting myself in your power. To balance the

scales." He drew in a breath and laced his finger with mine again. "I need you."

"To fight Titania?"

"One doesn't fight Titania. One struggles not to be consumed by her. She drives us, pushes us toward our darkest natures until we have nothing to resist with." His profile was stark against the gray sky. With the unmarked side of his face toward me, he could be almost human. "So I called you. I dreamed about you, in your world. I needed you to keep me from losing myself. If you hadn't been close to losing yourself, too, you wouldn't have heard me."

I pondered that.

"But it was the Dog who came to me."

"I can't control him." Rogue said it quietly. State secret.

"Isn't the Dog, well, you?"

Rogue laughed. "One aspect. He's part of me and yet not. Both older than I and younger." His indigo eyes flashed at me, hair sleek in the rain. "I believe you know what it is to have parts of you that aren't entirely in your control."

I didn't answer. I didn't have to.

"Exactly. But he—it—that part of me responds to you."

"That's why he came to me. And why I could pull you back out of him."

"Yes. You're learning, clever Gwynn."

"Why didn't you just tell me this before?"

He stopped. Turned me and pulled me to him. Now I could see both faces. The man and the wild creature. In front of me all this time.

"Aren't we the same, Gwynn? Both wanting the

power? No—you had to choose it and I didn't know how else to make you face that choice. Only something truly felt could break Titania's grip."

I laughed, the feeling bubbling up through me, chasing away the dark shadows. "Are you saying that love triumphs over evil?"

He searched my face, almost with childlike curiosity. "Do you believe in love?"

"I don't know." Maybe I did. My heart thumped. "You ask me what I wish for? I want this. I want to learn and grow. I want to be happy. I want the best part of what we are together—the back and forth, the partnership."

"I can give you that." He smiled that cat-in-the-cream smile. "You belong to me now."

"Only one part of me," I whispered.

Rogue smiled, eyes dark with triumph and something more. "True, my bold student. But in time, I will have all of you. Every part."

"I'll take every part of you in return then."

Rogue threw back his head and laughed in sheer delight. He pulled me tight up against his lean chest and dropped his face close to mine. I could feel the heat of his breath, the scent of mace twining through my blood, his lips were so close.

"Powerful Gwynn, I shall savor every moment of it."

Strangely enough, I knew that I would, too.

* * * * *

It is not wise to break an oath with a fae.
Read on for a preview of
ROGUE'S POSSESSION,
the sequel to ROGUE'S PAWN.

WE WERE LATE to the battle.

As I'd been promised, the Promontory of Magic enjoyed a spectacular view, though I wasn't there to sightsee. The finger of rocks thrust well out into the ocean, the water the unnatural blue of a resort hotel pool, despite the thunderous surf and driving rain.

Below, two fleets of sailing ships exchanged fire. They were conveniently arrayed on each side of the promontory, flanking me as if I were a Wimbledon line judge sitting at the net, ready to call faults and points. Except my power was even greater.

I would decide who lived or died.

Whether I wanted to or not.

My hair lashed against my cheeks, stinging me, and I pulled up the hood of my cloak, grateful for its warmth. A gift from Rogue, the cloak magically repelled water. Despite all I'd learned about controlling and stabilizing magic, Rogue's abilities far exceeded mine. The scent of sandalwood teased me, bringing up warm and sensual memories of his devastating kisses. Rogue managed to be both the bane of my life and the addiction I couldn't seem to shake. My life had become irretrievably intertwined with the fae lord's, though I hadn't seen him in days. His absence made my heart that much more vulnerable to the longings he stirred in me. I tucked them away, where they wouldn't distract me.

"Which side is ours?" I asked.

My fae companion, Puck—a vision in celadon polka dots that clashed quite alarmingly with his strawberry blond locks—gave me a goggle-eyed stare, as if I'd asked which way was up, and pointed at the left side. Good thing I'd asked—I'd thought maybe it was the other. One of the many disadvantages of being a human in Faerie was missing out on their hive-mind shared understanding.

"It's a fine day for a battle!" Puck gazed out over the ships with a gleeful expression and I tried to fake the same enthusiasm, despite the dread in my heart.

Of course, every day in Faerie was fine, in a purely aesthetic sense. The sun, which shone most of the time, did so with lustrous brilliance in depthless skies. The grass glowed an emerald green Oz would have envied. Even the rain shimmered like effervescent and musical drops of platinum.

Beautiful, gorgeous, yes.

Don't wish you were here.

Seriously.

In a place like Faerie, the pretty merely masked the reality, which could be horrible indeed. I hadn't liked my university job as a neuroscientist in the physiology department back in Wyoming, but being employed as a war sorceress sucked far more. Forget the glam sound of it—killing people at someone else's whim whittled away your humanity in hateful bites. Compared to that, my old tenure committee seemed like amateurs.

"You recall your instructions?" Puck bobbed his head as he spoke, encouraging me to agree.

"Piece of cake."

Puck cocked his head, puzzled, and I knew my idiom hadn't quite translated. Usually my intended meaning got through just fine via the telepathic network, but sometimes, particularly if I didn't pay attention, my good old American English slang created strange images in the fae mind.

Some gaps could never be bridged.

"Yes. Darling will inform me of the moment and I will sink exactly half of the enemy ships." I sent a questioning thought to Darling, my cat Familiar, to make sure he was still on board with the plan, especially since he provided my only long-distance communication access. When he felt like it. Imagine a cell phone company run by kittens.

"It shall be a battle to go down in history! Victory shall be ours!" Puck galloped off, leaving me alone with Darling's grumbling narrative in my head, which roughly translated as *bored, bored, bored.*

Darling had become my Familiar largely in a quest for adventure, and being stuck with the generals at battle HQ so he could relay information to me annoyed him to no end. He wanted real action. Sometimes his thoughts came across with a disconcerting manly point of view—especially since he communicated mainly in pictures and feelings. He also suffered from delusions of grandeur.

I had bigger problems, however. The terms of my indentured servitude to General Falcon as pet sorceress in his war dictated that I do as he instructed. The arcane rules of bargaining in Faerie gave me something of an out—as long as I stuck to the letter of our agreements, I could skate around what he really wanted.

In this case, the drowning death of half the humans in the opposing army. Or navy, I guess.

I sure as hell couldn't drown a bunch of innocent humans. The fae might regard their lives as disposable, but I knew the men on those ships had no more choice—

or stake—in Falcon's ridiculous war games than the
wooden vessels themselves. Rogue had warned me I'd
face this moment if I chose to honor my servitude instead of running off with him. Since I hadn't been eager
to exchange my status for an even more questionable
one with Rogue, I was well and truly stuck.

Don't think about him.

A white slice of anger at my current predicament
flared in me. Something sharp and alien enough to
take my breath away. I shuttered my mind, thinking it
came from elsewhere, but it continued its headlong race
through my heart and disappeared again, leaving me
rattled. This wasn't the first time I'd felt it since the last
battle—like the remnants of a fever dream after you've
awakened. I wasn't sure what it meant, but I knew giving it attention was probably a bad idea.

Instead I concentrated on my goals for the day:

1. Do what you're told.
2. Keep to simple agreements.
3. Stay alive.
4. Try not to kill anyone.

The four habits of highly effective sorceresses.

I found a rock to sit on, tucked the cloak around me
and watched the ships wheeling around, puffs of flame
and smoke exchanged, and not much else.

Maybe it was just me, but I found battle to be incred-
ibly dull. Especially from a distance. I had no doubt it
didn't feel that way for the people actually fighting. As
far as spectacles, however, it was terribly overrated.
And then knowing that people were losing their lives for

no good reason—it all made my stomach clench. There were few combinations worse than horrific monotony.

Darling had fallen asleep and I envied him the easy nap. To keep myself focused, I counted ships. Then counted again.

With a slowly dawning horror I realized there were nine enemy vessels. And I'd agreed in specific language to sink exactly half of them. No matter if I sank four or five, I'd be an oath breaker. My knotted stomach revolted as I thrust away the images of what I'd seen happen to those who violated their bargains. I couldn't let it happen to me.

Despite the chill air, a cold sweat broke out over my scalp.

Could I sink half a ship? And how would I make sure it was exactly half? The sailors and fighters on board would certainly count, and they'd be in motion. It would be next to impossible to make sure exactly half of them—no more, no less—went into the drink. And then how to keep them from dying?

I tried to make good use of the downtime, planning a spell that might simulate drowning. Darling, clearly just catnapping, showed me a mermaid giggling and cuddling him against her plump naked bosom. I seriously doubted he'd really found any mermaids, but he insisted on the tale.

Though…didn't mermaids save drowning sailors? Maybe I could work that angle.

Darling yawned and stretched. *Uh-oh.* He sent me an image of General Falcon conferring with the fae noble in charge of the navy. It had to be nearly time, though the battle below looked much the same to me. The fae both looked upset, however, pointing at the sky and growing red-faced.

From my vantage point, I tried to discern which way they were looking. And then I saw them.

Dragons.

Heart thudding up into my throat, I stood, squinting at the V formation of giant reptiles flying through the roiling clouds. They sparkled like jewels despite the gloom, glorious, impossible and terrifying. I'd encountered them only once before, but that had been plenty to convince me to keep my distance. Immune to magic, they were the enemy's trump card.

Darling sent a pointed poke, like a claw-swipe to my mind. *"Now."*

I reached deep inside for the place my trainers had taught me to find, that cool and remote spot where I existed without attachment to the world. It came from nothingness. The nothing I had become when they destroyed me before rebuilding me in their image. Almost.

My skills had been hard-won, paid for with pain and the kind of loss of self that comes only from torture and sophisticated brainwashing. I was frankly lucky to still be sane. If I truly was.

Carefully I shaped the idea of what I wanted. Precision was crucial if you didn't want unpleasant side-results. Like with organic chemistry, a slight error turned sugar to poison. To keep it simple, I focused on sinking four of the ships, holding the images of those particular ones clearly in mind. They would come apart with slow grace, the planks becoming sieves. Gently, they would lower into the water, allowing the people on board time to swim away. I added mermaids, beautiful and solicitous, carrying the sailors and soldiers to the beach.

A lot could go wrong, but it was a key discipline to keep any of those thoughts from contaminating my idea. Only what I wanted. Exactly what I wanted.

Once I had it, perfect, shining and precise, I pulled on the energy. It seethed inside me like my own personal churning sea. In this way, Rogue had done me a favor, staying away these past few days. My desire for him raged hotter than ever before. Our torrid night together, dream world or not, had barely touched the roaring need he stoked in me. All I had to do was open the door to it and it poured through, setting fire to my idea and making it reality.

The world shimmered, shifted as the new reality settled in, and the four ships I'd selected began sinking into the waves, like ladies in fancy ball gowns dropping into a gracious curtsy and continuing forever.

The size of beetles from my perspective, men poured overboard, jumping into the water where mermaids popped up, drawing the swimmers to shore.

Sometimes I impressed even myself.

"Lady Sorceress!" My page, Larch, was shouting, his blue fists knotted in my cloak as high as he could reach to get my attention. He pointed to the dragons. Which were headed directly toward us.

They glittered in the sky, enormous lizards with leathery wings, the moisture in the air steaming off in streamers as they dove.

With a rumble like a 747 on takeoff, the lead dragon dropped, man-high talons outstretched. I flattened myself, and the claws whistled through the air over my head.

"We have to get down!" Larch shrieked over the dragon-thunder and the pounding surf. He practically dragged me over the side of the point, letting me go at my own pace only once he was sure I was following him through the slick, sharp-edged boulders.

Another dragon dive-bombed me, the wind of its passage rocking my tenuous grip on the rocks. Larch crawled under the shelter of one, but I kept going, working my way forward to where I could see the enemy ships again. Larch shouted incoherently after me, which I ignored. I'd rather get munched by a dragon than violate my oath. I still had half a ship to sink.

To get around the point of the promontory, I had to clamber up a bit. Going down wasn't an option. The surf boiled just below, the cold brine soaking my boots. It would have saturated the cloak if not for Rogue's spell.

A rumble of approaching dragon warned me and I dropped to the side. It barely missed me, the enormous talon snagging a rock just above and shattering it, the shards raining down on me. I really wished they'd go away—one wish that would do me absolutely no good whatsoever.

The hood of my cloak had fallen back, and my hair plastered to my head in the chill rain and surf splatter. As fast as I could before the next pass, I crawled up and over the point, spotting the five remaining enemy ships. I would just have to try for it.

The dragon caught me by surprise. No approaching thunder. It must have glided in somehow, because the tip of its talon caught my hood, lifting me into the air. I shrieked, a sound immediately cut off by the loss of air as the cloak strangled me. Before I could think to reach for the ties at my neck, a black object torpedoed through the air, knocking me off the point of the dragon's claw and dropping me into the cold waves.

The impact stunned me, knocking the breath from my body. Cold seemed to freeze my lungs, stopping me from drawing air immediately. Not sure which way was up, I thrashed in the water, tangling in the cloak and my own skirts. Pushing through the surface felt like a miracle, until I drew that longed-for breath and took in as much sea water as air.

I spluttered and coughed as a wave swamped me, carrying me toward the point. The cloak didn't drag me down, but it wasn't buoyant either. Remembering the riptide rules, I swam crosswise to the current that insisted on crashing toward the rocks. The water wasn't cold enough to induce hypothermia right away, but neither did it help. I let the next swell lift me a distance, then struck out again once it passed.

The rocks, however, were too close. The wave crashed on them with a boom. Another few minutes and that could be my body breaking. I frantically sorted through magical solutions. A flotation device wouldn't save me from the rocks. I couldn't just wish myself out of here without a specific plan or a dragon would get me. I did wish away the boots, which helped considerably. Maybe flippers?

Before I could form a clear image, a bigger wave caught me, throwing me sideways and into the sucking current around a looming boulder. Gasping as momentum scraped me against the sharp edges with bruising force, I choked on water that tasted oddly sweet and tried to hang on to the rock. But the force of the receding water sucked me back into the sea's mercurial grasp, pulling me under. I thrashed to the surface, tangled in the cloak.

This was not going well.

A black head popped up next to me, sleek as a seal but with a slavering mouth full of white teeth. The Black Dog seemed to grin at me, full of puppyish joy. It was he who'd knocked me out of the dragon's grip. He yipped at me and I reached for him, but lost the moment to another swell that pushed me down. Teeth fastened on my shoulder, yanking me from the water. I gritted my teeth against the pain and turned, wrapped my arms around the Dog and climbed on his back, anchoring my grip around his chest.

I'm not a big person, but the Dog is nearly as large— enough to lift me partially out of the water, all surging muscle beneath me as he swam for the sandy shore. In exhausted relief, I leaned my cheek against his wet fur, the heat of him burning through and warming me.

Most everyone was terrified of the Black Dog, but not me. For I knew his secret now.

He pulled me all the way through the tumbling surf, and I let go when we reached the sand, rolling off him onto my back. With enthusiastic affection, he licked my face, meaty breath washing over me.

Darling sent an urgent thought, an image of Falcon snarling in rage.

I sat up. "Jeez, I've been a little distracted, okay?"

A dragon wheeled overhead but kept its distance. The Black Dog fell outside a lot of the usual rules of magic—in ways I hadn't yet quantified—but it seemed the dragons were wary of him. I struggled to my feet, wishing my dress dry. An easy wish and that was so much better. The ships were farther out to sea now, sailing away, perhaps.

Down the beach, the soldiers and sailors who'd made it to shore seemed to have noticed my presence and were pointing in my direction, near as I could tell. They likely recognized me from previous battles. The tone of their shouting didn't sound like gratitude for the trouble I'd gone to in saving their miserable skins from drowning. Probably they were peeved about me sinking their ships in the first place. Some people.

And, of course, I'd foolishly left my weapon tied to my horse's saddle back on the promontory. My self-defense instructor would give me a tongue-lashing for that—and not the pleasurable kind.

At least I could do that. I wished for my dagger to be in my hand and it appeared. Not that it would do much good against the mob making its way up the long curve of the beach, but it gave me a bit of comfort. They had a good mile to go.

I concentrated on the ships, nearly out of sight, obscured by the blustering rain. Now to sink half of one. I'd have to find a way to seal up the opening, like a magician's trick when they cut the lady in half, to keep it afloat. Dammit—I didn't know enough about sailing ships, but surely that wouldn't be aerodynamic, or whatever the nautical version of that concept would be. The only real solution would be to keep it magically buoyant.

"A pretty trick, even for me," a voice behind me drawled. "Are you sure you can do it?"

ACKNOWLEDGMENTS

THIS STORY, MY FIRST long fiction work, took many years—and support from many people—to come into being. I wish I could remember every person who encouraged me and offered advice. I will no doubt fail. If I've forgotten you, ping me and I'll buy you a drink. Or something better.

Many thanks to Kevin Reitz and Valerie Moon Meiers, who read this novel in its earliest, grittiest stages and pronounced it good.

Special thanks to early reader Karen Koonce Weesner, who told me this was a book she would keep and read over and over. Only one of the many wonderful things she's said to me all these years of our friendship.

A heartfelt thank you to Lise Horton, contest coordinator for her RWA chapter, who reached out to me when this story received very high and really abysmal scores. She told me it was that kind of story and not to lose faith. I've never forgotten it.

Thanks to Tammy Doherty, another contest judge, who became my critique partner for a while at a time I desperately needed it.

Thanks to Alyson Hagy, who encouraged me to write fiction and who helped me with the beginning. Several times.

Deep gratitude to Laurie Potter, friend, colleague and day-job boss, who read this, encouraged me, and without whose support everything would be so much more difficult.

Thank you to Allison Pang, for always believing in this book, even when she got invited to the party without me.

Big kisses to Laura Bickle and Marcella Burnard, who seem to be there to hold my hand when I need it most and shout my successes louder than I ever could.

Thanks to the rest of the Word Whores, for their bawdy support and enthusiasm.

Many thanks to Catherine Asaro, who read this and told me a story about wading through waist-deep snow. I think my toes are thawing out now.

As always, many thanks to my insightful editor, Deb Nemeth, for loving this story, too. And for knowing which century Western saloons should be in.

Thank you to my family, for being so nice to me.

Finally and forever—thank you to David. You've been there with unfailing support. I wouldn't be here without you, my dear.